BREAD
and
DREAMS

Bread

and

Dreams

A NOVEL

Jonatha Ceely

DELACORTE PRESS

BREAD AND DREAMS
A Delacorte Press Book / October 2005

Published by
Bantam Dell
A Division of Random House, Inc.
New York, New York

Book design by Karin Batten

Delacorte Press is a registered trademark of Random House, Inc., and the
colophon is a trademark of Random House, Inc.

Library of Congress Cataloging in Publication Data
on file with the publisher.

ISBN-13: 978-0-385-33689-5
ISBN-10: 0-385-33689-6

Printed in the United States of America
Published simultaneously in Canada

www.bantamdell.com

10 9 8 7 6 5 4 3 2 1
BVG

Love, I thought, is stronger than
death or the fear of death. Only by it,
by love, life holds together and
advances.

—*Poems in Prose*
by Ivan Turgenev

PREFACE

WE FOUND THE handwritten journal on a summer day in the country house we—my husband and I—are remodeling. The house, which dates back to the 1830s we think, is an absorbing project that takes us out of the city every weekend. Together, we leave the workaday world behind and join in the cleaning, scraping, painting, tiling, that makes the house ours. When we are done—although it is the seduction of an old house that we may never find an end to it—we will have touched, caressed even, every inch of its surface.

All houses hold secrets, which they teach the patient learner. The obvious secrets are the hidden passage, the bolt-hole, the safe behind a picture. But there are other kinds of secrets. Even a new house, finished yesterday, has already absorbed into its fabric the emotions of those who built it. How could it not happen? I lived in a house once where baseboards were loose, hinges not screwed tight. At the most unexpected times a kitchen drawer pull would come off in one's hand. I learned from a neighbor eventually that the couple who built the house never lived in it. The wife and the builder had fallen in love over the plans, had an affair, gone off together. It was a wonderful house—light, airy, pleasingly arranged—but disconcerting to live in. There was interrupted love in every room.

The places we live change us even as we believe we are changing them. This house awakens us early because the bed must go where the rising sun strikes in across it. It lures us outside because the French doors open so conveniently to the porches. We must arrange the furniture as the house prefers because the floors dip a little here and there, making tables rock or chairs feel unstable if they are not placed as the history of each room dictates.

On the day we found the journal, we were stripping wallpaper in the dining room. We had been discussing which layer we preferred. I very much liked the second layer as appropriate to a dining room, burnt-sienna artichokes—fruit, leaves, and stems—turned into a vining plant that swooped in intricate circles against a pale mustard to brown background. We both admired the earliest layer, medallions of dark blue and paler blue dianthus and fernlike leaves on a cream background. Then, absorbed in our task, we had fallen companionably silent. The distant sounds of the world—the purr of a boat on the lake, a questioning crow in the meadow, the rise and fall of children's voices along the road—drifted in to us with the scent of roses from the bush by the porch steps.

My husband was working by the fireplace when he called to me.

"Listen," he said as he tapped the wall. "It's different here." He tapped to the left, and I heard a hollow sound.

I found a knife. By probing we found the edge between plaster and wood and cut through the layered papers to reveal the square shape of a small door. It was evident that a smaller cupboard existed directly above the wood cubby, matching its width exactly.

I felt a flutter in my stomach. Why would someone take the latch from a cupboard and paper over its door so that no sign of it remained?

"Shall I open it?" He looked down at me from the ladder. I could see the expectation, the excitement in his face.

"Of course," I said, sharing the pleasure of suspense with him.

He pried gently with the knife along the edge of the door and it swung open with a faint creak of old hinges.

"What do you see?" I asked eagerly. His head hid the opening.

"How strange," he said. "I thought I smelled thyme. Here. It seems to be a book. I'll pass it down."

I reached up and took a thick notebook.

Moments later we sat at the kitchen table and looked at a square, cloth-bound book. There had been nothing else but that and dust in the little papered-over cupboard. I touched the rough linen of the cover with one tentative finger. The house had given us a gift.

Together, we opened the cracking binding, turned the yellowing pages, and read. *Mina's Book,* it said on the first page in an old-fashioned hand. And under that: *A Gift from Mr. Serle: October 10, 1848.* The book was a journal and, we soon discovered, more than a journal. There were letters tucked into the pages and yellowed newspaper clippings. A sprig of thyme, a bay leaf, rose petals, pressed in the book, had stained some pages.

We were quite sure the book was authentic to the dates inscribed on it, of course, but we showed it to a historian anyway. Tests proved beyond a doubt that the ink, the paper, the glue of the binding, the cloth of the cover belonged to an artifact of the 1840s and '50s. The man who examined it was somewhat dismissive.

"It's not unique, you know." He signed his name with a flourish to the letter stating that he had examined family papers and authenticated them. "There are thousands of such things in attics and historical societies all over the country. Only something by a famous person or of genuine historical importance like a Civil War diary or a slave narrative has value. You won't get anything for this."

He did not seem to understand that we did not care about the money value. We have no plans to sell the journal—it belongs in the house that gave it to us. Like Mina Pigot, the author of her own life, we are not famous people. The river of history bears us with it, floating in its currents, seeing ripples and eddies, not the pattern of the whole. We live the particular, and Mina's journal opens one life, one experience to us. As we read and puzzled, that one life—familiar and yet estranged from us—emerged. In the end, we understood why a young woman hid the precious record of her life and her loves. Mina Pigot reached across time to speak to us of her journey to America, her struggle to understand herself and her new world—and her desire to love with an undivided heart.

MINA'S BOOK

A Gift from Mr. Serle:
October 10, 1848

My Journal

1848 to 1852
with
An Added Note
for the Year 1856

by

MINA PIGOT

From the wreck of the past, which hath perish'd,

Thus much I at least may recall,

It hath taught me that what I most cherish'd

Deserved to be dearest of all:

In the desert a fountain is springing,

In the wide waste there still is a tree,

And a bird in the solitude singing,

Which speaks to my spirit of *thee*.

BY GEORGE GORDON, LORD BYRON

PART ONE

THE ATLANTIC OCEAN

MY STRENGTH IS my own even if it be faint. On Wednesday, October 11, 1848, we—Mr. Serle and I—set sail from Liverpool on the ship *Victoria* bound for New York City. We have been on the ocean for almost a week now, and today, at last, I found time to begin my journal. Crouched between the foremast and the cookhouse, out of the wind, I balance my book on my knees and hold the bottle of ink between my bare feet so it will not slide away across the scrubbed planks of the ship into the great Atlantic Ocean—

I almost lost the ink bottle overboard as the ship suddenly tilted in a gust of wind. It would have gone if not for Phoebe, who caught it just in time.

"There you are, Daniel," she said, handing me the square glass bottle.

Even as I thanked her, Phoebe hurried away with her chin

tucked down. She is a young African girl, twelve perhaps, servant of Mr. and Mrs. Horatio Greene. Every morning she fetches their early tea, sparing me the trouble of carrying it to their cabin.

Perhaps I should write all that happened within the span of the last year, but the sadness of it daunts me. The green meadows of Ireland, the smell of rotting praties, the starving village, the fever deaths of my sister, Eliza, and of my parents, the burning of the house where I was born still come back to me in dreams, still wake me in the empty silence of the night. That and my escape from the burning ship, the *Abigail*, and from the Liverpool people who would have enslaved me, my finding my friend Mr. Serle in the bounty of the kitchen in the great house in England and his taking me as an apprentice cook—memory overwhelms me. In a future time of peace and reflection, I will record the aching pain and the birth of hope. Someday.

Today my pen scratches its way across this paper, and today is what I wish to capture. Today and tomorrow—the adventure and the fear of going to America.

And now the ship—I write quickly for there is much to do and moments such as this with calm seas and light sail hoisted are few. The passengers, the fifteen who sleep in the cabins, perambulate about the quarterdeck taking the air and stare down at the steerage passengers. Those one hundred and fifty or so poor souls who live crammed below in the steerage are outdoors on the part of the main deck they are allowed to use. Mr. Serle and the crew's cook, Seymour, handed out their rations for the day, and they wait turns at the two big galley stoves lashed by the main cargo hatches. Sailors watch them so no fire will escape.

Mr. Serle and I cook for the cabin passengers: special dishes such as boiled mutton with capers, apple and preserved cherry pies, puddings, and the punch and cakes that the gentlemen like after their evening card games. The fat, dark-skinned man called Seymour boils the crew's salt pork and cabbage, which he calls their grub. Seymour is half African and half Mohawk Indian and half Irish, he told me, and he laughed until his belly shook when I said that is impossible, he can't be one and a half altogether. He is mankind's child, he claims, and when he finds an oriental lady to marry, he will be complete.

We—Mr. Serle, Seymour, and I as cook's assistant—work around each other in the cramped cookhouse that is almost filled by the bulk of the great iron range. The owners of the ship told the captain—who told Mr. Serle—that it is important for a sailing packet to have a reputation for fine food so that cabin passengers will recommend it. The steamships take many of the wealthy travelers now, and the captain does not want to be left with the cargoes of emigrants and their diseases, even though there is great profit in the emigrant transport.

When the weather is good, everyone is hungry on a ship. We are up early to fry chops, bake hot bread, brew tea and coffee for the breakfast at eight. The cabin boy and I take morning tea to the passengers who have requested it while they are still in their beds. At twelve, we put out a lunch of cold meats, pickles, and sweet biscuits. At three o'clock, dinner is served at the table set in the saloon with the captain presiding and the chief mate paying special attention to the ladies. After dinner the gentry talk or stroll on the deck or play their games. Tea is brought in at seven-thirty in the evening. With all that to prepare, we cook and serve and clean and cook again from early to late.

Of course, when the weather is bad, only brandy and water and hard biscuit are called for. And—Mr. Serle calls me to carry out the luncheon platters for the buffet in the saloon. I must stop.

TUESDAY, OCTOBER 24, 1848

Last night I fell asleep quickly and slept sound for a time. Then in a dream I am wide-awake. A noise disturbed me—the slap of waves against a wood hull. I am on a ship, sailing on a sea of restless rollers, tossing froth up to a milky sky. The horizon is a blank. Where am I? I ask myself in the dream. Where am I? As I ask, yearning toward the direction the ship moves, land appears, a gray mass against gray sky, but rapidly the colors sharpen, the land greener and greener, the sky bluer, as the ship approaches.

The ship docks. Where am I? I ask again. No one answers. I can see a path, winding up a green velvet slope toward a cleft between lush hills. I trudge my way into the country, my feet bare in the sun-warm dust as they used to be. On a stone bridge I cross a stream and see that, as the road bends, the white crofts of my village line the road. Gladness rises in me.

I hurry forward, calling, "Mother! Father! Eliza! Daniel! I am come home!"

Figures appear at the cottage door. I see my mother, my father, my sister, and my brother. They are thin sticks, clad in blowing gray rags.

"Go away, Mina! Go away!" my mother warns me.

Smoke rises through the charred rafters of the cottage roof. They are starving in this ruined place. As I hasten toward them, my mother, my father, my sister become as the smoke that rises. First their limbs disappear, then their bodies, but I can see their faces still. Then those too begin to fade. I will lose them forever.

"Come back!" I cry. I reach to them and discover I hold a bundle in my arms. "See the child." I try to raise the cloth-wrapped infant. No answer. Only my brother stands at the door.

"Follow me, Mina," my brother calls as he runs out into the dusty road. "Follow me!" he calls as his figure dwindles smaller and smaller ahead of me into the distance.

The child in my arms begins to cry, a thin, mewling wail. I stumble along the road, trying to keep my brother's fleeing figure in view. A hand touches my arm. Someone is bending over me, his face close to mine.

"Mr. Serle!" I cry. "Mr. Serle! Help me!"

Mr. Serle's calm voice speaks quietly at my ear, "There is nothing I can give you, nothing I want from you, Mina."

I awake then, startled, and, forgetting where I am in this narrow, low bunk, sit up and crack my head on the shelf above me. Mr. Serle, behind his canvas curtain on the other side of the storeroom, must have heard my cry of surprise and hurt, for he mutters something in his sleep. But the creaking of the ship, the rush of water under us, blurs all sound, and he does not awaken.

I have thought about my dream all day. I feel the sorrow of it still. And also that my name was spoken in it.

Here is the truth: I am pretending to be Mr. Serle's nephew, pretending that my name is a boy's name. I claim to be Daniel Serle, the last name loaned to me by my friend, and the first name Daniel my brother's name and also that of Mr. Serle's son who died in Rome three years ago. Really I am Mina Pigot.

Even though he spoke coldly in my dream, in waking life Mr. Serle helps me—first last spring by giving me work as a cook's apprentice in the great country house where he was master chef, and now as his assistant on this ship so we can earn our passage to America. Mr. Serle saved me from assault in Liverpool. Except for my brother in America, he is the only one I trust. And that will seem strange to some, for he is a Jew.

When we made our plan to travel to the city of New York, where I hope to find my brother, Daniel Pigot, and where Mr. Serle looks to find work and freedom, I asked if we could marry. I thought it would bring safety in a dangerous world. Mr. Serle said *no*. At fifteen, I am too young yet to marry, he told me. He grieves for his dead wife still, he said, and even when he is ready to love again, he will never marry out of his religion. And he said another thing, which I have puzzled over: that marriage is not safety, although we may be taught to think it so.

I asked him about it this morning. While we talk, I sit on a stool in the corner of the cramped galley, seeding raisins—always a tedious task—and Mr. Serle shows me how to cut vegetables in fancy shapes to garnish a boiled beef.

"You see," he says, slicing a turnip into neat batons. "I trim this into a three-sided stick, and then I cut across to make even triangles, which I will sauté in butter."

"I see," I tell him, and then, because I have been thinking of his words, "Why is marriage not safety?"

Mr. Serle looks up at me, startled perhaps at the change in subject. He scoops the vegetable trimmings into the stockpot before he speaks. "Love opens us to pain," he says in his quiet way. "I loved my wife and could not cure her sick body or her despairing mind when our son drowned and she fell ill, blaming herself for our loss. The greater the love, the greater the pain of knowing that we are helpless to save another soul. Nothing is more terrible."

"Would that be a reason not to marry?" I ask him, feeling the sorrow of his words like an ache in my throat.

Mr. Serle considers the question, his knife poised in the air over the cutting board, his dark eyes intent on some picture in his mind. "No," he says at last. "No. But love requires courage." He sighs. "What shape shall I make next?" he asks, and I hear he cannot bear to discuss love anymore.

"Can you make a carrot into squares?" I ask, and he shows me how easy it is.

"And this," he says, his knife moving swiftly to shape potato hearts.

On land, where there was time and privacy for talk in the quiet evening kitchen of the great house, it all seemed right. On this tossing ocean, where we are a cargo of souls pent up together, I wonder. As I rely on the sailors to keep the ship safe, I came in those months in England to rely on Mr. Serle for some balance in my heart. He encouraged me to talk of the past and to see the good that countered the evil. He told me of his dream of a new life, free of the hate that made the Pope's laws for the Jewish quarter in Rome. He confessed to me his yearning to have his own restaurant some day, a place of peace and plenty by a beautiful lake. I learned—and I felt hope in sharing thoughts with him. Now, as we journey, the wild waves and the fearful, endless waste of water all about us confuse my feelings. What seemed safe and secure blows away like the thin, high mare's-tail clouds that stream across the sky before a gathering storm.

Well, I cannot seem to explain clearly. I am trying to make my book a record of truth, but I do not know yet what my truth is.

NOVEMBER—

I had no opportunity to write again until today. In the early evening the wind has died, the ocean is calm. We are moving, gliding almost, the motion of the ship seems so smooth now, to the south. We can see America! To our right a low shore lies with a great sunset, flaming up deep apricot, crimson, and pale gold above it. It will be clear and cold tomorrow, the sailors say. But we will not care about the weather anymore, because at dawn the pilot will come out to board the ship and guide us safe past the reefs and islands into the harbor of New York City.

When I think to the coming days, I yearn for my brother. My heart twists in my chest with the fear that he is dead or gone from reach into a wild country. With today's work done, I turn to my journal to pass the time rather than imagine disaster. Here in the slowly fading warmth of the cookhouse, Mr. Serle sits also, reading one of his novels. The swaying light of the gimbaled oil lamp throws a glow about his dark head as he bends over his page. We are close together, and yet he seems far away, absorbed in some imaginary place that gives him comfort.

"What are you reading?" I asked him moments ago as we settled ourselves.

"It is called *Jane Eyre*," he said. "It was much talked of last winter in London. I took the liberty of borrowing it from the ship's library tonight."

I do not read novels myself. Indeed, Mr. Serle has pointed out to me that I do not read at all so far as he can tell. As if he were a real uncle and responsible for my education, he admonishes me to improve my mind.

"Do you like the story?" I ask.

"I do not know yet," he says. "The beginning seems to be about a child."

The teller of a story knows from the start which events will be significant for the characters and can shape the tale accordingly. In the real flow of life we have no foreknowledge. I must write down what matters to me tonight and wait for time to tell me if I tasted flavors that will blend at last in a refined and finished meal or only heaped, from a buffet of coarse dishes, ill-assorted viands on my plate. In my journal, I speak to myself only; nevertheless, I will begin again properly as a story should.

The ship, with her great sails unfurled, mastered the terrifying beauty of the green waves with their curling, frothing crests. The first days seagulls followed us, but they soon left, flown back to the safety of the land, I suppose. Certainly they were wise to go, for we had rough seas and a cold wind blowing against us. We passed Cape Clear, the land's end of Ireland, without being able to see a blade of green grass or a gray stone of it beyond the heaving water. The steerage passengers had hard times then, with the spray of ocean waves threatening to drench their fires even on the days they were allowed to cook.

Taking tea to the cabins and helping to serve at meals, I came to know the passengers. The famous English writer Mr. Simpkens always has a kind word and a smile. "Oh, Steward," he says to me, winking to show he knows I am not really the steward. Another famous passenger, Madame Anna Moses, an opera singer, travels with her daughter, Stellina, which Mr. Serle says means *little star* in Italian—a very romantic name. Her maid, Luly, and a bearded man, Mr. Sadick Meyer, who is Madame Moses's brother and a pianist, accompany them.

Madame Moses is a beautiful woman. She is taller than I am and has a fine woman's figure, which I cannot claim, being thin as a broomstraw. Her hair is very dark, and she wears it drawn in two smooth wings that sweep back into a great braided knot pinned high enough to reveal the white nape of her neck. I suppose I would admire it more if I did not know that the half of it is a switch that lies like a black snake on her cabin table in the early morning. Her eyes are dark too and set wide apart. Her skin is very pale. She wears black always, a simple wool with black braid trim for morning and a full-skirted black silk cut low to show off her white bosom when the cabin passengers dress for dinner. She is in mourning for her husband, who died fighting for freedom in Paris this past spring—so Mr. Serle says. The only color to Madame Moses is her gold earrings and her rosy lips.

Mr. Serle likes to look at her. He stands quietly at the door of the cookhouse sometimes when she is walking on the deck with her black fur-lined cloak wrapped around her. He makes special dishes for her too. The cow gives little milk in rough weather, but he makes blanc mange flavored with orange flower water for her because she said she liked it.

When Madame Moses is not seasick, she practices her music in the saloon. Her brother, Herr Meyer, as Mr. Serle calls him, accompanies her on the piano. The other passengers gather to hear her and murmur their admiration, which makes her smile. One quiet day when I was setting out the condiments for the dinner table, she sang an *Ave Maria*. It made the tears stand in my eyes. One could forgive much in a person who brings such beauty into the world.

Madame Moses leaves the care of her child to the maid Luly. When I take in morning tea, Luly and Stellina are playing together. Often their play is with Stellina's doll, or Luly is teaching Stellina the alphabet and little songs. Madame Moses looks at them and smiles her approval, but she seems most occupied with her own thoughts and her music.

One of the first days out, Luly and Stellina and I had the saloon to ourselves at mid-morning. The steward was busy in his pantry, and most of the passengers were in their bunks, too ill to eat because of the rolling of the ship in choppy seas. Luly and Stellina took advantage of the freedom to play a game of hide-and-seek. Luly closed her eyes and counted to twenty while Stellina rushed about looking behind chairs for a hiding place. When I pushed open the saloon door to return to the cookhouse, Stellina, shrieking, "Can't catch me!" ran past me to the deck.

The waves rose higher while I was inside. Sailors scramble aloft in the rigging, taking in sail. Perhaps the helmsman turns the ship, perhaps a wild wave catches us. As Stellina runs out, the ship rolls sharply, and the crest of a wave, climbing over her dipping rail, sweeps across the deck. Caught, the child slides with the surging water. I hurl myself after her and seize her but cannot regain my feet. The heavy push of the comber tumbles the two of us in its embrace across the tilting deck, first toward the ship's stern and then across the deck again toward the opposite rail, which dips down in its turn to drink the dark water. I think we would both have been emptied overboard like two bubbles in a bucket of wastewater, only, as we tumble up against the rail, I hook one arm into the rigging that lashes the backstays to the chains and then hold to Stellina with both arms about her as another sea drenches us.

I am not sure what happened exactly. I felt the heave and roll of the ship and the frothing crest of yet another surge toy with us. I clutched Stellina tight, shouted in her ear to hold her breath as the water tore at us, gasped myself, and hung on. The ship steadied. There was shouting and men lifting us.

"There's a brave lad," a rough voice said. "Safe to ease off now. We have a rope around you."

Someone large and strong and smelling of tobacco carried me across the deck. The saloon was a babble of sound and a crush of people. Stellina and I lay in pools of water. Luly called Stellina's name. Coughing, I struggled to sit up.

"My darling!" I heard Madame Moses's ringing voice. She was cradling her daughter in her arms.

"My dolly is saved," Stellina said solemnly, pulling the sodden toy from her pinafore pocket and hugging it to her breast. "Daniel saved her."

I began to sob then and could not stop myself.

"What is wrong with the lad?" The hoarse voice sounded troubled.

"Get the cook, Flint," said the steward. "He's a relation to the boy."

Someone stooped beside me and patted my shoulder. "There, there, lad," murmured a man's voice, Herr Meyer's. "No need to carry on."

But I could not stop.

"Hush, hush," said Mr. Serle at my ear. "Come with me, child."

My cries calmed a little then. Mr. Serle put his arm about me and helped me from the saloon to the cookhouse. The hoarse-voiced sailor named Flint came too. The seas had died, but, even so, the sailors had strung a rope on the deck to hold to. Mr. Serle had much ado to keep his grip on me and on the rope, for I still wept as I clung to him. I think Mr. Serle carried me, and Flint helped Mr. Serle. In the warmth of the cookhouse, Mr. Serle eased me down and spoke to Flint.

"Will you fetch the blanket from my bunk below?" he asked him. "You must take this wet clothing off and warm yourself," he said to me.

Mr. Serle helped me take off my sea-soaked smock. When he opened the grate to add wood to the range, I cried out in fear at the sight of the licking flames.

"What is wrong, child? What is so terrible?" He knelt beside me. "You saved the little girl. You saved yourself and her both. You did well. What is wrong?"

Through the choking sobs, I try to tell him. "It was like the *Abigail* again," I say. "I saw a child fall from the ship when it was on fire, I saw her body afterward in the hulk where they laid out the dead. The man put her little doll on her chest. It came back over me. The world is only danger and death, death and danger. And I have no mother to hold me anymore."

Mr. Serle wraps a blanket and then both his arms about me. "You are safe," he says. "My dear, you are safe now, thank God. Not all danger ends in death."

He held me tight until my weeping eased a little.

"Come," he said, cradling my head in his hand, "you need a hot drink to warm you."

The door of the cookhouse banged. Mr. Serle started.

"Ouch!" I said.

My hair was caught on the button of Mr. Serle's coat. We had to let Herr Meyer untangle the curl and free us. His deft musician's fingers made quick work of it.

"I came to be sure the lad is well," he said when we were apart.

"He is wet through and still shocked," Mr. Serle told him. "He is going below to change while I make a hot toddy for him. I need something myself. And you too, sir," he said, looking over to the sailor, Flint, who stood awkwardly by the stove.

The man shook his head. "I promised Zip to teetotal," he said. "If the lad is recovered, I will go."

He blundered out the door. I could not regain my voice to thank him for his help.

"What is your name, boy?" Herr Meyer asked me.

"Daniel," I say, hesitating. It seems strange to say it even though I must.

Mr. Serle catches his breath and puts his hand out to my head again. I am all soaking wet, as his young son Daniel was when he found him drowned after the flood in Rome. The tears, which dried when the pain of my hair being pulled distracted me, run again on my cheeks. I take Mr. Serle's hand.

"I did not drown," I say.

Mr. Serle grips my hand in both of his for a moment.

"Dry clothing," he says to me. His voice is severe, but his face looks kindly at me. "Take a light down with you."

In the storeroom I rub my wet head with a cloth and change slowly with trembling hands. When I climb back up the ladder into the cookhouse, Mr. Serle and Herr Meyer are talking quietly as if they have known each other a long time.

"The child survived the wreck of the *Abigail*," Mr. Serle says. "She saw horror."

I am upset. Mr. Serle must be upset too. He is forgetting my disguise.

"I brought my wet things," I say. I feel dazed still. "I must rinse them in clean water to take the salt out."

Mr. Serle tells me to do that later. Now I must sit. He gives me a mug of hot, sweet tea with brandy in it. The spirits make me cough, but the warmth slips into me. My heart unknots a little.

"Well!" Herr Meyer said. "Our hero does not look triumphant as he should."

He does not show whether he noticed Mr. Serle's slip. Herr Meyer has a thick, silky brown beard, which he strokes when he is thinking, and shrewd eyes. He came to see that I am well and to give me a gift for saving his niece. The gift is gold coins. I do not want them. I do not want money for a life. Besides, it was the sailors saved both Stellina and me. Herr Meyer persists until Mr. Serle says it is my right to refuse.

"My sister and I would like to show our gratitude," Herr Meyer tells Mr. Serle.

"The child will take your word for that," Mr. Serle replies.

To my surprise, when the talk is done, Mr. Serle tells me I must go to my bunk.

"But there is work to do," I say.

"You are shivering still. I will not have you ill for want of a few hours of rest when you most need it," Mr. Serle says. "Come back to help with tea later."

Herr Meyer is taking off his coat and rolling up his shirt-sleeves.

"I am going to be the assistant for dinner," he announces. "There will not be five people up to eat it anyway. I am bored with this journey."

Mr. Serle laughs and accepts his offer. He touches my head lightly as I pass him to go down the ladder. "Wrap yourself in both your own blanket and mine," he says. "Warm yourself and return when you are rested and calm."

By the next morning the ocean was quieter, and my mind too. I stopped on the deck to thank the sailor Flint for rescuing me from going overboard. In his gruff way, he told me never mind, it was a sailor's life. After that, we stood beside each other, watching the steamship *Pride of Boston* pass us. Dark smoke poured from her stack, and her great side wheel beat the sea to froth as she plowed ahead.

"She'll be in New York when we get there." Flint spat over the rail, a dark stream of the tobacco he chews constantly. "She makes passage in two weeks."

"Do you wish you were on her?" I ask.

"Me?" Flint looks surprised at the question. "I'm a sailor, lad, not a coal stoker."

From that day Flint stopped to talk to me whenever he saw

me. Not that the conversations are long or about much at all. I am always hurrying to take tea to a cabin, throw garbage over the rail, carry full dishes into the saloon or empty dishes out again.

"Good morning, Daniel," he says in his rough voice.

Flint surprised me with a present one morning, a continuous chain whittled all of one piece of wood. There are eight links to it; what once was a straight and rigid stick now moves and bends. It is a strange little thing, useless, I suppose, but finely made, smooth and gleaming with oil rubbed into it. Flint crouched down very close to me where I sat near the rail, scrubbing out a cooking pot. He smells of tobacco and tar and sweat.

"Here's something for you," he said, pushing the chain into my hand.

I felt frightened somehow but pleased to have a gift. "Oh," I said when I looked at it. I must have sounded puzzled.

"I made it," Flint said hurriedly. "See, it is all from one piece of wood. No glued places. I made it for you."

"For me?" I said. "Thank you."

Flint looked around quickly. No one was near. "Well, give us a kiss, then," he said.

Startled, I leaned over and kissed him on his rough cheek.

"Thank you," I said again.

"Good lad." Flint clapped me on the shoulder and was gone.

Looking at the toy in my hand, I had time then to be surprised. What have I done? I thought.

Later that same day, I remember, I talked to Phoebe. After dinner, I went to the stern to throw slops overboard. She was standing there with her brown hands gripped tight on the rail, staring back at the foam trace the ship leaves for barely a moment in the trackless ocean. I toss the contents of my bucket over.

"What are you doing here?" I ask her.

"Could I swim back to England, Daniel?" she says in a forlorn, small voice.

"You would surely drown," I tell her. "The waves would swallow you in a minute."

I am glad to hasten toward America. I feel the impatience of it even now as I write.

"Why would you want to return to England, Phoebe?" I ask.

"Mr. Meyer spoke to me." The girl looks at me. Her eyes are wet, whether from the wind or sorrow I cannot tell. "He asked why I did not stay in a country where I am free."

"Oh," I say. "I did not know you are not free."

"I belong to Mrs. Greene," Phoebe says, gazing out at the waves now and not at me. I have to bend my head down close to hear her words. "She had my mother and me from her own mother. Last year Mr. Greene sold up everything, keeping only me to be maid to Mrs. Greene. Then we went to England. I think it was to get money from his family. He must have got some because now we are going back to Richmond."

"Perhaps you will see your mother then." I am very unsure what to say.

"No, no," Phoebe says in her soft voice. "My mother is sold away."

"I am sorry," I say.

Which is sadder—to know certainly your mother is buried in a green country churchyard or to wonder without hope where her head lies?

"Mr. Meyer said that if I had run away in England no one could make me go back to Virginia." Phoebe speaks as much to herself as to me, I think. "Why did no one tell me?"

I am silent. I do not know.

"Did you have friends in England?" I ask at last, awkwardly.

Phoebe shakes her head no. "Only the servants in Mr. Greene's father's house. The housekeeper gave me extra sewing to do and paid me money for it too."

Phoebe's face brightens a little as she speaks.

"You must sew well," I say.

"I do." Phoebe smiles suddenly. The flash of her white teeth in her brown face is pretty. "The woman gave me clothes she did not want. I can fix them for myself. Or, maybe, I will sell them."

We are silent. I see that Phoebe has a darker mark staining

the soft coffee color of her cheek. Mrs. Greene strikes her, I know without the telling. Phoebe looks up at me, and her face changes.

"What is it?" I ask her.

"Oh!" she says. "With the sun behind you, the red curls of your hair seemed on fire."

The shock I feel must show in my expression. I remember what it is to burn.

"I mean it is beautiful," she says quickly. "I wish you could see."

I cover my confusion by letting down the bucket to rinse it. It takes care to tie the knot of rope secure to the rail and to the bucket handle. By the time I have finished and coiled the rope again, Phoebe has disappeared.

A few days after I talked to Phoebe, the *Victoria* turned toward the south. Land lay out of sight on our right hand. Somewhere over the horizon rose the cliffs of a great island, Newfoundland. We sailed into thick fog, and the sailors took turns ringing a bell all day and all night. Even when it stopped, the sound banged on in my head. When the air cleared, birds came, wheeling gulls that dive and scream when anyone throws garbage overboard. We saw fishing boats on the horizon, but none near enough to hail.

I think that I can smell land, but when I say that to Mr. Serle, he only smiles and says he has not noticed it himself.

"What does it smell like?" he asks.

"Like burnt sugar and toasted almonds," I tell him.

"Better than the odor of tar that gets into everything on board this ship," he says as he lifts the porridge pot from the fire. "I will welcome the change."

We had scant time to enjoy the idea of our journey's end approaching, however, for after breakfast was served and cleared away, the weather changed again. Before dinner a violent storm came on us.

Warned by the watch aloft, the captain turned out all hands to prepare the ship. The steerage passengers—who had tumbled up eager to see the birds and the fishing boats—were herded back into their hold. Mr. Serle and I and the steward secured the spirit chest in the saloon and made sure the cabin passengers had biscuits and water jugs for the time that we should all be penned in our places with the ship's hatches battened over us.

"I like it," said the steward. "The wind will blow hard from the northeast. If we are not carried in on the shoals to leeward, we will see New York all the faster."

Mr. Serle stared at the steward. "I would as soon die a dry death," he said.

We made sure all of the fires were completely dead and that no lamps were lit. No one may smoke a pipe or a cigar until the storm has passed. The captain has forbidden it. Anything that can burn is dangerous in rough weather. When Mr. Serle and I finished in the saloon, we hurried forward across the deck to the cookhouse and the storeroom below it. Dark clouds piled up to the north and east and the south too, moving thick and strong from horizon to zenith. The ship was sailing straight into a wall of black.

Sailors scrambled through the rigging of the ship and across the deck where lines were strung for safety. Before a storm the sailors strap on belts. They tie themselves to a line so they cannot be swept away in the breaking waves as Stellina and I almost were.

"Pumps ready," shouted the second mate.

In the cookhouse, Mr. Serle cleared the ashes from the iron range, soaked them in seawater, and threw them overboard. After I stored all of the pots and pans in the empty range, I moved the chicken coops inside the cookhouse. Mr. Simpkens will want his breakfast egg just the same after the storm passes. Then I went down to be sure the storeroom was ready. A sailor came to hurry us.

"Down the hatch with you both," he said roughly. "I saw half the cookhouse carried away in a nor'easter once. Down the hatch and let me secure all."

Moments later Mr. Serle and I are closed up in the dark. I grope my way to my bunk and, lying down in all my clothes, wrap myself in my blanket. At first, the sounds—the creaks and groans of the ship, the thump of feet on the deck above us—are familiar.

Slowly the whistle of the wind and the reverberation of the waves against the hull blot out all else.

Mr. Serle does not speak. The motion of the ship is not so bad yet, and I doze off. Minutes or hours later, I have no way of knowing, I awaken with a start. The ship labors in heavy seas. Like wickerwork under a restless sleeper or a bonfire of dry twigs, the *Victoria* crackles and snaps. Every timber of her cries with its own shrill voice, a chorus of agony. At any moment her planks will part and the sea rush in on us. Or fire will spring up, I fear. All will be lost.

I lie in the confine of my bunk and feel my heart beat in my chest. I do not know if the roaring in my ears is the pulse of my blood within or the sound of the wind and sea a few feet away. Sewn into my shirt, which was once my brother's shirt, is the gold ring with the red stone set in it that my mother gave me before she died. I pull at my shirt until I can hold the little round lump of it in my hand. This ring, my mother's ring, connects me to the goodness of the past and comforts me. I doze again.

A crash awakens me. The ship shudders and rolls right. Another crash and she lurches left, throwing me from my bunk to the rough planking of the floor. In the frightened, noisy dark, I crawl on the pitching floor of the storeroom. My shoulder hurts. I cry out. In the tumult, I am not sure even if it is the wind or myself that cries.

"Mina! Mina!" I hear my name.

"Oh God! What is it?" I gasp. And then, "Where are you?"

"Here, I am here." It is Mr. Serle. "Are you all right?" he shouts.

"I fell," I say.

I grope about. Here is the edge of my bunk, here the flat door of the locked storage cupboard. I crawl across the space toward Mr. Serle's bunk. I reach out. A strong hand grasps mine.

"I am here," Mr. Serle says.

"I am afraid." My throat is almost closed to speech by the constriction of terror.

Mr. Serle says something I do not understand.

"What?" I say. I am on the floor huddled by Mr. Serle's low bunk. I hold tight to the hand that he stretches out to me.

"I have been praying." Mr. Serle's voice makes a quiet center in the howling wind.

"I will pray too," I say, but I do not let go of Mr. Serle's hand.

Even though it is dark, I close my eyes tight. We speak our own words, Mr. Serle in the Hebrew language of his religion, and I in English as my mother taught me at her knee. The wind wails and the ship cracks, drowning our voices.

When our voices die away, I feel calmer. I cling still to Mr. Serle's hand. He must be lying on his side in his narrow space with his left arm stretched out and over my shoulder, holding me secure against the motion of the ship. In the dark, his face is very close to mine. I smell bay leaves and the spicy scent of his shaving soap. When he speaks at last, I feel his breath against my cheek.

"Are you all right?" he asks me.

"My shoulder hurts," I tell him.

"Perhaps you would be safer in your bunk?" Mr. Serle says.

"I will stay here," I say. "I do not want to die alone."

Before Mr. Serle can speak, terrible screaming begins somewhere beneath us in the ship. We recognize the pain of human voices even amidst the inhuman cry of the storm.

"Oh God," I say. "It is a keening. A poor soul is dead."

What can we do? We are confined within this coffin of a ship. I close my eyes against the dark and hold the strong hand that protects me. I imagine Mr. Serle's face: his black eyes with their hooded lids, the arch of his black eyebrows, the taut line of his cheek, the ironic curve of his smile, the way his dark hair curls on his high forehead. I wish I could put both arms about him and rest my head on his breast. I am so tired.

When I awaken, the noise of the ship has calmed, and the hatch is open, letting in a cold draft and a thin ray of daylight. I am lying on the floor with my blanket tucked about me for warmth. Mr. Serle must have done that.

I kneel where I am by Mr. Serle's bunk and say my prayers to thank the Blessed Virgin that we are safe. Above me, I can hear

Mr. Serle's low voice in the cookhouse and Seymour's growl as he clatters pans. I must hurry up the ladder to help them. No one has eaten a meal since yesterday morning. They will be complaining.

The ship came safe enough through the storm. One of the masts was a little damaged when rigging was torn away in the winds, but the sailors repair that, perched above our heads, calling to each other like birds in a forest.

In the steerage an old man died. Perhaps he was ill, perhaps his heart failed him in the dark. One of the sailors sewed the corpse into the blanket that had warmed him in life. They put a stone from the ballast in. Before the cabin passengers were all out of their beds, there was a service on the main deck. The captain read a prayer; the sailors lowered the bundle into the sea. Someone—a son or daughter perhaps—flung out a little cross that was soon lost to sight in the waves.

That was the worst of it. Bad, but not the worst, was that in the midst of the storm with sleet driving across the deck, the sailor Flint fell and struck his head against the capstan. He was carried unconscious to the forecastle. Seymour says he is awake now, but the captain gave permission for him to lie in his bunk for a day or so. I felt a sadness in my heart that Flint should suffer. I remember his strength as he carried me to safety.

It is thrilling that land lies so near. We are closer now to safety for us all. Very early, a boat, scudding out from one of the islands, hailed us and followed alongside. They offer milk, cream, and vegetables as well as fresh fish. Our cow, seasick, gave nothing since the storm. The captain approves purchases. Soon a milk can swings aboard and then a canvas sack of root vegetables. Mr. Serle is pleased with the produce of our new country.

The cabin passengers ate little but tea in the evening as the storm abated, and not all of them appeared for that. In the morning at breakfast everyone was up and gathered in the saloon, talking excitedly of their terror. Little Stellina Moses looks very pale still. I smile at her and give her a piece of toast with sugar and cinnamon sprinkled on it. She whispers her "Thank you, Daniel," and her mother, Madame Moses, nods her approval to me. The saloon's stove is alight again, and the place is snug and warm. The ship scuds south in light seas under billowing sails.

"Winter is coming," Mr. Simpkens says when I set his oat porridge before him. "See how our little steward's cheeks are rosy from the brisk morning air."

I do not correct him to say that, if I am red, it is from standing over the fire in the cramped cookhouse. Instead I say, "Here is cream at last, sir," as I set the pitcher beside him and retreat. Since the first week of the voyage, he has complained that there is not enough cream, only salt butter and molasses for a condiment to his oatmeal.

Remembering Mr. Serle's pleasure when we tasted the first food of America, I look over at him. He notices that my pen stopped scratching, for he glances up.

"You have been scribbling away like a little Pamela," he says.

"Who is Pamela?" I ask.

"Never mind," he says. "Just a character in a novel I read when I was teaching myself English."

"Did the child in *Jane Eyre* grow up yet?" I inquire.

"Yes," he tells me. "And now she has troubles. I am going to read a little longer."

Mr. Serle reaches to adjust the wick in the lamp and bends his dark head to his book again. I dip my pen and return to my own story.

During the storm, as I recorded, Flint slipped on the icy deck and hit his head on the capstan. Seymour reported that all day Sunday and Monday Flint lay in his bunk complaining of headache. Tuesday he appeared on deck at last.

"How are you?" I asked.

"Good morning, Daniel," he said. His voice sounds rough, but his manner is formal. "I am hungry." He leaned on the mop with which he had been swabbing the deck.

"I can get you a basin of oatmeal porridge," I offered. "There is some left from breakfast."

His face lit up at that. "I would take it kindly," he said. "I could not stomach the burgoo earlier. My head is bad again, I will lie down in the forecastle for a little."

"I will bring it to you shortly," I told him. The sailors eat only in their own quarters. It seems to be a rule with them.

Seymour was polishing brass on the deck, and Mr. Serle was nowhere to be seen, so I heated the oatmeal, added some butter and molasses to it, put a clean dish clout over it, and carried it forward. I can understand that Flint would not want the burgoo. It is a heavy Indian corn mush that Seymour does not bother to stir smooth and serves with uncooked lumps in it. Even a whole jug of molasses would not make it palatable.

The forecastle was deserted save for Flint lying cramped in his bunk. He is a large man, fleshy, almost soft looking, and yet very strong. The others make him anchor man at the end of the rope when they are hauling sail. His face is darkened from the sun. In honesty, it is also dirty and usually stubbled with his beard. He has a raw scar across his forehead. It is not very recent—the scar, that is—and yet it does not have the dead white look of a long-ago wound. In his right ear he wears a gold earring in the shape of an anchor. For all that Flint looks big and powerful and rough, there is a childishness to his face. He is not very young nor very old. His unlined cheeks, well-muscled arms, and work-rough hands make him something over twenty, I suppose. His sadness makes him old, and yet the yearning look of his eyes is young. He seems uncertain somehow.

"I brought food," I say. "Do you have your spoon?"

Flint eased himself from his bunk and seated himself at the triangular table that filled the center space of the forecastle.

"Here you are, then," I said, setting the basin before him.

"Thank you, Daniel," Flint said. "Will you sit?"

"A moment," I said. "Are you American born?" I ask, for something to say.

"Born in Uncas Falls, New York," he says, "but Zip has a house in Albany now."

He sounds proud of these facts, but he does not offer more

information. There is something in his manner, a distance, a confusion, that makes me want to question him and yet to hesitate. I might be intruding on a private world. It might be a world I should fear to enter.

"I must be off," I said. The place and the suffering man made me uneasy. I put my hand on the ladder that leads to the sunlight and the deck.

"Are you afraid of me?" he asked. His face turned toward me in a mournful look.

"No," I said cautiously, "but I have heard of men who prey on boys."

Flint shakes his head slowly, and then presses his hand to his temple as if the movement hurt. "I am not that kind, lad. I—" He breaks off.

There is a long silence. Flint stares down at the basin before him but does not eat.

"I must go to my work," I say.

"Give us a kiss before you go, then," he says.

He looks so bereft. I cannot believe evil of him. I brush my lips against his bristly, tobacco-smelling cheek and hurry away up the ladder. When I gain the deck and glance back, I see that his right elbow is on the table, and his head is supported by his right hand. He spoons up milk and porridge slowly with his left hand.

In the cookhouse I tell Mr. Serle where I have been as I begin my tasks. He is stirring and seasoning a beef stew. It is almost the last of the meat that was in the ice chest. I am coring and slicing apples for a pie for dinner.

"What does he want of me?" I ask Mr. Serle.

"You should not encourage him," Mr. Serle tells me.

"But I have done nothing," I reply indignantly. "He seems to beg for kindness. He is like someone asking a child for a good-night kiss."

"Are you a child?" Mr. Serle raises a dark eyebrow. "You told me you are not."

"But—" I begin. I stop.

Mr. Serle tastes his stew and makes a wry face. He adds

thyme to the pot and stirs again. "Sailors live rough lives. You do not know who this man is or what he has experienced. You are too quick to take pity, too quick to trust."

"But—" I start again.

"You cannot go about the world kissing strangers because they ask you to," Mr. Serle tells me. There is a flush of color across his cheekbones. "That is beyond foolish. Whether a boy does it or a girl, it is stupid and dangerous."

I sigh. Mr. Serle is right, no doubt, but I do not think he understands completely.

"Shall I grate cinnamon bark or nutmeg in the apples?" I ask.

"Cinnamon," Mr. Serle says, "and put in plenty of sugar."

When I went back to the forecastle for the basin, Flint still sat at the table, his head bowed in both his hands. He barely nodded to me when I spoke. He did not ask me for a kiss, and I was soon up the ladder again with the empty basin in my hand.

I doubt that Mr. Serle was angry about Flint even though he called me foolish. Sometimes I think my problems amuse Mr. Serle or sometimes make him sad. When I think back over what he said, I know he is right. I must not trust too easily. Certainly, I must not kiss anyone just because he asks.

The quarrel about Madame Moses happened on a day when fine, cold, penetrating rain fell, but there was little wind and the seas had calmed after a rough night. I carried morning tea to Madame Moses's cabin as usual. The place is a chaos of clothing and objects. Madame Moses wears a red flannel wrapper half-open over her petticoat and chemise. Her uncombed hair straggles on her shoulders. Her public elegance seems all forgotten.

"Set the tea by me, boy," she snaps, "and take away Luly's cup. She deserves nothing this morning."

I think I look shocked. I look at Luly, whose lips are pressed in tightly. I set the tray down and, leaving it all, back toward the door.

"I told you to take the cup," Madame Moses says. She picks it up from the tray and throws it at me. The thing shatters on the door frame.

I stare at her, openmouthed. She must be mad.

Indeed she must, for she cries, "I hate this ship. I hate feeling ill always. Go away, you wretch!"

As I flee, I hear her cry out again as if the words are pulled from her. "Why did you die, Isidore Moses?" The weeping of Luly and Stellina joins her sobs. Torn between fear of her anger and sadness for her grief, I close the cabin door as gently as the rolling ship allows.

In the cookhouse Mr. Serle looks up when I come in. I go to the range. I will throw a pinch of flour into the oven to see if it is hot enough yet to bake my bread. My hand is shaking, and I touch the hot iron by mistake.

"Oh!" I exclaim, startled by the sudden pain.

"Are you all right, child?" Mr. Serle says quickly.

"Oh yes," I assure him.

I do not wish to talk of the unhappy woman berating me, who helped her child, and Luly, who loves Stellina. Perhaps she is truly ill with sorrow. It is just this once that I have seen her temper. I feel a wrongness, and yet I cannot say it. It is a surprise to me. I speak of almost everything with Mr. Serle. But Mr. Serle admires Madame Moses.

Later in the morning, I gave the potato peelings to the hens. The pig was sacrificed the day after the storm. We are eating some of him for dinner today. As I stand in the cold rain, looking at the poor, doomed hens shivering in their coop, I have an ugly thought of the ship eating its way through the ocean like an animal. The planks and ribs are the skeleton, the sails and ropes the skin and hair. And the passengers? We are the digestion of the monster, taking in our stores and spewing out a trail of waste behind us.

I shiver, and then I hear Mr. Serle's voice. I cannot make out his words. Mr. Meyer's speech comes loudly enough, however.

"My *prima donna assoluta* will persist in having her walk on the deck this morning," he says. "I tried to tell her it is too cold and slippery, but she will not listen."

"I have my umbrella and your arm," the lady says. Her voice carries clearly. "I am starved for air."

"But I am freezing," the brother exclaims. "I came out without my greatcoat."

Perhaps they are facing toward me and Mr. Serle away, for I do not hear his words. What he said is evident enough when Mr. Meyer says, "Thank you for taking my place for a moment. I will return in a trice."

"Come under the umbrella with me," Madame Moses says. "It is large enough for two."

I move nearer the entrance of the cookhouse. My hair and shoulders are wet; I want to go in to the warmth.

"You have been thoughtful, sir," Madame Moses says. "I am grateful to you. I have been so wretchedly ill on this voyage."

"No, no." I can hear Mr. Serle now. "It is a privilege to serve an artist."

Madame Moses faces me, and I think she sees me. I know it is rude, but I cannot stop watching. There is something in the way she tilts her head and widens her eyes that tells me she likes an audience.

"Would you hold the umbrella for me?" she asks. "I fear I am bumping your head."

I see Mr. Serle take the thing, raising the black dome higher.

"My brother likes you," Madame Moses says.

"I am grateful for his interest in me," Mr. Serle says.

"Of course he is interested. You are one of us." Madame Moses reaches out her gloved hand and almost touches Mr. Serle's cheek. "Your attention comforts me. You are a good man," she says.

"Madame!" he exclaims.

I cannot tell if he is shocked or pleased. His back is to me, and I cannot see his face, just the lady's gloved hand hovering at his shoulder. Now I am ashamed to have heard so much, and since I cannot go into the cookhouse without interrupting them, I hurry to the saloon where I can pretend to busy myself. My heart hurts. I wish he would not like her.

Later, when we were storing the uneaten food and cleaning, I asked Mr. Serle about Madame Moses. I thought I might tell him after all of her throwing the cup at me.

"I overheard her brother call her *prima* something," I said. "What does it mean?"

Mr. Serle did not comment on my eavesdropping. *"Prima donna assoluta,"* he answered me. "She is a singer of the highest rank, a master of her art."

"Oh," I say.

"She is a great artist," Mr. Serle insists, as if I have questioned his word.

"I suppose," I say.

I can hear that my voice is sulky, childish.

"Is something wrong?" Mr. Serle asks.

He regards me with curiosity in his eyes. I feel the color rise in my face.

"You are mistaken in this woman," I tell him. My voice shakes.

"You know my opinion of her?" Mr. Serle's voice sounds cold.

We stand close to each other in the cramped cookhouse, and yet he seems, suddenly, far away.

What do I know? It is a feeling, I want to tell him. This woman is different in private with her daughter and her servant than she is in public to others. In my own mind I blame Madame Moses that Stellina and I were almost drowned. But that, I admit to myself, is not just. Stellina ran out as she might have done no matter who was tending her. Stellina is just a three-year-old child. No mother can prevent her child from danger entirely. It comes to me that I feel envy. But of whom? Of Madame Moses that Mr. Serle admires her, or of Stellina that her mother lives?

"Well?" Mr. Serle urges my answer. It is unlike him to push silence into speech.

"The lady does not love her daughter very much," I say. "She leaves her care to a maid."

"So do many women," Mr. Serle says.

"But we are on a sea voyage," I object. "There is little for any of the passengers to do. I see other women on the ship teaching their children."

"The little girl seems happy," Mr. Serle points out, "and her mother has suffered much in the rough weather."

"Her white skin and red mouth are paint," I say, remembering spilled powder in the cabin.

"Many women use a little powder," Mr. Serle says.

He sounds amused now.

"Madame Moses's brother should not boast about her fame, calling her a *prima* something."

I realize as I say it that I do not know anything about how artists behave. Mr. Serle does not hesitate to draw this to my attention.

"I think you know nothing about the matter," he says. "In this lady's case it is a matter of professional importance."

"Why?" I ask.

"Why? Because she is a Jew with a Jewish name. She faces prejudice."

"Her brother must have a Jewish name too, and she does not give him boasting titles," I object. I think about it further as I set biscuit tins in their places. "She sang a Christian song, to Mary, *Ave Maria*," I remind Mr. Serle.

"That is art," he says. "Her name is Jewish, not her singing."

"I use your name," I say. "I suppose it is a Jewish name. I do not care. I am glad to use your name, Serle, and Daniel, which connects me to my brother and your dead son too."

Mr. Serle's face flushes red.

"You do not understand," he says.

"Perhaps not," I concede, "but I should not like to work for people who judged me only by my name."

"Sometimes we have no choice," Mr. Serle says.

I know it is true, and I am about to say so when he adds, "Madame Moses has suffered. Her husband was a hero who died nobly in the cause of freedom. She is in mourning still, yet she rises above her pain to make great art. I admire her courage. She is an educated, accomplished woman and very beautiful."

"I thought you loved your wife only," I say.

Even as I speak, I know I should not. Perhaps because Mr. Serle called Madame Moses beautiful, I feel a devil in me. Mr. Serle's color goes. He looks gray and tired.

"Enough," he says.

He is honing a knife on the stone. His head bends to the task. He does not look up.

"I am sorry," I say, frightened.

"Enough," he says again. "Finish your work."

I have a few tarts to put away in a tin and then the breakfast manchet bread to knead. It is so cold now that I set the morning bread after tea and let it rise overnight. It is easier then to finish when the range heats up the cookhouse in the morning. As I work, I feel the silence of Mr. Serle. I do not know how to make things better, so I am silent too. It took me a long time to go to sleep that night, although I asked the Blessed Virgin to forgive my anger and then held my mother's ring and thought of her loving face.

It is late here in this place that is almost America. The lamp burns low. The wick will flare up, smoke, and die very soon. Mr. Serle, absorbed, turns the pages of his book. Tonight we share a peaceful quiet. The cookhouse smells faintly of grease and clove and of the anise seed in the rolls, rising for tomorrow's breakfast. I yawn. I am almost finished with my writing now.

Last night I cleared the tea dishes in the saloon as Phoebe came in to fetch the work bag Mrs. Greene left by her chair. Laden with the great basket I use to carry things across the deck, I struggle with the door. Phoebe steps out to the deck to hold it for me.

The cold wind makes my breath catch in my throat. The ship is a great bird in flight with sail aloft. Stars wink their icy light behind the blowing clouds. Phoebe wraps her brown woolen shawl tight about her arms and lifts her face to the night sky.

"How close to us the stars look," she says.

"I wonder where we are," I say. "The end of our journey must be near."

"I wish it would never end," Phoebe cries out.

"But why?" I ask. I am so tired of cramped space and heaving water.

"We are not in America here on the ocean, only traveling," Phoebe tells me. "I feel free in this no place. If I die here, I die free. I would give anything to die free."

"Anything?" I ask.

"Yes, anything," she says. "Do you know an *anything*?"

"I can tell you a secret," I say.

She turns her face up to me, and the wind blows her hair in its tight-curled strands about her forehead.

"Tell me," she says. "Quickly."

I tell Phoebe that I am a girl like her. I tell her that being a boy made me free to work and move in the world as girls cannot. I tell her that—nevertheless—I have a fear that I will do wrong to meet my brother as I am. I have boy's clothing; Phoebe has a woman's dress, so she told me days ago. I will trade clothing with her. Perhaps in New York she will have opportunity to slip away from the Greenes. Seymour told me that there are no slaves in New York. We speak quickly and low, only enough to agree that we will make the exchange and to promise each other secrecy.

"Oh, Daniel," Phoebe says, "I am so glad you trusted me."

She smiles at me, showing her pretty teeth, and then she is gone back to the saloon and the passengers' cabins.

I make my way fearfully across the tilting deck. It would be terrible to be swept away in the wind so close to our new country.

I wonder, now that I have written, if I should have recorded what we said. Perhaps this book, this gift from Mr. Serle, is a treacherous thing, luring me on into a dangerous desire to keep a history of speech and action. Writing makes a truth where none existed.

PART TWO

ELIZABETH STREET

WEDNESDAY, NOVEMBER 15, 1848—EVENING

WE ENTERED THE HARBOR of New York yesterday afternoon. First the white wing of a small boat came flying out to
us. Then a man in a trim uniform—the pilot, Flint said—came
nimbly up a rope ladder to the deck. The captain and the chief
mate greeted him, and he in turn handed a stack of papers to the
chief mate.

I spent as much time on the deck as I could steal from work.
Flint pointed out a low spit of land lying in the ocean to our left.

"That is Sandy Hook," he said. "See the bones of the wrecked
ships along her shore? That is the fate of fools who run for port in
stormy weather with no pilot."

Ahead of us lay a narrow strait with high land on the left-
hand shore. There is an old fort on it, ruined now. On our right
hand was lower land and another fort, not so derelict, built out in

the water. Then I had to carry lunch dishes to the saloon. The cabin passengers were in a state of great excitement. Many of them ate sandwiches out on the deck and watched the land growing and the traffic of the ships multiplying about us. I was glad for the excuse to go out to be sure that plates and cutlery were collected.

When we passed the narrowest place between the islands, we could see a yellow flag flying on a great pole in front of low white buildings. The ship received a signal and all sail was dropped. Another small boat came out to us from the shore.

"Don't cough or sneeze now, lad," Flint said as he paused near me. "It's the quarantine officer come out." He hurried forward where an anchor was being set.

When I retreated to the cookhouse, I found Mr. Serle and Seymour perched on stools, reading newspapers the pilot had brought. I went out again and saw the steerage passengers assembled on the main deck. The medical examiners emerged from the steerage hold as I watched and strolled among the people stopping to question one or another. The chief mate stood by, silent, with his arms folded across his chest.

At last, the medical men with the chief mate following mount the ladder to the quarterdeck. The captain greets them. They shake hands all around.

"A good sight," says Flint's hoarse voice at my ear. "We will weigh anchor as soon as they are off."

"There are no sick, then?" I am suddenly afraid.

Flint steps to the rail and spits over the side. "This is a clean ship," he says. "They don't overcrowd the steerage as some do."

I duck inside to tell Mr. Serle and Seymour the news and then hurry out again. The harbor of New York is a crowded, bustling place. We will lie at anchor for tonight in quiet water offshore and dock early tomorrow.

The city rises north of us. The ships crowded at the piers raise a forest of masts along the shore. Beyond that thicket are the chimneys of three-, four-, five-story buildings, houses and warehouses and factories, with the church steeples pointing up white fingers above their roofs toward the sky. The sun is low in the west

as the sailors throw out the great anchors fore and aft and set a little sail to catch the wind—just enough to hold us steady in our
place. The rays of the bleak November sun strike across the water,
illuminating a sail here, a glitter of copper roofing there in cold,
pure light. Everything is sharp, outlined. We are very near our
journey's end, and yet land is still so far away that we seem to look
out at a toy harbor and a toy city, a miniature of life before us.

The air smells different here. The pines of the shore, the coal
and wood fires of the city, the tar and animal smells of the ship. I
notice them now that we are still. The wind wraps odors in eddies
around us instead of blowing through and away.

On the ship, the steerage passengers huddle in quiet groups.
They are cooking the last of their provisions without the angry
cries and arguments of past days. The crew are cheerful. They
hurry about their tasks and make bawdy jokes about how they
will celebrate the end of our voyage. The cabin passengers grow
more gregarious and sociable suddenly, exchanging addresses and
commenting on the news they missed while traveling.

A fleet of smaller boats bustle out to us in the fading day.
Many of the cabin passengers pay their fees and go ashore to sleep
on dry land tonight. Mr. Simpkens is one of the first to leave, but,
before he goes, he seeks out Mr. Serle and thanks him for his fine
cooking. He gives Mr. Serle his card and says that if he ever finds
himself in London and in want of a position to call on him. They
shake hands heartily, and then Mr. Simpkens gives me a half sov-
ereign.

"Here is a tip for the bright, brave, redheaded steward," he
says with a wink.

Mr. and Mrs. Greene also go ashore, leaving Phoebe to be
fetched next day with their baggage. As soon as Mr. Greene's
blond head disappears over the side, Phoebe turns away, wrapping her arms in her shawl.

"Tonight in the cabin, Daniel," she whispers as she passes me
near the saloon door.

We make a final dinner for the few remaining cabin passengers. There are fresh oysters from a passing fishing boat, the last of
the beef, excellent turnips from America, and a spice cake. Mr.

Serle and I try the oysters and are impressed with their great size and briny flavor.

"I should not eat this," he says.

"Why not?" I ask. "I thought it was pork you cannot have."

"Nor fish without fins and scales," he tells me. "But it is hard to be a cook and avoid such things. When I worked in Paris, I learned the taste of oysters and lobster and shrimp. America is famous for her oysters, and I can understand it now."

"Is it a sin?" I ask him. Mr. Serle never talked of not following his religion before.

He shakes his head, but his words contradict his motion. "Yes," he tells me. "It makes me less a Jew. Less what I would wish to be."

"But if you were starving, you would have to eat shelled fish," I argue. "It would be a greater sin to die when you could choose to live."

"But I am not starving," Mr. Serle says. "I do not have that excuse. Only my work and that some believe the old laws out-of-date in this modern age."

"When you have your own restaurant, will you serve oysters?" I ask, but before Mr. Serle can answer, Seymour comes in. We leave our conversation and turn to our tasks. Mr. Serle adjusts the dampers on the range while I stir the soup. The meal we serve is a supper and tea combined, really, for it is so late. Madame Moses and her brother are among those still aboard.

"My sister will not trust her wardrobe to be brought ashore without her," I hear Herr Meyer tell another passenger.

After all is cleared and cleaned, Seymour tells us he is going to row in to shore. Not all hands are needed tonight. Some of the sailors are going to a tavern in the city.

"And you'd best be stowed away in your bunk when they return, lad. Some of 'em will be wild with drink and in a state to fuck a knothole when they return. Lock the lad up tonight, Mr. Serle."

Seymour, in his clean clothes and red neckerchief, does not wait for a reply.

"Did you understand him?" Mr. Serle asks me. He glances up

from stoking the fire in the range. He is heating water in one of the great cauldrons.

"Yes," I say. "I will be out of the way when the sailors return soused."

"Good," Mr. Serle says. "Tomorrow—" He stops short.

"Tomorrow," I echo.

My heart turns over at the thought.

"Have you given thought to tomorrow?"

"A little," I said. "The *Washington,* the ship that I believe took my brother up and carried him here, might have an office at the wharf. My brother will have left a message there if he was able."

I know inside myself I have not asked because I do not dare think of no office and no message.

"I spoke to the chief mate," Mr. Serle says. "The *Washington* is a Frost and Hicks packet. Their New York office will be very near where we dock tomorrow. We will inquire about your brother. If there is no word, we will decide then what next."

"Thank you," I say.

"And now," he says, battening down the lid of the flour barrel, "we are done here for the night. We will have the list of stores to check after the crew's breakfast tomorrow, a final cleanup, and we are done with sailing. I am heating water so I can shave and bathe. Can you find something to do elsewhere?"

"Of course," I say. "I have clothing I must brush and secure the buttons on for tomorrow. I will go find Phoebe and talk to her as I work."

When I tap on the door of the Greenes' cabin, Phoebe opens it a slit and peeks out.

"I am here," I say slipping in.

Phoebe latches the door safe, and we set to work. I have brought my good pants and jacket, both of which were my brother's. The pant legs and the jacket sleeves must be shortened for Phoebe. She has a linen smock—she calls it a blouse—that will do to wear underneath. I give her my cap. It costs me a pang because I bought it in Liverpool with Mr. Serle's advice. Boots we cannot exchange, for, to our surprise, her feet are larger than mine.

For me, there is the skirt and bodice that the housekeeper gave Phoebe in England. To my pleasure it is a fine wool that is smooth to the hand and a beautiful golden-brown color. The housekeeper must have been my height but very stout. While Phoebe is turning up cuffs on her new-old pants, I take a whole breadth of the fabric out of the skirt so that it can be gathered in on its strings to fit my waist. The bodice is a greater problem. It would be a day's work to unpick it all and fit it to me properly. We decide that if Phoebe pins the seams at the sides and the back for me, and then I stitch them as flat as possible, it will do. The result is somewhat lumpy, in the back especially, but the front looks neat enough. With Phoebe's dark brown shawl over my head, I will be respectable.

"Don't forget to put your hands in your pockets and walk easy like a boy," I tell Phoebe. "You will feel freer as soon as you wear pants."

We lean into the circle of light from the lamp and sew away frantically. There is no time for talk. We are both excited by what we are doing.

When we finish, we put on our new clothes to show each other. With her braids tucked up under the cap, Phoebe is a convincing little fellow. We look at each other.

"Oh, Daniel," Phoebe says, "I am so glad you are a girl."

We both dissolve in helpless giggles at her speech.

When we are sober, we begin work on our hair. We lay out a blanket. Phoebe takes the ribbons from her braids, and I clip her head all over. Then she stands while I brush her down. Phoebe has laid out some hairpins and a blue ribbon. She shows me how I can pin up the back part where my hair is long enough, and then let the curls in front spill over the ribbon. I will never have smooth wings of hair over my ears. Phoebe tells me that I should not try such a style.

"It does not suit your beauty," she says.

After I have put on my boy's work clothes again. I roll the skirt, bodice, and shawl carefully with the hairpins and ribbon and stow all in the bag I used to bring my things to Phoebe. My good pants and jacket are hers now. I have only the kitchen things

I am wearing to be a boy in. I pray I will be content and safe to be a girl again tomorrow.

"I will come very early in the morning," I tell her with a bravery I do not really feel, "with some food for you—and I will see you off the ship."

We are sober now and perhaps more frightened than happy at what we have done and what the morning will bring. Silently we kiss and hold each other for a moment. I hear the lock snick closed behind me as I leave the cabin and cross the saloon where a few passengers sit in the lamplight writing letters or reading.

When I emerge from the saloon onto the deck, Mr. Serle and Herr Meyer are leaning against the rail, looking out at the myriad lights of the city. They smoke cigars. I can smell the pungent odor that carries an undernote of sweetness. Lamps are lit about the *Victoria* and on all the ships in the harbor. As the ships rock, the lights swing, spitting out wavering tracks of gold on the dark water and on the deck and then swallowing them back. I see the two men in light and then shadowed.

Herr Meyer sees me and calls out jovially, "Come here, lad."

"Oh!" I am surprised. "If you will excuse me, sir, I will take my bag down to my bunk and come back."

"Of course," Mr. Serle says in his calm way.

"Are your buttons all in order, Daniel?" Herr Meyer says with a laugh when I return and cross to them. He smooths his brown whiskers with his left hand. His right hand holds his cigar.

"I believe so," I reply cautiously. What can Mr. Serle have told this man?

"Don't look so worried, child." Mr. Serle can read my thoughts, it seems. "Herr Meyer has invited us both to join him at his brother's house tomorrow night. We can be assured of a room there."

He raises the cigar to his lips. I think he is watching me from behind the rising smoke. Even though the lamp beside him swings a little so his dark head gleams in its rosy light, I cannot see his eyes.

"That is kind," I say.

It seems very strange to me to be standing in my boy's work

pants and smock before these two men, smelling the sweet odor of their tobacco. Moments ago I was twirling in a skirt and Phoebe put a ribbon in my hair.

"You aren't very enthusiastic." Herr Meyer smooths his beard again, as if the wind might have rumpled it. He does not sound insulted, only amused.

Mr. Serle watches silently. The red coal of his cigar end gleams in the dim light.

"I am grateful," I say. "Only I hope to find a message from my brother tomorrow. I came to America to find my brother."

"Well, well," Herr Sadick Meyer says. He glances askance at Mr. Serle as if surprised he did not mention it. "So you have a brother, Daniel. Does he look like you?"

"Oh yes," I say. "We both of us have our father's red-gold hair and blue eyes."

"Hmmph." Herr Meyer makes an interested sound. "Can you sing?"

"Of course I can," I tell him. "But simple songs, not famous ones such as Madame Moses sings."

"Enough, Sadick," Mr. Serle says in a lazy tone. "Don't tease the lad."

"He doesn't mind. Do you, Daniel?" Herr Meyer has a low, rich-sounding voice.

"I don't mind," I say, and that is true. If Herr Meyer is a friend to Mr. Serle, offering him a place to sleep in a strange city, I am glad to talk to him.

"What can you sing?" he asks me.

"My mother taught me 'Strawberry Lane,' " I say promptly. "She knew it as a girl in Falmouth, England."

I sing a verse for him. I like the first refrain: "Every rose grows merry betimes." When I was a child, I puzzled about the meaning. How can a rose grow merry?

"Hmmph." Herr Meyer looks down at the stub end of the cigar in his hand and turns it. "A very sweet soprano. Your voice has no crack in it yet, that I can hear. How old are you, lad?"

Before I can speak, someone among the steerage passengers on the deck begins to sing the rest of my song. The tenor voice rises pure as my father's did. "And then he will be a true lover of mine," he sings. It is a gay song, yet I shiver and tears come to my eyes.

Mr. Serle turns and throws the end of his cigar into the water.

"You were a long time with those buttons," he says. "Best go to your bunk now."

I am not reluctant to obey him. The wind is chill on the deck, and I am tired.

"Good night," I say to them and go down to my bed.

I cannot settle myself for sleep. The lamp is still lit for Mr. Serle, so I crouch in my bunk and write this.

I will wear my new clothes tomorrow. I will begin in the New World as myself—Mina Pigot. Even if I wear hastily sewn skirts with my old shirt. I worried what my brother might say if he saw me in a lad's pants and cap. He might not know me in a boy's costume and that would break my heart. He might be shocked or disapproving. I feel shame when I think of telling him of my mistakes. I do not look forward to explaining how I was tricked and threatened before I disguised myself and found Mr. Serle.

Only I would rather have the shame of explaining everything than not find my brother at all. I push the fear away. My bag is beside me in the bunk. The dress and shawl are at the top so I can take them out tomorrow. My money and my ring are sewn into my shirt. I touch the ring. Now I will put this book away and say a prayer for my mother and my father to watch over me and bring me safe to my brother.

SATURDAY, NOVEMBER 25, 1848

Today is Evacuation Day. This is the very day the British troops who fought to keep America a slave to England withdrew from the city to their ships in the harbor. They sailed away, and the great General George Washington, the father of America, riding on his beautiful horse, led his army in a parade all down Broadway. America was won. There was a parade again today to remember and celebrate. I feel almost as if New York is holidays and fun just for my arrival. Everything celebrates Mina in America.

But it is days since I wrote in my book. I want to set down my happiness.

On Thursday, November 16, 1848—I cherish the day—I walked on America for the first time. There was no breakfast served to passengers on the ship that morning. Only the sailors got their usual burgoo. Mr. Serle drank his coffee with milk and sugar as he always does. He urged me to have some, but I was too anxious to eat or drink. The ship weighed anchor well before dawn. As pale light broke, we were at the city wharf, the ship's bowsprit reaching out over a cobbled street, South Street they say, near Maiden Lane, where all is bustle and confusion.

While the sailors lash the ship at the pier, I slip down to the cabin where Phoebe waits. She is ready in her boy's clothing, and I am still wearing my kitchen pants and smock for this morning's work. In this space of time we are both boys together for the world. I made a packet of bread and salt herring for Phoebe. I put it in her hand, and she smiles at me. We do not speak as we hurry out through the empty saloon.

Everyone who can find a place is at the rails, looking down to the city. Shouting people crowd the road in front of the ship. Phoebe, with her bag over her shoulder and my cap pulled down about her ears, joins the steerage passengers surging about the deck. I see her move close to a distraught-looking woman surrounded by children and bundles. In a moment she has a child in her arms and is clambering with the others from the ship.

Then she is on the road, helping the woman assemble her things in a heap, guarding them from pushing carters who want to seize them. A man comes rushing to the woman. They wrap their arms about each other. Phoebe gives the child she has been holding to the largest of the other children. Then she slips away among the crowd.

Mr. Levi Meyer comes aboard and embraces his sister and little Stellina. He embraces Herr Meyer too, and then shakes hands heartily with Mr. Serle when Herr Meyer introduces him.

He has hired three carters: one for Herr Meyer's, Stellina's, and Luly's things, and two for Madame Moses's trunks.

Herr Meyer comes over and grasps my hand. "Thank you again for saving our little Stellina," he says. "If ever I can repay you, call on me. And Stellina wants to thank you."

Luly holds Stellina up.

"Good-bye, Daniel," Stellina whispers in my ear and kisses my cheek damply.

"Thank you, Daniel," Madame Moses says graciously. "We are grateful to you for our darling."

Herr Meyer turns to speak to Mr. Serle, and Madame Moses approaches him also.

"Come to us soon," she says. "My brother Sadick likes your company."

She lifts one black-gloved hand as if she will touch her finger to his cheek and then withdraws it. As they all go, Luly and little Stellina look back, see me watching, and wave good-bye to me.

The sailors and the longshoremen make short work of unloading the cargo. The ship rises higher as the weight is lifted out of her until we look into the windows of the warehouses across the road, where men in eyeshades sit at desks, hunched over ledgers.

Our own accounts are written up, and with the others we go aft to the captain's cabin to receive our wages. The captain and the chief mate dole out piles of notes and coins; we sign the book to show we took our pay. As the sailors go tumbling out the door, the captain asks Mr. Serle to stay a moment. Trembling with impatience, I wait too.

"Will you reconsider?" the captain says. "The cabin passengers were mightily pleased. Mr. Simpkens confessed to me it was quite a surprise to have your dishes. I will increase your wage if you will ship again with the *Victoria*."

"Thank you, Captain," Mr. Serle says. "If I find myself wishing to cross the ocean again, I will come to you. To speak honestly, I do not anticipate it."

The captain sighs and shakes his head. "The owners will be disappointed," he says. "These are strange times, with sail overtaken every day by steamship packets. I do not like their belching smoke and the noise. There is no beauty to them."

Mr. Serle agrees politely, and they shake hands. At last we are on the deck again.

"I must change to my good clothes and comb my hair," I say.

"I will be here," Mr. Serle tells me.

In the storeroom, I quickly pull off my work pants and smock and don the golden-brown dress. In the cookhouse, I do my best to dress my hair as Phoebe showed me, but managing the ribbon is hopeless, and I give it up. On tiptoe, I look into the scrap of shaving mirror that Seymour keeps on the shelf above the range. I can see just a part of my face, a curl of red hair at my temple, straight eyebrows, and my blue-green eyes that are like my father's and my brother's. My breath catches. My brother. I must hurry.

I look out from the cookhouse door carefully. I must not appear suddenly before sailors who thought me Daniel. Mr. Serle stands at the rail, waiting, gazing out at the city.

"Mr. Serle?" I call.

He turns and sees me. His eyes widen. He looks shocked, I think, as he sweeps off his hat and holds it like a shield before his breast.

"Mina?" he says.

"Is it all right?" I cross the deck to him.

"You did not tell me," he replies. "How did you do this?"

"I got the dress from Phoebe," I say. "She had it as a gift in England. Phoebe took my boy's pants and jacket and cap in exchange." I pause. "She has gone off."

Mr. Serle looks grave.

"That is very serious for her—and for you—if she is caught," he tells me.

"I want so much to step on the land of America as myself," I say. "My brother will not want to have his sister turned into a boy. And I remember what it is to be afraid of someone. Mrs. Greene whips Phoebe."

I am pleading with Mr. Serle to understand. I think he does, for he does not say anything further on the subject. Indeed, he stands silent a long moment and stares at me. If it were not Mr. Serle, it would be rude.

"You are lovely, Mina," he says at last.

Together, we make our way down the steep ladder from the *Victoria*. I hold on with one hand and keep my skirts tight about me with the other, remembering that I have no drawers and no petticoat underneath. At last we stand on this first cobbled road of America. I stoop and touch it quickly with my hand.

"We are really here," Mr. Serle says.

We make our way along the busy pier, where coils of rope and barrels are heaped and horse-drawn carts are being unloaded. Avoiding a cart, I almost walk into a porter swinging a bale to his back. Mr. Serle seizes my wrist to stop me. He hesitates a moment holding on to me, and then he takes my arm in his. He protects me as if I were a lady. It is a shock to feel the steel-wire strength of him. We lived so near each other, and yet we rarely touched.

On the second floor of a red brick warehouse, the shipping offices of the *Washington,* we stand before a polished wood counter. Mr. Serle explains our business. I cannot speak for fear.

"Miss Mina Pigot?" The man at the counter stroked his mustache with one forefinger and stared at me. "Let me see if we have a message for Miss Mina Pigot."

He took a wooden box from under the counter and set it solemnly before him. Wetting his thumb, he began to go through the file of papers. I wanted to shout at him to hurry, hurry, or to climb over the counter and do his job for him. Mr. Serle must have felt my need because he pressed my arm a little closer to him.

"Ah!" says the mustachioed man. "Message for Miss Mina Pigot."

My heart turns over in my chest.

MAY 12, 1848

My dearest sister Mina,

I have little hope, but if you are reading this, I thank God. I am a waiter at the Columbia House Hotel at Broadway between Vesey and Barclay Streets in New York City. I pray for your soul every day.

Your loving brother,
Daniel Pigot

"It is good, I think," Mr. Serle says, looking at my tearful, smiling face. "I am glad for you."

"Read it." I press the wonderful letter into his hand. Without waiting for him to finish, I ask the man at the counter for paper and a pen. "I must write to my brother," I tell him, full of joy. "My brother lives."

Mr. Serle and the man with the great mustache help me to sit and calm myself enough to write without my hand shaking so much that I blot all. The shipping office has a runner who takes the message and brings the reply. My brother will come to the *Victoria* within the hour.

We make our way back along the crowded, roiling waterfront. As we are about to climb the ladder to the *Victoria*, I see the name written along the bow of the ship beside her at the pier.

"Oh, look!" I cry to Mr. Serle. "It is the *Cushlamachree* beside us. It was an omen."

Mr. Serle looks puzzled.

"It is an Irish ship," I tell him. "Her name means *joy*."

Mr. Serle smiles at me. "A good omen indeed," he agrees.

I carry my bag up to the deck. I stand by the rail where I can see the bustling street. I imagine the first sight of my brother's bright head moving swiftly through the crowds of people coming and going, past the piled burlap bags, stacks of lumber, horse-drawn drays, and handcarts. Every minute Daniel is closer.

I am frantic with impatience, peering over the rail, walking up farther along the deck to see if I can see my brother coming. Mr. Serle sits down on his trunk.

"Rest a moment, Mina," he says. "You will be tired out before your brother comes. I am tired watching you."

I stop beside him. "I am Mina now," I say. "Is it strange to call me Mina?"

Mr. Serle sighs. "No," he says. "You look very much a girl today."

How can he look sad when all is sun and joy? Before I can question him, Flint comes from the forecastle.

"Oh, Flint," I say. "I am waiting for my brother."

"That's good," he says in his vague, hoarse voice. He blinks in a bewildered way as if the weak November sun dazzles him.

"Are you off, then?" I ask. "Are you going to celebrate the end of the voyage?"

"No, no," he says. "I took the Pledge last spring. I will go to the Mission here in New York or maybe I will dare to go to Albany. I am not strong as I should be."

He looks dismal. The only bright thing about him is the little gold anchor in his ear.

"Good-bye, Flint," I say. "Good luck to you."

I wish he would go and not stand there, looking like a rainy day.

"Well, give us a kiss, lad," he says.

I lean to him and kiss him lightly. He stinks of sweat and tobacco. Without saying more, Flint slings his sea bag to his back and goes down the ladder to the pier. He does not seem to have noticed that I am no longer Daniel in pants and smock but a girl in a long dress with a shawl about her shoulders.

"You see," I say to Mr. Serle. "I could not explain what he is like."

"I see indeed," Mr. Serle tells me.

"What does it mean?" I ask.

"I do not know," Mr. Serle says. "I think the man is addled. Was he like that before he hit his head in the storm?"

Mr. Serle comes to stand beside me. He leans his arms on the railing and gazes about at the crowded wharves. Before I can reply to say that no, Flint was like that from the beginning of the voyage, we hear someone shouting from the street.

"*Beniamino! Beniamino!*" The voice is robust, loud, joyous.

Mr. Serle makes a startled sound. On the pier a man is waving both his arms at us.

"*Beniamino!*" the man cries again. He is burly, strong-looking, with a mop head of dark-brown curls and the rough clothing of a longshoreman.

"Guido!" Mr. Serle shouts now. He too is waving.

The man comes swarming up the ladder. They wrap their arms about each other and kiss. I never saw men embrace like that. Mr. Serle grips his friend's shoulders tight. Like a sailor holding to a safety line when the ship tosses in a storm, he clings to this man whose name he says over and over—*Guido! Guido!* When they finish kissing, the man crosses himself. They both speak at once in a strange language. Between watching for my brother and trying to understand what is happening, I am beside myself.

At last, Mr. Serle turns to me. Tears brim in his eyes. "This is Guido," he says. "Guido, who knew my father and who saved my life after my brother died. Guido, who helped me leave Rome and my terrible life there. This is my friend Guido."

Guido looked at me and smiled. *"Che bella!"* he said to Mr. Serle.

It sounded like something nice to say. I smiled at him.

"This is Mina. I mean to say Miss Pigot," Mr. Serle says. "Guido, Guido, Mr. DiRoma—Miss Mina Pigot."

"How do you do, Mr. DiRoma," I say.

"Ahhh," Guido says, drawing the sound out in a long breath. "Miss Mina Pigot. Mina *di mièle. È la tua móglie, Beniamino?*"

"No, no, not my wife." Mr. Serle seems upset. Red flushes across his cheekbones.

"Innamorata?" Guido wrinkles his brown forehead and looks at Mr. Serle as if he is surprised and puzzled both.

"No, no, no," Mr. Serle says. He looks at me with an uncertainty in his face, as he did when he first saw me in my woman's dress. He and Guido talk. I do not understand a word nor even get a feeling from it except that they are friends.

"Miss Pigot?" Mr. Serle is speaking to me.

How strange, I think. I am child and lad and Mina and now Miss Pigot.

"I am so glad you have found your friend," I say. "What luck that he saw you."

"Guido works on the docks," Mr. Serle tells me. "He has a

room in a place not far from here. We have both found great good fortune today. Your brother lives, and I have met an old friend in a new country."

"How wonderful," I say, and then a terrible thought comes over me. "When will I see you again?" I exclaim. "What will I do?"

To my surprise, Mr. Serle's dark eyes brighten with tears again. "I think you might forget me soon," he says gently. "Your brother will wish to care for you."

"But you are my friend," I say. Tears well in my eyes too. I am happy and grief-struck all at once. "We worked and lived together for almost eight months. I can never forget you."

Guido says something quickly in his language.

Mr. Serle nods. "This new world confuses me," he says. "I had not thought ahead to parting from you. I will write down the address where Guido lives. You and I will both have much to learn in America. I shall be glad to hear how you get on."

I put the piece of paper safe next to my rosary and my housewife in the pocket of my new skirt, and as I do so, I hear my brother's voice, calling my name.

And then—well, how does one write joy?

"I brought your riding boots," I say as I throw my arms about him.

The solid flesh and blood of him against me blocks all the noise and tumble of the city. We are in a pool of light and quiet where love drenches the parched heart. I do not know how long I cling to Daniel, wordless, but at last he pushes me from him so he can look into my face.

Then all the world comes back. Cries from the wharf and the docked ships, the creak of rope against wood posts, and the clatter of rigging in the wind. Mr. Serle's friend has his arm over his shoulder as they lean against the rail. I introduce Daniel to Mr. DiRoma and Mr. Serle, but he seems to pay little attention, looking only at me.

"Hurry, Mina," Daniel says. "We must go to Elizabeth Street."

He slings my bag to his shoulder. Mr. Serle smooths a curl back lightly at my temple as he says good-bye and smiles at me. I feel tears rise again, but before I can think or speak, I am clamber-ing down the steep ship's ladder once more and walking, almost breathless with the wonder of it, with Daniel through the city.

I can see Daniel looks well. Since we were parted in the spring, he has gained flesh and strength. He no longer has the starved, almost transparent look I saw in the emigrants on the ship. He is become denser, more opaque, ruddy, not pale gray. He is taller than I, of course, and lanky. Besides the color of our red hair and blue eyes, we share the shape of our father's long-fingered, strong hands. Daniel has Father's long face too—a horse-inspired face, my mother called it for a joke, because my father loved horses so.

"Being a waiter agrees with you, Daniel," I say, hurrying to keep up with him. "I am so glad to find you in health."

Daniel slows a little then, and we talk as we go. All intent on him, I saw nothing of the streets or the sights we passed. Daniel likes his work at the Columbia House Hotel on Broadway. He lives there in attic rooms set aside for the cooks and waiters and kitchen boys. There are hundreds of guests, and all of them must pay to eat their meals at the hotel. Daniel serves rich travelers and businessmen from Wall Street and hears their talk.

After Daniel brought me to Mrs. Redburn's boardinghouse, where I sit and write just now, he went back to work immediately even though I begged him to stay.

"No," he said. "I must not risk my job. It pays well."

"Surely they will understand that you have just found your sister whom you lost," I say. "You can tell them."

"What a goose you are, Mina," Daniel says, hugging me to him again. "You are prettier than I remember, although your hair seems very short and you are too thin."

Then Daniel hurried off. He will take an omnibus down Broadway to the hotel and serve suppers until late this evening.

On Sunday, at last, he came back again. The evening supper at the hotel on Sunday is simpler, so the waiters are not all needed. They take turns having a few hours for themselves. Daniel ex-changed with someone so he could see me.

"You look more rested now, Mina," he said after he kissed me in greeting.

"I did nothing but sleep for two days," I say. "I am afraid to go out."

"We will take a walk together," Daniel says.

I wrap myself in my shawl, and we go down the stone steps of the boardinghouse. How wonderful to link arms with him and to see the city. We walk a little north on Elizabeth Street, looking at brick-fronted houses and small shops, and then along Prince Street, where Daniel points out St. Patrick's Church to me. It is a great stone pile with a stone wall along the street and then iron railings in front.

"See how close it is," Daniel says. "You can easily come here by yourself."

"Why does the church have a wall about it?" I ask. "Our chapel in Ireland had no such thing."

"For protection," Daniel says. His voice is bitter suddenly.

"But why?" I ask.

"There are those who hate us," Daniel says. "It is the same as Ireland for that. The elite claim the Catholics are ruled by the Pope and cannot truly be Americans. Our churches and our grave-yards too have been attacked."

"How terrible," I say and shiver with the thought. "I thought there is freedom here."

"Oh yes," Daniel says. "There is freedom. The greatest thing is that when we are attacked we have the freedom to stick to-gether and resist. We fight for each other and for our rights. It's not like the old country, where the hungry man was offered his lordship's boot to lick for a dinner. We are for each other. Don't you forget that, Mina."

"Yes, Daniel," I answer.

We turn left on Mulberry, then left again on Spring Street. We stop to see the horses at a livery stable. I take a deep breath. I love the warm smell of the stable. Daniel warns me that I must not go farther south on these streets.

"They lead into the Five Points, a dangerous part of the city," he says. "Stay near here and the church. Walk west to Broadway if you wish to go downtown."

Soon we are back at Elizabeth Street and Mrs. Redburn's.

"Shall we go in?" Daniel asks. "You look cold."

"I am chilled," I admit. "Besides, the streets are dirty, and I have just this one dress."

Mrs. Redburn let us use her private parlor to talk. The main parlor for the boarders is full of lounging young men reading their newspapers and joking with each other on a Sunday afternoon. The young men work as clerks in shops or counting houses, Mrs. Redburn told me. They stare when they see me in the hall or at supper.

At first Daniel and I sat silent in the warmth of the parlor. Just to be near him stirs my heart.

Daniel took my hand in his firm grasp and said, "I thought you were dead, Mina. I wept for you as I sat in the fishing boat that rescued me. Did you know I was alive?"

"After the first day I believed so," I tell him. "I always believed I would find you."

"What happened to you?" he asks me.

It is wonderful to talk to Daniel. His face is so alive and humorous, and always in his expression too are my mother's way of furrowing her brow in thought and my dead sister Eliza's curling smile. And so, watching him the while, I tell him as simply as I can of how I searched for him and saw his name as one of the rescued on the lists posted in Liverpool; how I lost all my money to a cheating man who sold me a ticket for America on a ship that did not exist; how I was offered passage and maid's work by evil Mrs. Hatton and then overheard her and her husband plan to sell me away as a brothel slave; how I put on his boy's pants and jacket from the bag of his things that I held to even when I jumped from the burning ship, the *Abigail;* how I made my way to the country thinking to work with horses and ended as a kitchen apprentice to Mr. Serle; how, still as a boy, I worked on the *Victoria* to come to America.

At this last he furrows his brow ferociously. "Well!" he says. It is an explosion of breath. "I am glad you are done with that. I thought you came across on the *Victoria* as a passenger, like a lady."

"But, Daniel," I protest, "I thought I was doing right to work

· 58 ·

and save. I thought all the time of our dream to have a farm and horses."

Daniel squeezes my hand. "How good you are, little one," he says.

"But I want to work," I say. "I want to be your partner in the world. Do you think we will search for a farm soon?"

"I gave up that daydream." Daniel speaks as if brushing a cobweb from his face. "I have a friend at the hotel, John Deegan. We will buy a saloon together. We will rise."

I remember the hopeful talks Daniel and I had when we planned to have our fine farmland and horses. I bite my lip. He has lived in America longer than I have.

"A saloon?" I ask. "I will cook." I hurry on before he answers. "I will help you. I learned so much from Mr. Serle in the great house in England. I can bake and roast and make fancy cakes—and even sugar nests for custards."

Daniel pats me on the shoulder. "I am glad, Mina. You will be a fine manager when you marry. Only I do not think that fancy cakes will be wanted in our New York saloon. Pickled eggs and pig's feet, perhaps."

"Oh!" I say, disappointed. But then, "I know a recipe for pickled eggs," I tell him.

Daniel is thinking of something else entirely. "Who were the men with you at the ship?" he asks me. "I forget what you said. I was thinking only of finding you."

"And I of you," I assure him.

"Who were they?" he asks again.

I wonder if there is something uneasy in his tone.

"The brown-haired man is Mr. Guido DiRoma," I say. "I met him only five minutes before you came. The other man, the darker one, who looks slight but is very strong for all that—that is Mr. Serle. He gave me work and saw that I was paid for it. He taught me. He is a very great cook, trained in Paris and London. He helped me cross the ocean safe to find you. Because of him I am here and have gold coins sewn into my shirt for savings."

"Where are these men from?" my brother asks. "Surely they are not Irish?"

"Oh no," I say. "They are both from Rome, where the Pope lives, in Italy. I do not know all of their history, but they know each other from boyhood."

I think for a moment. "They are very different," I tell Daniel. "Mr. Serle is a Jew and more educated. Guido DiRoma works as a longshoreman here. He is a Catholic, like us. Just the same, Mr. DiRoma and Mr. Serle are friends."

"A Jew?" my brother says. His brow furrows. "You trust him?"

"Of course," I say. Tears well in my eyes. I want Daniel to understand.

"It's all right, Mina," my brother says. "I know you are a good girl."

I am not happy, and yet, to explain further, to protest, will be how it was when I tried to tell Mr. Serle about Flint. Some things cannot be explained in mere words; some things in life are seeing and feeling purely.

Mrs. Redburn's little clock on the shelf tinkled the hour, and Daniel rose and hugged and kissed me. He told me he would visit again on Thursday, which is a special holiday. The president of America, President Polk he is called, declares Thanksgiving Day to the people. Everyone goes to their church and gives thanks for the great country that is theirs.

I have thought about it since Daniel explained it. He did not say what I just wrote.

He said, "This great country that is ours."

"Ours?" I exclaimed.

"Yes, ours, Mina," Daniel said. "Seventy years ago the people took it from the damned British. It is yours and mine now. I am a citizen. I voted Locofoco this month, and I voted for the men who rule this city too."

"But—" I begin. It takes five years to be a citizen. Mr. Serle told me.

"Never worry," Daniel tells me. "I know smart men who see I have my rights and advance. John Deegan and I will have our saloon and be runners for the Democrats besides. Our man did not win for president this time. Old Rough-and-Ready Taylor will be sworn in next spring—he is good enough for now. We will win in fifty-two."

I am proud that my brother could vote so soon, and I tell him so.

"Never mind, Mina," he says. "It is something for a man to do. I want you to brush up your clothing. We will go to the church I showed you, St. Patrick's, and be glad that we are together. Do you have a bonnet?"

A bonnet? I have just given up wearing a boy's cap.

"No," I reply. "I have no bonnet, just a shawl."

Daniel sighs. "Never mind for now," he says. "But I want you to look like a lady, not a poor immigrant just off the boat."

Kneeling in the great church with its high, many-paned windows and the voices of worship echoing around me, I remember Daniel's words about the iron fence and who we are. Hate. Freedom. The Irish stick together. Daniel believes in justice. He has not really changed. The father raises the host at the altar. This is a day for thanksgiving.

After the service, Daniel greets some men he knows. They are very well dressed. One of them, a tall man with a thick neck almost bursting his white collar, looks over at me and nods as Daniel speaks.

"Who are they?" I ask as we walk back to Elizabeth Street.

Daniel smiles. "Important men," he says. "Mr. Branton thinks you pretty."

At Mrs. Redburn's we sit in a corner of the parlor to talk. The young men are disbursed on this holiday and all is quiet.

"I told you about what happened to me," I tell Daniel. "What of you?"

Daniel sighs. "I do not like to think of it," he says.

"But I am your sister," I reply. "Tell me. It cannot be worse than what I imagine."

Daniel takes a big breath. "I was on the deck of the burning *Abigail*," he says. "I saw you at the broken rail. Your braid was unpinned, and in the wind and smoke I did not know if what I saw was your red hair or flame. As I reached out, you disappeared in a burst of fire and smoke. You were there and then you were not. You were lost to me, Mina. Not caring whether I lived or died, I jumped from the ship into the cold sea."

"Oh, my brother," I say and reach for his hand.

"I do not know how long I was in the water." Daniel grips my hand. "Someone was with me, struggling. I think he helped me. Then we were in a boat, gasping among a load of fish like gaffed fish ourselves. The *Abigail* was a burning hulk on the horizon."

He stops a moment and, letting go my hand, walks restlessly up the parlor and back again. I wait for him in silence. I know the pictures that flame in his mind. Sorrow cannot be hurried.

"The fishermen had taken several of us from the sea. With fish and people the small bark wallowed low in the waves. One of the men took off his white shirt and flew it as a flag. A ship hailed us, the *Washington,* westbound for New York. They would help by taking anyone willing to go with them. The captain had mail and many passengers and would not turn back."

My brother takes my hand again. I grip it tight.

"I thought you dead, Mina," he says, "else I would have gone back. Perhaps I was not thinking clear. My arm was burned, my mind blurred with smoke and grief."

"You did right, Daniel," I tell him.

"Well," Daniel sighs, a sad breath, "the choice is gone. The ship's boat came across. I boarded the *Washington.* The chief mate told me to sleep in the steerage with the other immigrants. I asked for work. He asked if I knew anything of sailing. I lied and said I did."

"Oh, Daniel," I say. "You were brave."

Daniel takes his hand from mine and rubs his face with it. It is a weary gesture somehow. He rubs his head until his red curls are all in disarray.

"I did not feel brave," he tells me. "Only desperate. There I stood in my dripping clothes, one sleeve to my jacket gone. My only possessions were our baptismal papers from Father Fintan, the few small coins that you sewed into the lining of that jacket, and my pocket knife that was Father's."

Daniel falls silent again. Then—"Brave or not, the mate did not believe me," he says. "They told me to find a place in the steerage. The ship's doctor came and looked at me and said I must be but a lad and should be issued half-rations as a child under fourteen—and I a starving man of twenty. Unless I gave him every penny I had, he could do—would do—nothing for the burn on my arm."

I want to cry out, to curse at the injustice of it. Daniel is not looking at me now, and his hand lies lax in mine. He is inside his story.

"It was a terrible ship, the *Washington*. Nine hundred steerage passengers, two iron grills on the deck for cooking for all that horde, mates that kicked and cursed the people, short rations. Oh, Mina, if it had not been for two good families from our home county, I should have starved and died. They let me cook with them; they found a spoon for me, so I could eat from the pot. I did all I could in return, helping to seize our supply of brackish water when it was doled out and holding the place at the cooking grill. Of course, there were days when we could not cook. We had rough weather."

I shudder at the thought. My poor brother ill and hungry in the stifling dark with the roar of wind and wave beating in his mind. I bend to kiss his hand in pity.

"A man in the steerage hurt his hand in the storm. He had huddled up against the hull planking so as not to be thrown from his bunk. The planking gaps when the ship leans one way and closes when it leans another. He must have put his hand out as the ship changed course and then was caught there with his little finger between two planks, screaming in agony. When the ship heeled to the other side, he was freed at last. I will never forget the sound of his cries. I hear him in my dreams."

"I know, I know," I say softly.

"The weather calmed and grew hot, and that was worse," Daniel says. "Fever took the oldest and the youngest. We lost eighty of us. Every day, every day, the bodies were flung into the dark water. And there was no priest on the ship. The people refused to have the captain read a prayer. He and the mates said we were ignorant, Popish fools, but we knew that no man who served a people so could be a Christian. We did not want the devil praying over our dead."

Daniel wipes his eyes on his sleeve.

"At last we came to the New York harbor and the pilot came aboard. The mates forced the people to throw all their dirty bedding and many of their goods overboard. Well, that was nothing to me. I had a bit of old sail that I had filched from the junk stores. That is what I wrapped myself into for a bed. The terrible steerage hold was scrubbed and fumigated so the inspectors of New York would not see the truth of how the people suffered. It was unjust to the end of the voyage."

"But you are brave and strong, and you are here," I say to Daniel. He moves as if he will rise and pace the room again. I wrap my arms about him to hold him still.

"I am here," Daniel replies, kissing my cheek and then pushing me away. "Irish men came on the ship in the harbor. They helped those of us in need to find a place where we would not be cheated. The society helped me to find work too. One of the men urged me to leave the letter for you. Even though I thought you dead, he counseled hope."

"I am proud to think of our good countrymen," I say.

Daniel passes his hand down his face as if he is wiping thought away. "Now I have told my tale. I will never talk of this again, Mina, never. You must never ask, never speak it. Promise me."

"I promise," I tell him.

And so I kissed my brother and saw him to the door. After eating a little at the noisy supper table, I took my candle and went to my room. I wrote my brother's story. I will never speak of it, but I have this private record. I will not forget.

Now I have arrived in my accounts at today, Evacuation Day. I walked down Broadway by myself to meet Daniel. I crossed to the west side of the thoroughfare and made my way among the crowds. I suppose if I had a purse I would have worried about pickpockets. As it is, my coins are all sewn tight in my shirt and are safe under my skirts. My brother told me to walk until I met him coming up, but to go no farther than A. T. Stewart's shop at Reade Street. I would not miss the place, he said; it is all shiny marble. Indeed, I found him arriving there just as I reached it. He was with his friend John Deegan.

"My sister, Miss Mina Pigot." Daniel introduced us.

I forgot I am a girl, reached out, and shook hands heartily with my brother's friend.

"I am glad to meet you," I said, and then remembered and felt awkward.

"What a pretty girl your sister is, Daniel," Mr. Deegan remarked, holding my hand.

I loosed my hand from Mr. Deegan's grasp. He stared at me, and I pulled my shawl more closely about my head.

"Are you cold, Mina?" my brother asked.

"No, no," I said. "Only I do not like the wind in my hair."

I surprised myself with my own words. It is not really true. On the ship I liked the freedom of my bare head. The sound of band music in the distance interrupted the need for conversation. The crowd surged forward and the three of us with it, Daniel on one side of me and Mr. Deegan on the other.

John Deegan is not quite my brother's height and of a slighter build. His hair sticks out under his hat in a light brown thatch. Hay-colored hair, I call it. His nose is straight, his features open. He has a strutting sort of walk. He has a handsome face, and yet—I am uneasy at his standing close to me in the pressing crowd.

My uneasiness vanished into the cheer and excitement of the approaching parade—firemen pulling a shiny water cart, marching bands, an artillery company hauling a cannon, men with banners, men shooting up Roman candles with a bang and a swoosh of red sparks that make the horses of the drays waiting in the side streets shy and neigh in terror. With the others, I call and shout. At the end of the parade comes a tall man dressed in the old-fashioned clothes of General Washington, riding a great, prancing white horse. The man waves his three-cornered hat and the people cheer themselves hoarse.

Then the parade is gone by. The music drifts back to us faintly as an odor of roses will scent a summer wind. The crowd noise subsides to talk and laughter. It is over.

"Honored to meet you, Miss Pigot," John Deegan says. He takes my hand again, although I have not offered it.

"Good-bye," I reply politely.

I wish I had gloves. I wrap my hands in my shawl.

"I am going to walk my sister a little on her way," Daniel tells Mr. Deegan.

"All right," Mr. Deegan says, turning downtown, whistling cheerfully as he goes.

Daniel and I walk together in silence for a moment.

Then—"Did you like my friend John Deegan?" Daniel asks me. "I think women find him handsome."

"Yes, he is handsome," I admit.

"He is my friend," Daniel repeats. "Perhaps if you like him, you might marry him."

The thought takes my breath away.

After a moment Daniel pinches my arm. "Are you awake?" he asks.

"I am not ready to marry," I protest.

"Well, when you are, consider John. He seems to like you." My brother squeezes my arm and laughs. He is only teasing me.

At Grand Street, Daniel sees me safe across the bustle and confusion of the carriages and carts and omnibuses on Broadway and then turns back to hurry to his work. I walk up Broadway slowly, wondering at the fancy-goods shops. At Broome Street I turn right and then go left on Crosby Street to continue up the town. Perhaps I will see Madame Moses or little Stellina out with Luly the maid. It is strange to be in a place with so many people, and yet, where I see no one I know for days at a time.

I wonder if Mr. Serle saw the parade today.

As I wrote the last sentence, the bell rang downstairs. I must hurry or I will miss the meal. Americans eat so fast that I am often just seating myself as they are rising. The noise and rush in the dining room tire me. I have little appetite for the boiled meat and lard-heavy pies.

Monday, December 4, 1848

I am finally used to being on land again. When I lie down at night, my head no longer swoops up and down and up and down in endless waves as if I still traveled the ocean on a sailing ship. I walk to church and back and then around the block past the livery stable with greater confidence.

I talked to Daniel about advertising for a job as a cook or a cook's assistant. I would like to live in a comfortable household and cook for people of refined tastes. Daniel wishes me to wait. He is looking out for a job for me that will let us see each other more often than if I am in service. He will have word for me very soon.

Meanwhile, I need clothing beyond this one ill-fitting dress and Phoebe's shawl. This morning I screwed up my courage to a sticking place and climbed the steps at the dressmaker's two doors up from Mrs. Redburn's. I noticed the pretty sign, black lettering on a pale blue ground, in the first-floor window last week.

FINE DRESSMAKING, FASHIONABLE MILLINERY
MISS H. CORBETT

There is another sign in the same style in the window on the other side of the center door.

ART LESSONS FOR LADIES, PRIVATE INSTRUCTION
MISS J. CORBETT

If it is too dear for me, I can say I was mistaken and go elsewhere, I told myself as I rang the bell. Miss H. Corbett ushered me into a bright room with a worktable and a long rack with dresses and parts of dresses hung on it. On the far wall opposite the door from the hallway is a stove with its hod for coal and wood. The stove must serve for both heating and cooking, for it has a kettle on it and next to it a set of shelves with a curtain over them. I imagine the neat array of clean pots and dishes stored there. Beside the stove are two comfortable chairs and a small table supporting a polished oil lamp. There is a rocking chair near one of the windows on the right. The dressmaker must sit where the light is good to work in the daytime. On the left-hand wall is a tall, three-paneled mirror and a doorway to some inner room.

The place pleased me immediately, for all was clean and orderly. Miss Corbett too emanates a sense of order. She is a short, plumpish young person, neither fat nor thin. Her shiny brown hair is drawn back from her face into a braided knot that is secured low on the back of her head. Her forehead is high, and her nose short and tipped a little. Her gray eyes have a lively expression. Her dress is very plain, a blue wool without trim and no flounces to the skirt; only the front is very finely tucked and sewn.

"How can I help you?" Miss Corbett asks me.

Like her simple-looking yet refined dress, she gives the impression of completeness, of polish, yet hers is not a hard surface shine but a glossy depth.

"I am come to inquire about having a dress made and also refitting this one I am wearing. I need a petticoat and a night shift. I do not have much money," I tell her.

"A dress? For day or evening wear? Home or visiting?" Miss Corbett has a brisk, businesslike way of speaking. She sounds very American. "Sit here," she says, indicating the chairs by the stove. "Take off your shawl. We will confer."

"A dress for day," I say, taking the chair she indicates. "Perhaps for working. I do not know. I thought something simple and plain. Black maybe."

Miss Corbett leans back in her seat. She picks up a pen from the table beside her and taps it against her front teeth. She looks at me consideringly.

"My dear," she says, "you do not want a black dress. With your bright hair and pale skin, you will make a sensation. You will not be able to walk down Broadway without turning heads. For evening, yes."

She never takes her eyes from me as she speaks. It is as if she is seeing me as I am and as she imagines me dressed, both at once.

"Not black?" I say faintly.

Miss Corbett shakes her head decisively. "No," she says. Suddenly her face is closed and dreaming. "Or maybe for an evening dress. Black silk, cut low, white lace at the sleeves, kid gloves, pearls." She stops and shakes her head. "Never mind me, my dear." Her eyes crinkle with her laughter. "Let us start again. You need a dress for day. And practical."

"Yes, and this one must be refitted. I do not have the skill to do it myself."

"Well," Miss Corbett says. "Let us begin by stepping into the inner room—if you will be so good. I need to take your measurements. Then we can talk of fabric and prices with confidence. If funds are limited, we will want to be sure of cost before we start."

To my horror and shame, I respond by bursting into tears. Miss Corbett says nothing. When I catch my breath and look up at her at last, she has picked up some work and is calmly sewing, her hands busy, her face serene. Now that I am quiet, she lays aside her work and looks at me.

"Can you tell me what is the trouble?" Miss Corbett says gently. "Miss—perhaps you will tell me your name?"

"I am Miss Mina Pigot," I tell her. Now I have the hiccups.

Miss Corbett takes a ledger book from the table and opens it to a blank page. She draws the inkwell toward her. "One *t* in Pigot or two?" she says, her pen poised.

"One," I tell her.

"Ah," she says, writing. "Well, Miss Pigot, your first purchase will be two cambric handkerchiefs." She blots the entry, snaps the book shut, and, rising, goes to her worktable. From a box she takes the white squares, brings them, and sets them in my lap.

While I am wiping my eyes and noticing that the handkerchief I hold is finely hem-stitched, Miss Corbett takes a cup from her store and pours water from an earthenware pitcher on the windowsill. She sets it by me without speaking and seats herself quietly.

"Can I help?" she asks. "Or can I send a message to someone for you?"

"I am so sorry," I say. "I feel very foolish. I have been in America less than three weeks. I am bewildered still. And you asked me to take off my dress for measurements." Tears start to leak again, and I sniff and mop my eyes. "Really, I am crying because I am ashamed that I have no chemise, no underthings at all, only a tattered boy's singlet under an old shirt and my dress."

"I understand." Miss Corbett's face is sympathetic.

As I learned in all our conversation today, she takes anything to do with clothing very seriously indeed—and other matters with easy humor. I sip the water, which is cold and clear. My hiccups stop. My eyes dry. Soon I am explaining everything. And then I am standing in the inner room, which seems to be Miss Corbett's bedroom. I shiver in the ragged singlet over which Miss Corbett tsk-tsks as if it were an injured animal.

"You have a lovely figure to dress," Miss Corbett says when we are seated again and she has written figures in her book. "When you are more recovered from your journey and have added a little flesh, you will be elegant. Now, let us consider how to proceed."

Together we make a very long list of all I need. When Miss Corbett makes some calculations and tells me the cost, I feel dizzy.

"I cannot do that," I tell her. "I am so sorry. I have troubled you for nothing."

"Slowly, Miss Pigot, slowly," Miss Corbett says. "Can you do simple sewing?"

I tell her that I can and that I have my own housewife with needles and a scissors.

"What do you need the most?" she asks.

"The flannel petticoat," I say promptly. "The flannel vest, and a warm night shift. I am cold all the time."

"And the weather will be even colder soon," Miss Corbett says. "You are a sensible young woman."

She speaks as if she were a grandmother, but with her glossy hair and smooth, clean skin, I think she cannot be more than a few years older than I am.

After that she lays out a plan. She will cut a petticoat and night shift for me, and I can do the sewing myself. She will cut a vest too, but I must sew it under her supervision and have a fitting. The price she gives me seems very low, but when I try to thank her, she says she is looking forward to more business later when I have work.

I left at last, much relieved of my worries, carrying the cut material for the petticoat wrapped in an end of muslin. I will return on Wednesday to work on the vest. While I do that, Miss Corbett will take the bodice of my dress apart and refit it. I shall have to stay until it is done, of course, since I have nothing else to wear except a boy's cooking smock.

At supper tonight, I remembered that Miss Corbett said I would be elegant if I added a little flesh. I tried hard to eat more, but really, the food is coarse, and the young men seize the broiled chops as soon as the platter is set on the table, leaving the greasy mutton stew and overboiled salted pork and cabbage for those who are not so quick.

Now I must lay aside my pen, wash my hands in the basin, and begin my sewing.

FRIDAY, DECEMBER 8, 1848

I spent my Wednesday afternoon with Miss Corbett. We sewed and talked quietly. Miss Corbett refitted the bodice of my dress to perfection. I no longer look like a hunchback when I remove my shawl. She will show me how to make a pair of false sleeves with an end of cambric from her store of fabric pieces. I will not need to wear my old shirt anymore. Miss Corbett says she will help me make a *berthé,* a sort of capelet to wear over my dress to vary the look of it. She says *berthé*s are very fashionable.

We did not talk only of clothing. I told her of my brother and how glad I am to have found him. I told her of how Mr. Serle helped and protected me and of my sadness that I may never see him again in this vast new country. Talking made me feel less lonely.

Miss Honor Corbett is like me. Her parents are dead. On her table she keeps a watercolor portrait of them in a carved wood frame. The picture shows her pretty, delicate-looking mother seated in a chair and her father standing with his hand protectively on the mother's shoulder. Honor's only living relative is her aunt, Miss Jane Corbett, who painted the picture and who occupies the other front room across the hall. Her aunt is her father's sister, who took her in and raised her. Miss Jane Corbett teaches art to young ladies at their homes or in her studio. She and Honor cannot share one space because they each must welcome customers—and in Honor's room women must be able to shed their garments with a sense of privacy.

This afternoon I went to show Miss Corbett my finished petticoat and began my sleeves. She laid the pieces out and gave me instructions. After Miss Corbett carefully wrapped the work in the muslin that I brought back, there was a surprise.

"I wish you to meet my aunt," Miss Corbett said. "We will have tea together."

Miss Jane Corbett is a slim woman with the same glossy brown, intricately braided hair as her niece. She also wears the same sort of simple dress with fine needlework finishing. The color is a deep green that brings out the richness of her hair and the blue of her eyes. Truthfully, she is prettier than her niece although she is older and worn looking and a little stiff in her manner.

Miss Honor Corbett brought the rocking chair from the window and set the kettle to boil. We talked of all sorts of things—family and my first confused impressions of New York and America. Miss Jane Corbett was born in New York; Miss Honor Corbett was born in Hartford, Connecticut, but has lived in New York with her aunt since infancy. The city is changing very quickly, growing every day, they both say. It is built up all the way to Thirty-fourth Street now.

After we had drunk our tea and eaten a biscuit each—cookies, a Dutch name, Miss Jane Corbett calls them—I began a polite speech to thank them for their kindness to me. Miss Honor Corbett tapped my arm to interrupt me.

"We wish to talk to you, Miss Pigot," she said.

"Oh," I exclaimed, surprised.

Miss Corbett's eyes crinkled with humor. "Well, of course, you are thinking we have been talking," she said, "but that was the hors d'oeuvre, not the meat of the conversation we wish to have."

"We have a proposal to make," the aunt says.

I feel a shiver of caution.

The change must show in my face, for Miss Honor says quickly, "Do not be apprehensive, Miss Pigot. It is a respectable proposal to which you can say no immediately without hurt feelings."

I nod and try to smile.

"We wonder if you would like to live with us?" the aunt asks.

"Oh, my!" I say.

"Wait, my dear," Miss Honor cautions. "Listen."

The aunt continues, "Honor will have explained that we maintain both of our rooms to conduct our business in a professional way. It is an expensive arrangement for us."

She looks sad. It is hard for her to talk of being poor.

"I like you, Miss Pigot." Miss Honor goes to the heart of the matter in her frank way. "If you would share my bedroom with me and pay a portion of the rent, we could all manage more easily."

"Honor tells me that you are a respectable, well-brought-up young woman and that you like to cook. We can all economize if you do the shopping and cooking until you have other work," the aunt says, sitting very straight in her chair and speaking formally. "A Polish family has the basement rooms here. Their boys bring in water and wood and coals and take out the ashes. The wife cleans for us twice a week. That is included in the rent. We do not do the heaviest work."

"I have noticed you looking longingly at the stove," Miss Honor says. She smiles at me in her sweet way.

"I miss cooking," I admit. "I would like to work as a cook. It will be an advantage to me to shop at the markets here before I seek a position."

"It will be an advantage to us to be able to work late with the assurance of a pleasant meal at the end of the day," Miss Jane Corbett says in her genteel way.

"We hope you will say yes," Miss Honor adds.

"I must talk to my brother," I tell them. "It is such a kindness of you. You do not know how the noisy young men and the gobbled meals at Mrs. Redburn's make my head ache—for all she is a kind and honest woman."

"Naturally you must consult your brother," Miss Jane Corbett says.

"May we call on you Sunday afternoon?" I ask. "I should like you to meet him, and he will wish to meet you."

We agree to the plan. I think Daniel must approve. The sum the Miss Corbetts named is much less than the full board at Mrs. Redburn's. I am so happy. It is as if little iridescent soap bubbles of gaiety, winking and bursting in the light, are all about me.

FRIDAY, DECEMBER 15, 1848

I moved my things to the Corbetts' yesterday morning. There was little enough, just my bag and blanket. In the afternoon I ventured out with a direction from Miss Corbett—Aunt Jane, I will say. After our meal last night, she asked me to call her that just as Honor does. Now I have bought and had delivered a tin trunk banded in brass in which to keep my possessions neat. The brass looks somewhat like the banding on Mr. Serle's trunk.

I arranged everything in my new trunk. Here is all that I have: my store of money; a china mug decorated with blue flowers that was my mother's; a horn spoon; the linen shirt that was my brother's and that I wore thin these last months; two old singlets; my mother's little prayer book that is all swollen and ruined from being in the sea when the *Abigail* went down but that I cannot bear to throw away; my blanket, which I do not need just now, for Honor—I call her Honor and she calls me Mina—has two quilts and a feather bed on the bedstead we will share. These are the things I brought from Ireland except my housewife and my rosary, which I keep in my pocket.

Also in my trunk are a pair of boy's work pants, two smocks, and the kerchief I tie over my hair for kitchen work. Mr. Serle gave me those when I became his apprentice in England. I have another very old and tattered kerchief with apple seeds from the orchard in England knotted into the corner of it. Of course, I keep a store of rags for use during my monthly bleeding, but with me it is not every month. On the sea voyage it did not happen at all. It will be a relief to talk with Honor or her aunt about such things. I know very little, and when I think of being a woman, I miss my mother and my sister so.

My new flannel night shift lies ready on top of everything. I decided on rose-pink ribbons, not buttons, for the front. All my other clothing, I am wearing.

"Slowly, slowly," Honor says. "Rome was not built in a day, and a wardrobe should not be either."

Honor will help me make what I need over the next weeks and months. Besides, I must see what work I will have and choose a dress to suit the job. Aunt Jane is teaching me to knit. I must have warm gloves and a hood when the snow comes. A bonnet is too expensive for now.

There are three last items in my trunk. There is the little wooden chain that Flint gave me. It is such an odd thing—like him. I have two papers. One is the water-stained certificate of Father Fintan, saying I am baptized *Mina Pigot on November 19 of the Year of Our Lord 1832*. It is much damaged and hard to read, but my brother says I should have the keeping of it. The other is the letter from the baron in whose kitchen I worked in England. It says that Daniel Serle served honestly in his employ as assistant cook in the year 1848 and that Daniel Serle is a gifted baker. I do not know what use this can be to me since I am Mina Pigot again, but even so I treasure it.

The most important of all—my mother's gold ring with the red stone—I have sewn into my new undervest so that it is just over my heart.

SUNDAY, DECEMBER 17, 1848

Daniel came to visit me at the Corbetts' this afternoon. He brought his friend John Deegan with him. His face is handsome, but John Deegan's hay-colored hair sticks out like tufts on a poorly thatched roof when he takes his hat off. Daniel and Mr. Deegan drank a great deal of tea and ate all the biscuits. They talked almost the whole time of the gold discovery in California. A man in the Columbia House Hotel dining room was showing around a real gold nugget on Friday night.

Daniel upset me by saying that he thinks of going out to California to seek his fortune. Mr. Deegan talks of going too. When I thought of coming here to find Daniel and then losing him again, I wanted to cry. Aunt Jane and Honor were very comforting after Daniel and Mr. Deegan left. They think it unlikely that many people will go to California chasing such uncertain reports as the newspapers are publishing.

Earlier this week, I sent a note to Mr. Serle at the address of Mr. Guido DiRoma, telling him where I am living. Yesterday, I received a kind letter in return. Although—well—I will paste it in my book. Here it is:

Dear Miss Pigot,

Thank you for your note of Tuesday.

You ask about my prospects. I am already employed. Indeed, to my surprise, I had a choice of employment. I encountered an old colleague from the Paris restaurant where I worked before you knew me. He has made my way easier, and through him, I am engaged as one of the chefs at a great dinner and ball at a private house on the sixteenth of this month. It is an excellent opportunity to work with someone who knows this country, its produce, and its tastes.

After considering positions at several of the great hotels, I have chosen the Columbia House Hotel on Broadway. I hope my kitchen staff there will prove as quick and skillful at their tasks as was my young assistant this past summer in England and on the *Victoria*.

Americans seem to work very long hours, but I hope occasionally to be able to see friends and attend concerts. My dear Guido, who is commenting as I write, asks to be remembered to Miss Mina Pigot. He thinks I should ask if we may call upon you in your new home. You must decide if you wish that.

Yours respectfully,
Benjamin Serle

I am grateful to be in America tonight, sitting on a chair in a real bedroom, writing at an oak table. Honor's voice conferring with a client makes a pleasant murmur of sound in the workroom. The prospect of a peaceful evening meal with Honor and Aunt Jane is one of dear companionship. Only, only—if the voices were Mr. Serle's and Guido's, I should be glad also. If I were to consult Mr. Serle about our meal and work beside him as we made it, I would feel more appetite.

Mr. Serle writes as if calling on me is his friend Guido's idea. And *yours respectfully* sounds like something from a business letter. I feel a strange confusion. In my own heart I am still disguised as a boy; Mr. Serle is still my uncle and I am still his nephew, Daniel, his child that he protects. But perhaps I do not live so in his heart. It makes me sad to think that he might be forgetting our time together so soon. I wonder if Mr. Serle has found a church to attend with his people. I wonder if he is truly well. I wonder what concerts he will hear, who will perform, and if he will like them.

SUNDAY, DECEMBER 31, 1848

I am writing in the bedroom with my shawl about me, for we have numbing cold on this last night of the year. Honor is finishing a dress for a woman who came hurrying in on Thursday, carrying a bundle of silk and saying she must have something special for a great dinner party tonight. Honor set an extra fee for the rush of the work. She is pleased to have the money, and she loves making a fancy dress of beautiful crimson silk with a cream silk under-skirt and real lace trim. The woman is here now with her carriage waiting as Honor checks the final fit and adjusts the flounces just so. I hear laughter.

I too have work. I am the tobacco girl at the Columbia House Hotel. It is all arranged by Daniel. The tobacco girl sells cigars, pipes and pipe tobacco, chewing tobacco, and snuff at a place in the hotel Daniel calls a kiosk. I have not seen it yet. I will meet the manager of the hotel and begin work the day after tomorrow, Tuesday morning.

To celebrate I am making a special supper for Honor and Aunt Jane. I went out yesterday in the snow and purchased a fine, fresh young chicken with white flesh and pale yellow feet. As soon as the woman leaves with her dress, I will sauté it *à la Marengo* as Mr. Serle taught me. We will have a delicate soup first, of stock from the chicken feet, wing tips, and neck, with vermicelli and fine-chopped carrot added at the last. I cannot bake here easily, so early this morning I made little pots of chocolate cream. They are waiting on the cold windowsill. I purchased some biscuits with orange peel in them at the confectioner's to eat with the cream. After all that, we will drink our tea by the stove.

Daniel cannot join us. He is earning extra money by serving at a ball tonight. Every day of work brings his saloon nearer, he says. And in two days I will be at the Columbia House Hotel. I will see Daniel every day. I shall always know he is well and be glad.

My pen hesitated after I wrote that. I have not told my truth. I am sad because I should have liked to end this year with a glimpse of Mr. Serle. I miss him so. When Daniel told me that there is work for me at the Columbia House Hotel, my heart beat harder in my chest. I think my cheeks flushed red. Before I even thanked my brother or asked what the work would be, I thought, Now I will see Mr. Serle, my friend.

I went out to St. Patrick's Church this morning. After I gave thanks for my life, I prayed for the souls of my parents and my dear sister. Perhaps they know somehow that we remember them. I prayed they know we have enough to eat.

I listened to the jubilant music of the choir and the chanting of the priests. Incense hung in the air, making a haze through which the figures at the altar loomed large as angels performing their rites. The musky scent is the perfume of the soul opening to God as the rose opens to the sun in a summer garden.

PART THREE

THE COLUMBIA HOUSE HOTEL

SUNDAY, JANUARY 21, 1849

THE WEATHER IS COLD and miserable. For a week it was so frigid that we all moved our feather beds into Honor's workroom to sleep in the warmth.

Last night I made a dish of scalloped oysters for our evening meal. Afterward we were three ladies together. Honor sewed, and Aunt Jane worked on the etchings of children and dogs that a publisher hired her to tint with color. I read aloud to them from Honor's copies of *Godey's Lady's Book*. Mr. Godey's ladies do not walk down Broadway to their work. They exercise with dumbbells to develop beauty and grace. Jenny Lind bonnets, whatever they are, are going to be popular in the spring.

I began my job as tobacco girl three weeks ago. I admit to my book only that it is not all I hoped. The manager of the Columbia House Hotel was kind enough when I went with Daniel to meet him. Honor and Aunt Jane helped me dress, and Honor loaned me a pair of gloves to wear. Aunt Jane was most worried about my hair.

"We must put it up in back over a form to make it look longer," she told me. "You do not want questions about why it is so short and whether you have been ill or worse."

"Worse?" I asked.

"Women who go to prison have their hair cropped short." Honor does not hide behind vague words. "You can tell sometimes when you see them on the street with their shawls slipped down. The rough b'hoys taunt them if they notice."

"I will have my hair up over the form," I say quickly. "I am glad you told me."

It must have looked all right, because neither my brother nor the manager mention it. The manager looks me up and down and then asks me my name and my age. He wants to know if I can read and do addition and subtraction. When I say yes, he turns to my brother and says, "She speaks well, and her manner is ladylike enough but not overrefined. Mr. Branton recommended her. She will do. Eight dollars a month without board. Nine in the morning to seven at night. Sundays the kiosk is closed; we do not sell tobacco on Sundays. Pay given at the end of every month."

"Thank you, sir," I say.

"Here is the key," he says, giving it to my brother. "You pay a fee if you lose it. Miss Roget will stay an hour to show you what to do. Good day, Miss Pigot, Mr. Pigot."

"Who is Mr. Branton?" I asked Daniel.

"An important political man," Daniel said. "He saw you at church on Thanksgiving Day. When I asked his advice, he said he would recommend you here."

The tobacco kiosk is in the lower level of the Columbia House Hotel opposite the broad marble stairway that comes down from the entrance hall. The gas lamps on the walls glow and hiss all day and evening. On either side of my kiosk, corridors go left to the kitchens and right to the bathing rooms for guests. The windows high up in the walls let in little light. There are big brass spittoons at the bottom of the stairs, and brown stains on the marble floor where men have missed their target. The cleaning men mop often, but the floor is never entirely clean.

My brother introduced me to Miss Katy Roget. Then he hurried away.

The tobacco girl works inside the kiosk, a tiny pantry with locking cupboards on three sides and a counter in front. I go inside it by swinging up the counter on a hinge and then lowering it again. I feel suddenly like a caged bird when I am inside. Katy Roget, a cheerful girl who must leave because she is marrying, shows me where everything is and how to measure and cut the plugs of chewing tobacco neatly.

"Purchase a couple of pairs of cotton gloves," she suggests. "You will want something to keep your hands from being stained."

I will sell six kinds of cigars. The Ramon Allones are the most popular Havana style. There are Spanish cigars, chewing tobacco, pipe tobacco, and snuff also. Miss Roget shows me how to set the scale with the customer's snuffbox and how to add snuff without spilling. The kiosk does not sell the small cigars called cigarettes. Only doxies in the brothels on Mercer and Greene streets that everyone calls "ladies' boardinghouses" smoke such things, Miss Roget sniffs.

Before she left, Miss Roget spent some time warning me about the customers.

"Do not choose a cigar for a man and light it for him, even if he is most charming and persistent," she tells me. "They consider it an invitation to further attention if you serve them so. And avoid looking men in the eye."

"What should I do?" I ask, perplexed.

"Lay out a choice of two or three cigars. Do not engage in conversation beyond comment on the weather. Be cheerful and quick." Katy pats my hand. "You are a pretty girl. Guard yourself. Who knows, you may find a rich and respectable husband here."

How one avoids looking men in the eye, talks only of the weather, and at the same time finds a husband, I cannot imagine.

The work is easy—but tiring because it is always the same. A pleasant part of the day is the morning shopping. Sometimes Aunt Jane comes with me to take a little air. It is enjoyable to confer with her about chops and cheese. I store the things and go to work. I walk across to Broadway among the hastening throngs and down to the hotel. The best part of the day is seeing Daniel. Every morning he comes hurrying from the passageway that leads back to the kitchens. He has just been serving breakfasts.

"Good morning, *acushla,* dear heart," he says, just as my father used to do.

If no one is around, he leans over the counter and kisses me on the cheek. We exchange a few words of news. I always ask him if he slept well, and he always answers yes, although I see in his eyes and drawn face that it is not always the truth that he is telling me. In the afternoon I often see him again. Sometimes he can only pause and tell me a quick story about an interesting customer—last Tuesday he served a man who had traveled all the way from the island of Australia. If he can, Daniel watches me lock up and walks me up the stairs and out to Broadway where I begin my journey home.

I walk or take the omnibus up Broadway to Spring Street. I must not board an omnibus when the driver is obviously drunk, Daniel warns, but wait for another, safer one. I vow to myself that, when the weather is warmer, I will always walk.

I do not mind the serving and selling much. The people are interesting to observe and generally kind. What I mind greatly is the smell of the tobacco. It gets on my hands and in my clothing; after several hours with it I feel choked. Before I bought cotton gloves as Katy recommended, my fingers would be stained brown at the end of the day. I would scrub and scrub at night to get them clean. Now I have gloves, and I am making a pretty smock to wear over my dress to protect it from the smell.

I treasure the moments with Daniel. It does not matter that we say little. In seeing him full of motion and energy, I see hope for the future.

Friday, January 26, 1849

I saw Mr. Serle and spoke to him. It was almost time for me to close up; I had begun to put the stock away. Cigars must be carefully stored, or they lose their savor. I would not care except that they will not sell if they are stale and dry. I heard a step on the marble floor, and when I looked up, there he was. I am safe now, I thought suddenly. Here is the one who anchors me because he knows me best.

Mr. Serle was wearing his dark suit and an overcoat. He carried his hat and gloves. When he saw me, he came over to speak to me. His white collar came up stiffly under his chin. His dark hair curled on his forehead, and his eyes looked alert and wide.

"Miss Pigot," he says. "Are you well?"

"Yes," I say, which is not entirely true. The cold weather makes my hands and feet ache, especially the side of my right foot where a pony's stepping once hurt it. "And you?" I ask him.

He nods. "I am satisfied with life here in America," he says.

"You look very . . . very elegant," I tell him. I remember his letter. "Are you going to a concert?"

He smiles and shrugs his shoulder. "I am going to the opera," he says.

"Oh," I say. There is a pause, but he does not say good-bye and go. "Perhaps Madame Moses is singing?" I ask.

"No," Mr. Serle replies, "I am meeting Herr Meyer. He has undertaken my education in the arts. Tonight we will hear an opera by the composer Gaetano Donizetti."

"Do you think you will like it?" I ask. I have seen handbills posted with sketches of the famous singers, but I am not sure what an opera might really be.

"I do not care if I like it," Mr. Serle tells me. "It is still strange to me that I must come to America to have the freedom to hear the art of one of my countrymen. I will absorb the pleasure of that before I decide to like or dislike the music."

"How is Mr. DiRoma?" I ask.

"He is well," Mr. Serle tells me.

He stands looking at me. I pick up my cloth to polish the counter but do not use it. I am happy just to be still and look at him.

"Thank you for your letter to me," I say. "It was kind of you."

"I am glad you have found friends," Mr. Serle says.

I summon courage. "Will you call on us? I should like you to meet the Miss Corbetts," I say. "Perhaps when you have a Sunday afternoon free, you will tell me. I can ask Aunt Jane if it suits her."

"Aunt Jane?" Mr. Serle sounds surprised, almost annoyed.

"She asked me to call her that," I say. "They are good people."

"I am sure," Mr. Serle says quickly. "I look forward to meeting them." There is another pause, and still he does not go.

"Do you ever see little Stellina Moses?" I ask. "Is she well?"

"I see her," he admits. "She asked me about Daniel recently. She remembers him and how he rescued her."

I feel the red in my cheeks and a constriction in my heart. I want to ask Mr. Serle what he remembers of the Daniel that I was, but I cannot.

"It seems a long time ago." I can turn my face down as I polish the counter. "And yet it is only ten weeks and a day since our ship docked in New York and I found my brother."

"That was a day!" Mr. Serle exclaims. Then he sighs. "Well, I must go, child."

"Good-bye." I hold my flannel cloth tight in my hand. "I hope you enjoy your opera."

"Good evening, Miss Pigot," he says.

I watch him swiftly mount the stairs.

SUNDAY, FEBRUARY 4, 1849

We work hard at Elizabeth Street, and our fortunes are rising. Honor has several orders for spring costumes. Then Aunt Jane unexpectedly received a great order of work from the maker of prints who hires her. She has a thousand fashion plates to tint with color by next week. I help in the early morning and evening, and Honor is going to work too as soon as she finishes the walking dress and cloak she has in hand. Aunt Jane will share the money with us.

I am very glad for money. I have a secret. I told Daniel that

Mr. Serle rescued me from the man who would have beaten me and sold me for an evil purpose. I did not tell Daniel—I have not told anyone—that Mr. Serle rescued me not just by breaking Mr. Hatton's whip and frightening him but also by buying the bond that Mr. Hatton claimed made me his indentured servant for five years.

I owe Mr. Serle the thirty guineas he paid to release me. It is a strange thing. When I worked with Mr. Serle, the debt did not weigh on me; I hardly thought of it. Only now, when we are in this new world and I see him rarely and by chance, I feel the press of what I owe. Mr. Serle gave from his precious savings, the savings for his dream of owning a restaurant by a lake. I have stolen from his dream.

There is another reason too that I am determined to repay the money. Aunt Jane sets great value in propriety. I complained one evening that a man who bought a cigar at the hotel told me to keep the change for his purchase but then thought he had bought my attention for his talk. Aunt Jane says that the worst thing that can happen to a woman is to be indebted to a man who is not related to her. The man will always have a power over her after that, she claims. It destroys all trust. She said she could not respect a woman who takes money from a man. Honor begged to differ. She said the circumstances determine the meaning of an action. I could not listen well to their debate. I was horrified that Aunt Jane or Daniel or Honor might think ill of me.

Until I came to know Aunt Jane, I did not think of myself as someone who might be respectable or not. I thought of my need and my own soul, not of society. Now when Aunt Jane talks of etiquette or Daniel says he wants me to look like a lady, I see that I have much to learn. What we are and what we seem must both be weighed.

As I look back, perhaps I have wanted to believe that Mr. Serle is my uncle. Relatives love each other. I thought a disguise for convenience was a truth and accepted being a child because it made me feel safer.

Now I must stop writing and tint fashion plates.

When Daniel came to see me today, he talked the whole time about prospecting. A ship, the *Crescent City,* arrived in New York last Monday with a cargo of gold. I thought it was the influence of John Deegan that made Daniel eager for California. Now I must admit that it is Daniel himself who wants to seek a fortune.

Everywhere people talk of the gold to be taken from the rivers and the earth of California. The men coming to buy their cigars speak of it to each other. Even an old lady buying snuff yesterday asked me if I had heard the news.

"America is a great country," she told me. "Just think, we took California away from the Mexicans, and now it will make us all rich. My grandson is going west. He promises to send me a real gold nugget as soon as he has dug one up."

I told Daniel that I hoped he would not leave New York.

"Sea travel is too dangerous," I said.

"I will go by land," he replied. "It is but a tenth the cost of a ship."

"But there are wild beasts and Indians, and they say the Mormons do not like strangers crossing their territory," I argue. "People die in the terrible mountain passes in the trackless snow. Honor told me of the horror of a party of travelers who are rumored to have eaten each other."

Daniel laughed and shook his head. "I would not go in winter, Mina. If I leave this spring, I can cross the mountains in summer. The problem is the money for a kit and finding a trustworthy companion. I prefer not to go alone."

"I thought John Deegan wished to go," I said.

Daniel looked at me thoughtfully. "Would you regret his going?"

"No, not at all," I declared. "It is your leaving that I fear."

"John Deegan is a very city kind of man," Daniel said. "The gold tempts him, but not the adventure of it. He cares more for the idea of owning a saloon and rising in the eyes of the politician Mr.

Matt Branton. Now that I know him better, I doubt him. He is the kind to sell the skin before he kills the bear."

"You do not think anymore of a saloon?"

I felt the pull in Daniel this way and that. I do not like to think of my brother selling rum, and yet it would keep him here, near me.

"I hate the idea of being any man's thing to command," Daniel said abruptly. "Come, Mina, let us walk a little before the sun is down."

Without waiting for my reply, he began to move toward the door in his restless way. So we went over to St. Patrick's Church. Incense from the Mass still hung in the air. I lit a candle for the memory of our parents and Eliza. On the way back, we talked of life at home and the bay horse our father had for a while before the bad times came. Now, as I write this with my right hand, with my left I touch the ring my mother gave me where I keep it sewn in my undervest above my heart. I pray the future brings us joy again.

MONDAY, MARCH 12, 1849

In late February we had bitter weather. The Croton water froze, and we were desperate for several days. Then in early March, spring promised. To celebrate, Daniel and I walked all the way down to the Battery to look at ships in the harbor and blue sky.

Of course, many other people had the same idea after being cooped up in their rooms for all these frigid weeks. We saw babies in carriages, and a man and his son flying a kite. One young lady walked a tiny dog, which wore a red and green plaid blanket that matched her cloak; they looked fashionable enough to please even Honor.

Daniel was pointing out Castle Garden to me when I heard a child's voice exclaim, "It is Daniel, Mama. See Daniel!" And then, amazed, "There are two Daniels now!"

Coming toward us are Mr. Serle and Madame Moses and

Herr Meyer. Stellina is jumping up and down and holding on to Herr Meyer's hand. When they come level with us, Stellina drops Herr Meyer's hand. She runs about us in a circle and then stops in front of Daniel and me. She turns her head from one of us to the other. Her mouth is open in an O of wonder.

Herr Meyer too looks back and forth between us as he fingers his brown beard. Mr. Serle looks dismayed at first, but then he smiles and greets us.

"Miss Pigot," he says. "Mr. Pigot. I am glad to see you out on this lovely day."

He shakes hands with Daniel. Madame Moses jabs the ground with her umbrella and looks out at the water. Her brother continues to stroke his beard and smile.

"May I introduce you to my friends?" Mr. Serle asks me.

I think this is not quite right. Aunt Jane reads to me from her etiquette book. Mr. Serle should ask Madame Moses if she wishes to know us, because she is older. I remember her open passion on the ship when she thought me only a servant, and I do not care what is polite or not. I have met them all anyway. Why should I object to meeting them again? Besides, friends of Mr. Serle must have good in them.

"Of course," I say to Mr. Serle. "We are glad to meet your friends."

We are Miss Pigot and her brother, Mr. Pigot. They are Madame Moses, her brother Herr Meyer, and her daughter, Stellina. Herr Meyer shakes Daniel by the hand and makes a little bow to me as if he never saw me before in the world. I remember that Aunt Jane's book says it is not genteel for ladies to shake hands. Madame Moses and I nod and smile politely to each other.

"But which of you is Daniel?" Stellina demands.

"How old are you, Stellina?" Daniel asks her.

"I am four now," she says.

"I am twenty-one," he tells her. "I am more than five times as old as you are."

The child refuses to be distracted. "But are you Daniel?" she asks.

"Yes," my brother admits, "I am Daniel."

"Then who is that?" She points at me. "She looks like Daniel from the ship, but she is wearing a dress today. You are too tall."

"That is my sister," Daniel says. "Are you sure she was on your ship?"

"Yes," the child says. "Daniel on the ship saved me when a wave tried to push me overboard. He made me toast with sugar on it. Luly and I love Daniel."

Madame Moses is as white and lovely as ever as she looks from me to Mr. Serle. Her face is framed in the soft black fur that lines the hood of her black cloak.

"I see that my brother and his friend have secrets from me," she says in her clear voice that rings like a bell sounding on a frosty night.

"Now, Anna." Herr Meyer smiles.

While I try to think of something polite to say, Madame Moses changes her mood suddenly.

"Never mind which one is Daniel, my sweet," she tells Stellina. "We are always grateful for your life."

"Yes," cries the child, "and, Mama, I will be twice as safe now that there are two Daniels to help me."

Madame Moses smiles down at her daughter and then looks inquiringly at her brother. He nods to her.

"I am giving a musicale next Sunday," Madame Moses says. "It is at our brother's house on Crosby Street. You must both join us."

"You are a musician, Madame?" Daniel asks.

"I sing," Madame Moses tells him. She looks at me as if she wonders that I have not boasted of her fame. "I have engagements with the opera here next month."

"She sang on the ship, Daniel," I say. "She sang *Ave Maria* to perfection."

Madame Moses looks gratified. Stellina has lost interest in us all and watches a seagull peck at a fragment of biscuit on the path.

"Come next Sunday," Madame Moses says.

"I am not sure—" I begin.

"I insist," Madame Moses interrupts my speech in her decisive way. "The rescuer of my daughter, and friends of Benjamin Serle must always be welcome with us." She takes two cards from her muff and hands them to us with her black-gloved fingers. "I will expect you," she says. She turns to Mr. Serle. "If you would be good enough to give me your arm, sir? Sadick, take my umbrella."

She hands him the long black thing without waiting to hear him speak.

Mr. Serle smiles at me. He seems very pleased.

"Good day," he says and tips his hat politely.

He offers the lady his arm, and they walk on. Herr Meyer bows to us, takes little Stellina by the hand again, and follows his sister and Mr. Serle. Stellina turns and waves.

"Good-bye, Daniels," she calls.

We watch them walk away. Even though they are just four people, Madame Moses creates the feeling of a procession.

Daniel and I walked slowly in the opposite direction for a while, but the sun was going over, the air grew damp, and the breeze gusted up. Daniel said I looked pinched, and even though I denied it at first, I had to admit that, after having so little air for two months, I felt tired by the wind. Daniel treated me to a cup of hot chocolate in a place just below Mr. P. T. Barnum's Museum on Broadway. It was warm there, and Daniel cheered me by talking of the funny habits of Americans—he sees elegantly dressed people at the hotel putting their knives in their mouths. Then he said I look much better now than when I arrived in America.

"You are tired, I know," he said, "but you have color in your cheeks today, and your figure is improving."

We have agreed that we will go to Madame Moses's musicale next Sunday. Daniel is very curious to see how such people live. All afternoon he did not mention gold once.

We went, Daniel and I, to the musical concert that Anna Moses gave at her brother's house on Crosby Street. Honor and Aunt Jane were very pleased when I told them about it. Honor wanted to make me a new dress, but I refused. A second winter dress would be a luxury. Honor and I compromised on a *berthé* of cream cambric with brown velvet ribbons and a new set of sleeves with the same ribbon that are much fancier than the plain pair I wear to work.

When I was dressed and ready, Honor looked me over carefully.

"I wish you would let me lend you a bonnet," she said. "Your knitted hood is a pretty enough frame for your face, but not so elegant as a bonnet with white roses and ribbons to match the trim on your sleeves would be."

"The hood matches my outdoor woolen gloves," I say. "It is cold again today. I think I am better being warm instead of fashionable."

Honor looks quite sulky. "Something is missing," she insists.

I feel as if I am a dish she has just cooked that lacks salt or seasoning.

"What do you think, Aunt Jane?" Honor asks.

Aunt Jane looks at me critically. "She needs a brooch at her neck," she says. "She is all soft browns and cream and the red of her hair. The dress needs a touch of something else near her face to make an emphasis."

"Of course," Honor exclaims. "Why did I not see it? What would I do without your artist's eye?"

She kisses Aunt Jane on her worn cheek. Aunt Jane looks happy, as she always does when Honor pets her. Honor rummages in the box of ornaments she keeps in her workroom for use when her customers are trying their new clothes, but she finds nothing that satisfies her. She goes into the bedroom and returns with a black mourning brooch.

"No," Aunt Jane says when Honor holds it at my throat. "It is too heavy looking. Wait a moment."

When she comes back from her room across the hallway, she has a brooch in her hand. It is an oval piece of a dark green stone set into beaded gold metal.

"Oh," I exclaim when I see it. "I cannot borrow anything so valuable."

Aunt Jane shakes her head. "It is not of great value, Mina," she says. "This is jasper, not a precious stone, and the metal is gold wash only. I do not think you would lose it, anyway. It has a secure catch."

"It will do very well," Honor says, which settles the matter.

When Daniel arrives a moment later to fetch me, he declares himself proud to be seen beside such an elegant creature. I think he looks magnificent in his checked trousers and neat, skirted coat. He is wearing the dark-green silk cravat that I made for his present at Christmastime from an end of fabric Honor found for me.

When we arrive at the house in Crosby Street, there are two carriages at the door and a crowd inside. A maid invites the ladies to go up to a room on the second floor to leave their cloaks and shawls. I descend the stairs slowly. I feel shy to push in where I know no one, but Daniel takes my hand in his. We go into the parlor.

Mr. Serle comes through the crush of people to speak to us.

"I was glad to see you on the Battery," he says to me. He turns to Daniel. "You are wise to take your sister out of doors. I fear her place at the hotel is not healthy for her."

Daniel looks annoyed. "She has not complained," he says.

"I am very well," I lie to Mr. Serle. I do not like that he should talk about me with Daniel. "I walk every morning and evening. I enjoy the bustle of the streets."

"She takes care of herself," Daniel says in a challenging voice.

"Where is Herr Meyer?" I ask to change the subject, looking about at the eagerly conversing ladies and gentlemen.

"He will not speak to anyone until after he performs," Mr. Serle explains.

A bell rings in the hallway. The talking dies to a murmur as people seat themselves. The ladies arranging their skirts make a rustle of silk. Of course, my wool dress and muslin petticoat are silent. I feel pleased when Mr. Serle sits down beside me. Even if I am not the most elegant person present, he is still my friend.

"What will she sing?" I ask him.

"Herr Meyer will announce the program," Mr. Serle tells me in a low voice.

"What is he saying to you?" Daniel demands on my other side.

"Ssh," someone in front of us admonishes.

Herr Meyer has come out with sheets of music in his hand and is waiting to speak. I can see from the corner of my eye that Daniel looks annoyed at being hushed. He leans back in his chair and crosses his arms over his chest. On my right, Mr. Serle has done the same. I fold my hands in my lap. With these two swelling their chests on either side of me, I do not have a great deal of space.

Herr Meyer speaks soothingly about what we are to hear. He holds the music in one hand and pulls on his beard with the other as if he is checking to be sure it is real and his. The musicale will begin with Madame Moses singing an English folk air and then two songs called "Sympathy" and "She Never Told Her Love" by the composer Franz Joseph Haydn. She will also sing three songs by a composer whose name sounds like *cluck,* although I do not think it could be that. When Herr Meyer stops speaking, everyone claps their hands. He bows and goes to sit at the pianoforte.

Now Madame Moses steps out. She wears a low-cut black silk dress with what Honor calls a basque bodice. The skirt has two tiers, with the top one caught up to the side with a crimson silk rose. The lace at the neck and short sleeves is black. She wears white kid gloves that reach above her elbows, and glittering ear-rings. An ivory and black lace fan hangs on a white silk cord from her left wrist. I try to memorize everything to tell Honor. Madame Moses's face and bosom are very white. Her hair and her dress are very black. The only color is her red lips and the red rose on her skirt and the flashes of light at her ears as she turns her head.

On my left Daniel drops his arms and leans forward. He looks interested now, his self-consciousness at having spoken too loud forgotten. Mr. Serle does not change his posture. He is contained inside himself. I know so much about him—and so little.

Madame Moses looks at Herr Meyer, smiles, and nods. The first note sounds under Herr Meyer's fingers. How strange, I think, to stand before a room full of people and all of them staring, watching you, and waiting to hear you make a sound for them.

When Madame Moses opens her lips and throws back her head, the little rustling noises of the people in the room and the street sounds of carriages, clopping horses, hawkers' calls, fade away. The piano ripples and makes beats under Madame Moses's soaring, quivering voice. I do not know what the words mean in most of the songs, and yet I feel sad and afraid and teased and joyful by turns. Madame Moses, who I am not even sure I like, made me feel this way. When Mr. Serle said she is a great artist, that must be what he meant. Everyone claps their hands very loud when Madame Moses stops, bows, and goes out.

Herr Meyer announces that he will play *Opus 62* of Dr. Felix Mendelssohn-Bartholdy. "These are called 'Songs Without Words.' There are six of them," he says. He looks about at the audience, and his eyes smile. "There are six, but they are short. The great composer coached me himself in the interpretations when I was his student at the Leipzig Conservatory."

There is a murmur of approval from the audience. I listen carefully. It is not like the singing of Madame Moses. The feelings are quieter when it is just the piano alone. The sounds push me into myself. I remember the water rippling against the ship as we sailed in quiet seas. I think of the march of people on Broadway for Evacuation Day. The last song is light and graceful—spring is coming soon.

Madame Moses returns. She will sing from an opera by Rossini. I am interested to hear a song from an opera. Now I will know what Mr. Serle has been learning. The songs are very dramatic. Madame Moses sounds upset and sorrowful for what seems like a very long time. This music is more suited to her than the gaiety of folk song. Her voice says heartbreak more easily than joy. Perhaps Mr. Serle hears that and thinks he listens to her true self. When the applause died and Madame Moses and Herr Meyer had retired to another room, there was intermission.

Daniel asked me, "Would you like to go out and get some air, Mina?" at the same time that Mr. Serle said, "Here is Mr. DiRoma come to speak to you, Miss Pigot."

Guido DiRoma shakes my hand vigorously and asks after my health. Mr. Serle introduces him to Daniel.

"Are you a cook with my *Beniamino*?" asks Mr. DiRoma in his frank way.

Daniel looks puzzled.

"He means Mr. Serle," I tell Daniel.

"Oh!" Daniel says. "No, sir, I am a waiter at the Columbia House Hotel. And you?"

"I was on the docks at first. Now I work for my cousin in his business, delivering ice and coal. I am a very strong man." Mr. DiRoma laughs and clenches his fist to show us its weight and power. He leans to Daniel and says confidentially, "I am a fish out of water in this house." His voice is rather loud. Several people turn to stare, but Mr. DiRoma does not notice. "Do you like your work in America, Mr. Daniel Pigot?" he asks.

Daniel shakes his head. "I have been in New York almost a year, and I plan to leave for California soon," he says. "There are fortunes to be made there."

Mr. DiRoma looks interested. "I too have been thinking of the fortunes to be made in California," he tells Daniel.

I sigh. Now they will talk endlessly of gold.

Mr. Serle goes away, and I stand next to Daniel and Mr. DiRoma, but their conversation—tents, panning, gold dust, guns—moves briskly on without me. I wish that I knew some women here. Near us an older woman and a younger one are talking together. They look neat in their silk dresses and small bonnets. The younger one glances at me. I smile. Perhaps she will speak, but she looks me up and down slowly and then turns her back. Perhaps I should have borrowed Honor's bonnet after all.

Daniel and Mr. DiRoma continue their conversation. They are well matched, I think. Daniel tall and loose-limbed, Guido DiRoma sturdy, shorter in the legs, and broader across the shoulders. I can see that neither one is so well dressed as the other men here. It is their faces that I like—the openness, the humor in them. They burst with energy. They will tear their destinies from the earth of California. It makes me almost tired to contemplate them. I perch on the edge of my chair and wish I had a fan I could yawn behind, pretending to be a society lady.

At last, the bell rings in the hallway, and it is time to sit and listen again. Just when I think that the seat beside me will be empty, Mr. Serle appears. He nods when I turn to see him, but he does not speak.

The second part of the musicale is introduced by Herr Meyer again. First there is an arrangement of songs from an opera about love, *L'Elisir d'Amóre*.

"*The Love Potion*," Mr. Serle murmurs in my ear.

One song is called *Quanto Amóre*. *Amóre* means love. Madame Moses sings sweetly and flirtatiously with a Mr. Windmuller, who has a rich voice and a comic manner. There is great applause after Madame Moses's voice climbs to the soaring, icy peaks of the last high notes. Next, Herr Meyer announces he will play a work arranged by a man named Franz Liszt, *Hexaméron,* or six variations on a theme by Bellini. Herr Meyer must like the number six, I think. He played six songs before. I watch his hands flying and am amazed that ten fingers can make such a complicated, ever-changing sound.

Now the last part of the concert will be Madame Moses singing arias by Mozart. That is what songs in operas are called, *arias*. When Herr Meyer says *Batti, Batti* and *Porgi Amór,* there is a sigh of contentment from the audience. Madame Moses's voice is very supple and floating. I feel in a kind of dream of love and a beseeching pleasure.

At the end there is a kind of quiet pause as if everyone together is listening for the last sweet note as it dies away into the air above the city. Then there is much clapping of hands and calls of *Bravo* and *Brava*. Madame Moses looks at Herr Meyer and he nods. Then she sings the *Ave Maria* as I remember it.

"You were right, Mina," Daniel whispers to me at the end. "That is very beautiful."

Madame Moses and Herr Meyer bowed graciously. The child Stellina came forward from the back of the room and presented her mother with a bouquet of red glass-house roses. Madame Moses stooped to kiss her, and Stellina looked surprised. "So sweet," a woman said, and everyone applauded even more loudly. Then Herr Meyer thanked everyone for attending and said that refreshments were served in the room across the hall.

"I am going to talk with Mr. DiRoma again before we go," Daniel said to me. "Can you amuse yourself for a few minutes?"

"Yes, Daniel," I told him.

People are moving about and talking to each other. Voices rise, full of laughter and life. Across the room I see Mr. Serle speaking to Madame Moses. She is slowly stripping off her gloves. When she is done, he takes her hand in his and kisses it. My heart turns over in my breast.

"Did you enjoy the music, Miss Pigot?" Herr Meyer has appeared beside me.

"Yes, very much," I say cautiously.

"And did you have a favorite piece?" he presses.

"It is all so new to me," I say. "I liked everything. Perhaps I was most glad to hear the *Ave Maria*." Then I think that it is inconsiderate of me not to pay him a compliment. "I thought your playing on the pianoforte very . . . very precise and masterful. I liked best the 'Songs Without Words.' "

"Thank you, Miss Pigot." Herr Meyer sketches a bow. There is a pause. "I recall you sing sweetly, with a true pitch." Herr Meyer's eyes are smiling as he strokes his beard. "I appreciate your praise, for I think your ear must be good."

"My ear?" I have an instinct to touch my ears, which I resist.

"Have you thought of music lessons and performing?" he asks. His eyes narrow; he looks sly suddenly. "You would look well on a stage in either boy's or woman's dress."

"No, no," I say. "I do not wish music lessons."

Herr Meyer is suddenly very sober. "Excuse me, Miss Pigot. I have a foolish way of talking. I remember vividly the beauty of a night on calm water with the lights of America before us. When I see it in my mind's eye, it is always with the sound of your pure voice accompanying the picture. I should thank you for giving me that memory, not bother you with unwelcome suggestions."

"Are you teasing this girl, Sadick?" says a voice behind me.

It is Madame Moses. Mr. Serle is speaking to someone else now. Herr Meyer does not answer, only raises his sister's hand to his lips as Mr. Serle did a moment ago.

"I have told you once, and I tell you again: you were brilliant, my dear," he says.

"It was very beautiful singing, Madame Moses," I say politely. "Thank you for inviting us to your musicale."

The lady looks me up and down.

"Ah," she says, her red mouth smiling, "Benjamin Serle's little boy-girl charity case. You sell cigarettes now, I hear."

I see Herr Meyer stiffen. I feel the blood rise in my cheeks.

"I work at the Columbia House Hotel," I say, "where my brother and Mr. Serle are both employed. I think you are confusing me with some one of your friends."

Herr Meyer makes a sound between a cough and a laugh.

"Anna," he says taking his sister's arm, "you need a glass of champagne. And I see Mr. Nathaniel Willis across the room. We must thank him for attending. Charming to meet you again, Miss Pigot."

He shepherds his sister away as fast as he can conduct her through the throng.

"Would you like a glass of champagne or something to eat, Miss Pigot?" Mr. Serle is addressing me. "Can I help you?"

"No, thank you," I tell him.

"I saw you speak to Madame Moses. She is lovely, is she not?" Mr. Serle says.

"She is very well dressed," I say stiffly. My head is aching. "I must go. My brother is waiting for me. I would like to be out in the air."

"Of course," Mr. Serle says. He is not listening to me really, but gazing across the room to where Madame Moses is laughing at something a tall gentleman has said to her.

Madame Moses's contemptuous words make my heart hurt. And Mr. Serle sounds distracted, not like himself. Everyone is pretending to be a lady or a gentleman here.

In the hall I remember that I must fetch my outdoor things. When I come down the stairs again, holding my woolen gloves in my hand, I do not see my brother or Mr. Serle. Herr Meyer stands at the foot of the stairs. He seems to be waiting for me.

"I apologize for my sister," Herr Meyer says as soon as I am on the last step. "When she performs, her emotions come to the surface. She is very volatile."

"It does not matter," I tell him. "I am only surprised a lady would speak to an invited guest so rudely."

Herr Meyer sighs. "Benjamin Serle was emphatic in your praise when he explained the mystery of the two Daniels," he tells me. "Anna likes a challenge, but I am afraid she is looking for a meal she will never digest with your Mr. Serle."

"He is not mine," I say.

Herr Meyer raises an eyebrow. "Excuse me, Miss Pigot, but I thought he is your protector."

"Oh!" I say. The memory of the past and Mr. Serle holding me during the storm comforts my heart. "Mr. Serle protected me, indeed. He helped me leave England and travel to America. I will always be grateful to him for his protection."

"I see," Herr Meyer says. "But your liaison is ended?"

I stare at him. "Liaison?"

Herr Meyer strokes his beard and stares at me in a considering way. "My sister and Benjamin Serle are not suited, but, still, I do not like to see her misled."

"This is not a proper conversation," I say. "I do not understand it."

"I apologize, Miss Pigot," Herr Meyer says. "I seem to be always on the wrong foot with you. Would you allow me to call sometime when you are at home? Perhaps I might explain myself better in a quieter setting." He smiles at me and tugs at his chin.

I wish to say no and no again. It is rude for him to ask to visit me. Aunt Jane's etiquette book is very clear on that point. It is up to me to invite him.

"It is better not," I tell him.

"Ah," Herr Meyer says. "I understand."

He takes my hand in his and raises it to his lips just as Mr. Serle did before with Madame Moses. His mouth is rather pink in the brown nest of his beard. A gentleman never kissed my hand. Only I wonder if Herr Meyer is a gentleman. Before I can think what to say, a stout man with a black beard down to his second shirt button accosts us.

"Sadick Meyer!" he says, as if Herr Meyer might not know his own name. "A very excellent concert."

Herr Meyer bows to him. "Excuse me, sir," he shouts as he backs away. "Miss Pigot, our distinguished music critic, Mr. Cyrus Taub. Apologies. I must excuse myself."

The man turns to me. "What did you think?" he demands.

"It was very fine, Mr. Taub," I say.

"Eh?" He cups his hand at his ear. "Speak up, my dear. The noise is abominable."

"It was very fine!" I repeat.

"What about the andante movement of the *Hexaméron*?" the man asks. "Do you consider it characteristic of Chopin?"

"Andante? Characteristic of Chopin?" I repeat his incomprehensible words.

"Ah, you are a harpist," Mr. Taub bellows. He beams at me. "Charming. Will you perform in New York soon?"

"I must go," I say. What can he think I said?

"I see you have taken no refreshment," he goes on. "I do not blame you. Ham sandwiches and such trash. Our people forget the ways of our fathers and excuse it as becoming American. Even some of the rabbis call themselves reformers and say old rules of *kashruth* are not important in this modern age. I am glad to see you hold to your own principles."

"I—" I begin. I should say—or rather shout—that he is mistaken in thinking me a musician or a Jewess. Of course, it does not matter, because Cyrus Taub is not listening.

"This concert was a pleasure for me, but—"

I can see my brother with Mr. DiRoma by the door that leads out to the vestibule.

"Thank you," I shout to Mr. Cyrus Taub. "Good-bye!"

I leave him still talking and hurry to my brother.

"Please, Daniel, let us go," I say.

"There you are, Mina," Daniel says. "I wondered where you were. Did you eat?"

"No," I say. "The heat and the crowd took my appetite."

"The ham sandwiches are good," Daniel says. "Guido and I have eaten several."

Life is ridiculous. Rude Madame Moses, sly Herr Meyer, deaf Mr. Taub, people who welcome ham sandwiches, people who reject them.

"If you have eaten, then perhaps we can go," I say to Daniel. "Mr. DiRoma will understand that I am tired and you must walk home with me."

"Well, I must go," Daniel says to Mr. DiRoma.

"We will continue another time," Mr. DiRoma says. "Think about what I have proposed, eh?"

"Indeed," Daniel says. "What about talking again on Tuesday night? Shall we meet at Hoxey's near the Fulton Market? Nine o'clock? Will that suit you?"

Mr. DiRoma shakes Daniel's hand enthusiastically.

"Tuesday night," he says. "I will talk to the men I mentioned about our ideas." He turns to me. "Good-bye, Miss Mina Pigot," he says. "You look charming. *Bellisima.*"

His directness is neither bold nor yet impersonal. Unlike Herr Meyer, who seems always to be addressing some version of me that he is inventing while he fingers his beard, Guido DiRoma is—it is hard to find the words—he is here. He exists in the world in the present moment.

When Daniel and I come out of the house, the air feels cold and raw after the heat of the rooms. The streets are muddy from the spit of sleet earlier. I pick my way carefully. It is very tedious to sit in the chilly hallway to clean my boots every night.

"Did you like the music?" I ask Daniel.

"It was well enough," he says. "The folk tunes make me easier in my heart than the high-flown opera songs. And the lady is certainly lovely to look at. I can see why your friend Mr. Serle is smitten with her."

"He is?" I speak so faintly that Daniel does not hear me.

"Tell me again how you know Mr. DiRoma, Mina," my brother says. "You told me, but I forget."

"I met him just once before. Mr. Serle knew him from

childhood in Rome, Italy," I say. "Remember the day you came to the ship to find me? Remember that he was there?"

"I like him," Daniel says. "We talked of California. He has very sound ideas."

"What ideas?" I ask.

"He understands the risks of the gold fields," Daniel tells me. "Some claims are full of gold, but some are completely barren. Mr. DiRoma thinks a wise man would take supplies to sell to the miners and examine conditions before venturing out to prospect."

"He does sound sensible," I concede.

"I like him." Daniel says with satisfaction in his voice. "I look forward to talking to him again. He might be the partner I want."

I wish we had not gone to the musicale. I hope that Mr. DiRoma will not want to go to California. I hope that Daniel will not go. I feel afraid, and angry too, when I think of Daniel choosing to leave me.

SUNDAY, MARCH 18, 1849

On Thursday, when it was quiet in the late afternoon, Mr. Serle stopped at the kiosk to ask if he might call on Sunday. I told him that I would ask Aunt Jane if it was convenient for her and tell him Friday. Of course, Aunt Jane and Honor said yes. I consulted Aunt Jane before I shopped early Saturday morning. Aunt Jane suggested that I make chocolate creams and buy some cookies.

"You make delicious creams, Mina," she told me. "Smoother than any I've had before. And chocolate is *my* favorite."

It rained last night and more today. I was sure that Mr. Serle would not come in such unpromising weather. After I made the chocolate creams in eight little jars, I paced about and peered out the rain-streaked window at the street until Honor, who was working on the turn of a collar, told me that I was distracting her and to sit down and do my crochet work. When Mr. Serle arrived, we were surprised to see he had brought Mr. DiRoma with him.

I introduce Mr. Serle to Aunt Jane and Honor, and Mr. Serle introduces Mr. DiRoma to us all. He seems to have forgotten that

I have met him twice already. We have to bring an extra chair from Aunt Jane's studio across the hall, so there is confusion as we all settle ourselves. Aunt Jane and Mr. Serle are sitting near the stove. Honor is by her worktable. I do not think she is even aware that she has unfolded cloth and is beginning to sew. She cannot in her nature sit with her hands unoccupied.

"Mina told us of your kindness to her, Mr. Serle," Aunt Jane declares in her flat, American accent. "We are glad to welcome you and your friend." She lowers her voice a little so she is addressing Mr. Serle only, although standing by the stove to make the tea, I can still hear her. "Thank you for bringing Mina safe across the ocean to her brother and to us," she says. "You must be a man of great delicacy of feeling. You not only earned her trust but deserved it too."

Mr. Serle's color rises.

"You are generous, Miss Corbett," he replies.

"We are very fond of her," Aunt Jane says, to my embarrassment.

The kettle is boiling at last, and I can bring the blue and white china teapot to Aunt Jane, who pours out the cups. Aunt Jane and Mr. Serle talk of the weather in the city and how difficult it is to get about on foot when the streets are either frozen with slippery ice or ankle deep with noisome mud.

Guido DiRoma looks restless. He twists in his chair to examine the room.

"May I look about?" he finally asks Honor, who sits closest to him.

"Of course," she says.

Guido walks about the room with his hands behind his back. He looks out of the window. He throws back his head and stares up at the plaster medallion of curved leaves in the center of the ceiling. He walks down the rack where Honor hangs the bodices and skirts of dresses she is working on. She threw a sheet over it as she always does when we cook in the room.

"May I see?" Mr. DiRoma asks.

"Yes," Honor says, "but do not touch anything, please."

He twitches aside the cloth. *"Che bella,"* he says.

"What does that mean, Mr. DiRoma?" Honor asks.

"Lovely," he answers, looking at her and not at the hanging garments. "What do you call this cloth in English?" He points to a gray velvet skirt with black silk ribbon trim.

"That is velvet," Honor tells him.

"It is like your eyes. I will remember velvet," he says, putting the sheet back over the rack as he found it. He moves on and examines the spools of colored silks and ribbons on the big worktable.

The rest of us watch him. Aunt Jane seems suspicious, I think, but Honor follows his movements with a thoughtful look. Her mouth turns up at the corners as she uses her little scissors to clip off a thread. Mr. Serle too appears amused. He seems at ease. He holds the cup of tea that I handed him, his long fingers curving under the blue and white saucer.

Guido turns from his contemplation of the room and its contents to see us watching him. He smiles.

"Ma cóme è gentile qui, Beniamino," he says. *"Tranquillisimo."*

"Please speak English, Mr. DiRoma," Honor says demurely.

"He says it is pleasant here," Mr. Serle tells her. "Civilized."

"And the fabrics," Guido says. "You know, Miss Corbett, this fellow, my *caro Beniamino,* and I worked once for a fabric warehouse in Rome. Such colors, such textures."

"Indeed," Mr. Serle speaks with pleasure at the memory, "we imported brocades from the east, silks and fine wools from the north."

"You make us feel at home, Miss Corbetts, Miss Pigot," Guido said and bowed to us. "We thank you. Perhaps you will allow my friend here to cook something for you another day to show you how grateful we are."

The frown clears from Aunt Jane's forehead.

"You are quick to volunteer your friend's labor," she says.

"Ah, but my *Beniamino* will surprise you with what he can do," Guido says. "He makes *pesce all 'Ebraica* to make you think you are in heaven."

"What is that?" Honor asked.

"Fish," he said, "vinegar and honey and raisins and little *pignoli*—I do not know the word in English."

"I would like to try it," I say.

Guido does not allow Mr. Serle an opportunity to offer to cook for us. "Your beautiful dresses and ribbons remind me," he says. "We have a saying: *Vesti da Turco, mangia da Ebrèo.* Dress like a Turk, eat like a Jew."

"Oh!" Honor says. Her needle is still, poised over the fabric she was about to pierce. The dreamy look I recognize from the first day I met her peeps out of her face. "I should like to see Mina dressed as a Turk," she says. "Red silk gauze trousers, I think, shot with gold thread, falling from a gold-embroidered low waistband and caught at the ankles with the same embroidered bands. Her feet bare. A small red and gold vest, low cut and sleeveless, and wide gold bracelets set with rubies on her upper arms. Her hair loose and—"

"Honor!" Aunt Jane is horrified. "Honor! You are embarrassing Mina. You are embarrassing us all."

Mr. Serle's teacup rattles in the saucer, and he sets it down on the table beside him.

Guido is staring at the ceiling again. "It is a good thing my English is poor," he says.

"I am sorry," Honor says. "I forgot myself."

But she is smiling and watching Mr. Serle. She does not look sorry at all.

I feel shy suddenly, but pleased somehow. Honor made me feel that I might be very different from the girl in the high-necked dress I am today or the disguised boy that I was just a few months ago. I could become someone beautiful even.

"I apologize for Honor," Aunt Jane says to us all.

"I know," I say. "When Honor begins to dream of clothes, nothing will stop her."

There is a silence. Honor returns to her sewing and Guido to his perambulations. Mr. Serle picks up his teacup cautiously and drinks a little. I do not know what any of us would have said next. We are spared because a bang comes at the door, and there, unexpectedly, are my brother and John Deegan with him, shaking rain from their hats.

Then, of course, the talk is all of gold and fortunes and the best route to California. Sea or land, they all sound terrifying. Mr. DiRoma and Daniel speak enthusiastically. Mr. Serle listens to them, asking an occasional question. Other conversation is impossible.

Later, when they had all left, we talked about the visit.

"I like your Mr. Serle," Honor commented. "He is just as you described him, very attractive. And, I think, deep," she adds.

"He seems a gentleman despite being a cook and a Jew." Aunt Jane sounds condescending, but that is her way. "Not someone I would wish courting you or Honor, of course, but a respectable acquaintance. He has lovely manners."

"Mr. Serle would not court us," I say. "He will marry in his own religion."

There is a pause. Aunt Jane purses her mouth and does not comment. Honor looks down at her teacup and smiles at some thought of her own.

"I was surprised to see Mr. Serle's friend, Mr. DiRoma," I add. "He did not mention it when we talked."

"I did not mind. Not at all." Honor spoke quickly. "I found him amusing."

Aunt Jane looked apprehensively at Honor, but when she spoke it was not about Mr. DiRoma. "That friend of your brother's, Mr. Deegan, ate the extra chocolate cream," she said. "I thought it greedy of him."

SUNDAY, MARCH 25, 1849

When Daniel came to call today, he spoke politely to Aunt Jane and Honor in greeting. Then he asked abruptly if I would walk out with him and talk.

"I was just going across the hall with Aunt Jane to look at some prints she will be tinting," Honor said smoothly. "Why go out? Be comfortable here for your conversation."

"Thank you," Daniel replied.

We were silent as they went out and closed the door.

"I am going to California." Daniel took my hand but did not meet my eyes.

My heart freezes with despair.

"Why, Daniel?" I cry. "Why must you go?"

"I wish to rise in the world," Daniel says.

"You said your work at the hotel pays well," I tell him.

Anger chokes me. My brother will leave me. My brother does not need my love.

Daniel stood up and began to pace the room.

"It is a waiter's job," he replies. "Where will it lead? I might become captain of the waiters. I might even rise after many years to manage a hotel, but that is doubtful. I can never earn the money on a waiter's pay to own a hotel myself."

"But your saloon," I remind him.

"It will be twenty years before I have the money for that," he says, "or else I must take on debt with such men as Matt Branton. They take more than interest back on debts. I will not break my back and give over my conscience to be the prop of another man's power. No, Mina, my soul requires freedom. I will make my own fortune."

I clench my fists so my nails hurt my palms. Crying to him that his freedom is my pain, that he is abandoning me, will be useless.

"If you must go, I will go with you," I say.

"It is no place for a woman," he replies, frowning.

"I will go as a boy," I argue. I can see from his face the moment I speak the thought that he sets his mind against it. "I will cut my hair. I can cook for you and repair your clothes. I am a very good traveler."

It gave me pain to speak of cutting my hair again. It is just now long enough to put up easily. I will do anything for my brother, though—if only he loves me enough to take me with him.

Daniel sits down and holds my hand in both of his.

"Mr. DiRoma and I will take passage on a ship going to

Panama," he says. "I cannot have you in a steerage with a crowd of men. It would shame you and me also."

"What will I do without you?" I cry.

"But you have your friends," Daniel says. "I talk with Mr. Serle at the hotel, you know. You were right in how you described him. He has your welfare in mind as an uncle would. And I thought you were happy with the Miss Corbetts. I am proud of you for the ladylike way you earn your bread."

In his voice is his impatience that I be content and let him go with a clear mind.

"Will you come back?" I ask him. It comes out as a pleading.

"Of course I will come back," he says. "I will come back with a great fortune."

He stands, paces the room, and returns.

"But what if there is no great fortune or only a very little one?" I ask. "What then?"

"You can join me," Daniel says, and then he thinks and adds, "I will send money for you to hire a maid and travel as a lady. Or, perhaps, I will return to fetch you myself."

"Yes." I try to smile. "It is always easier to make a journey with someone who knows the way."

"I will write to you, Mina," Daniel promises. "I will write to you, and as soon as possible, I will send money. I want to care for you."

"I would like the comfort of being with you better than money," I say.

"You are a good girl, Mina," Daniel says as he seats himself beside me again. "I could not bear to go without your blessing."

"You have that," I say, "and my prayers always." And my tears, I think, but I do not speak the words. "When will you and Mr. DiRoma go?" I ask.

"We go Thursday on the *Salsette*," he says. "Yesterday was my last day at the hotel. I am living with Guido until we leave."

"Thursday!" I am appalled. "But that is four days. It is too soon. What about all the things you need? I must make you a new shirt."

He goes Thursday, and he told me only today. It is easier to be practical than to talk of feelings when one's heart is frozen in one's breast. I make a list of all Daniel's needs that I can prepare. Daniel will be busy with the business of his journey. He and Guido DiRoma purchased the supplies they plan to sell and are arranging for them to be shipped on the *Salsette* with them.

A thought worries me. He is my older brother and knows more of the world than I do. These are a grown man's affairs, and yet there is something unaccounted for.

"You are going by the route you told me was too expensive and are buying stores to sell," I say. "Is Guido DiRoma rich? Is he paying?"

"Oh!" Daniel seems surprised that I must ask. "I forgot I did not tell you. Guido is not rich at all. Between us we found we could raise enough for one passage through Panama, the fastest way. We have investors for the rest."

"Investors?" I am puzzled.

"Guido talked to his friend Mr. Serle and to Mr. Serle's friend Mr. Meyer, who is a banker's son. And Guido's cousin owns an ice and coal business. The three of them have each advanced us money. We are a business with five owners. As Guido and I earn our way, we must share the profits with the three others. We made an agreement."

"I did not know Mr. Serle had so much money," I say.

Daniel looks at me sharply, furrowing his brow. "He seems willing and at ease."

"I wish I could invest too," I sigh.

Daniel laughs and takes my hand kindly. "If something happens to me and the business survives, you will be a partner with the other four. I have written it down. They each have a copy of the paper."

"You are a good brother," I say with my mouth, even though, God forgive me, I did not feel the thought in my heart. "God keep you safe."

"There was one surprise in the business," Daniel says. "Guido DiRoma cannot read or write except to sign his name. I am pledged to teach him on the voyage."

We talked a little more. Daniel believes our parents would approve his venture. I suppose he needs to think that. Soon I went to fetch Honor and Aunt Jane, who were pretending still to be busy in the other room. Honor is going to help me with the things Daniel needs. She asked particulars about Mr. DiRoma and said that it is almost as easy to make two shirts as one if he needs outfitting.

I am bereft. And yet—later, after I calmed myself and talked quietly with Honor, I can admit that I feel the desire for adventure in Daniel. His face lights when he talks of making his way against the world. He is like the falcon that must fly high and look wide to see its prey.

FRIDAY, MARCH 30, 1849

Daniel and Mr. DiRoma ate their last dinner in New York with us on Wednesday night. I went out to market very early in the morning and then closed the kiosk at five to hurry home. I made a boiled beef with mustard sauce and roasted potatoes in their jackets. I was lucky to find good ones at this time of year. I served them with cream poured in and onions stewed in butter. There was chopped salad of early greens from the farms in New Jersey, and then oranges sliced with sugar for a sweet. I think it was cooked well enough, but I could only pretend to eat.

Daniel liked everything.

"I do not suppose we will eat so well for a long time," he said.

"Or enjoy the company of such pleasant ladies," Mr. DiRoma added.

I wanted to ask, "Then why do you go?" but I knew that I would only sound sulky.

"We will miss the company of such pleasant gentlemen," Honor said. She sounded very demure, but her eyes crinkled at the corners from her smiling. "New York will be the usual wasteland of bad manners without the two of you."

Everyone laughed then, and the mood eased.

"Would you like to see my pistol, Mina?" Daniel asked me.

I admired it with caution. Daniel reassured me that he did not intend to fight with anyone, only to have it for protection. He bought the thing yesterday near the Fulton Market and went up to the open land above Forty-fifth Street to practice using it. We joked that he could have shot us one of the pigs that infest the alleyways for our dinner.

"He is an excellent shot," Mr. DiRoma assured us. "I will trust my life to him."

"You will not take a gun?" Honor asks.

Mr. DiRoma shakes his head emphatically, *no*. "It is not in my nature," he says. "I should make some terrible mistake. I would shoot Daniel or myself. I carry my friend, my bowie knife, which serves to cut my food. If I have to kill a bear with it to protect myself, I will use it for that too."

"He will talk the bear to death," Daniel jokes. "It will be begging me to shoot it before Guido is done."

Aunt Jane asked about the journey. The ship will take them from New York to the city of Chagres, a terrible, unhealthy place. They will cross the Isthmus of Panama to the Pacific Ocean. There they must embark again and sail north to San Francisco, the city nearest to the gold fields. Daniel will write to me from Panama if he can. It may not be possible to send a letter until he reaches California. If all goes well, that will be in June. But, of course, the letter will then have to find its way back to New York, Daniel reminds me.

I must not expect word too soon, everyone says. I must be patient. The hard part will be that I cannot direct a letter to Daniel until I have word from him. I must keep this book carefully so that I have a record of my news and thoughts to share.

At the end of the evening, when it was time for Daniel to go, I had a surprise for him. I gave him his new shirt and showed him how I sewed a gold piece, an American eagle, into the sleeve of it.

"You must have a secret resource against want. You will take gold to California as well as find it there," I tell him. "Now I am an investor in you too."

Daniel kissed me then and held me to him. I think we both

had the unspeakable knowledge of his terrible journey on the *Washington* in our hearts.

"You will have a return on your investment," he said. "I promise."

"Wait," I said, "there is another present."

I gave him a little portrait of me, painted by Aunt Jane. It is a head and shoulders and of a size to fit in his vest pocket. The expression looks very like me, everyone says. Daniel seemed more than pleased. He kissed me again.

After Daniel and Mr. DiRoma left, Honor sat in her workroom for a long time.

Daniel and Mr. DiRoma sailed very, very early Thursday morning. Aunt Jane and Honor and I went down to see them off. Mr. Serle and—to my surprise—Herr Meyer were at the pier. Herr Meyer seemed barely awake. Mr. DiRoma's cousin and the cousin's wife came too. The cousin looks like an older version of Mr. DiRoma, bluff and vital, but with gray hairs in his disordered brown curls. His wife is stout, gets out of breath easily, and speaks little English. She and Aunt Jane talked to each other mainly with signs and gestures.

Last night when she sat up late, Honor made a gift for Mr. DiRoma. She gave it to him as soon as we arrived at the ship. They walked a little way apart down the pier. She put a packet in his hand and they talked. When they came back, Mr. DiRoma was smiling, but Honor's gray eyes were bright with unshed tears.

I do not know what anyone said, really. I was distracted with worrying whether Daniel had everything he needed for the voyage, thinking of the dangers he will face, and trying not to cry at being left behind.

Daniel put his arm about my shoulders for the last embrace. "Don't be anxious, Mina," he says. "Remember that you are with me."

He pats the pocket where he stowed my picture. I look at his dear face, his blue-green eyes, and the long line of his jaw. His face holds not just himself but the ghosts of my parents and my sister. What will I have of him—of any of them—when he is gone? The wind from the water blows a lock of hair across his forehead.

"Please, Daniel, may I cut a curl of your hair?" I ask.

"Yes, but hurry," he says. "We must go aboard."

I take my housewife out and fumble with the scissors. The tears are starting now, and my hands are shaking. I drop the scissors. Then someone is there—Mr. Serle.

"Let me," he says. "You do not want to stab your brother by mistake." He retrieves the scissors, cuts the lock, folds all into the housewife. "Here," he says. "Put it away safe in your pocket, child."

"Thank you, sir." I hear my brother's voice. "Will you give her your arm? I fear she will faint."

"I am all right," I say, but Mr. Serle takes my arm anyway.

"Good-bye," Daniel says and kisses my cheek again. "Pray for me, Mina."

Through the diamond prisms of tears I see Daniel and Guido DiRoma running toward the ship's ladder, clambering up. There is shouting, hauling of ropes, cries of farewell. White handkerchiefs are waving from the deck of the ship and from the people on the shore.

"Here is my handkerchief," Mr. Serle says. "Your brother is waving to you. See?"

The ship is under tow, slipping away from the pier, down the river into the harbor, and away toward the narrows that lead to the sea. Like a woman donning her finery for a ball, she unfurls her sails about her, and her pennants stream bright as bonnet ribbons in the wind. At last we cannot see even a flicker of white from her deck. I sigh and give Mr. Serle back his handkerchief.

"Here," he says gently and blots the wet from my cheeks. Then he folds the cloth and puts it away in his pocket.

The others are talking. The world that tipped and wobbled about me is returning to a dreary steadiness.

"Will you go home with Miss Corbett now?" Mr. Serle asks me.

"Oh no," I say. "I must go to my work. I left a notice at the kiosk yesterday, saying it would be open today but later than usual."

"Are you sure?" Mr. Serle asks. "I can change the notice for you."

"I would like to be busy," I say.

Herr Meyer comes over to us.

"May I offer to drive you home, Miss Pigot?" he asks. "I have a carriage waiting. I am taking the Miss Corbetts to Elizabeth Street."

"I wish to walk," I say. "If it is all right, I should like to walk quietly to the Columbia House with Mr. Serle."

"Of course," Mr. Serle says.

Herr Meyer bows to me, and then he surprises me by taking my hand and kissing it.

"*Au revoir,* Miss Pigot," he says.

"What did he say?" I ask Mr. Serle. "I did not understand him."

"He spoke in French," Mr. Serle explains. "He said, 'Until we see each other again,' which means he does not wish to say good-bye."

We do not speak again for a time. It is so easy and comforting to walk with Mr. Serle. The day is brightening steadily. We turn our backs to the sea and go up Battery Place to Broadway. The grass within the iron railings of the Bowling Green across the street glows in the early sunlight with the brave promise of spring.

"Did you know there were crowns on those railings once?" Mr. Serle asks me.

"No," I say. "Where did they go?"

"They read the Declaration of Independence for America against England here in the year 1776. The crowd listening were so inspired by the words that they broke off and took away the crowns, the signs of monarchy."

"I did not know," I say.

"We should learn these things," Mr. Serle comments. "We should know our history as Americans."

We walk on tranquilly until we come to Trinity Church and the entrance to its cemetery.

"Let us stop here a moment," Mr. Serle suggests. "Have you been here? The churchyard is a peaceful place."

"No," I say. "Is it all right for us to go in?"

"Certainly," he replies. "Here is more of the history of our country."

The trees above us swell with their first delicate tracery of leaves. Snowdrops bloom along the wall of the church. We walk down the gray gravel of a path among the monuments. Mr. Serle stops in front of a white stone pyramid. The name *Alexander Hamilton* is carved deeply into its base.

"Who is Alexander Hamilton?" I ask.

"He was a founding father of America," Mr. Serle informs me.

"Oh?" I say. "What did he do to be a founding father?"

"I have no idea," Mr. Serle tells me solemnly. "But it must have been important, because he has a large tombstone."

It makes me smile at last.

"You are a very poor guide," I say.

"But I know more than you do," he points out.

"Barely," I say. Then I sigh. "I am a stranger here. When will we feel American?"

"Soon," Mr. Serle says. "Just think, when your brother is in California and you are here, you will stretch out your arms to him and hold the whole country between you. It will be yours."

"I wonder," I say.

It is a strange thought. My brother on the shore of the Pacific Ocean and me, here, on the shore of the Atlantic. What miles of prairies and rivers and wooded mountains will lie between us.

"I wonder," I say again.

"I do not," Mr. Serle tells me. "This is your country."

There is a pause.

Then—"You are wearing a pretty pin."

I see that Mr. Serle regards me with a sort of considering expression in his face.

"It is a loan from Aunt Jane," I tell him. "Honor is so particular about how a dress looks, and they are both kind to lend me things."

"They are very kind," Mr. Serle says. "But wouldn't you like your own brooch?"

"I might buy a simple brooch to keep the lock of hair my

brother gave me," I say. "I am not sure how to choose an honest place to purchase such a thing. Do you know?"

"I will inquire for you," Mr. Serle says.

I stood alone as we contemplated the tomb of mysterious Mr. Hamilton. Now Mr. Serle tucks my arm into his again. We make our way out of the quiet of the gravestones and the overarching trees to the clamor of Broadway. The business of the morning is under way. As often happens, there is a street accident. At Fulton Street a wain loaded with empty beer barrels locked wheels with a cart carrying bricks to a building under construction. All is a chaos of rolling barrels, spilled bricks, plunging horses, and shouting drivers. We make our way very cautiously around the mess. I am relieved to see that none of the horses is injured.

"Thank you," I say to Mr. Serle at the steps of the Columbia House Hotel. "I love Honor and Aunt Jane, but you are my truest friend. You tie together past and present for me because we know each other's hurt."

"You are welcome," he tells me. "You are always welcome to whatever I can do for you. I value your friendship and your trust."

We enter the great building, where last week I saw my brother every day. He is gone. I take a breath and let it out slowly. Now another life begins.

"Do you like Herr Meyer?" Honor asks me at night as we brush our hair, preparing for bed.

"Not really," I say. "I do not like the way he strokes his beard. One would think it was his pet cat. He is much nicer when he plays his music; then both his hands are busy on the pianoforte."

"Such a picture," Honor laughs. "What do you think of Mr. DiRoma?"

"I like him," I say. "I trust him to be a good friend to my brother."

"Yes," Honor says in a thoughtful voice, drawing out the sound into a sigh.

"Did you give him a gift?" I ask.

It is impossible to resist asking.

"Yes," Honor says. She brushes her hair quite violently. "I gave him two handkerchiefs, one for use and one with a square of gray velvet sewed into the corner."

I almost say that I do not understand, that she had met him only twice. But I do understand. Honor would know what she wants very quickly; that is who she is.

"You were kind to give him a gift," I say.

"Do you think he will ever return to New York?"

I hear a little tremble in her voice. I look at her, but she has lowered her head and is brushing her hair down from the nape of her neck in sweeping strokes. Of course, I cannot see her face.

"In honesty, I do not know," I tell her. "I do not know."

Honor does not speak further about the matter, but asks me to blow out the candle after I say my prayers.

THURSDAY, APRIL 19, 1849

Mr. Serle came to the kiosk as I was closing the cupboards. I saw him rarely in the winter, but since Daniel left, he passes by and greets me almost every day. Usually he is very brief, more as if he is looking to be sure I still exist than seeking conversation. Tonight I could see when he approached that there was something more of deliberation in his aspect. He was dressed in his dark suit. His shirt gleamed with starch. The dark oval of his face was like a sharp-cut cameo above the white.

"Good evening," he said.

"Good evening," I told him. "Are you going to an opera tonight?"

"No," he said, "Herr Meyer and I are escorting Madame Moses to a concert."

"I wish you a pleasant time," I said, locking the last door and putting the key into my pocket.

"Thank you," he said. "I brought you something," He set a little pasteboard box on the counter between us.

"Oh!" I looked at it, surprised. "What is it?"

"Open it and see," he says.

I wipe my fingers on my handkerchief before I touch the box. When I lift the cover, I see a brooch pinned to a scrap of white silk. It is an oval bound in a gold band. The brooch itself is a picture of a red rose with a green leaf against a dark blue background. The whole is made of tiny, tiny pieces of what look like different-colored stones.

"It is so beautiful," I say. My breath catches.

"Look at the back also," Mr. Serle tells me. He picks the brooch up and turns it over. "See, here is a place to put your brother's hair."

He shows me how the pin opens and closes like a locket. The back is a transparent crystal, so I will see the red of my brother's hair. It is a perfect thing.

"How did you find it?" I ask. "How can such tiny pieces be fitted so smoothly?"

"It is *piètra dura,* mosaic work, from the city of Rome where I was born," he says. "The stones are lapis and jade and coral."

"But I do not have money for such a valuable thing!" I exclaim. "When I asked you about a place to buy a brooch, I did not—" I stop. Mr. Serle must have misunderstood.

"No, no," he says. "It is a gift. I wish to give this to you."

"A gift?" I ask. "For me?"

"Yes," Mr. Serle says, "a gift for you."

"It has a secure catch," I say. "I will not fear to lose such a lovely thing." A terrible thought comes to me. I will be doubly in debt to him. "Is it all right to take it?" I ask hesitantly. "Is it proper to accept?"

"What are you worried about, child?" Mr. Serle asks.

"I am not sure," I say in some confusion. "Aunt Jane has warned me—and then my brother said—and sometimes the men who buy cigars—it is such a pretty pin—" I stop again.

I have no idea what I want to say. And Mr. Serle is not one of the men who buy cigars. He is not just anyone. He is my friend.

"We could consider that I was your uncle once," Mr. Serle says in a dry tone.

I am afraid I have hurt his feelings.

"I am glad the brooch was made in the place where you were

born," I say. "I will ask Aunt Jane if it is respectable to accept such a gift. I hope she will say yes. I think my brother's hair would be well protected in it."

Tears come to my eyes when I think of my brother, and of Mr. Serle's son, dead these many years, who was called Daniel too, and of Mr. Serle thinking to choose such a gift for me.

"Please do not cry, *cara*," he says, his voice softer now. "I did not mean to make you sad. I thought you would like something of your own, not borrowed."

I wipe my eyes with my handkerchief.

"You did not make me sad," I tell him. "It makes me happy to know you thought of me—and my brother too," I add.

"Then why are you crying?" he asks me, reasonably, I suppose.

"I am a little tired," I say, "and then I thought of your family and mine who are dead, and my brother traveling ever farther from us as we speak—and your kindness to me."

I replace the pin in the box and put the cover in place. As I do so, Mr. Serle sets his hand over mine.

"It distresses me that you are tired," he says. "You are too young to be cooped in this dark place all day."

I look at his hand curved over mine. His long fingers with their clean, trimmed nails are beautiful.

"Truly, I am not so sad," I tell him. "You are very good to me. It is like having a guardian angel, I think."

He looks into my face for a moment.

"What are uncles for?" he says. "I must go. I will be late."

"*Au revoir,*" I say carefully. "Thank you."

He nods and goes.

Aunt Jane hesitated about whether it was respectable to accept the brooch. I could not help beginning to cry again with tiredness and disappointment, although I tried not to, and then she quickly said I could keep it. I was so glad. It would be terrible to have to choose to be a lady instead of a true friend. Aunt Jane conceded it is all right too if I make Mr. Serle a silk cravat like the one I made for my brother. I have chosen a lovely piece of dark blue silk with a red and black figure in it from Honor's basket of ends. The blue is just the color of the blue stones in the brooch, I think.

WEDNESDAY, MAY 2, 1849

We had unseasonable heat today. In the late afternoon the oppression broke into a thunderstorm. I heard the growl from the clouds. The first rumble was followed by a bang and clash as if all of the pots and pans had fallen from their shelves in the hotel kitchen. And then came crash after crash until my head rang with the noise.

I heard the sweep of rain down Broadway even from my work. A cold gust of air blew down the stairs. The gas lamps along the wall flared up and flickered. The relief did not last, however. The thunder died to a far-off rumble like wheels on cobblestones, and the air came hot again, but worse now, carrying the steamy stink of the streets. I began to put the stock away, thinking how good it would be to be home in an hour. I was wondering too if it was raining still and whether I should take the omnibus uptown.

John Deegan startled me. I turned to see him leaning on the counter. He had come to invite me to Niblo's Garden tonight, he said. There are acrobats and ropedancing and a trombone band. I told him no. When he pressed me, I told him that, even if I wished to go, I would not without a chaperone.

"You do not seem to be an Irish or an American girl," John Deegan protests. "You seem to think you are some proper English miss. Believe me, you are not. Nor one of the elite who swans it at the opera either."

"It does not matter what you think of me," I say indifferently.

"Modern girls are free to go out as they please with their beaux," John Deegan says.

"Then I am clearly a modern girl," I point out. "I feel free to do as I please. Besides, you are not a beau of mine."

"Your brother believed our people should stick together," he says.

"Off with you," I say. His words sting me. If my brother believed we must stick together, he would not have left me here
alone. And then I say, in relief because it is true, "A customer is
coming."

"You must miss your brother," John Deegan says with a sudden kindness in his voice. "I did not mean to press you. Forgive me?"

"Yes," I say, and he goes off, looking pleased—with himself
or me I cannot tell.

The customer, who comes down the marble stairs from the
hotel lobby, is a short, stout person, well dressed, but reeking of
rum or whiskey. He makes an endless business of asking my advice about cigars and choosing among the three I lay out for him.

"Will you clip it and light it for me?" he asks.

I can see that he has his own cigar clip hanging on his gold
watch chain. I set the box of matches on the counter.

"I do not do that," I say. "Matches cost extra."

When I take his money and try to return the change, he refuses it.

"Keep it, dear," he says. "Buy yourself something."

"No, thank you," I say. "I do not accept tips."

"Then let me take you to a supper," he says. "Oysters and
champagne and ices. Your hair is a red-gold summer sunset. A
lovely girl like you should have a treat."

"No, thank you," I say.

"The theater?" he offers.

"No, thank you," I repeat.

After offering Niblo's, a concert, the minstrel show at
Mechanics' Hall, a ferry ride to New Jersey in the moonlight—a
ridiculous thought in this weather—at last he gives up and I can
close the kiosk. Now I am very late. Last week a young woman
disappeared from Mott Street. Honor says that she probably
eloped, but Aunt Jane is not so sure. I do not worry much about
being carried off. Robbery or insulting accusations from the street-
walkers of trying to take their trade are more likely.

To my dismay, the stout man with his gold watch chain
stands smoking by the door of the hotel when I emerge.

"Miss," he shouts at me. "Miss! I will escort you home."

Sam, who calls cabs for people, is not in sight. If I wait for an omnibus, this man will bother me. If I begin to walk, he might follow me.

"Go away or I will scream," I say desperately.

I turn to go back into the hotel. Mr. Serle is coming down the steps. The sweep of the searchlight from the roof of Mr. Barnum's Museum catches and illuminates his face for a small moment. It is a revelation of safety.

"Good evening," he says.

"Will you wait with me until a car comes?" I ask. "A man is bothering me." Before Mr. Serle can answer, the man lurches toward us.

"I saw her first," he says.

Mr. Serle looks him over.

"Are you staying at the hotel?" he asks.

"Yes," the man says. He seems surprised.

"You had best go in," Mr. Serle says in his calm way. "I can smell the spirits on you from here. You will not have that gold watch chain long if you stay on the street."

We do not wait to hear the man's response, for Mr. Serle takes my arm in his and hurries me along to where a horse cab is waiting. After he hands me up, he gives the driver my address and climbs in beside me.

"I am sorry," I say. "I did not know what to do."

"You were doing right by going back indoors," he tells me.

There is a silence.

"Do you carry enough for cab fare?" Mr. Serle asks suddenly.

"I do not know how much it is," I reply. "I never thought to take a cab."

"I will speak to Sam," Mr. Serle says. "He will always find you a safe driver. You should not be alone on the street after dark."

"Thank you," I say. "I am later than usual tonight."

I do not think I would spend the money for a cab, however little it is. I am saving to pay Mr. Serle back and to have enough for passage to join my brother in California.

"You are kind to see me home," I say. "I am sorry to take you from your evening."

"I am going uptown anyway," Mr. Serle says. "I have an appointment to call on Herr Meyer." There is a pause. "On business," he adds.

Despite the rain, the side windows of the cab are down. It is so warm that even the muggy air is welcome, because it moves a little. The evening sounds of the city come in to us mixed with the clatter of the horse's hoofs on the stones. The lamps cast their pools of light. Black umbrella tops glistening with wet gleam under the lights and then disappear into the darkness between the lampposts.

Sometimes it is easier to recognize a person walking away from you than it is to recognize him coming toward you. Near the corner of Broadway and Reade streets, John Deegan prances along behind a larger man, a bear of a man, who strides purposefully. Mr. Deegan beside him is like a dog trotting with its master.

"There is Mr. Deegan," I say. "He is with someone."

Mr. Serle leans forward just enough to see as we pass. "That is Matt Branton," he says, "a political boss."

"Oh," I say. "My brother said he recommended me for my work at the hotel."

I turn to look at Mr. Serle. It is too dark in the cab to see his expression. Only as we pass a lamp, I can see the beauty of his profile.

"I am very glad you do not wear mustaches or a beard," I say without thinking.

"Thank you for your approval, Miss Pigot," he says. "I shall keep your preference in mind for the future."

I think from the sound of his voice that he is amused. There are so many things I would like to say. Both the sadness and the comfort of the past come pouring in on me when we are together. I would like to ask him important questions about whether he holds to his dreams. I read a few days ago that there was a disturbance of Germans objecting to the burial of a Jew in a cemetery on Long Island. I would like to ask Mr. Serle if that overturned his ideas of America. I cannot find the words to begin such a subject.

Mr. Serle does not speak. He is lost in some thought of his own. I do not wish to babble foolishly at him. Besides, I am too tired to make up conversation. It is good to sit near to a person one trusts and be tranquil. In easy silence we arrive at Elizabeth Street.

"Wait for me," Mr. Serle tells the driver. "I will see the lady to her door and then go on to Crosby Street."

He helps me down to the sidewalk. It is not raining now, but the air is heavy with the threat of it. There are people about on the street as usual.

"Flowers, sir! Flowers! Daffodillies and tulips!" a girl's voice pipes.

Two children advance along the street toward us, carrying a bucket containing flowers. The gingham-clad girl has a pretty, rounded face and rosebud lips, but her left eye rolls in to squint at her nose. The boy is taller than she but not by much. His white shirt gleams bright against his dark skin. His hair springs up above his forehead in short, tight curls.

"Why, it is Phoebe!" I exclaim.

The little girl giggles. "That is Phil," she says.

Phoebe is looking at me wide-eyed. I think she is afraid.

"Oh! Of course, he is Phil," I say. "I am mistaken."

"Buy our posies." The little girl turns her head to look at me with her good eye.

Before we can say more, either to refuse her or to give a coin to send her on her way, a man and a woman come up to us. The woman has a severe face, long jawed, long nosed, straight brows above narrowed eyes. She is tall for a woman. She wears an old black poke bonnet and a tight black bombazine dress of old-fashioned cut that must be stiflingly hot in this weather. She holds a furled black umbrella in one hand and printed sheets in the other.

"Without holiness no man shall see the Lord!" she says without preamble. "Are you saved?"

She thrusts a tract into Mr. Serle's hands. To my dismay, the little girl and Phoebe begin to back away. Mr. Serle folds the paper and addresses me.

"I will see you to your door," he says. "I must go."

"Hello, Daniel. Good evening, Mr. Serle, sir."

It takes me a moment to realize that it is Flint, even though he speaks as if he has seen us just this morning. He stands a step behind the woman, looking as vague and lumbering as ever he did. The gold anchor earring gleams at his ear. He too is carrying a bundle of papers. It must be more of the tracts the woman is giving out.

"I have taken the Pledge again," he tells us.

"Good," says Mr. Serle. "Miss Pigot?"

"Repent! Repent!" the woman exclaims fiercely. "Sinners, will you not stay to hear the word of the Lord?"

"I must tell my friends I am back safe," I say.

Mr. Serle hurries me up the steps.

"If you talk to this woman, you will never get free of her," he tells me in a low tone.

I am in confusion. I call toward Phoebe, whom the tall woman has seized by the arm. "Wait. I will come back."

"I am late," Mr. Serle says frankly. "I cannot keep the cab waiting longer." He opens the door for me. "Be careful, my dear," he says. "Good night."

"Good night," I tell him. "Thank you for seeing me safely home."

Mr. Serle runs down the steps again, and I go in to tell Aunt Jane and Honor I am returned. Then I must go back to give a coin to Phoebe, but when I look from the steps, Phoebe, the little girl in gingham, Flint, and the tall woman too have all gone. The street is empty. Thunder growls in the distance. The rain pours down again. The streets steam and stink. I go in to tell Aunt Jane and Honor that I had a tiring day, ending with a moment of peace and the appearance of apparitions.

TUESDAY, MAY 8, 1849

As I walked down Broadway this morning, the newsboys shouted of riot and mayhem at the Astor Place Theater. I unlocked my cupboards and was about to read the news in the *Mirror* before I set out my stock, when John Deegan came to the kiosk.

"How are you?" he asks.

His hand on the counter looks grubby.

"I am well," I say, putting aside the newspaper and setting the scales for weighing snuff and pipe tobacco on the counter, with the little box of brass weights in their velvet compartments beside it.

"I need your help," he says in a low voice.

I look at him properly for the first time. He has dried blood on his neck. His right ear is red and swollen. The sleeve of his jacket is torn. I am about to ask him what is wrong when Mr. Serle comes over to us.

"What happened to you, Mr. Deegan?" Mr. Serle asks him.

"I defended the honor of our country against the Codfish aristocrats and their damned puppet actor," he declares belligerently.

"So you were one of the rioters last night," Mr. Serle says.

"Of course," John Deegan answers. He raises his voice in a defiant tone. "I am bound to fight against those who beat working folk down. The rich find their pleasure in crushing us under them."

"The newspapers are stirring up a foolish quarrel between actors to build their own sales." Mr. Serle speaks quietly but with contempt. "I suppose a newsman or one of the political bosses gave you a ticket for the theater last night."

"Bigger men than you or I saw how I answered the call to fight," John Deegan says.

"So personal gain inspired you?" Mr. Serle asks calmly.

"I came to ask Mina to sew my sleeve," John Deegan tells us. He looks sullen. "I cannot report for work like this, and my mother is angry at me and will not do it."

Mr. Serle regards him as if he were a saucy child.

"Has Miss Pigot given you permission to use her name?" he asks. "I do not imagine you would address her so if her brother were present."

"I told her brother I would take her off his hands and marry her," John Deegan says. "I call her as I please."

"No, you do not!" Mr. Serle sounds very angry. "You call her as *she* pleases. Miss Pigot, what do you wish?"

"This is a place of business, Mr. Deegan," I say. "I will be called Miss Pigot. Now, give me your jacket; I will mend the sleeve for pity so you do not lose your place. Mr. Serle will bring the jacket to you in a moment."

John Deegan looks as if he will argue, but then he shrugs, takes the jacket off, and goes away with his strutting walk. My housewife is in my pocket, of course, and I make quick, rough work of the repair. Mr. Serle stands, watching as I stitch. Luckily it is still early and no customers come.

"Would you really consider marriage to such a ruffian?" Mr. Serle asks me.

"No," I tell him. "Daniel liked him at first but turned away from him. I did not know John Deegan had a mother. How sad she does not care for him."

There is a pause. "I do not think he would make you happy," Mr. Serle says.

Surprised, I look up. Mr. Serle regards me with a frown, and then red flushes across his cheekbones under the olive brown of his skin. My heart jumps in my chest. He cares that I am happy.

"I promise I will not marry John Deegan," I assure him. "But I am not ready to marry anyone, yet." I finish my work and clip the thread. "Here is the jacket," I say, smiling at Mr. Serle. "Wash your hands after you deliver it. It is dirty."

Mr. Serle takes the jacket in two fingers and goes down the passage to the kitchen.

THURSDAY, MAY 17, 1849

The newspapers say it all began with insults directed at an English actor from hired bullies. The actor—that is, the English one—is the rival of an American actor. The insults were last Monday night. Then the newspapers talked and talked about it, with the newsboys crying special editions that predicted great violence if the English actor, Macready his name is, performed as he planned on Thursday night.

When I walked down Broadway to my work last Thursday

morning, all was calm enough. The usual rushing crowds, the beggars, and the hawkers clogged the sidewalks. I look ahead and do not gawk or dawdle even when I see a shop window crammed with oriental goods or Indian people in their leather tunics and beads. Some New York women wear heavy veils to prevent attention, but I notice they draw more comment from the idle boys than those who dress modestly and go their way quickly.

So all was as usual in the morning. The return should have been a lovely spring evening walk among people hurrying home to their suppers or sauntering out in the air after an early meal. I try always to be on my way during the quiet before the trulls and the loungers take the street corners. Last Thursday evening I was in good time, but as soon as I stepped out of the front entrance of the Columbia House Hotel, I felt the city boiling. Both sides of Broadway were clotted with groups of men and boys hurrying north. Some brandished fistfuls of handbills that they passed about to others.

"Hurry, Pat!" I heard a man say to his companion. "The fun will start without us."

"What is it?" I asked Sam, who stood at the hotel entrance.

"They are going up to Astor Place to stop the play there," Sam said. "Watch yourself on the streets, miss. It is a dangerous crowd."

At first, I felt safe enough. I kept to the side of the shops and houses so that I would not be pushed to the gutter by the heedless mob. When I came to a block of buildings under construction, it was more difficult. The mob grew thicker, and I was shoved aside and stumbled down the steps of an areaway. The place stank dreadfully of garbage and dead things. Something rustled behind a broken barrel. I did not dare to look.

As I came back to the street again, another group of men hurried by. One of them glanced aside, and I recognized John Deegan. He saw me too and paused, staring back.

"Mr. Deegan?" I called to him.

He shoved the handbills he was carrying into another man's hands and came back.

"What is it?" he asked roughly.

"I am trying to go home to Elizabeth Street," I said. "Could you help me make my way? I am afraid I will be pushed and fall."

He shrugged as if he would say *no,* but then he straightened his shoulders and reached for my hand.

"I will escort you," he declared. "Come. We must hurry."

The crowd thinned a little, and then groups, hastening from behind us, caught up and the mob grew. We came to a building being demolished. Lathe and brick and broken plaster lay strewn about. A man ahead of us stooped to seize a length of wood and brandished it about his head.

"Beat the devils," he shouted. "Beat the Codfish aristocracy!"

The mob parted around him so as not to be hit by his stick and then, as he began to run faster, speeded with him. John Deegan pulled my hand, and we were running too.

At the next cross street, we turned right out of Broadway. The crowds were pouring up Orange Street from the Five Points, ragged men and even more raggedy boys. There were women too, racing with the throng or trying to hold a son or husband back.

"Come back, Adam, come back," an old biddy shrieked, trotting after a clot of boys. "You'll be killed. Come back."

The hardest place to cross was at Broome and Mulberry Streets, where the railroad tracks come in and the cart traffic going downtown turns. People and horses and vehicles were in confusion everywhere. I prayed that the train would not come down into us. Someone screamed a warning. A fast-moving gig with the young driver lashing his horse scattered the crowd. Mr. Deegan put his arm about me for protection, almost lifting me along, and we were quick enough to escape the horse's hooves and the rattling wheels.

"Codfish!" someone cried out, an Irish voice, and threw a stone after the gig.

Luckily no one of the mob milling in the street was hurt. Yet, at that moment, I would not have cared. We ran. My heart beat strong in my chest. John Deegan's hand is strong and warm about mine. We are stars shooting across the night sky, sparks of light among the scintillating millions of the Milky Way. I am a part of all the crowd of people, moving, bursting with light, burning with an icy fire. It is a strange and dangerous joy.

We turn aside into Spring Street, cross Mott, and pause to catch our breath by the livery stable. I feel the elation of the mob, and at the same time that I do not want to be caught in this wave when its force crests and breaks.

The smell of the horses comes out warm and familiar from the stables. We lean against the wall, both of us short of breath from our run. I am no lady now, and, lifted still in the freedom of the moment, I do not care.

"Do not go farther, Mr. Deegan," I say, panting. "Leave the riot to others."

John Deegan shakes his head. "This is my quarrel," he says.

"How can you fight about an actor in a play?" I ask.

"You are wrong," he tells me, breathless still. "This is not a quarrel about actors. We fight to be Americans; we fight for rights against the elite."

"What will it benefit us to throw rotten eggs or burn a theater?" I demand.

"We stick together," he says stubbornly. "We show we are a power in the city."

"I would rather know you will be alive in the morning," I say.

We had been leaning our backs against the wall, our chests heaving as we caught breath, but now he turns. I lean back still, but he stands in front of me with his arm at the wall beside my head. His handsome face lightens into beauty.

"You could care that I am alive tomorrow?" he says, as if the thought is something extraordinary, honey in the mouth to be savored.

"Life is better than death," I say.

I do not know if he would have calmed and walked me soberly the rest of the way home. As I speak, the sound of a beating drum and the high thrill of pipes swells louder and louder from the direction of Broadway. John Deegan's face changes again. A different taste is in his throat now.

"The militia has come out." His voice is fierce and glad. "We will have battle."

"Oh no!" I exclaim.

"You are close to home here," he tells me. "You are safe enough."

He goes without waiting for my words, running—leaping almost—up toward Astor Place as if to mount a stairs to paradise.

"What is going on out there?" one of the stablemen asks me, leaning on his half door as I pass.

"A mob is going up to Astor Place," I tell him. "The militia is out."

The man looks sour. "A bad night," he says. "It is bad for business."

"Indeed," I say, still feeling the pull and power of the crowd.

Elizabeth Street is quieter compared to the noise behind me on Mott and Mulberry streets and the shouts I can hear from the Bowery beyond. I want to be indoors. My heart still pounds with the strange muddle of fear and exhilaration. I see the neat signs for the Miss Corbetts' businesses. Order is possible again.

Honor was watching for me at the window. She opened the door and hugged me. I hugged her too. We waited on the stoop, arm in arm, for Aunt Jane, who came at last, breathless, clutching her portfolio and with her bonnet askew. Her walk from Washington Place, where she gives a drawing lesson, was a struggle, but she was safe.

Later in the evening, after our meal, we heard explosions in the distance, great shouting, the crash of breaking glass, and the tolling of fire bells.

"Guns!" Aunt Jane exclaimed as the noises echoed.

Honor peered cautiously from the window. No one and nothing was to be seen on the street. We talked of sitting up in case of fire and then decided that Elizabeth Street was safe enough. Attacks on our houses, if they came, would be against the rich who signed a public petition in favor of the English actor.

I had just drifted into an uneasy dream of my brother standing by the iron railings of the Bowling Green, arguing with a great bear with Matt Branton's face, when Honor shook me awake again.

"Someone is banging at the door," she said. "Someone is shouting your name."

We dressed hastily and went out. Aunt Jane met us in the hall. She had lit her oil lamp. Outside was dim night. The moon was dark, and the flickering streetlight at the corner made the figures on the steps into wavering silhouettes, black shapes against gray. Aunt Jane raised her lamp. We could see a little crowd of men, eight or ten perhaps.

"What is it?" Aunt Jane asked in a quavering voice. "What is this disturbance?"

"Miss Mina Pigot?" a voice asked.

"Yes?" I said and stepped forward.

"We have brought John Deegan," the voice said. "He is shot. He asked for you."

I hurry down and kneel beside John Deegan on the steps. Someone comes from the house with another lamp. Even in the warmth of lamplight, John's face is waxen white. A thread of blood trails from the corner of his mouth and down his chin. His coat is torn over his breast and soaked in blood.

"This man needs a surgeon and a priest," I say.

"We stopped at St. Patrick's," the voice from the darkness tells me. "The priest gave the rites to him and two others. The others are already dead, but John Deegan would have us bring him here. Until a moment ago he could speak."

Perhaps he hears his name, for John Deegan sighs a deep breath that makes a bubbling, gasping sound in his throat. I bend over him.

"John?" I say. "How can I help you?"

Someone brings the lamp closer. John's eyes are open, gazing at nothing. I touch his cheek, and his eyes turn back to me from a faraway place. I think he knows me, for his face lightens a little as it did when we talked by the livery stable. His lips move.

"I am here," I tell him.

"You are right," he murmurs.

"Right?"

I shiver in the night air. Death has come to find me.

"Life—" he says quietly, and then with a question in his voice, "Forgive—"

John Deegan stares at me a moment, and then his gaze, like lamplight rippling on water, stretches out past me to another place. A bubble of bright blood blooms on his lips. I reach out and stroke the rough thatch of his hair.

"My dear," I said, "my dear. God give you peace. I do not know what you wish to forgive or have forgiven. Whatever it is, God grant it. I think nothing but good of you in this moment."

He raised his hand as if to ward off a blow, and the death rattle came in his throat. He died on the steps with my hand on his head and the silent crowd of strangers about us.

At last—"He is dead, miss," said the man who had spoken before.

I knew without knowing how it happened that my face was wet. "What must we do?" I asked. Time and feeling are frozen in this dim night.

The man shrugged.

"His mother lives down Mott Street in the Five Points," another voice spoke out of the dark. "I know Mary Ann Deegan."

The first man shrugged again. "We will carry him to his mother, I suppose."

"Honor," I said, "please bring the blanket from my trunk."

When she came out again, I spread the blanket on the walk by John Deegan's body.

"Here," I said. "I brought this from the old country. What better use for it now. We will wrap him in it so you can carry him in decency to his mother, poor thing."

Aunt Jane closed John Deegan's eyes, and then the men lifted him to the blanket so we could fold it over him. Honor found a length of cording to tie the covering. We laced it about the wrapped body to make a bundle with three loop handles on either side. I crossed myself as six men stepped up to take their burden. Then, as shadows, they moved away south into the darkness of the night and disappeared.

The next morning I was very ill with a terrible flux. Honor took care of me. She made me drink chamomile tea, and then, when I did not recover, she consulted the chemist and dosed me with an elixir of paregoric and chalk in brandy.

On Saturday, as she helped me down to the privy for the third time, I told her that I could not imagine a better friend.

She answered in her easy way, "I think you are purging sorrow, Mina. I like you for not having a romantic illness."

"I did not love him," I say. "I am not proud of that."

"I know," Honor says, "but loving is not in our control. And whether you loved him or not, his death is a sad and stupid waste. Now—you can go into the privy by yourself, but call to me if you feel faint."

As I lay in bed for all those days, resting between the privy, the medicine, and the nourishing broth that Honor insisted I must attempt, I thought over what had happened. Aunt Jane came in to tell me the newspapers were full of reports and blame. The soldiers fired on the mob that threw paving stones at them and refused to disperse. Maybe as many as fifty people are dead. God rest their souls. And all for a cry of "Codfish!" from hired ruffians. I felt a need in me to understand it.

When Stellina and I almost drowned, I grieved for past sorrows and pushed away the fear of the moment. Now, thinking of John Deegan dying, the tears run on my cheeks again. His death is present loss.

And yet beyond the sadness of his death—I must tell my truth whether I like it or not—John Deegan has left me a gift of thought and feeling. I understand now the excitement in danger. A person might give herself to the mob, caring for nothing but to be one drop melted into all the power of the surging motion, one atom of water in the ocean wave. I felt it as a kind of death, and yet, in the moment, I did not care that I was dying. I loved my death. One could not be lonely if one gave oneself up. I wonder if that seduction drew John Deegan to his fate. I wonder if he felt the danger but believed himself immortal. I wonder if my brother and Guido plunge into their lives with this exhilaration in their hearts. I knew grief, but I did not know before that this other emotion, which pushes grief away, existed. I soared like one of a flock of birds that dips and wheels as one in the autumn sky while winter gathers. But I can see the flock and myself too. I feel lonely and bereft perched on a branch, solitary. And yet—another truth beyond my liking or disliking—it is my nature to choose so.

This morning—Thursday—I was well enough to go to early Mass. Today is Ascension Day. After the service I bought food for our meal tonight. I found some tender spinach and herbs and good fresh eggs. I will make omelets. Aunt Jane was hesitant about my going to the hotel, but I insisted. I must earn my way, and she herself was going out to give her lessons. We walked over to Broadway together. The streets were quiet, although we could see here and there that paving stones were torn away or brickbats left in the gutters.

When I arrived at the Columbia House Hotel, Mr. Serle came down the passage from the kitchen almost immediately.

"Good morning," I said.

"Are you all right?" he asked. "I heard that John Deegan is dead."

"It is a terrible thing," I say. "He came to Elizabeth Street for help, but we could not help him."

"Oh, my dear," he said. "Will you tell me what happened?"

When I finish the story and wipe my eyes, Mr. Serle looks at me with concern.

"You must feel your loss," he says.

I tell him the truth.

"I have a sorrow," I say. "But I cannot feel John Deegan's useless death as my great loss. John Deegan knew my brother. He connected me to a little part of the past. I am sorry for his mother. Perhaps I weep more for myself than for him."

"How so?" Mr. Serle asks quietly.

"I recognized that John Deegan was lonely the day he died," I say. "I never liked him until that one moment, and then he was gone. My heart is a closed door."

Mr. Serle stands silent. He looks inward at some thought he is not ready to speak.

At last—"I do not think you know yourself yet," Mr. Serle says. "Someday you will awaken to the joy in a man, not just embrace his sadness. That John Deegan could not move you would have been his sorrow, not yours, if he had lived."

I think of running with John Deegan and the fleeting glimpse of his beauty.

"I wish to know myself, to be grown inside as well as outside," I say. And then I have a confused thought. "How will I recognize myself if I do not know who I am?"

Mr. Serle's mouth turns up at the corners. He might be trying not to laugh.

"You will know when the time comes, my dear," he tells me, and then he shifts the subject. "You have not been at work since last Thursday," he says. "I saw the manager's notice on the kiosk when I looked for you."

"I was ill for three days. Then Aunt Jane would not allow Honor or me to go out on the streets until today because of the soldiers and the ruffians."

"Good," he says again. "I am glad you are in health again. I am very glad you are safe."

"Well!" I sigh as I begin to open my cupboards. "A customer is coming. Work will steady me."

SUNDAY, JULY 22, 1849

No letter yet from Daniel.

I wear my rose brooch every day. In the morning when I pick it up to pin it on, my heart gives a little jump of happiness to see the red curl of Daniel's hair and to think of Mr. Serle's hand protecting mine.

The brooch looks very well with my muslin summer dress, which is white with a dark blue and a light blue line in it. Honor has almost finished a second dress, which is white with a rose-red line. The hot, dirty weather makes two dresses necessary if I am to keep clean and fresh. The temperature reached over ninety degrees last week. All three of us go about the house in our petticoats and chemises in the evenings. We stay up late because the heat makes it so hard to sleep.

I gave Mr. Serle the cravat I made for him. He seemed very pleased. He said he will wear it the next time he goes to a concert.

"Herr Meyer will be envious," he said.

I put a note in with the cravat thanking him again for the brooch. He notices that I am wearing it, I believe, but he has not mentioned it.

Mr. Serle stopped by yesterday for just a moment. Disease is sweeping the city. He warned me not to eat shellfish—even cooked—and to be scrupulous in boiling everything when I prepare meals. After he said that, he hesitated for a moment and then added, "It is wise to rinse down the privy with lye if you can. I say it because I wish you to be safe."

When I told Aunt Jane and Honor, Aunt Jane pursed her mouth and her cheeks got a little pink. She said it is not right for a gentleman to mention a privy to an unmarried girl.

But Honor said, "Nonsense, Aunt Jane, such gentility is ridiculous. Mr. Serle shows his care for darling Mina that he said it. Really, to put etiquette before common sense and even our lives is wrong."

Aunt Jane looked hurt, and Honor apologized for speaking pertly. She did not, I noticed, say her point was mistaken, only that her manner was impolite.

Poor souls die in the city to the south of us every day and in the rich neighborhoods to the north too. They say the Quarantine Hospital out on the island is full. Business in the restaurants and saloons is down, especially the oyster houses.

I have been very busy, though. Tobacco is a good preventive against disease. All the men are smoking cigars or pipes. Drugs are useful too. Aunt Jane purchased some laudanum in case one of us becomes ill. She says that calomel and laudanum in combination are very good against the *cholera morbus*. But it is better not to become ill in the first place. I rinsed the privy with lye water. Yesterday, I also fumigated it with tobacco, even though I loathe the smoke and the odor.

At night, I touch my ring. I kneel and pray for the safety of my brother far away and for the health of those I love here in this city.

SUNDAY, OCTOBER 14, 1849

At last—a letter from Daniel.

JULY 4, 1849

San Francisco

My Very Dear Sister,

Today I have a moment, paper, and pen all together to write to you. All is well with me and Guido DiRoma. We arrived here in San Francisco in early June. The journey—in particular the grim and anxious slogging transport of our goods by mule across to Panama City on the Pacific Coast—was not easy, but we won through and fortune smiles on us. We were lucky to find a ship from Panama to San Francisco quickly. Some we met must still be waiting there for passage north.

I will not tire you with all our business dealings, only say that we are doing well but not by mining. Gold comes to us, we do not go to it. Guido was right. Here in the city, we have a saloon, store, and sleeping quarters for those preparing to stake their claims. It is already profitable in three weeks. I would not have believed it if Saint Patrick himself had promised it before we left the east.

Part of our establishment is still only canvas-roofed. Soon, when we have improved the store here, we will take turns to go up the river, ferrying men to the mines and selling supplies. We have a boat already and are waiting for coal to fuel the boiler and more goods. There is great opportunity here for those who are willing to work hard and who are not dazzled blind by the yellow of gold.

This city is a growing, thriving, struggling place. You would be shocked by some of what we see. I do not always believe it myself. We celebrated the birth of our country here today with a band and speeches and a cannonade. Now there are pistols being shot off in celebration too. Myself, I am saving my ammunition.

> Pray for me, Mina.
> Your loving brother,
> Daniel

In a postscript he gave me the direction to write to him and asked me to write soon. My letter is sent already. I have begun another one too.

I neglected to write in my book these past months because I was so anxious. Looking at the date and recording no letter from Daniel made me feel ill.

SUNDAY, NOVEMBER 11, 1849

A second letter from Daniel arrived on Wednesday. He and Guido DiRoma continue well. Of course, Daniel does not have my reply to his first letter, so he did not answer my questions about what he eats and what the city of San Francisco looks like.

In the letter was a little folded paper with a pinch of gold dust inside. I did not know what to do with it. I asked Mr. Serle when I saw him.

Mr. Serle says I need an account at a bank to save from my wages and to deposit the gold dust and any other gold or money my brother sends. For now, I keep the folded paper with the gold in my trunk with my money. My brother touched this treasure; I do not like to give it up to a stranger in a bank.

The walk down Broadway this morning was frigid, and my feet ached by the time I reached the Columbia House Hotel. I was opening the kiosk when I heard a voice on the stairs. Daniel has come to say good morning to me, I thought, looking up with joy. Then, of course, I remembered. Anger and sadness swept over me.

My hands felt heavy suddenly, and even taking a cigar from a box became an enormous, fumbling task. I spilled snuff, I misheard an elderly gentleman and tried to give him twice the weight of pipe tobacco he wanted, and then I dropped a clay pipe when I took it from the shelf to show him. I suppose it was lucky that I did not break a really valuable meerschaum one. In the late morning, Mr. Serle stopped to speak.

Mr. Serle frowned at me. "You do not look well," he informed me.

"The weather is changing," I said. "And I miss my brother today. I have not seen you for almost a month."

"I keep long hours and take extra work for private parties too," he said. "After the terrible summer of heat and illness, people are making much of the holiday season."

"I see," I tell him and begin to fiddle with the brass weights in their velvet case.

"Miss Pigot," Mr. Serle says.

I looked up at him, but he did not speak, only stared at me with a troubled look in his face. Someone must have opened the great door upstairs, for a cold draft sweeps down the stairway, making me shiver. A cleaning man comes through with his bucket and mop and swabs at the floor around one of the big brass spittoons. I can see from where I stand that the water he wrings from the rags is brown and vile.

"Miss Pigot," Mr. Serle says again.

"Yes?" I say.

"I am leaving the Columbia House Hotel," Mr. Serle tells me. My heart twists in my breast. I hold to the counter tight.

"Why?" I ask him.

"I have taken a new post," Mr. Serle says calmly. "I will earn more with the Delmonicos. The cooking is more varied and interesting also—not the infinity of broiled beefsteaks we serve here."

"When do you go?" I ask.

My voice is not mine but someone else's—a calm person who feels nothing because to feel is too much trouble.

"At the end of the month," Mr. Serle says as if my world is not a scrap of paper that he tosses carelessly into a fire and watches burn to ashes.

"I see." Tears gather behind my eyes. I pinch my wrist; I must not weep.

"I am pleased," Mr. Serle says, remorseless. "It is an opportunity for me."

"I am very glad, then," I lie to him. "I will pray for your success."

"Thank you," he says. He reaches to touch my hand. "I will try to stop by here as my work permits. I like to know how you get on."

"I like to see you," I tell him. "Perhaps you could call on us some Sunday."

Mr. Serle looks uncertain. "I am not sure, my dear. They have me working seven days a week just now. Perhaps when I have a new schedule. We will see."

The cleaning man clatters his bucket and mop about the other spittoon. A family who live in the hotel come down the stairs. The father will buy his cigar now as he does every day before dinner. Mr. Serle opens his lips as if to speak again, closes them, and goes.

Toward the end of the day Mr. Branton stopped at the tobacco kiosk. I was not sure who he was at first, and then when he turned his head, I remembered seeing him in church and on the street. He is a massive person, tall and broad both, with a neck that rises out of his collar like a thick post.

Mr. Branton took his time to purchase a cigar. I could feel him watching me as I laid out samples of Havanas from Cuba,

Spanish panatelas, and a mild cigar with an American Piedmont wrapper as well. He picked them up one by one and sniffed them. At last he chose the largest, a fat Havana, paid for it, put it in his mouth, and lit it. He did not move but stood there like some great rooted tree, watching me put away the choices he had declined. Something in him made me wish to resist him and yet to know it was a foolish thought. If he wanted me to speak, I would be forced to it.

Finally he asked if I knew his name.

"Yes," I said. "I believe you are Mr. Branton."

"Your brother is Daniel Pigot, isn't he?" he said.

Smoke wreathed up about his face with its strong features, broad forehead, and close curling black hair.

"Yes, sir," I said.

Mr. Branton cannot be so old, thirty at most, which is about Mr. Serle's age. Like Mr. Serle, he has a force that comes from inside himself. Mr. Branton continues to stare at me. He has beautiful clear, light hazel eyes. What does he want?

The silence hangs, and then Mr. Branton speaks abruptly. "John Deegan died for you, and you never came to his funeral," he says.

"I could not," I say. "I was ill. And he did not die for me. He died because he insisted to fight about an actor and was shot."

Mr. Branton shakes his head as if a fly is annoying him. "You are forgetting who you are, miss. You should stick with your people."

"I go to church," I say.

Mr. Branton does not bother replying to that.

"Do you like your job here?" he asks me.

"Well enough," I say.

"I want to know you better," he says. "I have some pretty cousins who would like you to call on them. They wish to comfort John Deegan's girl. What do you say?"

What is the answer to that? There is power in this man to bend others to his will and make them like their service. He could make me feel an honor in being the lion's prey.

Mr. Branton takes the cigar from his mouth.

"Your hair was very short when I first saw you," he says. "I suppose you were a jailbird before you came here."

"No!" I say. "No! I am an honest girl!"

Mr. Branton appears to think. There is another silence.

"I hear your brother is doing well in California," he says.

"Oh yes!" I say, too eagerly perhaps. I am proud to think of Daniel's rising.

"Well," he says after another pause. "Write to him. Tell him I am interested in his good fortune. Tell him we talked."

He begins to move away at last, but then turns back to me. His bulk fills my vision, blocking out the rest of the world. His hazel eyes shade to gray as the slant of the light changes. They are clear and very cold.

"Remember, Miss Pigot, I do not like the word *no,*" he says.

He turns and strolls away to the stairs. Before he goes up, he pauses and stares back at me once again.

The rest of the day is a confusion of customers. I make mistakes and do not care. It is a relief, finally, to close up. I hesitate and then go down the passage toward the kitchens. When the corridor branches, I am unsure which way to go. The clatter and steam of the kitchen seem to lie ahead. Offices and storerooms are perhaps down the hallway to my right. A kitchen lad comes by, carrying a cloth sack of some lumpy vegetable, turnips or potatoes maybe.

"Where will I find Mr. Serle?" I say. "I have a message for him."

He stares at me saucily but nods down the hall to the right. "Third door," he says.

I tap at the door.

"Come in," his familiar voice says.

I open the door and stand on the threshold.

"Mina!" Mr. Serle rises from his chair behind a table.

I want to speak to him, but I cannot seem to make the words come out. My head feels very strange, as if the room is a ship's deck, tipping under me. Mr. Serle must see that I am not well, for he takes my arm to support me.

He pours some water from a carafe on the table into a glass. When I try to drink, the water spills. Then he takes the glass from my hand and sets it back. He puts his arm about my shoulders and holds me to him.

"My dear," he says. "You are safe. Rest a moment."

His arm is an iron band of strength. It is as if he draws a circle that I can stand inside and breath in peace. At last the dizziness eases. Mr. Serle's arm relaxes a little.

"Have you eaten today?" he asks me.

"I had coffee this morning," I say, "with a piece of bread and cheese."

"I remember your pieces of bread and cheese," Mr. Serle says. "They are of a size a mosquito would cut for a blanket and pillow. And you have eaten nothing since your scraps of bread and cheese at—what time?"

"It was before dawn," I say.

"Sit here," Mr. Serle says. "You need to eat." I must look frightened, because he adds, "I will lock the door. No one will come in."

He goes out, and I hear the key snick over smoothly in the lock. The square room has one small window glazed in pebbled glass high up on the wall. There is a plain table where Mr. Serle sat with his account books before him when I entered. There is an oil lamp on the table. He must prefer that light, for the gas jet on the wall is not lit. The place is very clean and spare.

The key turns in the lock again, and Mr. Serle returns, carrying a tray, which he sets on the table.

"Pull in your chair and try this," he says.

On the tray is a tall, slim glass with a little fluted foot. Beside it is a long-handled spoon and a white napkin.

"Try it," Mr. Serle urges.

He sits down behind his table and folds his arms over his breast. I set the napkin over my dress and pick up the spoon. The top of the glass is a white puff of whipped cream and under that a pale gold custard with little darker flecks in it. I taste it. The soft custard is scented with vanilla, and the darker flecks are nutmeg. I try another spoonful. Something makes a tiny tickle on my tongue.

"Oh! What is it?" I ask Mr. Serle.

"See if you can tell me," he says, smiling.

I take up the spoon again and taste.

"It is very cold," I say. "It is like a creamy cloud and then a snowflake on the tongue. A sensation, not a taste—like an atom of ice."

"Very good, Miss Pigot," Mr. Serle says. "It is indeed ice."

"How do they make it?" I ask, eating more and considering the contrast of textures.

"The soft custard is just a soft custard," Mr. Serle explains. "Easy enough, as you well know. The ice is made by dribbling cold water into tiny trees on a metal sheet and setting the sheet on an ice block to freeze. After that, the custard goes in the glass, the spine of ice is pushed in, and the whipped cream finishes it off. Easy when you know."

"Very easy, once someone thinks of it," I agree.

"We had a gentleman yesterday who ate four glasses and still could not identify the effect that gave him pleasure," Mr. Serle tells me. "You knew in two spoonsful."

I am finished. I lay my spoon on the tray and set the folded napkin beside it.

"Do you feel better?" Mr. Serle asks.

"Yes, thank you," I say.

Mr. Serle pushes the tray with the empty glass, and then his account books, to one side. There is nothing between us on the table. The lamp makes a warm pool of light.

"What happened?" he asks.

"I have been sad today," I tell him. "I miss my brother and you are leaving—oh, I understand," I say when I see Mr. Serle about to speak. "You are right to better yourself. Only now I think of being here without a friend, and Mr. Branton suddenly seems to want something from me. I felt so frightened and alone just now."

I describe the strange conversation with Mr. Branton.

"You do not want the attention of such a man," Mr. Serle says.

"I do not wish it at all," I say. "I wonder that he should notice me now."

"He mentioned your brother," Mr. Serle reminds me. "They say the gang bosses here want more influence in California."

"Surely, my visiting his cousins will not gain him influence in California," I say.

"He has an interest in several women's boardinghouses on Greene Street," Mr. Serle tells me. "Perhaps he thinks if he controls you, he can get at your brother. His cousins would most likely be some of his doxies, pulling you into their life."

"I do not think Daniel would admit he knew me if I sank to vice," I say.

"I agree," Mr. Serle replies.

There is a silence then.

"I will look for another job." Saying the thought makes me happier.

"Good," Mr. Serle comments.

"I should go now," I tell him. "It is late."

Really, I would like to stay here in the quiet with my friend.

"Since we have this moment, I must ask you a question that has been troubling me," he says. "There is another matter, Miss Pigot."

"Yes?" My heart twists. This day brings only evil.

Mr. Serle takes a breath; he seems to find it difficult to speak.

"My dearest innocence, what the devil did you say to Sadick Meyer at the music recital last March?" he asks at last.

I think back to that afternoon with my brother. The image of Madame Moses slowly peeling her long white gloves from her white arms and Mr. Serle kissing her hand comes to me. Madame Moses insulted me. Surely, Mr. Serle is not asking about that.

"I told Herr Meyer I admired his piano playing," I say.

"What else?" Mr. Serle is considering me. His dark eyes gleam in the lamplight as he leans back in his chair with his arms crossed before his breast.

I think again. Daniel and Guido talked of gold. The deaf man shouted at me. Before that I came down the stairs with my wool gloves in my hand.

"Oh yes, I remember now," I say. "Herr Meyer asked if you

protected me. I said of course you did, and I am very grateful. He asked to call on me, and I said *no*. I thought him very rude."

Mr. Serle drops his elbows to the table and his head to his hands. It looks almost as if he is clutching his hair.

"You must know what it means when a woman refers to a man as her protector."

"I don't read novels," I say. "I never talked to gentry in my life until we traveled on the ship to America. What is so wrong?"

"You understand the threat of Matt Branton. How could you not know this? You cannot be so innocent. *Sórci verdi!* It is not possible."

"I felt Mr. Branton wanting to control me. I did not understand his words until you explained about his cousins," I tell him.

"How old are you now, *cara?*" Mr. Serle asks gently. "I forget."

"I was baptized in November 1832. I am just seventeen," I say.

"Herr Meyer thinks you told him that you are my mistress," Mr. Serle informs me. "To him a protector means a man who gives money to support a woman, takes her sexual favors, and does not marry her."

"Oh!" I say. Tears swim in my eyes. "But you gave money for my bond. You pretended I was your nephew. You did protect me."

Mr. Serle holds his head again. "To think that I have been proud of my self-control, that I congratulated myself for resisting temptation. Now I am damned for the sin without the pleasure of committing it."

For a moment I cannot breathe. I have been a temptation to Mr. Serle. Even when he called me "child," he knew he might possess me. He told me once I am too young to marry. Perhaps he needs to keep me a child so he can feel a safe kind of love. He cannot realize what he has just said, for he looks across the table at me frankly, as a friend who shares a problem with his friend.

"But surely Herr Meyer respects you even if he thinks ill of me?" I say cautiously. "Should I write to him? Should I explain to him there are no sexual favors?"

Mr. Serle seems torn between laughter and despair. "God preserve me from an honest woman," he says. "What could be more dangerous?"

"I am sorry I did not understand," I tell him. "Do you care what Herr Meyer thinks?"

"Yes, I do," Mr. Serle replies soberly. "He and Guido are my closest friends, and Guido is gone. I owe much to Herr Meyer in friendship and as a brother in religion."

"If he is your friend, he will honor your word," I say. I think about Herr Meyer. "It is bad for me to be thought a mistress; it invites insults. But for men it is different. Herr Meyer might admire that you have power over a woman."

Mr. Serle looks at me, surprised. "I should not like you to be insulted, Miss Pigot."

I do not tell him that Madame Moses—and Herr Meyer too, apparently—have already attended to that.

Mr. Serle sighs. "I will talk to him again. Now I should take you home, my dear nephew or niece or whatever you are. The Miss Corbetts will be worried."

"They will be very worried," I say. "I must hurry."

"It is quicker to go out the back of the hotel," Mr. Serle says. "The cabs often wait at Church and Barclay streets in the evenings now. The warmth from the kitchen reaches them there, and Sam whistles round the corner to them when he has a fare."

"I can go alone," I say. "It is not right of me to take you from your work."

"I am finished for today," Mr. Serle replies.

"You are better than a real uncle," I say in a rush. "I am sorry I upset you. It would be terrible here without you. You are so patient, and you always help me. I never know how to thank you."

"To feel needed is gratification enough for me," Mr. Serle says in a quiet voice.

He extinguishes his lamp and locks his door. He shows me how the turning, confusing corridors lead around the kitchen, past storerooms and more offices until a door leads out to the back alley where deliveries come.

"I must find new work immediately," I say when we are in the cab, and the horse—cajoled to motion by the cheerful driver—is clopping his way uptown.

"Why immediately?" Mr. Serle asks.

"I am afraid of Mr. Branton's power to corrupt me," I tell him frankly. "And now that my brother is gone and you are going, I will have no friend here to protect—I mean, to brighten my days. I feel like a caged bird in the kiosk. And I truly hate the smell of tobacco. It spoils the taste of everything."

"What would you like to do?" Mr. Serle asks me.

"I would like to be a cook in a pleasant household," I say. "I will study the advertisements."

"You will want a character," Mr. Serle tells me. "I will write one tonight and bring it to the kiosk for you tomorrow."

"Thank you," I tell him. "You are very good."

Mr. Serle takes my hand in his to steady me as the cab sways, turning the corner into Spring Street.

"Do you still have the ring you showed me in England?" he asks.

"Yes, I keep it safe," I say. "I have sewed it into my chemise, here over my heart."

After I have said it, I am uncertain of propriety. Probably a lady does not say the word *chemise* to a gentleman. But Mr. Serle does not seem to notice.

"You are right to make a change," he says. "You will use your talents better as a cook."

When we reach Elizabeth Street, Mr. Serle lets the cab go, but although he stands a moment more talking to me on the steps, he will not come into the house. He is pleased about his new work, he says, happy to be beginning to feel part of life in America. When I thank him again for helping me, he shrugs his shoulder in his old way. I must take care of myself, he says. And then, abruptly, he tells me I must go in. He will walk in the frosty night and study the moon, which hangs like a ripe, golden apple in the sky, he says. He needs air and space.

Yesterday, when I came in, Aunt Jane and Honor were worried about me. Indeed, Aunt Jane was so upset at my being late that I did not speak much of the difficulties of the day. I did not want her to fret herself even more. I just said that a man had bothered me again and that Mr. Serle had kindly seen me home in a cab.

Aunt Jane talked on and on about the dangers for young women in the city, while I heated the oxtail soup I had made in the morning and Honor toasted bread to eat with it. Another young woman has disappeared. This one has been gone three days now. Her parents have posted notices and asked the neighbors to watch for her. Aunt Jane was so concerned, she actually said the words *abduction, rape,* and *brothel* to us.

When Honor and I were preparing for bed, I told her more of the truth. She agrees I should go to other work as soon as possible. To my chagrin she thought the confusion with Herr Meyer about Mr. Serle's being my protector was amusing.

"Anyone who knows you, Mina, would never think such a thing," Honor says. "Herr Meyer's fantasies must cloud his brain."

She asked me the same question Mr. Serle did: why I felt impropriety immediately with Mr. Branton but never thought of Herr Meyer's sly meaning.

"I am not sure," I said. "Perhaps it is how Mr. Branton looks at me, as if I am a horse he is about to bridle. And then, when I spoke to Herr Meyer, I was thinking only of how we both are friends of Mr. Serle."

"I do not understand why Mr. Serle has not asked you to marry him," Honor said.

"Oh no, his religion will not permit it," I say. "Even if he felt temptation, he would resist such love."

Honor looks skeptical.

"I would not have thought it from the way he studied you when he visited, or from his concern for you the day your brother left—" She stops. "I am sorry, Mina, I do not mean to intrude. I hope he does not make you unhappy."

"No," I say. "I am seventeen now. I suppose I could marry,

but somehow—well, I do not know, but I am not unhappy about Mr. Serle."

"Good," Honor says and settles herself for sleep.

I pull the quilt to my chin and close my eyes. I fall asleep but it does not seem so. I go direct from pulling the quilt to my chin to a dream in which I am lying in a bed pulling a quilt to my chin. In my dream my bed is warm just as the real one is, but the room in which the bed stands is cruelly cold. A bell tolls in the far distance.

"Rise!" Madame Moses's ringing voice speaks sharply in my ear.

Reluctantly, I let the quilt fall away. I set my bare feet on the floor and immediately recoil. The slime of icy tobacco spit is everywhere. I curl up my toes in disgust, but I am compelled. I must follow the tolling bell.

Shivering in my night shift, I cross the dirty floor and open the door. Down a vaulted hallway of stone, a procession of black-veiled figures comes toward me. They are barefoot like me, and their feet are stained brown. Only their filthy feet and the candle that each holds in a cold hand is visible against their fluttering drapery.

"Follow," says the familiar voice.

The figures lead me to an echoing cavern of a room. All is shadow, all is frost-rimed. The figures walk to the end of the cathedral space. Each sets her candle down and passes to the side. They turn to watch me come, empty-handed, to the altar.

"She is here," Madame Moses's voice says.

Hands reach for me. I push the hands away.

"Cut her hair," Mr. Branton's deep voice speaks. "She is a prison bird now."

I see the flash of scissors by my face.

"No! No!" I cry. "Stop!"

"Mina?" Honor's sleepy voice is in my ear. "Why are you thrashing so?"

"I am sorry," I whisper. "I had a bad dream."

"Never mind," Honor grumbles. "Go back to sleep."

When I woke up again in the thin gray just before dawn, I lit a candle and wrote a note to the manager of the Columbia House Hotel, saying I must return the key for the tobacco kiosk and collect my wages at the end of the day.

As I walked up Broadway this evening with my money and Mr. Serle's kind letter in my pocket, I saw the moon again, an orb of brightness between two dark buildings. My heart sang in me. I will change my life.

SUNDAY, DECEMBER 23, 1849

In January I become cook to the Westervelt family in Fourth Street, with a kitchen maid under me and a parlor maid to serve the meals. I will live on the top floor of the house—in my own room because I am the cook. It is the first time—except for the few days at Mrs. Redburn's—I have slept in a room by myself alone. The maids share a room. I will have every week from after Sunday dinner to Monday breakfast for my own. The maids have only every other week free.

I made a calculation of my resources; I have the money from England, from the ship, and from the tobacco kiosk. The extra work painting colors into fashion plates to help Aunt Jane earned me more than fifty dollars through the year. I have just enough to pay my debt to Mr. Serle and to make the wash dresses, aprons, and caps that I will need for my new position. I will wait until I have my wages in February to buy new winter boots, even though the old ones are worn and leak a little in the wet.

After I counted up my money, I wrote Mr. Serle a letter.

Dear Mr. Serle,

I enclose the money that I have owed you since October of last year when you bought my bond for me. Please accept it. It is not respectable for me to owe you money.

The two gold sovereigns in the packet are the very same that you gave me for my wages when we left the great kitchen in England and that I sewed into my shirt for safety on the sea voyage. When I look at them, I think of all your care for me and bless you.

Thank you for all you taught me and for the character you gave me. I have already found new work. In January I begin employment as a cook for a private family. The house is on Fourth Street, very convenient for shopping at Tompkins Market.

Perhaps you will be good enough to tell me that you have received this package safely.

I think that without you I should have been dead or ruined before now.

> Your grateful friend,
> Mina Pigot

I am sure I have done right.
Mr. Serle replied immediately.

My Very Dear Miss Mina Pigot,

The package you sent arrived safely. I hope that you have not deprived yourself of any necessity of life or even of any pleasure in setting aside this money. Be assured that you have never been under any improper obligation to me.

I am touched that you remember our work together. I hope your new position suits you as well. If I can help you in any way, please write to me or come to me.

> Yours respectfully,
> Benjamin Serle

I have paid my debt. I am respectable, yet I do not feel happier for that. In repaying Mr. Serle, I flew free from obligation but also from the net of kindness that binds the present back into the past. Instead of feeling a release, I feel loneliness. I am a bird that perches solitary on its branch in shivering winter twilight.

Well!

The Miss Corbetts and I will have an American Christmas. They are selling pine trees at the market. It must smell wonderful to have one in the house, but that is too great an extravagance. A venison stew and chestnuts to roast on the stove in the evening will be our treats. I have never eaten venison. Perhaps I will feel more American, cooking and eating the game of the great forests.

I am glad to be done with the Columbia House Hotel—its echoing marble hall, flaring gas jets, leering men, the smell of tobacco always in my clothes, and the memory of poor John Deegan. I hope to be safe from the anger of the world in my new work.

SATURDAY, DECEMBER 29, 1849

The newspapers report a terrible fire in San Francisco. Aunt Jane did not want me to read about it, but Honor said that was wrong. I told Aunt Jane that I must know the news even if I have nightmares after. The *Tribune* says there are few deaths and rebuilding has already started. I pray that Daniel and Mr. DiRoma live.

PART FOUR

THE HOUSE ON EAST
FOURTH STREET

I HAVE A CHRISTMAS LETTER from Daniel, written in November. Perhaps this is the last letter I will receive if Daniel perished.

My dearest sister Mina,

I am glad to have your news from New York and to know you are well. Business continues very vigorous. Guido is just back from taking a boatload of miners past Benicia and then upriver on their way to Sutter's Fort. I stayed here to sell our goods, tend our hotel, and to receive a shipment of shovels and chains and another of rum that came in on ships sailing around the Horn. It took much persuasion to get the sailors to unload the cargo. No sooner had they done so under threat of being shot than they disappeared to the gold fields. Many ships are now abandoned in the graveyard of boats in the bay. Guido and I have been trying to think of a way to take greater advantage of the materials they present. So far, only the canvas has been worth the salvage.

You asked about our food and also about the presence of women here. Prices are very high, of course, but the beef is excellent. The women for the most part are not respectable. You would find none with whom a lady, such as I hope you are, could associate. I do not wish you to travel here as you suggest.

Guido and I talk of you and all our friends in New York City. It will be a sad Christmas if I do not have a letter from you. I hope you will go to Mass on Christmas. Pray for me.

Your loving brother,
Daniel

He enclosed more gold dust. I have added it to the pinch I had before. I tried to set aside my fears that he is lost in the fire and replied to him immediately. My heart is hopeful, but I must accept that he may never read my thoughts and love for him.

MONDAY, JANUARY 7, 1850

I began my new job last week on January 2. The Westervelts' kitchen has modern water taps that run hot and cold into a deep zinc tub and a huge ice chest for which the ice is delivered six days a week by the DiRoma Company—Guido DiRoma's cousin's business. I was pleased when I learned that. The range is big enough to cook a dinner for twelve at least. The previous cook did not leave the kitchen so clean as Mr. Serle taught me is correct, but Bridget, the kitchen maid, and I are setting all to rights.

Before I record my thoughts about the people I work with, I wish to say something about the Westervelts and how I was hired here. I answered an advertisement in the *Tribune* for an experienced cook. I was very nervous about it because two of the notices that sounded promising said *No Irish*. Five others asked for *Protestants only*.

Mr. Serle wrote an excellent character for my work in England. He mentioned especially that Miss Pigot is a skillful baker and pastry cook. I was a little nervous that I might have to explain that I have been selling tobacco this past year and only cooking at home. Some employers might think being a tobacco girl not respectable enough. Perhaps—like Madame Moses—they will see opportunity for insult in my having worked in such a public place as a hotel. Or they might not care about the tobacco but expect me to have a character from the Columbia House Hotel too. I did not think the manager would write anything helpful for me after I left so suddenly.

Finally, I took from my trunk the letter that the lord in England wrote for me at Mr. Serle's direction. It is very beautiful, with a crest and a great scrolling signature. Perhaps two characters will be more impressive than one, I thought. Of course, the name on the lord's letter is Daniel Serle. With my pen and ink I very carefully added a small *a* to the end of Daniel to make *Daniela*. It was perfect, and I felt it was all right since I truly earned the character, and it would be useless otherwise.

Mrs. Seton Westervelt received me in her morning sitting room for an interview. I did not lie to her very much, really. She asked me some questions about my family and where I live. She did not seem especially interested in my answers. She asked nothing about what I cook and what techniques I use. At last, she wanted to know if I had a character from my last household. I said yes, I have two, but here is where I did not say the truth. I told Mrs. Westervelt that my name was first Daniela Serle, that I married a Mr. Pigot the week before I came to America, and that he died a month ago, which is why I seek work. That is why I am Mrs. Pigot, but my character from the lord is for Daniela Serle. She looked suspicious until I handed her the letters. She did not question the strange name Daniela, which I was prepared to account for with a foreign grandmother. She barely glanced at Mr. Serle's statement. Instead, when Mrs. Westervelt saw the lord's letterhead with its crest, she put her hand to her breast and looked as if she might faint for pleasure.

"A baron!" she exclaimed. "What sumptuous meals you must have prepared, what myriads of servants, what china, what plate there must have been."

I kept my mouth shut tight then, only smiled and nodded.

"Well!" she said. "May I keep this one to show my husband tonight? I am sure he will approve you. If you will return tomorrow at eleven, we will settle your wages."

I told her then that I should want every Sunday afternoon for myself and that I do not do laundry. She did not make any objection at all. When I returned the next day, she was all graciousness as she handed back the character from the lord. Her husband had approved me willingly. I have my wages paid every month, Sunday afternoons and evenings free, my own room and my board of course, and no laundry. I was so happy.

I wanted to sit and talk to Mrs. Westervelt about what the family likes to eat and if they have dislikes or prejudices. She was not interested in my questions at all but told me of her family, which are the Archers, of very old English descent, she says. They were probably related to royalty, she claims, and she complained that her grandfather was accused of assisting the English in the War because he was known to be of distinguished lineage. I finally had to almost interrupt her to ask when I should move my things and what day and meal I would commence my work.

Mrs. Westervelt is an ample woman with a distracted air about her. She is blond, with regular features and a rather pink complexion. She dresses in a great deal of pastel colors, with crinolines and lace and artificial flowers. Honor said she sounds too fussy for true elegance when I described her. She is vague not just in her manner but in her words. I had much difficulty determining even how many people are in the family—herself, her husband, a young miss daughter, and a grown son, resident just now at a college in Massachusetts—and no success at all in conferring about budget and menus. I am to cook what I please and not spend too much. Mrs. Westervelt is much more interested in writing her poetry than in what her family and servants eat.

One of her verses was printed in the *Star Herald* last week under the name *A Child of Old New York*. The poem is called "New Year's Effusions for Our Mother City."

Let us to the great isle of Manhattan
Seized from the savage and insolent Powhatten
Cry our New Year's praise.
With our pure state cider let us our bumpers raise
Press'd to succulence divine.
All hail our mother on whose island bosom we recline,
As babes in the cradle of liberty
Where our founding fathers trod to make us free.
Huzzah Manhattan! Huzzah!

There were ten other verses like that. Mrs. Westervelt asked me to read it when she was supposed to be giving me her directions for the menus this week. I said "Very nice" politely, but privately I thought it would do to wrap fish in. I prefer Lord Byron. Aunt Jane warned me of his immoral life but gave me a little volume of his poems for my Christmas present anyway. I told her I admire his love for freedom and his beautiful verses, not his other choices in life.

I have seen Mr. Seton Westervelt just once. Saturday morning I came down the servants' stairs and was turning in to the kitchen as he walked along the corridor from the back of the house. I was surprised. The family have their water closets upstairs, and the privy in the yard is for the servants' use. Mr. Westervelt is a tall man with smooth brown hair, graying at the temples, and a clean-shaven face. His eyes have a kind expression, but they are made sad looking by circles under them, as if he does not sleep peacefully.

"Mrs. Pigot?" he asked.

"Yes, sir," I answered. "Perhaps you are Mr. Westervelt?"

"Indeed," he responded. "I am sorry if I startled you. I have just been to look at the boiler with Jacob. He has been having trouble regulating it."

"I hope it is all right," I said.

The thought made me anxious. Many house fires begin with exploding boilers.

"It is working properly." Mr. Westervelt looked for a moment as if he would question my concern but then decided not to ask. "By the by, my wife may have neglected to tell you that I will be home for lunch today."

"She did not mention it yesterday," I replied. "Perhaps she intends to tell me when I go up for her orders after breakfast."

"No doubt," he commented, rather dryly, I thought.

"Since I have seen you," I said after a hesitation, "is there anything that you particularly wish me to cook? Mrs. Westervelt has not made any suggestions, but perhaps you have a request."

Jacob came through the passage with a load of wood for the kitchen range. Mr. Westervelt and I stepped aside for him to pass, which brought us closer together.

"You are much younger than I thought." Mr. Westervelt spoke abruptly. "No, I have no requests now, but in April I am partial to shad roe. You might keep that in mind."

"Of course," I replied.

"Since we have seen each other, do you have any requests of me, Mrs. Pigot?" he asked politely. "My wife may have neglected to make some point clear."

"Oh!" I said, remembering. "There is a point. I have been arranging with the tradesmen for quarterly bills because Marie says that is what the previous cook did. Should I give the account books and the bills to you or to your wife at the end of the quarter?"

"A good question." Mr. Westervelt sounded pleased that I asked. "Mrs. Westervelt reviewed the kitchen accounts in the past—if they were reviewed at all. I will ask her if she wishes to be relieved of the responsibility and let you know. Meanwhile, your meals have been excellent. Not one dish of sauerkraut yet, for which I thank you. Good day, Mrs. Pigot."

He went quickly up the stairs to the parlor floor. He has a very erect figure and a brisk way of walking. I thought him pleasant enough. I made a note to myself to find out about shad roe. It must be an American dish. I wonder if Mr. Serle knows a recipe.

Tonight I made a dinner of clear soup, oyster patties for the fish course, a roast chicken garnished with potatoes and turnips and carrots cut in fancy shapes, a salad of shredded beet and orange, and an almond tart for a sweet with some lovely, fragrant pippins for those who wanted fruit after. For the first time, Mrs. Westervelt sent down a note with Marie to say that she was very pleased. Marie said that Mr. Westervelt dictated the note, and that he used to eat out of the house three nights a week all last year. He has only been out by himself once since I began to cook, and she thinks that night he had to go to an encomium dinner.

Even though I am tired, I can stay up tonight and write because the Westervelts are going to his mother's house for dinner tomorrow, so I will have an easy day. I think I have described Mr. and Mrs. Westervelt both. The other member of the family at home is Sarah Westervelt, the daughter. She is a rather colorless girl who takes lessons in the mornings and goes out or sees visitors with her mother in the afternoons. She came down to the kitchen once to ask for some saleratus to apply to an itch on her arm. I think she is about thirteen at most. Usually she rings for Marie when she wants something.

Marie is the parlor maid who does the light cleaning and serves the meals after they go up to the pantry in the dumbwaiter. Her whole name is Marie Lepettit. Her family is French. They lived in the north in the French land near Montreal for generations, only her grandfather came south to New York when war threatened in 1812, because he refused to defend the interests of the damned English. Marie has been in service with the Westervelts for ten years. She says it is an easy house. Two women come in twice a week for heavy work, and the laundry, except for Mrs. Westervelt's lace, goes out. Marie is much older than I am. She has a little wattle of loose flesh under her chin. She is rather small, but strong enough for lifting trays. She is very neat in her ways, and she looks composed and younger than she is in her black dress and white apron and the pretty white cap that hides her graying hair.

Bridget Cosgill, the kitchen maid, is seventeen, she says. When she told me, I said, "Hmm," or some such sound and tried to look older than that. She has a more ample figure than Marie or I and thick blond hair that is always coming down from under her cap. Her looks are spoiled a little when she smiles because she has a broken and discolored front tooth. Bridget is a very willing worker. She confided to me that she has a family in the Five Points. Bridget and her brother, who works as a hod carrier as he can, give almost all they earn to their mother, who has three younger children to feed on her earnings from hawking apples. Bridget is very afraid that her mother will not be able to pay the rent for her second-floor room and will be forced to a basement. The rats are worse in basements. The father talked about the gold in California and then disappeared five months ago. They fear he has gone forever.

The day after I came here, I noticed that Bridget had very red, chapped hands that seemed to pain her, for she was always wrapping them tight in her apron. I laid out a bottle of sweet oil on the shelf by the sink and told her that she must rub some in her hands every morning and night and always after she has worked with her hands in water. When I have time, I will make a better ointment with beeswax and rosin for us all to use. I also showed her how to skim the grease carefully when she washes up. I told her we will share the money the rag-and-bone man pays for the kitchen waste. The previous cook kept it all. Bridget seems pleased with the care for her comfort.

The other person who works in the house is Jacob. He is a very silent German man. I do not even know his last name. He lives next door and tends the boilers and the yards of both houses. He takes his meals one week with us and the next with the other house. So far, he eats a large amount very fast, grunts *Danke,* which Marie says means *Thank you,* and disappears. The Westervelts do not keep horses but use the livery stable down the block. I was sorry at first since I would like the chance to pet a horse, but now I am glad. Flies are problem enough without the stable right at the back door.

The only person who seems uneasy about me in my new job

so far is Aunt Jane. She knew about the work in general, of course, but had not heard any particulars of the place. On my first Sunday off, which was the sixth of this month, she asked me to describe it all. She seemed glad at first when I talked about the house, the convenience of the kitchen, and how few people it would be to cook for. Then I said that I found Mrs. Westervelt a little scattered about business. Aunt Jane's face, which is naturally pale, looked even paler and very anxious.

"Westervelt?" she said in a pinched sort of voice. "Are you sure?"

"Of course she is sure," Honor said. She must have thought she sounded rude, for she set down the sleeve and the lace she was sewing and said more gently, "What is wrong, Aunt Jane?"

"Nothing," Aunt Jane said. She was looking at the teakettle steaming on the stove, not at Honor or me.

"You sound troubled," Honor persisted. "Do you know the Westervelts or something about them that makes you concerned for Mina?"

"No," Aunt Jane said in a sort of dispirited way. "I went to school long ago with Julia Archer. I remember how pleased she was when she became engaged to Seton Westervelt. We all thought him very handsome." She hesitates, a long pause, and then says quickly, "He had a reputation for breaking hearts."

"I do not think you should worry about anything improper in the way Mr. Westervelt speaks to me," I said. "He seems more interested in avoiding sauerkraut and looking forward to shad roe than in me. Besides, he is quite old."

"You must be careful, Mina," Honor says. "Women in service do not have the protection of their families. Remember that if anything at all troubles you, you must come back to us immediately."

Aunt Jane brightens suddenly. "Honor is right," she says in earnest tones. "You must not stay even an hour if you are not treated with complete respect."

I promise them that I will heed their words, and then our talk turns. Aunt Jane begins to worry about the weather. She feels in her bones that a storm is coming. Honor and I teased her that she cannot be content unless she has something to be anxious about.

MONDAY, JANUARY 21, 1850

It turned out that Aunt Jane was right about a storm coming. Only it was today that it came, after two weeks of quiet weather. I walked back from Elizabeth Street to Fourth Street before dawn this morning into a fierce north wind, which swept snow in under my hood and my skirts. I was very glad to go down the areaway and into the warm kitchen, where Jacob had the fires blazing, and Marie, who was up earlier than usual, had put the kettle on. The howling of the wind in the chimney awakened her, she said.

Tonight, I am sitting in my room after a busy day, and the wind that died has risen again. The lamp smokes in the draft. I must go to my bed soon. I do not know why I love the routine of my days now. At the hotel I dreaded the sameness of the hours and the predictability of when business would be brisk and when it would slow. Here all is routine, but every day brings differences too. I rise before six and set out the servants' breakfasts. Breakfast for the family goes up at seven-thirty o'clock punctually, because Mr. Westervelt must be walking down the front steps to go to his office on Wall Street at eight-thirty. I send a light lunch up to Mrs. Westervelt and her daughter at one o'clock. The servants' dinner is right after. Dinner for the family is at six and tea goes up to the parlor at eight, unless the Westervelts go out to a concert or other entertainment—which they frequently do.

On Sundays, the family attend church, and then dinner with both soup and fish as well as the usual entrées, roasts, entremets, and desserts is served at one o'clock. I leave a supper ready to heat for the evening. Marie and Bridget must tend to this preparation on their alternate Sundays, but the family serve themselves. Marie seems not to mind, but Bridget is always very nervous about the responsibility.

On Tuesday nights Mrs. Westervelt usually goes out to sit

with an invalid friend. When Marie told me that was why there was rarely tea on Tuesdays unless Mr. Westervelt requested something in his study, she rolled her eyes.

"Why do you look like that?" I asked.

"Don't ask," she said. "What we do not know never hurts us. Her husband does not inquire closely, so why should we?"

Bridget giggled. I am not sure what is a proper example for the cook to set about gossip. Perhaps I frowned as I was thinking, for Marie said, "She is a fool, that woman. As if I would not notice the special care she takes with her dress when she is going out to her poor sick friend. I wonder why she wants me to brush her best muff instead of asking you for a jug of nourishing beef tea or some of those delicate little sponge cakes you make so beautifully?"

"Oh well," I say, "it is not for us to judge a lady," and we let the subject go.

Mrs. Westervelt is so satisfied with the cooking and the order in the kitchen that she has invited three other couples for a dinner next Saturday night. I told her that I am pleased to plan it with her, but that, when there are more than eight at table, we must have extra help in the kitchen and a second maid to assist Marie with service.

Mrs. Westervelt asked if that was true in the household of the baron in England. I told her, "Yes, but there were never fewer than three of us in the kitchen, and the baron had valets to take the dishes up and a butler to set them out for service *à la française*." Mrs. Westervelt smiled and looked vague. I could see she was afraid to ask me what service *à la française* meant.

SUNDAY, JANUARY 27, 1850

The dinner party last night went off smoothly. Marie reported that there was comment on the elegant presentation of the dishes, so the extra time I spend trimming carrots and frying glass-house parsley was worthwhile. Even though the dinner for eight was served at five-thirty and the light supper was set out at ten, we had not finished clearing and cleaning until after midnight. It made a very tiring day. I am still learning to schedule tasks and to use the cooking range efficiently.

I sent a note to Honor and Aunt Jane this morning by Peter, the boy at the livery stable who runs errands for me, to say that I am well but tired and will see them next week. As soon as the Sunday dinner was served, I went upstairs. I have slept all afternoon.

Perhaps I am tired also because there is no word from California. I often awaken from an evil dream of fire and have difficulty sleeping again.

MONDAY, FEBRUARY 4, 1850

Honor was waiting for me at the door yesterday with a letter from Daniel in her hand. She knew he is all right, of course, because she saw his handwriting. As soon as I opened it, though, she asked if he mentioned Mr. DiRoma.

I scanned the pages quickly. "Yes," I said. "Look here. There is a message for you."

At the end of Daniel's letter were some lines in a different hand.

To my dear friends, the Miss Corbetts and Miss Pigot, it said. *We are well and richer every day. I send best wishes from the land of gold.* Il tuo amico, *Guido DiRoma.*

The signature was written with a great flourish.

"See," I said, "he has learned to write, Honor."

"If you wrote your answer to your brother today," Honor said, "I could add a message at the end. I think it would be rude not to acknowledge Mr. DiRoma's best wishes, don't you?"

"Just let me read Daniel's letter," I told her, "and then I will sit down and write."

It was good we read Guido DiRoma's message first. Daniel's letter was not so cheerful. They lost all their store in the fire on last Christmas Eve. Luckily, he said, most of the payment they had was in gold dust and nuggets. Once the fire had passed, they sifted the ashes of their business and had their gold again. *Guido thinks we have even more than we had before the fire,* Daniel wrote, *because there was a great lump of fused gold in what must have been the corner by the ruined chimney, which is not where we kept our money box. Guido thinks someone hid gold there and forgot it.*

Daniel makes little of the fire. He says that everyone rallied to raze structures in the path of the blaze and so contained it. He thinks the onset of the rainy part of the year will help to control the danger. *By the time you read this, my sister,* his letter continued, *our business will have risen from the ashes bigger and better than before. The phoenix will surely be the emblem of this place.*

He sounds very excited and confident, I think. I wrote him of our news before we sat down to our evening meal. There is not much to report, and Daniel does not ask me questions. I have to think of what might interest him. When I finished, Honor took the letter and stared at the space I left for her message for a long time. Then she wrote quickly and blotted and sealed the paper before I could ask for it again. We argued about who would take it to the mail office tomorrow. Finally, we agreed that I would give her the money, and she would post the letter.

The weather here is cold and dirty, with gray slush in the streets. My feet were wet by the time I arrived at Fourth Street this morning. It makes the side of my right foot ache terribly. I will have to buy waterproof boots before next winter.

This morning, soon after breakfast was sent up in the dumbwaiter, we heard a great roar in the distance. Almost immediately fire bells began to sound.

"Something has been torn all to flinders," Bridget said and crossed herself.

The afternoon papers report that a six-story factory in Hague Street has blown up, with terrible loss of life. They think it was a faulty boiler. I hope Jacob is doing his job conscientiously here. Danger hides, a monster in the ocean depths, under the tilting deck of this everyday world.

We had sun and mild days all week. I wake earlier every morning. I feel so much stronger now than when I worked at the tobacco kiosk. I went out to Tompkins Market before dawn this morning and was surprised to see Mr. Serle standing by the entrance, reading a newspaper. The Fulton Market is much larger and closer to the Delmonicos' restaurants. He saw me coming along the street, for he discarded his paper, swept off his hat in greeting, and then stood looking at me, staring really, as he did that first time he saw me in a woman's dress on the deck of the *Victoria.*

"You are examining me as if you have forgotten what I look like!" I exclaim.

He smiles and his eyes light. "I am pleased to see you in health," he says courteously.

"And you are well?" I inquire.

"Yes," he replies. "You like your work?"

"Oh yes," I say. "It is a pleasant household. The family has varied enough tastes that I can try new things. There is Croton water from the taps at the sink and a great range as well as spits for roasting. I make pies and cakes again easily. The kitchen is very modern. I like to work in it. I wish you could see it."

"I would like that," Mr. Serle tells me.

I describe to him where the house is on Fourth Street near Lafayette Place, not very far from here.

"When I am free on Sundays, I go to Honor and Aunt Jane and spend the night," I say. "They are my family. Besides, my brother is still sending his letters to me there."

"Come," he says. "Walk with me along the fruit stalls. You can tell me whom you like to deal with. I am looking for bananas. They do not have any at the Fulton Market this morning."

"I never tasted one," I say. "Are they good?"

"You must decide for yourself," he says.

We pass the butchers' stands. I greet Mr. Woodcock, of course, who supplies our regular needs and gives me sensible advice on economy. His boy delivered meat for today before I came out. Beyond the butchers are the vegetable stalls. Some of those have vegetables and fruit both. I stop at the stall of Mr. Romeo Larkins, whose produce I have found fresh and fairly priced. Mr. Serle waits while I add a bunch of parsley to my basket and make a note for my accounts. Farthest into the market building, where their wares are protected best from the weather, are the purveyors of tropical and hothouse fruits and other specialties.

Mr. Serle walks slowly along the aisle, telling me the names of fruits I do not know. He points out small greeny-yellow ovals that look like unripe lemons. These are limes, Mr. Serle says, and have their own distinct flavor. In New York, they are not so well known as lemons but can be used to make a pudding, a cream, or a drink in just the same way. He picks one up and rubs the rind a little so I can smell it. Then he tucks the lime in my basket and gives the stall man a coin.

"You will think of something to cook with it," he says. "It is even good with chopped parsley as dressing on a salmon or sea bass. Or just make yourself a refreshing drink. It is very healthy."

At the next stall, I recognize pineapples, of course. Mr. Serle shows me how to test them for ripeness by tugging on one of the spiny leaves at the top to see if it moves easily. That and the honeyed smell of the fruit tell us that these pineapples are ready to eat. Mr. Serle surprises me by negotiating to buy ten of them.

"Ten pineapples!" I exclaim. "Is it for a sweet at the restaurant?"

"Not this time," Mr. Serle says. "I am not in a restaurant kitchen every day but work on private parties and balls."

"Is that better for you?" I ask him.

"I am pleased so far," he answers in his calm way. "It gives me more freedom and variety. Tomorrow, for example, there is a fancy dinner for thirty-six at a new house on Fifth Avenue. I will have one of my assistants make pineapple ices."

"What else will you have?" I ask.

Mr. Serle looks amused. "Are you going to steal my menus, Miss Pigot?"

"Of course I would not steal," I say indignantly, and then I think he must be teasing me. "Well, I might," I say, "if it was a good menu and adapted for a family of three on Fourth Street."

"It will be an expensive menu," Mr. Serle says. "The dinner is given by a man who thinks a dish that costs a lot must taste delicious. And here are bananas," he says.

"Oh, they are like yellow hands," I say, looking at the curved fingers of the fruit that cup one over the other in rich layers around a stout stem.

"And that is what we call them, miss," the vendor says. "This is a hand of bananas." He holds up a cluster of the fruit attached together.

Mr. Serle and the vendor show me how the underripe bananas are green and light yellow with sharp edges to the rind. The unripe fruit will have a chalky edge to the taste. The ripe ones are rich gold and softer edged, with just a light freckle here and there of brown but not penetrating through the rind itself. The flesh inside is firm but melting. When the fruit is too ripe, it will have brown spots into the flesh and a slimy texture.

"It is an honest fruit," Mr. Serle comments. "The outer peel tells you what you will find inside. Would you like to taste it?"

"Indeed, yes," I say. "I am very curious."

Mr. Serle asks me to choose a fruit that I think is properly ripe. He and the stall man approve my choice, and the finger is cut neatly away from the hand it belonged to. Mr. Serle unfolds his own knife then and shows me how the fruit is prepared to eat. He cuts the peel across at the end of the banana and pulls back the glossy yellow into three petals to show the paler flesh within. The fruit is so cleverly made that it wears its own serving dish.

Mr. Serle slices a small piece crosswise. He deftly spears it on the point of his knife and shows it to me. "See how pretty it is when sliced?" he says. "It has a symmetrical design in the center."

"I like the scent of it also," I say. I reach to take the piece.

"It is a little slippery," he says. "Be careful. I do not want to cut you."

I am not sure I like the texture of the fruit in my mouth. But then the sweet, strange savor of it blooms on my tongue and pleases me.

"Try another piece," Mr. Serle says. He cuts a slice for me and one for himself.

"Good, hey?" the vendor says in a cheerful tone. "You can eat them out of hand, you know, like an apple. No need to cut them up."

"True," Mr. Serle says, "but politer to share this way."

Another customer comes before the stall man can comment on that. He has a glint in his eye that makes me wonder what he was about to say.

"What do you think?" Mr. Serle asks me.

"It is a lovely fruit," I tell him. "I cannot compare it to anything but itself. Perhaps the feel of it is a little mushy. It might be good to put it with some other crisper food."

"What would marry well with it, do you think?"

"Oranges?" I say doubtfully. "Or its oily sweetness might be offset with the bite of caramel or strawberries in season."

"What about chocolate?" Mr. Serle asks.

"Perhaps." I think about it. "It might have a heavy feel to it."

"What about slices of banana in a dish with pineapple ice and a chocolate sauce scented with brandy?"

"It sounds like an expensive dish. Add some toasted filberts and a mint leaf for a finish."

"Aha," Mr. Serle says. "Filberts, a *Coupe Mina*. The rich man in his great marble house on Fifth Avenue will be pleased."

"How is banana commonly served?" I ask.

"As a fruit alone or in a compote. With sliced pineapple and shredded coconut it reflects its home in the tropics and is very good. The emperor Napoleon liked banana fritters."

"I would prefer it with coconut," I say.

"I am going to give you one banana to take with you and buy a couple of hands of them for my dinner tomorrow," Mr. Serle says. "Don't cut your banana until the moment before you wish to eat it. The flesh turns brown quickly in the air."

When he finishes his business, he sets the banana in my

basket and we walk back toward the market entrance. It is so easy to be with him. I feel as if we have marketed together every morning for years.

"What will you cook for your dinner today?" Mr. Serle asks me.

"The family will eat fish soup and roast beef tonight. The other servants and I eat dinner at two. We will have vegetable soup and codfish cakes. It is Friday, and Lent too."

I look at him to see if he understands, and he nods. His head bends toward me and his dark eyes regard me attentively.

"I made coffee cream for the sweet already, and the family will have that tonight, but Marie and Bridget and I will eat coffee cream with thin-sliced banana and chopped almonds for a treat. I will certainly not share my gift with the Westervelts."

"Your work seems to suit you better now," Mr. Serle tells me. "You look well."

We are back at the butchers' stalls again.

"I must go," I say. "Thank you for the lime and the banana. I am so glad to see you and to learn new things."

"You seem—" Mr. Serle cuts his speech off and hesitates.

"I seem?" I am curious to know what he is thinking.

"You seem more grown, more a young woman suddenly," he says.

"I hope so." I feel a pleasure that he sees me changing. "I should not like to be a child always. Would you wish it so?"

"No, I think not."

Mr. Serle's voice sounds doubtful to my ear. I think that he would like to care for me in some way that does not trouble his conscience. I would like to ask him if I am right, but how can we talk of such things in a public market?

He does not say more, just shrugs and smiles and says, "Good day, Miss Pigot."

I was glad to walk in the market with Mr. Serle today. I had a happy feeling that we were companions for a space of time. He taught me—it is his nature to teach, I think—and listened to me too. But now I feel afraid as I write this. I see him so rarely. What if I never saw him again at all? That can happen in life. Like mist on a river dissipated by the heat of the sun, goodness disappears.

At Tompkins Market this morning I was thinking about vegetables. It is such a difficult time of year for fresh produce. It may be that I will have to settle for cabbage. If I stew it in cream, it will not be at all like sauerkraut. I am about to ask Mr. Larkins when he thinks we will have good head lettuces again, but he speaks first.

"He is back at Mr. Torrilhon's stall, discussing pâtés," Mr. Larkins says and makes a kind of knowing smirk.

"What?" I am startled from my thoughts.

"Your friend," he says. "He was here a moment ago. He said the watercress looks good for a soup and asked if you were by yet today. I think he is looking for you."

"Well, I must make my purchases before I have time for talk," I say as calmly as I can. My heart jumps in my breast. I did not expect to meet him again so soon. "The watercress soup is a good idea. I will take two bunches with me. Do you have parsnips or salsify?"

When I have settled my menus and made my notes of what Mr. Larkins will be sending and the prices, I walk on toward the specialty stalls. I feel a satisfaction, holding the certainty of talking to Mr. Serle in my heart. Like a good meal, pleasure should not be hurried but savored. Mr. Serle is where Mr. Larkins said he would be, talking to the man who sells pâtés, terrines, and galantines, all ready-made.

"There you are," he says as I approach.

"Here I am," I say. I look over the array of dishes set out on a tray of crushed ice. "You are not considering fruit today?"

"No," he says. "Wait a moment."

He turns and speaks with Mr. Torrilhon again. I have no idea what it is about, because they speak in French. I am beginning to recognize the rhythm of it. Marie sings songs to herself in

French when she is working, and she has taught Bridget and me a few phrases too. *"Je vais aller à l'église maintenant pour prier à la Vièrge,"* she says when she is ready to leave for church.

Mr. Serle is still talking. I move along to the next stall where the man sells snails and turtles. Poor things, I think, looking at the snails in their barrel. Their heads sprout two little stalks that waver about. Perhaps that is how they see. I am about to ask the man when Mr. Serle touches my arm.

"Are you well?" he asks me. He sounds anxious.

"Why, yes," I tell him. "Did you think I might not be?"

He looks at me and then away. Agitation is unlike him.

"I had a dream," he says.

"Oh." I am surprised. He never mentioned such a thing to me before. "I hope it is not an omen. Perhaps if you tell me, I can be careful of whatever was the danger."

"Never mind," he says. "It is bad luck to speak of it." His mood changes like sun glancing from behind the clouds as he smiles at me. "I like your bonnet."

"Honor made it for me," I say. "I wanted one so. My brother said a bonnet would make me look more like a lady."

I do not mention to Mr. Serle that I chose buying the bonnet and postponed new boots again.

"You look lovely." He speaks abruptly, as if he is uncomfortable with his thought.

When I look to see his eyes and what he means by such a compliment, he is staring at the poor snails wiggling their eyes—or maybe the stalks are their ears.

"Thank you," I say. There is a silence. "I forgot to ask you a question the last time we met. It is about cooking."

"Yes?" He is still regarding the snails.

"What is shad roe?" I ask. "Mr. Westervelt mentioned that he likes it, but I know nothing about cooking it."

"It is an American dish." Mr. Serle looks at me now. I am his apprentice again, and he is teaching me. He is at ease. "It is the eggs of a Hudson River fish that they catch in April and May. The roe comes in pairs in a membrane. Soak it in clean salted water, divide the two lobes, and trim them but do not remove the membrane before you cook it. Try it poached in court bouillon with a sauce of sorrel thickened with egg. Sorrel cuts the richness of the roe."

"Thank you," I tell him. "That is very helpful."

There is another silence.

"I may return to Italy," Mr. Serle says, changing the conversation again suddenly. His forehead is knit into a frown.

"But why?" I am upset. I feel my hand on the basket handle grow damp with fear.

"There will be a struggle there. The soldier Garibaldi is here in America. I went to Staten Island to talk to him. He is very poor, but he is gathering his forces. He will return to unite the pathetic fragments of our country into one. My conscience says I should follow him."

"But I thought—" I begin.

"You do not think of the larger world, do you?" Mr. Serle interrupts me, which is not like him. He speaks as if he is searching for something he can find wrong in me. "You do not read the newspapers. You do not think of the problems of our day."

"I did not think I should be called upon to solve such problems," I reply. "Can my knowing change anything? And you are not fair. I look at the newspapers when I can. I know there is great discussion of slavery. I hope Phoebe is safe when I read that. I read the news of California and pray for my brother. If you go to Italy, I will read the news about that place and pray for your safety too. Only I hope you will not go."

Mr. Serle's voice softens. "You are right to correct me, Miss Pigot."

"There are so many wrongs in the world," I tell him. "War and famine and fires and poverty. There is so little report of happiness."

"I feel a duty to the cause of freedom."

Mr. Serle's voice sounds troubled to my ear. I breathe in the smells of earth and blood that scent the morning air of the market. I wish I could help him. I think before I speak.

"I have duty enough here," I say. "To honor the past, to

comprehend this busy place, to care for my friends, to try to know myself. We cannot correct every wrong."

"But we can support the causes we care for." Mr. Serle seems to be arguing with himself as much as with me. "They raised money in my synagogue for relief of the Irish famine."

"How kind," I say. "In my church too we send money to those left behind. For me life every day is here. If I do not study the newspapers always, it is so I can use the little time I have to read something like Shakespeare that helps me to hold the memory of my parents' voices by the hearth. We choose in life. Today I will candy oranges and read a page by Shakespeare rather than worry about why men fight a war far away."

"You bought a book?" Mr. Serle sounds interested and calmer.

"I found a copy of *Twelfth Night* on one of the barrows," I say. "I have that and a few other books."

Mr. Serle nods. He seems not to be thinking of Italy now.

"Good." He puts his hat, which he has been holding in his hand as we talked, back on his head, hiding his dark, disordered hair. "Perhaps I will see you one morning next week, Miss Pigot."

I sigh and say good-bye to him. I must buy oranges. He seemed in a strange mood, restless, unhappy in himself. But when I think of our talk, I feel glad. He dreamed of me. He let me see his trouble. He spoke of uncertainty and himself. To know he changes makes him more real somehow, a friend like Honor, not just the silent figure who holds me tenderly in my dreams as he did on the ship and in his office at the Columbia House Hotel.

TUESDAY, MARCH 19, 1850

On Monday that was the eleventh, I went up after breakfast—as usual—to receive Mrs. Westervelt's directions, which consisted—as usual—of her asking me what I thought best for the week's meals. Mrs. Westervelt said she and her husband would be out for dinner Thursday. Just as I think that it will be an easy week, Mrs.

Westervelt says in a tone of great pride that she has invited guests for Saturday night.

"I wish a special meal, Mrs. Pigot," she says. "The dinner is in honor of a famous man, a writer from England."

"What do you mean by special?" I ask.

At last, I think, Mrs. Westervelt will have to be specific. I am wrong, of course. She flutters one white hand and says in her vague way, "Oh, you know, two soups, ice cream, that sort of thing."

"How many will there be?" I ask.

"Oh, ten, I suppose," she says.

"Ten including you and Mr. Westervelt or ten in addition to you and your husband?"

I want to shout at the woman. She takes a pencil and a piece of her blue letter paper from her writing desk.

"I wonder," she says. She begins to write a list of names. "Did I ask the Strongs?" she says to herself. "I think I did." At last, "Ten guests and then Seton and myself, so twelve altogether," she says triumphantly, as if she has performed some magic trick.

I am so nervous that I feel my stomach clench. Twelve for a special dinner. I have never been in charge of anything like that. I have been here for less than three months.

"Yes, Madame," I say. "With so many guests, we will need extra help in the kitchen and for serving upstairs."

"Arrange it as you think best," Mrs. Westervelt says.

In the kitchen, I take a deep breath and sit down with pencil and paper of my own to plan. I must begin today to prepare the stocks and sauces I will need. A dinner for twelve seems daunting. Two soups—one clear, one cream—four plates of hors d'oeuvres, four entrée dishes, two roasts, two salad dishes and two or three vegetable dishes, sweets, cheese, fresh fruit, and, of course, bread and butter and condiments.

I must not try too much, I think. It will be more special if it is dishes I know how to prepare done very well and carefully garnished. Having Thursday night almost free will help. When I am clearer in my mind about what I wish to do, I consult Marie and Bridget.

Marie is appalled. "I will ask the parlor maid next door to help serve, but I do not think we have enough china for a fancy dinner for twelve," she says. "Bridget will have to wash the hors d'oeuvres plates from the soup course in time for the dessert service."

Bridget is more cheerful. She can ask her mother to help, she says, and her brother too if we have tasks for him. The little ones will come along as well. "We can set them in a corner out of the way," she says. "They will be happy to watch the fancy doings."

"Who is ordering the wine?" Marie asks me. "Did Mrs. Westervelt say? The wines should match the food. Even if Madame does not care about such concerns, Mr. Westervelt surely will."

I go to the market on Tuesday to see that I can obtain the extra produce and poultry that I need. For a price, anything is possible, the stall men say, and so I make my orders. On Marie's advice, I write out the menu I have planned. When Marie serves breakfast on Wednesday morning, she will give the menu to Mr. Westervelt. I write a note with the menu asking him if he and Mrs. Westervelt will approve it. I add that I suppose he will order the appropriate wines and that I will need a bottle of Madeira and two bottles of claret in the kitchen for sauces.

No sooner has Marie gone up to serve breakfast and deliver the note than the bell for me rings frantically on the kitchen wall. I change my apron for a clean one and go upstairs. Mr. and Mrs. Westervelt are still seated at the breakfast table, the food uneaten before them on the table. Mr. Westervelt has my note in his clenched fist, which he appears to have been brandishing at the lady. The girl, Sarah, is cowering in her chair, staring at a portion of creamed codfish congealing on her plate. Marie is standing by the sideboard, her hand over her mouth—whether in shock at what she has heard or to stifle a laugh, I cannot tell.

"My wife has something to say to you, Mrs. Pigot." Mr. Westervelt's tone is grim.

Mrs. Westervelt is dabbing at her eyes with a lace-trimmed handkerchief although I see no evidence that she is actually crying.

"Really, Seton," she says. "Why all the fuss? You can just as well tell her yourself."

"Very well, Julia, I will," Mr. Westervelt says. "My wife apologizes to you for her scatterbrained behavior. She left you on your own to plan a dinner for twelve. I found out about it only now when I received your note. At least she mentioned it to you. When she would have condescended to mention it to me, I have no idea."

"I am sorry for the trouble," I say.

I hope Mr. Westervelt accepts the menu. His problems with his wife are no business of mine.

"Wait, Mrs. Pigot," Mr. Westervelt continues in the same angry voice. "Mrs. Westervelt has something else to mention. There is more that she forgot to say to either one of us."

"Really, Seton," Mrs. Westervelt says. "There is no call to be unpleasant. I gave the cards on the spur of the moment. We are entertaining a famous writer. You do not appreciate the honor."

She pats under her dry eyes and sniffs.

"Cards?" I ask. My heart begins to pound in my chest.

"My wife has not only invited ten people to dinner, she has requested the company of forty more after dinner for music, dancing, and supper," Mr. Westervelt says in a shout. "It is Wednesday today. The fact that she has not told you that you are expected to provide supper for fifty-two in addition to dinner for twelve, that she has not hired musicians, that she has not ordered wine, that she told me nothing about any of this until I had your note this morning, seems not to concern her. You belong in a madhouse, Julia."

"Fifty-two for supper?" I reach out and hold the back of the chair nearest to me. I will not faint, I tell myself. It would not be dignified for a cook to do so.

"You are making a great fuss, Seton," Mrs. Westervelt says. "I am sure Mrs. Pigot can arrange things. She is accustomed to the habits of great houses."

She prinks the lace of her sleeve complacently.

"I should refuse to allow Mrs. Pigot to do anything," Mr. Westervelt says. "I should make you stand at the door telling each of the people you invited that you made no plans and that there is no food, no drink, and no entertainment because you are too careless and too stupid to remember to arrange them."

"I do not think your pride will allow you to do that, Seton," Mrs. Westervelt replies haughtily. "I cannot imagine your expecting me to say such a thing to Mr. and Mrs. Cooper. Besides, as you point out, today is only Wednesday. There is plenty of time. Oysters, some pâtés, ices, a few cakes, punch, champagne. How difficult can it be? An evening party is the company, not the food, and I have taken care that the company will be the best. I do not see that I should be expected to do more. You have taken my appetite this morning and given me a headache. Congratulate yourself for that."

She rises and, skirts rustling, leaves the room. She does not bother to dab her eyes. Mr. Westervelt half rises and then sits down again heavily. His fists are still clenched.

"Sit down, Mrs. Pigot," Mr. Westervelt says. "You look ill."

I sit, even though I know it is not proper. When I have collected myself, I look at Mr. Westervelt. He continues to frown angrily. I think his wife has won. His pride will not allow him to shame her publicly.

"Dinner for twelve and fifty-two for supper," I say at last.

"Can you do it?" Mr. Westervelt says. "I can attest that you are a fine cook, but you look just a girl. How old are you?"

"I am twenty-one," I lie. I am tired of being a child. If I have to cook supper for fifty-two to prove it, I will be grown up.

"Twenty-one?" He looks surprised. Then he sighs and asks me if it really is possible to organize dinner and supper both by Saturday.

"If I purchase most of the supper refreshments ready-made, I think so," I say cautiously. "It will be very expensive."

"I will manage," Mr. Westervelt says. "So you can do it?"

"I think so," I say again. "But it is not just the food. I am not sure I have enough pots in the kitchen. And Marie and I have calculated that there is just barely enough china for the dinner service. Supper service for fifty-two is impossible. You will need more plates and forks. Mrs. Westervelt keeps mentioning ices. Marie says there are only twelve glass dishes suitable for serving ices. And there must be spoons and punch glasses too."

"Well," Mr. Westervelt sighs very deeply, "I will see to the china and tableware. Marie must give me a list. And the wine and musicians. You have my authority to purchase any kitchen utensils you need. What else?"

"Marie has found another woman to help serve dinner," I say. "But there must also be a third person at supper to keep things neat."

"And flowers," Marie adds. "Someone should purchase and arrange flowers on Saturday." Like the proper servant that she is, she has been standing silent by the sideboard all this time. And from the satisfied expression on her face, enjoying the upset.

"My wife can certainly manage that," Mr. Westervelt says, "or it will remain undone. And she can take the expense out of her personal allowance," he adds in an undertone. He looks at his daughter. "Eat your breakfast, Sarah," he says. "You will be late for your music lesson."

He picks up a spoon and cracks the top of a boiled egg smartly. It must be cold by now. His wife, not he, deserves my anger, but even so, I do not find in my heart the kindness to suggest sending up fresh, hot food for him.

I go back to the kitchen, sit, and make a list of all the tasks that must be accomplished by Saturday evening. I am still staring at it when Marie comes down.

"*Mon Dieu,*" she exclaims. "What a scene! I thought he would strike her after he read your note and she confessed that she had been at a literary *soirée* last Saturday and invited everyone there to be entertained along with this English gentleman. To think that she knew what she had done on Sunday and only mentioned it this morning."

"Marie," I say. "Can you find another woman to help you serve and clear? If I go over the menu with you, can you make a list of necessary china and tableware and give it to Mr. Westervelt by this evening?"

"Camille from next door will come, and we have another friend four houses down," Marie says. "As soon as I have put the dining room to rights, I will go down and speak to her. If her mistress is invited to dinner here, and she surely is, they will let her come."

I look at the daunting list. "All right," I say. "I will spend to-day making cakes and cookies and biscuits enough for both the dinner and the supper. I will make soup stocks and sauce bases to-morrow. I will go to the market very early on Friday to see what in the world I can find ready-made of galantines and pâtés for the supper. I must order extra ice starting tomorrow and remember to roast enough coffee beans."

"You will make a success of it," Bridget says in a comfortable tone. "My mother will come on Saturday and my brother too if you want him," she adds eagerly.

"I think he can crush ice for the ice cream maker and make the ices if I have the creams ready," I say. "Oh! And I must have salt as well as ice for the machine. Yes, write a note to your mother now."

And so Wednesday and Thursday were a blur of flour, but-ter, eggs, cream, nuts, rose water, currants, spices, and soup bones. The range blazed steadily. Delivery men came with oranges, lemons, bloody parcels of meat, bags of onions, six dozen eggs, and all manner of other things besides. The family upstairs got their eggs with sliced ham and toast in the mornings, smoked tongue sandwiches at lunch, and some roast pork and potato Wednesday night. I would make enough beef à la mode on Friday for supper upstairs and for an entrée on Saturday, I decided. We would eat omelets downstairs. I could make pastry on Friday for both a lemon tart for Friday night dinner and the patty shells for the oys-ters on Saturday.

It seemed possible until I went to Tompkins Market early on Friday with my list of how many pounds of galantines and ter-rines and pâtés I would need. Mr. Torrilhon's stall was closed.

"His wife is very ill," the man who sells snails and turtles told me. "He has been closed since Wednesday. He sent a note that his customers could place orders at a stall down at the Fulton Market, but it is certainly too late to fill orders for tomorrow."

I turned back to the front of the market with tears in my eyes. What would I do? I will go and ask Mr. Woodcock about a ham, I thought, although I will not have a pot free to cook it in un-less I sit up all night tonight and have it done before tomorrow.

"Good morning, Miss Pigot," says a familiar voice behind me.

I turn and can barely restrain myself from throwing my arms about Mr. Serle.

"Wait, wait," he says as I seize his arm and begin to pour out my troubles.

When I am calm enough to speak clearly, he listens carefully.

"What is your menu for the dinner?" he asks me. And when I tell him, "You really can do all that alone?"

"I made a dinner for eight by myself," I say. "It is only four more. And I have all my stocks and sauces on ice except for the egg-lemon to go with the sea bass. It is the supper I cannot manage now without Mr. Torrilhon's ready-made things."

Mr. Serle takes out his pocket notebook. "Let me see," he murmurs and writes a list. "You have ordered the ingredients for the ices, you say, and you are making a queen cake and brandy sauce. I remember you do that very well. So the sweets will be done." He closes his book with a snap and then opens it again. "The address?" he says. "I will be there at two in the afternoon with the rest of the supper, extra pots, and an apprentice who can run out for anything that is forgotten as well as help us both."

"But it is not right to ask you—" I begin.

"I wish to help you," he says. "Besides, I know you. Your kitchen must be overflowing with food and that means you will not eat. Did you eat breakfast this morning?"

I admit that I did not.

"You see?" Mr. Serle says. "I should take you to a cake shop. Only I have business to do, and you have work. I will see you to-morrow. The number of the house?"

I tell him reluctantly. I had thought he might tell me where to buy galantines, and now he is coming to cook with me. I feel great relief. And a sort of guilt too. I need him so, and he is always there when I want him. I ask too much.

"Good," he says. "Now go home and eat something. I do not wish to arrive tomorrow and find you fainted on the floor."

"I will," I promise.

It is not an easy promise to keep. The heaps of food over-whelm my appetite, but I manage some bread and cheese and, later, when I can see that my queen cake is a success, some soup. By the time Mr. Serle arrives on Saturday, I can attend to nothing but the heat of the range, the texture of the sauces, the order of dishes. The first thing I think when I see him is that he has brought a pot big enough to poach the sea bass.

"This is Jean-Claude," Mr. Serle says, indicating the dark young man carrying the pot. "Jean-Claude, Miss Pigot."

The young man bows and looks about. I introduce Bridget, who, overcome with the grandeur of these strangers, curtsies to Mr. Serle with her hand up over her mouth to hide her tooth. Bridget's mother comes in the door bringing her son, two little girls, and a baby in a basket. It is not surprising that the son does not have hod-carrying work this week. He looks to be about fourteen years old, and a puny fourteen at that. I am very busy, showing everyone their tasks. It takes much conferring with Marie to arrange matters so that there will be service platters for all the dishes as we need them.

Sometime after the soup, fish, and hors d'oeuvres have been cleared and all the entrée dishes as well as the roast veal, spring lamb with caper sauce, salads, and vegetable dishes have gone up, I am garnishing the plates of dessert cakes with candied orange peel. The kitchen is a chaos, and yet a sense of calm pervades. It is like the descriptions of maelstroms in the ocean when the winds and waves make a great circle of tumult and yet the heart of the whirlpool creates its power quietly. Jean-Claude, a sleek-looking, silent young man to whom Mr. Serle speaks in French, is juicing oranges for a punch bowl. Bridget's brother is cranking the ice cream machine for a chocolate ice. Mr. Serle is at the worktable opposite me, slicing bananas for a fruit compote. Bridget and her mother are washing plates at the sink. The two little girls have dish clouts and are drying spoons carefully, holding them up to see that they are perfectly shiny and admiring each other's work. The baby stirs in its basket and begins to whimper.

"I should feed the poor thing," the mother says.

"Of course," I say.

She dries her hands, takes a chair, and opens her dress. The baby begins to nurse, making murmuring sounds of contentment.

The heat of the range has dissipated for the moment. In half an hour we will have to build the fire again to brew coffee, and so Mr. Serle can start an oyster stew for the supper table. For now we are warm and comfortable. In the quiet of the kitchen, we can hear the distant voices and laughter from the dining room. The English gentleman must be a success.

Mr. Serle looks up at me and smiles. His knife flashes in his hands.

"I don't suppose you were able to find mint leaves for garnish?" he says.

"No," I answer, "but there is candied orange peel. Will that do?"

"What do you think? I wonder if it needs it?" he asks me.

I have finished my task; the cake plates are ready to go upstairs when Marie signals that she wants them. I go around the table and stand beside Mr. Serle to see what he has done. The slices of orange and banana are layered in circles in a great glass bowl. He has not added the shredded coconut yet.

"Put the coconut around the outside and just a little in the center. Here is candied orange peel. Put three strips in the center for the look, not the taste," I suggest. "It is pretty to see the rounds of the fruit. You cut and arranged them so beautifully."

"Yes, ma'am. Thank you, Miss Pigot," Mr. Serle says.

Jean-Claude starts to laugh and then stops himself. The dumbwaiter makes the whirring sound that signals its descent. Marie must be beginning to clear the table and remove the cloth for the dessert course. I go to unmold the vanilla ices and put the cherry sauce into its pitcher.

At eleven o'clock, when the last course is done, the dishes washed, the coffee and tea service sent up and then down again, and the supper buffet is all in place in the dining room, Mr. Serle says we in the kitchen must sit down for our own supper.

"I want to try the sea bass with the *agristada* sauce," he says.

We can choose among the left overs, of course. The two little girls, bright-eyed with fatigue, are yearning for ices. Bridget's mother and brother want beef à la mode, and I tell Bridget how to warm it for them. Jean-Claude wants oyster patties. I get two fresh pastry shells from the tin for him, because what is left from dinner is very soggy now. He exclaims in French, and Mr. Serle says it is that the pastry is so light. Bridget wants the last of the small birds in Madeira sauce.

"I never had such a thing before," she says shyly.

I urge her to have something else as well, and she has her bird and then a slice of veal. I warm watercress soup for myself. All of us share the last few spoonsful of the fruit compote. No one speaks as we eat; we are all so tired. It is a rest before the supper upstairs is cleared away and the final cleaning begins. I confer with Mr. Serle and then write a brief note to Mr. Westervelt, reminding him that I must pay the help at the end of the evening. I send it up in the dumbwaiter for Marie to deliver.

Bridget and her mother and brother are hard at work on the third—and almost final, we think—load of dirty supper dishes from the descending dumbwaiter when someone knocks briskly at the kitchen door.

"May I enter the sanctum?" a voice says.

It is Mr. Simpkens from the ship. Mr. Serle and I know this famous writer who thanked us so kindly when we reached New York.

"I thought I recognized that wonderful queen cake with brandy sauce," he says. "I asked if the famous Mr. Serle was in the kitchen with his redheaded assistant. The maid upstairs, Marie, seemed puzzled, but she said the cook is definitely redheaded and that a famous chef came to help this evening."

Mr. Serle rises, and he and Mr. Simpkens shake hands cordially.

"I am amazed to find you cooking here," Mr. Simpkens exclaims. "I thought you would be at one of the great hotels or with the Delmonicos."

"I am assisting Miss Pigot for this one night," Mr. Serle says. "She is the one you must congratulate."

Mr. Simpkens bows to me and then looks again and jumps in surprise. "You must be the twin of Daniel?" he asks in a puzzled voice.

"I have a brother Daniel," I admit, smiling.

While it was awkward and strange when Madame Moses and Herr Meyer recognized that they knew me from the ship, it seems a joke, a happy puzzle, with Mr. Simpkens.

"I feel as if I am in a play by William Shakespeare," Mr. Simpkens says. He sounds delighted. "Now, don't tell. Let me guess whether it was you or your brother on the ship."

He is interrupted by Mr. Westervelt's appearing at the kitchen door. He looks very much the master of the house in his formal dress with its glossy white shirt and silk brocade vest. He seems surprised to see Mr. Simpkens.

"Mr. Westervelt!" Mr. Simpkens greets him. "Come to congratulate the cook in person for her brilliant dinner, of course. Tonight I enjoyed the best meal I have eaten during all my tiring tour of America. Your Miss Pigot is a treasure, a pearl. And how fortunate you are to know a master like Mr. Serle also. He made the tedious sea voyage to America bearable. I dread returning to England next week without him."

Mr. Westervelt looks uncertain. He does not speak, only looks curiously about the crowded kitchen. He stares at Jean-Claude, who bows to him politely.

"Well, I must go up and say good-bye to my hostess," Mr. Simpkens says. "I have enjoyed this encounter. I shall amuse myself on the voyage home by writing a story that solves the mystery of Daniel and Miss Pigot."

He shakes hands with Mr. Serle again, bows to me, and bounds off, laughing.

"This is Mr. Westervelt, Mr. Serle," I say. "Mr. Westervelt, Mr. Serle has made the supper possible. He has rescued us all."

"I thank you," Mr. Westervelt says. He does not offer to shake hands. "I apologize for my wife's confusion."

Mr. Serle regards him coldly. "I hold you responsible for the well-being of my niece," he says.

"Of course," Mr. Westervelt says hastily. He looks at me. "You wished to ask me something, Mrs. Pigot?" he says.

"There is the matter of the payment for the supper and the extra help," I say. "Mr. Serle brought almost everything."

"How much?" Mr. Westervelt asks.

I turn to Mr. Serle.

"Thirty dollars for my outlay for supplies, for my assistant's wages, and for the kitchen help. The maids upstairs, I leave to you. I will take payment from you tonight," he says briskly.

Mr. Westervelt looks almost cowed. "The thirty does not include your wages?" he asks.

"No," Mr. Serle said. "I am here not in your employ but as a favor to my niece."

"I will have to go to my safe," Mr. Westervelt says.

Mr. Serle shrugs. "I can wait for you," he says.

After Mr. Westervelt has gone upstairs, Mr. Serle gives Bridget's mother and her brother three dollars each. He gives the mother another two dollars. "For the little girls," he says. The mother stares wide-eyed at Mr. Serle and then down at so much money in her hand. "Our Lord bless you, sir," she says. Mr. Serle suggests I wrap the remains of the beef for Mrs. Cosgill to take home. He chucks the sleepy baby under the chin. Bridget kisses each of her family and sees them out the door. Meanwhile, the assistant, the sleek Jean-Claude, carries the clean pots and pans he brought to the cab that he has summoned. Mr. Serle rolls his knives neatly in their flannel and closes them in their case.

"Well, my dear," Mr. Serle says, turning to me, "you must be very tired."

I nod. "Thank you," I say. "How can I repay you?"

"To be needed is gratification enough for me," Mr. Serle tells me. He has said that before, I know, but my tired mind cannot recall the day.

"It seems I am always needing you," I say.

He smiles at me. I think I am about to weep with exhaustion, but Mr. Westervelt comes in to give Mr. Serle the money. Mr. Westervelt looks as if he wishes to speak to me, but Mr. Serle stands calmly looking at him. He seems to be waiting for Mr. Westervelt to go back upstairs, and Mr. Westervelt does not challenge him.

"Thank you for your extra work, Mrs. Pigot," he says as he turns and goes.

Mr. Serle surveys the quiet, clean kitchen.

"You have done well," he says.

"Because of you," I say.

"No," he says. "Bridget and Marie work willingly for you and follow your directions well. That is not the result of one day. You planned the work for the evening brilliantly. It is not your fault it was too much for one cook. You have the talents of a master chef." He smiles at me again. "Not that the Delmonicos will hire a woman. Tell me, why are you Mrs. Pigot here?"

"Oh," I say. "I never told you." I remind him about the character from the lord in England for Daniel Serle, and then tell him about changing the name and saying I am a widow. "I thought it would sound older," I say.

"I am sure the last three days have made you old enough," Mr. Serle says. "I must go. Good night, my dear."

He surprises me by reaching over and giving a straying curl of my hair, which must have escaped from under my cap, a decorous little tug. He tucks his case of knives under his arm and hurries out to his waiting cab. It is like the fairy godmother in the tale, I think sleepily. I survey the clean kitchen as Mr. Serle did moments ago. There is food enough in the ice chest that tomorrow and Monday will be easy days. Fish pies, I think, maybe a curry. For now, where three hours ago all was chaos, everything is clean, neat, and in its proper place. And Mr. Serle ate all of his portion of sea bass and said it was seasoned perfectly.

I am going to paste the menu I made in my book. Of course, it is a little stained from being in the kitchen. Mr. Serle said it was quite varied given the problems of finding fresh vegetables and greens just now and our dependence on tropical fruit from Cuba.

I like to think that I might have managed the dinner myself if only the supper had not been added. It will be wise, however, to begin to train Bridget to learn more cooking tasks. Then, when there is a dinner for any number, we can have her mother and sisters to wash dishes while Bridget helps me. Also, I will have to be braver about refusing services that are too much for me. It was chance that I saw Mr. Serle and chance that he was free to help me. I must—I remind myself again and again—I must stand on my own.

It is hard to write tonight, but I have an urge in me to keep a memory-record of what happened. Perhaps if I begin slowly, it will be easier. Easter was last Sunday. It seemed simple to make the family dinner for just three people. The past week has been tiring, though. The spring cleaning had to be done. Hired men took down the stovepipes to clean them. Another service took away the rugs and washed the windows. It has been chaos and dirt and strange people coming and going for five days. It seemed in the kitchen that we cleaned and then repeated the same task immediately because dust and soot from the rest of the house filtered down on us.

Tonight all is finally quiet. The family went out for the evening. They ate an early dinner and went to sit with Mr. Westervelt's invalid mother. We had an early meal in the kitchen too. Marie went to church with her friend Camille from next door. I gave Bridget permission to go to her family tonight. She will be back before breakfast tomorrow, she promises. Her life will be easier now that she does not have to lay the fires upstairs again until next October.

I was sitting by myself in the kitchen. It is so rare to be alone except when I take a moment to write my life and then fall into my bed at night. I had the lamp lit and crochet work in my hands. I must have a new petticoat and chemise. I started the lace for them. Honor says it is a lot of work when machine lace trim is to be had for very little, but I like to do it. It helps me to remember my mother and her ways.

Soon Mrs. Westervelt, her daughter, and Mr. Westervelt's mother go to the family farm near West Point for the summer months. White sheets will cover the furniture in the parlors, and only the kitchen, the dining room, and Mr. Westervelt's study will be in use—and the bedrooms, of course. On the weekends, Mr. Westervelt and the son will travel to the country by Hudson River steamboat or by train to join the rest of the family.

I thought of the country and what it must look like. I have seen so little of America. Aunt Jane says the great Hudson River comes through beautiful mountains to our north. I glimpsed the cliffs of New Jersey across the river once. I wonder if they are as high as the great falls at Niagara. I must have dozed a little in the quiet, for I had a sort of half-awake dream of standing, gazing at a dancing fall of water. "Are you all right?" a voice asked. I recognized that it was Mr. Serle, but when I turned my head, I did not see him, only the tumbling, frothing water over gray rocks.

The sound of steps in the areaway and a tap at the door roused me. It was Mr. Serle himself, not a dream.

"I was walking and saw the light," he said. "Am I disturbing you?"

"No, no," I say quickly, "I am alone this evening for a little while. Come in. Would you like something to drink?"

"Thank you," he says.

He sits at the scrubbed table. I fetch lemon syrup and cool water and make a lemonade for each of us.

"To your health, my dear," Mr. Serle says.

There is a little, peaceful silence as we drink.

"Are you happy here in America?" Mr. Serle asks me.

I think about that. "Yes and no," I tell him. "I like that there is so much to learn, so much bustle and life to this city. I make my way. I have found friends. Still, the city overwhelms me, and I feel so lonely sometimes. I wish my brother would return."

I want to say also that I do not like sleeping in a room by myself at night. It sounds improper to say so to Mr. Serle.

Mr. Serle nods.

"And you?" I ask. "Are you happy in America?"

He looks down at his hands. "I am thrown into a stew of strange ingredients, boiling and bubbling. In my native Rome my life was limited—perhaps I am forgetting how limited—and yet I lived in my history, which, like the stones in a cellar under us, stayed in its place. Here I am all lost sometimes. The building on the corner of my street that stood solidly yesterday is pulled down today. A new hotel will rise there tomorrow. I walk out of my door into confusion." He stops, and his expression is rueful. "I am bubbling in the stew. The flavors do not melt into each other as they should. There is a seasoning missing."

"Everyone works very hard here," I say tentatively.

I am not at all sure I understand him. Perhaps he does not understand himself.

"Oh, work." He shrugs his shoulder in the familiar gesture.

"What, then?" I ask. "Do you mean that someone to share your thoughts with is the seasoning that you lack?"

Mr. Serle does not answer my question.

"I spoke to the rabbi at the synagogue where I worship," Mr. Serle says. He looks down at his hands again, and his eyelids hood his gaze so I am unsure of his feeling. "It is in Crosby Street," he adds, talking just to talk, I think.

"Yes?" I wonder what he wishes to say that he is reluctant to express. Why should he not talk to the priest of his faith?

"He tells me that four years ago—just the year before you and I came to America—the congregation decided that only those married under Jewish law can hold a seat in the synagogue and be buried in the community's cemetery. It is their rule."

He tilts his head, gazing at the golden liquid in the glass before him or at some unseen thing.

"I do not understand," I say.

He leans across the table to me now. "My people, my synagogue, are so important to me. I do not know who I would be if I let that go."

"Of course," I say. "You must think of your faith."

"I have met men in my synagogue with Christian wives. I thought that so long as they did not marry in a Christian ceremony it was acceptable. The rabbi tells me that this is no longer so."

"They have rules about such things?" I try to understand what he is saying and the meaning for me in his words all at once.

"You are so dear to me," Mr. Serle says quietly. I can barely hear him. "I am afraid to see you anymore. If it cannot be, I must stop now before I hurt you."

Tears well in my eyes. I cannot speak for the pain of it.

"I am so sorry," he says.

"You told me before you would not marry out of your religion," I say. "Truly, I did not expect it. Only, I cannot bear the thought that we cannot be friends. Why not?"

"My dear, I am not strong enough," Mr. Serle says sadly. "At least, not now. That you can think of me as a friend comforts me. It tells me that I have not misled you, not hurt you."

"No," I say. "You have not misled me about marriage." I have to stop because the tears choke my voice. I grope in my pocket, and Mr. Serle, understanding my need, silently hands his handkerchief across the table to me. I think then of the day my brother sailed and Mr. Serle giving me his handkerchief to wave and blotting my tears after. Like a child given one spoonful of honey for its bread, I have had my share of goodness.

"I am sorry," he says again.

I shake my head. Now I am angry at him. "You were wrong to tell me. You are throwing away an innocent love. You have destroyed everything."

The taste is bitter almonds in my mouth. To know that he has thought of me and that his religion tells him he must not—it is too much. Why could he not let us go on as we were? Talking to him in the market gave joy to my days. I do not want him to turn away.

"You were wrong to tell me," I repeat.

"Wrong?" Mr. Serle says. He looks down at his empty right hand, turned palm up on the table before him, not at me. "I want to be honest with you always. The world does not have so many people in it that we can trust with our selves."

"Your religion must be evil if it forbids love," I say.

I feel a wave of anger at the world rise in my breast.

Mr. Serle does not answer me. There is a long silence. The half-full glasses of lemonade gleam on the table, golden in the lamplight. Mr. Serle is looking at me with a hunger and a sadness in his face that I have never seen before.

"Well," he says at last. "I am going to leave New York for a time."

"Where will you go?" I ask. My head aches with crying, or maybe it is my heart.

"I have a good job with the French ambassador in Washington. Not the chief cook, but a chief assistant. I need to learn again, and this is a good opportunity."

"You are not looking for a restaurant by a lake in the country?" I ask. Where has hope gone? "What of your dream?"

Mr. Serle shrugs. "I do not think that will happen," he says. "It was a passing thought. Sometimes we have to live in the light of day, not in the moonlight."

"Oh no," I say. "It is a good dream. I would give anything, anything, to make your dream come true for you."

"You are very good," he says.

Tears run on my cheeks.

"It hurts me to see you cry, *cara*," he says in a helpless way that is not like him at all.

"I cry more since I am a girl than I did when I was your nephew," I say, sniffing.

"O Dio!" Mr. Serle says. "Forgive me, Mina." He starts to rise and then sits again. He reaches in the pocket of his coat.

"I brought you something," he says. "It is a very small present. I hope you can accept it."

He hands me a packet wrapped in thin paper. Inside the paper is a length of green silk ribbon. It is not just any green but a deep shining richness that speaks of grass and sky and summer rain.

I look at it for a long moment. It is hard to speak.

"Thank you," I tell him. "It is a lovely present."

I refold the packet and put it carefully in my pocket.

"I thought it might suit you," he says.

I cannot look at him.

"Well, I must go," he says. "It is getting late."

We walk into the passage and stand in the door to the areaway.

"Good-bye, Mina," says Mr. Serle.

"Good-bye," I reply.

What can I do? Weeping is useless. I thought of him too much; I was glad he talked to me of his changing thoughts. Now I am punished. He must go.

Mr. Serle leans over and smooths my hair back from my face. He kisses me gently on the cheek.

"Be well, my dear," he says, "be well."

And then he is gone up the steps into the soft spring night. I hear the click of the gate as he shuts it behind him.

"Does my mother allow you to entertain your lovers in our kitchen?" says a voice behind me.

I whirl about, my hand at my cheek.

"Who are you?" I say.

I did not hear the street door open or footsteps on the stairs while I was talking with Mr. Serle. The person who spoke comes down the last step into the passage and sketches a bow to me.

"Jasper Linwood Westervelt, at your service, madam," he says.

When he follows me into the brighter light of the kitchen, I see he is a young man, brown-haired, well grown, and healthy looking with rosy color in his cheeks. His ears are large for his head, but his eyes are small and close set. He must be the son, on a vacation from his studies in Massachusetts.

"My uncle came to say good-bye to me," I say stiffly.

"Your uncle, eh?" He sounds skeptical.

"Yes, my uncle," I say more sharply than I mean to.

I am upset by the talk of marriage. I am upset that Mr. Serle is leaving, I tell myself. I am upset that he kissed me in parting. Mr. Serle's handkerchief lies on the table where I left it when he handed me the ribbon. I sweep it into my apron pocket, feeling the damp of my tears in it still. It has nothing to do with this brash young man.

"You are much prettier than the last cook," Jasper Westervelt tells me. "Although your eyes seem a little red. If your cooking equals your looks, I think I will like you very much."

"I hope my cooking is satisfactory," I tell him, too pertly perhaps, but I feel unbalanced. "You look as if you like to eat."

"*Touché,*" he says, and laughs. "Can you not tell from my gaunt face and hungry eyes that I have just arrived from Boston and have not eaten for ten hours?"

"Was there no food at the stops?" I ask.

"If you can call those horrid buffets of pies and ale *food,*" he says. "I wolfed down something at New Haven and hiccuped the rest of the way home. And now," he actually looks sad, "no one is here to greet me, and the cook does not care that I am suffering the pangs of hunger. No, she must bid good-bye to her uncle. Can you give me nothing? Not even a sandwich?"

"Of course, I can give you a supper," I say. "They cannot have expected you tonight. Your mother did not mention having a meal ready for your return."

"Just like her," the son says. "She has no doubt been busy poeticizing and has not read my letters."

His small, bright eyes are watching me. I do not comment. It is not proper for a servant to discuss her mistress's flaws.

"Would you prefer to go upstairs?" I say to this Jasper Westervelt. "Marie is not here, but I can bring you a cold supper of boiled chicken and salad if you would like something quickly, or I can make a sauce and have the chicken hot if you are not in a hurry. I will have to stir the fire up to cook."

"A cold supper is good," he says to my relief. I did not really want to build the fire on this warm evening. "Only I am not in a hurry either. I will eat here in the kitchen. That will save you steps, and it will amuse me to watch you prepare my meal."

He pulls a chair out and sits at the table, looking at me with an expectant smile. Here is a young man sure of his own charm, I think. And he is charming in the way of a well-mannered child or a new puppy, firm in the certainty of its own importance in the world.

"You will have to be content with the servants' cutlery, then," I say.

All the time that I make the young man's supper, clean the things away, and climb the back stairs to my room, I think of Mr. Serle. He wished to marry me. And now he is gone. If he had not wanted marriage, he could have stayed. I cannot sleep, and so I sit in the cool air by the window to write this in the quiet night. The world is not what I thought.

SATURDAY, MAY 11, 1850

The Westervelts are out tonight, so I have a little time to myself. The newspapers are full of reports of another great fire in San Francisco. Three blocks of buildings are gone. Many other buildings were torn down to stop the progress of the flames. They say there were deaths. I have had bad dreams all week.

THURSDAY, JULY 4, 1850

I have not written in my book for a long time. Tonight I took it out for a companion, not because there is anything important to record.

In June there was yet another fire in San Francisco, even as the rebuilding from the fire in May was proceeding. No letter from Daniel has arrived. He may well be dead. If he lives, the new overland mail service could have a letter here in a month. Of course, my letters to him may be burned up. Perhaps he is waiting to hear from me before he writes. Or then, he may be forgetting me as he makes his life in a new place. It is understandable that such a thing can happen. There are so many miles between us now.

Tonight is the birthday of America. There were parades earlier today. Even in the kitchen, we heard the band music from Broadway in the distance. Now I sit at the open window of my room. Here on the fifth floor of the house I see the stars, thick as sugar crystals on a cake, in the night sky to the south and the blocks of dim buildings, stretching to the sea. People are letting off fireworks on the rooftops. There is an incessant sparkle of light and the distant explosions of sound all over the city.

I bought netting for my bed. In the heat of the summer, I open the window wide for air and am not plagued with insects. Just now I read back in my book for something that made me happy, but when I remember the joy of finding Daniel the day the *Victoria* came into port and docked beside the *Cushlamachree,* I begin to weep. Perhaps happiness must be shared to be real. For me, alone, the thought of it is hardly different from sorrow.

I made a change that comforts me. My mother's ring with the red stone is in my chemise for the day, but I wear it on my finger at night. Before I say my prayers, I kiss my mother's ring and ask her soul to pray for Daniel with me.

MONDAY, JULY 8, 1850

Mrs. Westervelt and her daughter, Sarah, and Mr. Westervelt's mother left today. They went to the farm the Archer family owns at Blithedale-on-Hudson, across the river from West Point. Marie also has gone to her people for two months. It is uncertain whether she will return. She hinted that she may find a husband, that marriage is the real purpose of her journey.

Bridget and I are left here to run this house. I cook breakfast and dinner Monday through Friday and then just breakfast on Saturday for Mr. Westervelt and his son, Jasper, who has finished his school and is working with his father now. They join the others in the country Saturday afternoon and Sunday. Jacob continues to come in to regulate the boiler for hot water. He is more taciturn and grumpy even than usual because he is on reduced wages for July and August.

When Mr. Westervelt told me about the summer arrangement, I explained to him that if Bridget and I are at full wages, we would work to stock the pantry with preserves, jams, and pickles against the winter. If he wished us to take reduced wages, I would give my extra time to my friend Miss Corbett and earn money by sewing. It is a matter of saving money for wages now or saving money for food later, I said.

Mr. Westervelt seemed startled that I had such a clear argument to make. He seemed surprised also that I mentioned my friend.

"You know a Miss Corbett?" he asked in a cautious tone.

"Indeed," I said.

I did not see that it was any business of his what I do with my time unless he pays me for the use of it. I was pleased when Mr. Westervelt agreed we should continue at full wages. Bridget wishes to learn more about cooking. I will be able to train her and build the resources of our pantry against the difficult times of year when fresh foods are scarce and expensive.

FRIDAY, JULY 19, 1850

I thought that the matter of the wages and of my sewing if I did not cook was ended, but Mr. Westervelt mentioned it again today. Usually, Bridget goes up to serve the dinner to the father and son, but she felt ill tonight. The heavy heat in the city is tiring. The kitchen was very hot and steaming also, because I had built the fire up and boiled a codfish. I made two sauces—one cucumber, one anchovy—for a choice. When Bridget said she felt dizzy and confessed that she had her courses too, I gave her a cold drink and told her to sit and rest while I served. I can help her with the cleaning after the gentlemen are finished and we have had our supper.

I washed my face in cool water, smoothed my hair, put on a fresh cap and a clean apron, and went up to serve. The soup was easy, and then I brought the fish and the plates for Mr. Westervelt to serve the portions. I was returning to the pantry to stack the soup service in the dumbwaiter when Mr. Westervelt called me back.

"One moment, Mrs. Pigot," he said.

Of course, I turned, met his eyes, and waited for him to speak.

"About your friend Miss Corbett?" he said.

"Yes?" I thought it was strange of him to broach the subject.

"Would your friend be a Miss Jane Corbett?" he asked.

"Miss Jane Corbett is one of my friends," I told him. "I also know her niece, Miss Honor Corbett."

"Have you known them long?" he asked.

The son, Jasper, sat looking from his father to me and back again. His close-set eyes give him a calculating, sly appearance.

"I have know them since I arrived in America two years ago," I said. "They are very kind to me."

Mr. Westervelt continued to stare at me. "Were you born in America?" he asked.

"No," I said. "In Ireland."

"But you are twenty-one?" he asked in a hesitating manner, as if he were aware that his questioning was strange in the circumstance.

"Yes," I said. I did not like to admit to my lie now.

"I see," Mr. Westervelt said in a vague sort of way. "And the niece is how old?"

"Twenty-two," I say.

"I see," Mr. Westervelt says again. And then he turned to his son and said, "Fish, Jasper? We seem to have cod. Let me give you the tongue."

I thought that was truly the end of it, but after I had cleared away the fish and then the cold beef and salad and set out a bowl of cherries and a plate of chocolate sponge cakes, Mr. Westervelt returned to the Corbetts again.

"Your friends, the Miss Corbetts, are well?" he asked.

I could hear that he was trying to sound as if we were having a normal conversation. Only one does not have conversation with one's cook during the service of a meal. Besides, why should he be interested in the Miss Corbetts? Jasper Westervelt seemed surprised by his father too, for he stared at him with a furrowed brow.

"My friends are well enough in this hot weather," I said. "It tires us all. And if you will excuse me, Mr. Westervelt, I will finish clearing and leave you to your dessert. I must go down to help Bridget. Please ring if you wish coffee or tea later."

I did not wait for further talk but went down to the kitchen. I do not want to think of trouble, but Mr. Westervelt's questions distressed me. The one person who can tell me if he is being rude or kind is Aunt Jane, and I remember her uneasiness when I first said the Westervelts' name.

WEDNESDAY, JULY 31, 1850

At last! I received a short letter from Daniel, written in late June. He survived the two terrible fires with only a burn on his cheek from a windblown ember. Guido DiRoma survived also and is well. Daniel did not write before because they were so busy fighting fire, sifting ashes for gold again, and then undertaking all the difficult process of finding materials and rebuilding their store. He has joined a committee to establish a firefighting company for the city.

The letter is disappointingly short; it is more a business letter almost. He says he intends to send a bank draft to me soon. I am grateful that he thinks of me. Only I would rather have the news of his life and his thoughts than a bank draft.

WEDNESDAY, AUGUST 21, 1850

Mr. Westervelt and his son went to the country last August 10 to be away for a week's vacation. Bridget and I stayed busy making pickles in the early part of the week. We were looking forward to a few days of ease for ourselves before the family returned.

The letter came by the early post last Tuesday, the 13th. It was written on Mrs. Westervelt's special pale blue paper with her initials *JAW* in fancy engraving in a circle at the top. I read it doubtfully.

Dear Mrs. Pigot,

The cook at Blithedale is ill. We wish you to travel here the day after tomorrow to stay for a few days. You will take up her work, so that she may recuperate. Train tickets and a schedule are enclosed.

Please advise me by note today which train you will arrive on. Jasper will meet you at the Blithedale-on-Hudson station, where you must descend.

Yours Sincerely,
Julia Archer Westervelt

The style seemed very direct for Mrs. Westervelt. Perhaps her husband dictated the letter, I thought.

I decided that the earliest train would be the best and posted back a note accordingly. The journey up the river in the dawn light was very beautiful. I had a seat by the window and gazed out at the ships on the broad water and the ever-changing shadows on the mountains rising to the west. It made me think sadly of Mr. Serle and his books about America. Two years ago I might have thought we would be seeing such scenes of natural loveliness together. He might have read to me some passage that would help me see deeper into the beauty around me. Our talk would have helped me to understand better our place in America. It was a child's dream to think that I would be cared for so, to believe his companionship would be part of my life forever.

When I descended at Blithedale-on-Hudson, Jasper was pacing to and fro on the platform. He seemed tangled up in himself, agitated.

"Did you have an easy trip, Mrs. Pigot?" he asked, and without waiting for an answer, "Is this all your baggage?"

When I said yes, he seized my valise from my hand, and we walked to the area where carriages waited for the few passengers who had descended at the Blithedale-on-Hudson stop. Jasper led us to a gig with a pretty bay mare in harness. He set my valise under the seat and handed me up. I wanted to ask him if I might pet the horse first, but that seemed not proper for a cook to ask of her employer's son. Of course, I would have liked to drive too. I have not had an opportunity to tend or ride a horse since I left England.

Jasper Westervelt used the whip to set the little horse going at a fast clip. I thought he used the whip too much, but he seemed a safe enough driver, slowing for turns and tipping his hat courteously when we passed a carriage going toward the station. I could see that he glanced at me nervously from time to time. He made no conversation, however. I was glad of that, for the country was beautiful on this part of the river also, rolling eastward into farmland with orchards. We soon turned into a lane with well-grown trees rising up to shade it.

"What kind of trees are these?" I asked.

I liked their great trunks and spreading, upthrusting limbs. They were like arms reaching toward the sky.

"The trees?" Jasper Westervelt seemed to have his mind on something else. "Oh, the trees. They are elm trees."

"They are very grand and handsome," I said.

We drew up in the dooryard of a dressed-stone house with windows opening to a terrace along the front.

"I must just speak to the housekeeper," Mr. Jasper said abruptly and swung down from the gig.

He did not even bother to throw the mare's reins over her head but disappeared around the side of the house, leaving me.

"Sally! Sally!" I heard him shouting.

The horse pricked her ears and moved restively. I picked up the reins.

"Who are you?" a voice asked.

A stout woman carrying a flat basket of garden produce had come into the yard.

"I am the cook from New York," I say. I gather the reins. "I had a letter to come. Where is Mrs. Westervelt?"

"Mr. and Mrs. Westervelt and their daughter went to Nahant to visit friends," the woman said in an angry voice. "No one sent for a cook here."

"There you are, Sally," said Jasper Westervelt.

"Who is this woman?" Sally said in an aggrieved voice. "We will not entertain your fancy woman from the city while your parents are away, Master Jasper."

"Oh Lord," Jasper Westervelt said. "I was looking for you to explain, Sally."

"There is nothing to explain," I said. "You have lied to me."

"Wait," he cried. "I want to talk to you."

He ran toward the gig, looking very agitated and upset. The mare, startled by his sudden movement, threw back her head and sidled away from him.

I shortened the reins and took the buggy whip from its socket.

"I am going to drive myself to the train depot and take the

next train back to the city," I said. "I will leave the horse in the care of the stationmaster. If you try to stop me, I shall whip you." I looked at the woman, Sally. "I am no fancy woman," I said.

I set the mare going so quickly that Jasper Westervelt had to jump smartly out of the way.

If I had not been sorely angry and distressed, I would have liked the journey back to the station and the satisfaction of controlling a horse again as I learned from my father in Ireland. Centuries ago I sat with his hand over mine on the reins, although it is less than five years, really. Driving the horse brought his presence back and calmed me a little. As the road turned, vistas opened up. Down the river to the south, clouds piled above a purple-shadowed mountain that pushed its flanks out to make the river bow about them. On the water, boats plied their ways with white sails set or plumes of gray smoke announcing their busy industry.

The stationmaster did not seem to think it strange that I handed the horse to his care to be fetched later. I paced the platform and then sat impatiently on a bench until the next train down to the city arrived. Luckily, it was very quiet, and no one bothered me.

Not until I was safely seated in the car did I draw breath to consider why Jasper Westervelt had tricked me into such a journey. Looking out the smoke-grimed window, trying to let my heartbeat slow and my thoughts ease themselves, I puzzled over it. Truthfully, he has paid no attention to me since that first night when I gave him supper in the kitchen. I would have said he sees a cook, a servant, when I am in his sight. The only time he seemed curious was when his father questioned me about the Corbetts.

I thought about Aunt Jane's telling Honor and me she knew Julia Archer at school. Perhaps they were both in love with Seton Westervelt. Perhaps he loved Aunt Jane at first. Or there may be some family connection, which Aunt Jane did not think it proper to discuss. She is so private and concerned about propriety too. I should respect Aunt Jane's privacy above speculation.

Perhaps this does not concern Aunt Jane at all. Jasper seems very sly and childish. College men might be like that. Until this summer he never worked for his bread, and now his father employs him and still pays for his keep. Tricking me might be a prank to boast of to his college friends.

I was turning the problem this way and that when the train came to a sudden stop, almost throwing me from my seat. A female shriek farther down the car suggested someone had indeed fallen from her place. No one seemed to know why the train halted—and so abruptly. Across on the right of the aisle, a man let down his window all the way, letting in a puff of smoke and cinders. He leaned out but apparently saw nothing, for he closed the window again and mopped his face with his handkerchief. He did not know it, but he left a large black smudge on his cheek.

We sat and sat. No conductor or trainman came through the car to explain. I thought more about Jasper but could reach no further conclusion. He is such a puppy. It is hard to take him seriously. Still, I must think about resigning my position, I told myself. Aunt Jane makes too much fuss about propriety sometimes, but she is right that I cannot stay where I am not treated with respect. I stared through the grimy window at the weeds and tree stumps beside the train. Farther off, cows stood in a field. They looked peaceful—as if their world was through another window after the train window and the ugly slash of the line and embankment.

At last, the car made a jerk back and forth and a great blast of the steam whistle sounded. My window showed more weeds, more stumps, and then, suddenly, a woman, her hair wild, her dress in tatters and rags so that her bosom showed, gripped by the arms between two men. Her head was thrown back as if she screamed something at the moving train. It was just a glimpse as the engine gathered speed, and yet it was a picture of horror. I leaned back in my seat, my heart pounding again in my breast. Something evil has happened, I thought.

"What was the delay before the station?" the man seated across the way from me asked the conductor as he came through to take tickets after the next stop.

"A poor Irish biddy—came over on a boat just months ago,"

the conductor says. "Her husband and three children all died yesterday of fever, and she alone survived. She tried to throw herself under the train wheels."

"Merciful heavens," the man exclaimed. "Is she saved?"

"She is," the conductor said. "Workmen saw her and seized her from the track as the engine bore down on her. The passengers in the car ahead took up a collection. The men will take her to a mission house in Peekskill."

"Poor soul," the man said.

The conductor passed on. I crossed myself and said a silent prayer for the dead and for the desperate lost woman, left alone in a strange land with none of her own to comfort her sorrow.

Although the train was into the city before dark fell, it made me uneasy at first to go back to the empty house on Fourth Street. I had told Bridget she could go to her family for three days while I was away. She had been glad to go off with the kitchen leavings. I slept poorly Thursday night, but when I went out to market on Friday, I found lovely raspberries and peaches. Friday and Saturday I spent quietly by myself making raspberry jam and two kinds of peach preserves, sweet and pickled. It is very important to lay by food against such want as we knew when the potatoes sickened and died. Even though I am stocking the Westervelts' pantry for them, really, not for my own need, I feel comforted and safe in the tasks.

I was afraid at first that Jasper Westervelt might follow me to the city, but there was no sign of him. When I went to Honor and Aunt Jane as usual on the Sunday, I did not mention what had happened. Aunt Jane always asks so anxiously how my work is going for the Westervelts that I did not want to distress her with the tedious tale of Master Jasper's prank. Perhaps I do not wish to talk about it anyway. Aunt Jane and Honor will urge me to find another place, but I love the kitchen here.

I told Bridget when she returned on Monday all eager to hear of my journey that it had been a mistake of Mrs. Westervelt's. The cook was fine, and I had come back directly the same day. Of course, knowing Mrs. Westervelt, she did not question that, only laughed and rolled her eyes to heaven.

Last Sunday afternoon Honor and Aunt Jane and I went down to P. T. Barnum's Museum. When I arrived at Elizabeth Street there was a letter from my brother, with a message at the end from Guido DiRoma too. The rebuilding of their city is going on apace. It looks almost as elegant as Dublin or New York now, my brother says. Mr. DiRoma's message makes Honor smile. He may return to take up business in New York. His cousin wants help and only trusts a relative. Nothing is certain. My brother does not mention the matter.

After we read the letter several times, we fell to talking about the wonders of New York. Aunt Jane does not believe that San Francisco could equal it. I mentioned that my brother once promised to conduct me to Mr. Barnum's Museum, but we never went. Honor said we should all go out to see the museum and then have a treat at an ice cream shop. We took the omnibus down so that we would not be tired for walking all over the museum—

I stopped writing just now and sat by the window for a time. The moon is dark. Only the lights of the city illuminated the autumn sky of blowing clouds and faint stars. I must try to understand the world as it is.

Almost as soon as we had paid our fee and begun to look at the exhibits, I saw Mr. Serle walking with Madame Moses on his arm. He is not in Washington. Madame Moses noticed me first, I think, for she said something to him and laughed. He did not laugh at all but conducted her across the hall to speak to me.

"Miss Pigot," he said. "I am pleased to see you out with your friends."

He looked a little flushed. When he asked Aunt Jane if he might introduce his fiancée, Madame Moses, she said yes, with pleasure, in her polite way. I must have looked shocked, for Honor pinched my arm and whispered, "Courage, Mina," in my ear.

"You are engaged to be married, then," Aunt Jane said to Mr. Serle. "Congratulations."

The lady looks the same as ever, smooth and pale in her black dress and pelisse and black bonnet with just a little white lace set in about her face. I wonder that she does not celebrate her marriage by turning to bright colors. I would if I were happy.

"I am glad for you," I say to Mr. Serle. "I will pray for your happiness." And for my own peace too, I think.

Madame Moses smiles condescendingly when she hears my words, but Mr. Serle says, "Thank you," quietly.

I turn to the lady. "How proud you will be to take the name of Mrs. Serle," I say. "You will have such a gifted and kind husband."

I sound foolish to my own ears. How does one talk when one must be pleasant and yet would prefer to run away and weep?

Madame Moses winces at my speech, but not to call it foolish. "I will use my name still for my profession," she says.

I do not dare to look at Mr. Serle.

"I am sure it will comfort Mr. Serle to have a wife," I say. "He works so hard."

"He works much too hard," Madame Moses agrees. "I wish he would give it up. I would love to have him with me when I travel." She taps Mr. Serle's arm affectionately. "He even neglects his friends for work. Why, just before Benjamin went to Washington, Sadick gave a dinner with a musical entertainment after on a Saturday night. I sang, but Benjamin wrote Sadick a note on Friday, saying he had to work unexpectedly. And soon after that, he went away all summer." She touches Mr. Serle's arm again, and says in her ringing voice, "I missed him terribly."

Mr. Serle does not seem to be listening to her or, despite her touching hand, looking at her beauty. He is regarding me with a question in his dark eyes.

"A good wife must always be concerned for her husband's well-being," I say awkwardly. This conversation is a terrible dream.

"Who is your dressmaker?" Honor suddenly asks Madame Moses in a low tone. "She has fitted you beautifully."

Honor draws Madame Moses away, complimenting her on her parasol, asking her opinion of a case of seashells. Aunt Jane drifts after them.

"Now, as a singer of the top rank yourself, what do you think, honestly, of this excitement about Jenny Lind?" I hear Honor ask. "Is she overrated, as people say? Do you think they will be disappointed when they hear her?"

"Oh no," Madame Moses exclaims. "I heard her in Europe. She is an artist one must respect, although no actress."

"You are well, Miss Pigot?" Mr. Serle asks me.

"Well enough," I say. "You did not like Washington?" I ask him.

"It is not a healthy place," he says, "and also, I had not anticipated the pain of walking by the slave markets. I did not like the atmosphere of the city."

"How terrible!" I exclaim.

It makes me think of Phoebe to hear of slaves, but Mr. Serle is thinking of something else.

"You know I am still your friend?" he says in a quick, low voice.

I close my heart against the kindness in his face.

"You should not say anything to me you do not wish your wife to hear," I reply. I am both glad that he is here and disappointed at what he has done all at once. "It is not proper."

"Madame Moses is not my wife yet," Mr. Serle says.

"But she will be," I remind him, "and everything should be open and equal between husband and wife. I cannot be the friend of one of you only."

"I am not married yet," Mr. Serle repeats, stubbornly, I think. "And if I am, I will not give up my friends."

"I do not know much about married people," I say. "Only I do not think it wise to lie about breaking dinner appointments."

Mr. Serle seems to be studying me. His brow furrows, and then his lips curve in his ironic smile.

"I have no regrets," he says.

Madame Moses must have noticed that Honor has been edging her farther and farther away from Mr. Serle, for her heels click on the floor as she wheels back toward us.

"We must move on, *carissimo,*" she says, seizing Mr. Serle's arm. "If you have *quite* finished your conversation, that is. I want to see the freaks before we go."

"*Au revoir,* Miss Pigot," Mr. Serle says to me.

"Good-bye," I say.

Arm in arm they walk away together. I wander along with Aunt Jane and Honor, staring into glass cases at minerals from South America, botanical specimens from Florida, a miniature model of the city of London, and I do not know what all. I cannot help thinking about Mr. Serle. He does not really seem at ease when he is with Madame Moses. Am I so evil that I am glad he will be unhappy in his marriage? What do I want of him? The only question I can answer is that I do not wish him unhappy. And I am glad he is in New York, not Washington. Perhaps if he is finally married to a woman of his faith, he can be my friend. It might be like having an uncle truly, or a second brother. But Madame Moses will not like such a thing, I can see. She looks at me with suspicion. Perhaps she believes her brother's fantasies about mistresses.

Honor and Aunt Jane leave me to myself at first. When I lag too far behind, staring blankly at a strange, squatting, stuffed animal—*The Alligator,* it says on a card—Honor comes back and takes my arm.

"Come, Mina," she says. "Unless you are determined to go stare at the snake woman and the man with no head, it is time to go to an ice cream parlor for refreshment. Aunt Jane is tired, I think."

I am surprised—when we are seated together in the kind of respectable place that women together can patronize—to find that Aunt Jane is quite agitated.

"Men are terrible," she says. "It is so unfair."

She takes off her gloves and twists her hands together as if they pain her.

"Perhaps he is in love," Honor says, but she sounds doubtful.

"Why are men terrible?" I ask.

I feel very cold suddenly. Is Mr. Serle just "men"?

"So selfish," Aunt Jane says.

She might burst into tears, I think. If she begins to cry, I will not be able to stop myself from joining her.

Poor Honor. She tries to soothe Aunt Jane and to help us

both keep our composure. She takes Aunt Jane's hand in hers to still her movements. When the waiter arrives, we both say we want nothing, but Honor prevails on us to order tea and cakes, at least.

"I will have a vanilla ice," she says. And when the waiter goes, she adds, "I see no reason for an engagement—even an ill-considered engagement—to spoil our outing."

"We should be happy for the happiness of others," I say.

I sound entirely insincere to my own ears.

Honor smiles at me. "Very good, Mina," she says. "I do not think you will lose your friend. I have a feeling about it."

"I would not mind his marriage," I say. "Indeed, I could truly be glad if I would gain another friend by it."

The waiter returns to set down the tea things and Honor's ice. There is a silence while we are served. Aunt Jane pours tea for us. She is calmer now. The ritual of the table soothes her. Honor picks up her spoon. I break a morsel of cake to taste it, but the crumb is dust in my mouth.

"I wish Madame Moses could be my friend," I say at last.

"She is uneasy with you, dear," Aunt Jane says. "Mr. Serle is so clearly fond of you. I fear she is a little jealous of his attention to you."

"A little!" Honor snorts. "She is eaten up with it."

Honor is remembering the protector story, I think. I would like to ask her if that might be why Madame Moses seems suspicious of me, but we cannot talk openly in front of Aunt Jane. She would be shocked.

"Why does he love her?" I ask.

"It is an old story, Mina," Honor says. Her tone is gentle, but as always, she does not soften her choice of words. "He wants company in his bed. His life must be lonely. Also, she appears lovely. She knows how to set her beauty at advantage, and she has the kind of figure that is very fashionable just now. Besides, she has a look of drama and passion. Men turned to stare at her at Barnum's." Then, being Honor, she adds, "I wonder if she is truly passionate or only enjoys suggesting that she will perform her role well."

Really, Honor thinks of things I never thought of before. It makes me smile and forget for a moment that I am sad that Mr. Serle has finally made his choice.

The sadness comes on me with great heaviness again as I write this. I must accept that Mr. Serle is lost to me. The talk in the kitchen on East Fourth Street is the last talk we will ever have as friends alone together—and that is not a memory of comfort. I must hold instead to the remembrance of the busy kitchen last March and working together—the quiet in the center of the storm.

THURSDAY, SEPTEMBER 19, 1850

Jasper Westervelt tried to make love to me. At first I thought he was merely mocking me. Indeed, I still believe it is a joke or prank with him to badger me.

His first attempt was this morning. I had been out to do the marketing and found that Mr. Larkins still had tomatoes, large, beautifully red, and dead ripe. When I admired them, he told me his wife's recipe for a tomato tart with cream and egg and nutmeg. I started a rich paste right after breakfast and was rolling and folding at my worktable while Bridget washed the dishes at the sink.

I did not realize Jasper Westervelt was behind me until he seized me, pinning my arms. He kissed the nape of my neck then, wetly, so that I wanted nothing more than to push him away and to wipe my neck with a cloth.

"Leave me alone!" I cried, kicking backward as hard as I could at his legs.

"Ow!" he exclaimed and let go of me.

Of course, Bridget heard the noise and turned from the sink to stare at us. She said later it gave her quite a shock, for I was turned and brandishing the rolling pin while Master Jasper hopped on one foot, attempting to rub his shin where I had kicked him.

"What are you doing'?" I demanded of him. "Why are you bothering me?"

"I am sorry, Mrs. Pigot," he said. He was collapsed on a chair by then, still rubbing his leg. "I could not resist an impulse. You are so beautiful."

It is very strange. He does not say it as if he believes himself.

"And you are insolent," I said. "Get out of my kitchen."

He looked as if he would argue with me but seemed to think he had better not. Because his eyes are so close set and small, it is hard to know what he is looking at, really. It gives him such a shifting appearance. I was glad that a thump outside in the areaway announced the arrival of the iceman. Bridget hurried to open the door for him, and Jasper Westervelt limped off upstairs.

I hoped that might be the end of him, but, like a counterfeit ten-cent piece, he turned up again. He entered the kitchen just when I was busiest before the evening meal. Again, I did not see him come in. Bridget warned me by saying in a loud voice, almost a shout, "Good evening, Master Jasper. What brings you back to the kitchen?"

I turned from basting the chickens at the fire. He was standing in the kitchen door with his hat in his hand. He must have just returned to the house.

"I am come to apologize," he said. "Will you let me come in and speak to you?"

"There is no need," I said. "We are very busy. I will accept your apology, and you can go. Ring for Marie if you need anything upstairs."

He turned his hat about in his hands like a chastened child.

"I should like to speak with you, Mrs. Pigot," he said. "Please."

"No," I said. I could smell that the tart was almost baked. I needed to look at it. "If you wish to speak to me, you must do so in the presence of one of your parents. Now I am truly busy."

I turned away then to take out the tomato tart. When I had a moment to look up again, Jasper Westervelt was gone.

Later, when Bridget and Marie and I were eating our supper, I asked them if Master Westervelt behaved so rudely before I came to the house. No, they said, but then, the previous cook was fifty if she was a day, and Master Jasper was away at his school and visiting his friends almost all the time until last spring.

"You must have led him on," Marie says flatly.

"Of course, she didn't," Bridget objects, glaring at Marie.

Since Marie returned from her summer journey, she has been very sour. She sees the worst in things and takes offense easily. It seems the marriage proposal she hoped for did not come. Bridget and I have tried to be kind with her, knowing that she is angry and disappointed, but she is not so easy as she was.

"And he never bothered you?" I asked Bridget when Marie was gone to take the tea upstairs.

Bridget is a pretty girl certainly, with bright golden hair and a graceful figure. She is appealing despite her chapped hands, which all my lotions cannot take the redness from, and the broken front tooth that spoils her smile.

"He never did," Bridget said. "I would not have thought it in his nature to prey on the servants. His father stays a gentleman, for all the grief he bears from his silly wife."

I sigh. I do not want to be driven from this place.

FRIDAY, SEPTEMBER 20, 1850

I sent a note up with Marie, asking to see Mr. Westervelt on a private matter. He sent word down that I should come to his study when he rang after dinner. I removed my cap and put on a fresh apron so as not to take the smells of the cooking fires upstairs with me. When the bell jangled on the wall at last, I went up. Marie showed me which door was the study, and I knocked and went in.

The room is not large, but comfortable and, unlike the parlor where Mrs. Westervelt interviewed me, not cluttered with small objects. Shelves filled with books line the walls. There was a red rug on the floor, two brown leather armchairs, and oil lamps lit on a table and on Mr. Westervelt's desk. A small fire in the hearth took away the evening chill.

"Please sit down, Mrs. Pigot," Mr. Westervelt said from his

seat behind his desk. He had not risen when I came in but only glanced up from his papers and nodded.

"Thank you, sir," I said, perching on the edge of one of the armchairs.

"What is it you wish?" he asked me, leaning back in his chair and making a steeple of his hands in front of him.

"I have a concern," I tell him cautiously. "I think I must speak to you now and not wait, but it is not a pleasant subject."

"If it is about Bridget or Marie, perhaps you should consult Mrs. Westervelt," Mr. Westervelt says.

He sounds uncertain. He must know that, if I have come to him and not his wife, it is some problem I do not consider her capable of resolving. I thought of Honor and how I admire her directness. I must say what I think and feel.

"It is about your son," I say. "Your son attempted to seize me and to kiss me. He came into the kitchen yesterday to bother me while I worked." I draw breath and go on. "I do not want Master Westervelt's attentions. Perhaps I cannot stay in this house."

"I would not have thought it of Jasper." Mr. Westervelt sounds truly surprised.

"Nor would I," I say. "Only it is not the first insolence he has shown me."

I tell Mr. Westervelt briefly of the letter and train tickets that were supposed to be from Mrs. Westervelt and my going to the country to find the family except for Jasper gone to Nahant. After I finish, there is a long silence. Mr. Westervelt's face looks drawn. The cast of light from the lamp emphasizes the dark circles under his eyes. He has dropped his hands, and now his right fist lies clenched on the desk in front of him. He gazes across at me as if he does not see me but something in his thoughts. Then he bows his head over his papers although he is obviously not reading them.

"Perhaps I must go," I say at last. "Perhaps it is wiser."

"I cannot wish it," he responds. "Since you came, I can bear the meals at home. There is order in your work and calm in the kitchen. Did you know that the previous woman would shout and swear at Bridget and Marie until I could hear her in this room? I had to let her go when my wife refused to interest herself in the affairs of the house. Your accounts are impeccable, your budget economical, your cooking excellent. All moves smoothly—and now this." He stops and is silent.

What did the previous cook berate Bridget about? She is always so cheerful and willing.

Mr. Westervelt hefts a glass paperweight in his hand and then sets it down. "Please stay, Mrs. Pigot," he says. "I will speak to Jasper. This behavior is not like him. I promise he will not bother you."

"I will wait another month to decide," I tell him. "Perhaps it is some foolish impulse of youth. Only, if he does bother me again, I must go to my friends at once."

"Youth." Mr. Westervelt somehow puts both sadness and humor into the word. "You are youth yourself, Mrs. Pigot. And younger than Jasper, I think, although wiser."

"Good night, sir," I say as I stand to go.

Mr. Westervelt rises also, as if I am a lady to be seen out of his office. "You mentioned your friends. Miss Corbett and her niece? They are well, I hope?"

"Yes, they are well," I answer briefly. "Good night."

"Good night," he says. "I will speak to Jasper."

MONDAY, SEPTEMBER 30, 1850

Usually I take my valise and go to Honor and Aunt Jane as soon as Sunday dinner is cleared. I go by way of Tompkins Square and pray in St. Bridget's Church, where I do not fear seeing Mr. Branton. I bring with me to Elizabeth Street such treats as I have had time to buy or prepare during the Saturday shopping and cooking. It would not be right to expect Honor and Aunt Jane to feed me as well as make me welcome in the warmth of their lives for a night.

Yesterday was a nasty, sloppy, wet day. I gave up on the idea of St. Bridget's almost immediately and turned south to Elizabeth Street. I spent the afternoon helping Aunt Jane tint fashion plates. She has another good order. Before supper we sat in Honor's workroom by the stove and warmed ourselves after the chill of the studio.

"I feel guilty still that it was so easy to give up church today," I say in the comfortable quiet. "I should not let bad weather stop me."

"If God wanted you to go to church, He would have given you stouter boots and an umbrella," Honor says. She looks at me. "I am sorry, Mina. I speak before I think. I wish I had your faith."

"But," I hesitate in puzzlement, "you are a Christian, Honor?"

"Oh, I suppose as much as I am anything," she says.

She does not seem to care. She picks up her needle and licks the end of a thread.

"But you are baptized?" I am afraid for her.

"No, not yet," Honor says. "Are you very shocked, Mina?"

"Why do you say 'not yet'?" I ask.

I feel despair. Why is it that the people whom I would most wish to love in heaven are the ones not saved?

"Would you like me to explain?" Honor asks me.

She has threaded her needle and begun her seam.

"Oh yes," I reply.

"Aunt Jane raised me carefully." Honor sets her work aside. "I had a sound moral education. She read the stories of the Bible and the myths of ancient Greece and the fairy tales of England and France and Germany to me. It is better to be honest than to lie; it is better to be generous than greedy. I must respect myself and those about me and my country too.

"Some years ago, Aunt Jane suggested we might go to churches in the city to know their rites and hear their messages. We went to Trinity and to St. Paul's and to St. Patrick's also. I liked the music and the candles well enough. I admired the embroidery on the priests' vestments and the elegant dresses the ladies wore. The poor sat at the back of the churches. The sleek ministers and their assistants gathered in money during the service. I could not understand why they did not hand it out again to the poor as they left at the end. Then I noticed that the poor gave in money too—and the priests scolded them for not giving more.

"I listened to the sermons and the readings. I heard the well fed berate the needy. I heard virtues extolled but did not see them practiced. I could not imagine one of these empty men baptizing me, saving my soul. I should merely get wet and gain nothing."

"It is my fault, Mina," Aunt Jane said sadly. "She does not mean to shock, but I allowed her to grow up speaking her mind."

"You are a Christian, Aunt Jane?" I ask.

How strange! I think. I never thought to discuss such things before. My brother is in California. Mr. Serle is engaged to marry Madame Moses and might as well be in China for all that I will see him again. Honor, Aunt Jane, and Bridget are my only friends now.

"I was brought up a Christian," Aunt Jane says calmly. "If it makes you feel better, Mina, I was baptized as an infant. I do not remember, of course. My mother said I was very good and did not cry when I was sprinkled with the holy water."

Honor picked up her work, and now she points her needle at me. "You are a picture, Mina," she says. "You look so relieved that one of us at least is not doomed to hell."

"Oh no, I pray it would not be hell," I say. "Not good people. It would be purgatory. They say only those baptized in the Catholic faith go direct to heaven."

"Would it upset you very much to know that I do not care for such things anymore?" Aunt Jane asks me.

"But why?" I wonder.

"I will tell you a little of my life," Aunt Jane says. "I know you are a kind girl and will not judge harshly."

"I will try to understand," I say.

"Listen, then," Aunt Jane says.

Honor sets down her sewing again and looks attentive. Her lips part a little. It seems that she is listening too for something Aunt Jane has not said before.

"I was brought up in a Christian family here in this city," Aunt Jane says. There is a long pause. She swallows and goes on. "After my father died, my mother and I were alone." She stops again.

"But you had a brother?" I am puzzled.

"Oh yes," Aunt Jane says. "I had a brother, but he and his wife lived in another place quite far from here, in . . . in Hartford, Connecticut."

She stops, and there is quiet. Honor looks down at her own idle hands in her lap and then at the picture of her parents in its place on the table. Her lips are set in sadness.

"Something bad happened in my life. I could not find a way to prevent it." Aunt Jane's pretty face looks as if it will crumple into tears.

I want to ease her pain and Honor's too.

"Honor's parents died?" I ask.

Perhaps if I say it, she will know she is not so alone.

Aunt Jane nods. "Death," she says. "Terrible death. In my grief I sought counsel of the minister of our church. I sought counsel and help and found nothing to sustain me. Nothing. I was more alone than before."

"I wonder—" I begin and then stop. I have no right to question.

A log cracks in the grate. Honor has begun to work again, and her needle flashes through the pink satin flounce she is hemming.

Aunt Jane continues. "You will tell me that one man is not the church, one man is not the voice of God. Only when I tried to pray after that, the cold speech of the man, condemning my weakness, interposed itself between me and God. I could not pray. I could not feel comfort. My faith was gone. To the pain of sorrow was added another depth of pain. When the responsibility of Honor came to me, I decided that her religion must be her choice. By the time she was twelve, she knew the principles of Christianity. If she is baptized, it will be of her own free will."

"And will you?" I ask Honor.

"Not yet," she says. "I am twenty-two now and I have not felt a need yet."

"But what if you marry?" I ask. "You husband might wish you to share his faith."

"My husband must take me as I am or not at all," Honor says. "I do not want a husband who would force my soul."

"Oh," I say. Actually, I am relieved. She believes she has a soul. "But should not children be taught to pray by their mother?"

"Some children seem happy so," Honor admits, "but my mother never made me pray, and I find myself happy."

She must see that I am pained, for she says, "If I married a man who had faith and he wished for us to teach our children kindly, I should not object."

Aunt Jane says quietly, "You do not think us evil, do you, Mina?"

"Not at all," I say. "I am only sorry for your pain and that you do not have the comfort of prayer."

"And prayer truly comforts you?" Honor asks in her honest way.

I tell them of praying with Mr. Serle, each in our own way, during the storm on the ocean when we were cooped below in the ship *Victoria*.

"Truly it comforted me," I say.

Honor regards me with curiosity in her wide gray eyes. "If you knew that you could be in your hell together with Mr. Serle, would you give up heaven for him, Mina?"

I am silent then. "I do not know," I say at last.

There is a long silence. I hear the rain tap at the window and the wind vibrate in the stovepipe.

I sigh and turn the subject. "Mr. Westervelt asked after you, Aunt Jane. He heard me mention my friends the Miss Corbetts, and he asked if you are well."

Aunt Jane gasps. "He knows you know us?"

"Indeed," I say. "As I said, he asked if you are well."

"What did you say?" Aunt Jane asks.

Her face turns white as fresh snow and then suffuses with pink as bright as the flounce Honor hems.

"I said yes, you are well," I tell her. "I did not think it proper to say more."

"Thank you," Aunt Jane replies.

There is a pause. Perhaps I should not have mentioned Mr. Westervelt's inquiry.

"I would not like Julia Archer to know that I am fallen in the world since we knew each other at school," Aunt Jane says at last.

Honor purses her mouth as if she would comment but is restraining herself.

"I brought chocolate sponge cakes, Aunt Jane," I say. "And I made a fish pie to eat first. I will warm it in the Dutch oven now so we can have our supper."

Later, as I was falling asleep beside Honor, a very wicked thought startled me into wakefulness again. If Mr. Serle lost his faith as Aunt Jane did, he could allow himself to love me instead of marrying Anna Moses. I tried to push away the terrible idea all day today as I worked. Now I admit my evil to my book and banish it too. I care for Mr. Serle as he is. He might become a person I could not love if he changed in that way. Life is very cruel.

WEDNESDAY, OCTOBER 23, 1850

Mr. Westervelt must have had an impression on his son when he spoke to him. Jasper Westervelt has not returned to bother me. Indeed, I have not seen him since the day he came into the kitchen in September, only heard his voice a few times in the hall.

There has been no letter from Daniel, although I have written to him twice.

The autumn weather here is very beautiful and clear. The newspapers are full of the anger in our northern states against the Fugitive Slave Law. I had a terrible dream in which Phoebe was held in chains that weighed her down so she could not walk. I could not go to her because two men gripped my arms.

"You must forget her," they said. "We are taking you to the mission house. You will be punished there for losing your family."

I woke in the dark with my heart pounding in my chest.

THURSDAY, NOVEMBER 21, 1850

The warm days of autumn are past, and winter winds whirl dead leaves and dirt into the areaway outside the kitchen windows. On Tuesday morning Marie and Bridget and I had eaten breakfast and were busy with our tasks. I was setting out the ingredients and utensils to make almond macaroons. Pounding almonds in the mortar is a warm thing to do on a chilly morning, and, besides, my tins of cakes and cookies are almost empty and need replenishing.

A thump at the door to the areaway signaled that the iceman had come, and Bridget hurried to let him in. I heard her voice saying that yes, this is the Westervelt house. I paused with the pestle in my hand to see who the new man might be and to ask if Pat is ill.

"*Dio in cièlo!* Miss Mina Pigot!" exclaimed a familiar voice.

"Guido DiRoma!" I said, dropping the pestle and flying to him. "What are you doing here? Where is my brother?"

My heart was beating so that I could hardly speak clearly.

"A moment," he says as if he too is breathless. "A moment. Let me put the ice where it belongs."

I hurry to show this wondrous apparition the cold pantry. I hover about him like a fluttering finch above a sunflower ripe with nourishing seed. Guido wears the rubber apron of an iceman and carries a great block of the stuff in an iron tongs. He puts the ice into our modern ice chest and—perhaps to hide his feeling— stoops to admire its convenient drain.

"Please, Mr. DiRoma, please!" Hungry for his news, I pull him back into the kitchen. "When did you return? What of Daniel? Can you sit a moment and talk to me?"

"Willingly," he says, turning the warmth of his smile to me, and—now he is free of the ice—planting a smacking kiss on my cheek.

"Let me fetch some tea," Bridget says eagerly.

My eyes brimming with the tears of sudden happiness, I introduce her. I can see that she considers Mr. DiRoma handsome, because she suddenly puts her hand up to her mouth to hide her broken tooth. He certainly looks well. His eyes are bright and clear and his skin still brown from his voyage. He appears stronger than ever with his broad shoulders and his sturdy legs under the great apron. His manner is as easy and courteous as I remember it.

As we sit and drink our tea, I calm my quivering heart. Mr. DiRoma tells me that he left Daniel in good health six weeks ago, that he made an easy voyage back, that he wishes to stay in New

York. He has used some of his fortune from California to become half partner in his cousin's business. That is why he is learning the delivery routes, and looking at customers' kitchens, and thinking how to make the company stronger. They may wish to sell ice chests as well as ice.

"But why did you not let us know you are here?" I ask.

Mr. DiRoma looks abashed. He makes a circle on the table with his forefinger. "I have been working on a letter for a week," he says. "Without Daniel I am very uncertain of my words. I did not want to embarrass myself before you and the Miss Corbetts."

"But Mr. Serle would help you," I say.

Mr. DiRoma makes a comical face. "I searched for him the day after I returned," he says. "I found him at Crosby Street with the lovely Madame Moses. It was a poor time for conversation. I will see him alone some evening soon. Perhaps we will eat together at an oyster house, or I will invite him to my cousin's home."

"I am sorry," I say.

It seems wrong of Mr. Serle to let Madame Moses separate him from his friend.

"I have a letter for you from your brother," Mr. DiRoma says, "and gifts for you and the Miss Corbetts too. It is all at my cousin's house. I had decided to call at Elizabeth Street, not try to write. Can I call on Sunday? Will you be there?"

Of course I will be there, I tell him. I do not bother to say I will ask Aunt Jane about the day and send a note. It would be cruel to us all not to welcome him as soon as possible. Unwilling to let him go, I walk out with Mr. DiRoma to the street and see his great horse that pulls the ice cart. I caress its nose, and it nuzzles my hand. Mr. DiRoma says he will be delivering our ice at least once a week. He wishes to learn his new business thoroughly.

Before he climbs back to the driver's seat of the cart, Mr. DiRoma looks at me as if he wishes to say something.

"What is it?" I ask.

"Is she—does—perhaps—" He stumbles over his words.

"Miss Honor is not married or engaged," I say. "I think she will be glad to see you."

Guido DiRoma does not say anything, only smiles broadly and climbs up to his seat. I wish it were proper to caress or to kiss Mr. DiRoma. I am so glad to see a friend.

MONDAY, NOVEMBER 25, 1850

I sent a note last Tuesday to tell Honor and Aunt Jane that Mr. DiRoma is returned. When I arrived at Elizabeth Street Sunday afternoon, Honor drew me into the bedroom immediately to help her dress.

"Is my crimson wool or the blue better?" she asked me. And then, before I could reply, she answered herself. "The blue, of course. The gray gimp trim is exactly the color of my eyes."

Before I could comment, she wanted to know how Mr. DiRoma looked when I saw him and whether he had asked after her. As I was assuring her that he looked very well and in health, she was already inquiring about how long he plans to stay in New York, whether he likes New York better than California, what news he brought of Daniel, and many other questions that I could not answer. And then, when the knock came on the door, I had to almost drag her out to answer it.

Mr. DiRoma came in with his arms loaded with parcels. When he had set them down and greeted us each in turn, I made tea. Honor sat speechless. She gazed at Mr. DiRoma with her lips parted and her eyes bright while Aunt Jane asked politely after his cousin and the cousin's wife. By the time the tea was ready, Honor had regained her usual composure, and we sat and talked of Daniel and of all that the partners had accomplished in California.

Mr. DiRoma says he hated the chaos of the life in the west. "Too much whiskey and rum," he says. "Too many knives and guns. Everyone is a gambler. And many of them do not even know when they have won their game but play again and again until they lose all, as if that is their goal."

When Aunt Jane says she heard that the land is quite lovely and the climate mild, he agrees. "But they are tearing the land to pieces," he says. "Where grapes for wine and fruit might grow, there are piles of gravel, mud, and disorder. Sometimes they find gold, but often not. Where the miners have searched, everything is left ugly and sad."

He gave us the gifts that he brought. For Aunt Jane there was a book of views of California. For me there was a pair of gold earrings from Daniel, and from Guido DiRoma an ivory fan painted with a scene of a waterfall, mountains, and clouds. Except for my brooch, I never had such ladylike things.

"It is from the east," Mr. DiRoma said. "There are many such things from the Orient in California. Traders bring them."

Honor's gift was from the Orient also—a coat of rich red silk brocade, lined with gold silk and embroidered all over with golden flowers. Honor gasped when she saw it.

"It is called a kimono," Mr. DiRoma said, rather shyly, I thought. "Both the women and the men of the East wear them. I could not find any velvet."

"Oh!" Honor said.

I could see from her expression that she wanted to kiss Mr. DiRoma. I looked at Aunt Jane, who had knitted her forehead into a frown. She seemed about to say something about propriety and whether an unmarried lady can accept valuable gifts. The kimono looks very valuable.

"It is so beautiful," I said quickly, before Aunt Jane could speak. "It is a perfect gift for you, Honor. Only you could appreciate such a thing. Mr. DiRoma has a wonderful understanding of what will help you in your profession."

Honor reached out then and touched Mr. DiRoma's hand.

"Thank you, Mr. DiRoma," she said. "You understand my tastes perfectly."

Guido DiRoma began to explain to Honor how he had found the kimono in a shop owned by a man who spoke no English or Italian, nor any language that Guido ever heard. He showed us how they had to make a pantomime of everything. He made us laugh. Poor Aunt Jane could not say anything then. It was too late. The gift was accepted.

In addition to the earrings, there was a long letter from

Daniel for me. He talked about how Guido has been his good friend and that he will miss him. He said that the business in San Francisco is successful beyond what anyone could have imagined two years ago. Folded in the letter was a bank draft for five hundred dollars. It took my breath away.

"But this is enough money to buy a house," I said. "What will I do?"

"We have done well." Mr. DiRoma smiled complacently. "I have letters for the other business partners as well. Do you want me to take you to the bank or shall I ask my *Beniamino* to help you?"

"No," I said. "Aunt Jane will show me what to do."

This afternoon I took time from my work, and Aunt Jane and I went down to the Chemical Bank on Wall Street. It is a small institution, and I feel more comfortable there than in some great marble palace of a place. Now I have an account and a little book that records my riches. No one at Fourth Street knows. I did not take the gold dust or the money from my wages to the bank. I wish to keep them in my trunk until I see what it is like to have a bank account.

I have written to Daniel to tell him everything. It must be lonely for him now without his friend.

FRIDAY, DECEMBER 13, 1850

Yesterday was the Thanksgiving Day announced by the President for the country. I had forgotten about it until Mrs. Westervelt said that the family would have turkey for the meal as is usual and that her uncle and his wife as well as Mr. Westervelt's mother would join them. I served the turkey with a chestnut sauce and cooked a glazed ham as well. I am glad to be busy; since Guido returned and we have talked of Daniel, I miss him terribly. I remember my first Thanksgiving two years ago, going to church with Daniel and wearing my lumpy dress, no underclothes, and the shawl that was once Phoebe's—and being content anyway.

Guido called at Elizabeth Street again last Sunday. He

brought his cousin's wife to call on Aunt Jane. Aunt Jane and I were kept busy entertaining the wife and teaching her the English words for the tea things. Guido DiRoma and Honor walked over to the windows and talked more privately. Aunt Jane kept looking over at them, frowning and losing the thread of what we were trying to say to the cousin's wife.

I finally left Aunt Jane to eavesdrop on Honor and Guido and exchanged the English lesson for an Italian lesson. I have learned *tazza* for cup, *grazie* for thank you, and *grazie per lo biscòttino delizióso* for thank you for the nice cookie. If I should ever see Mr. Serle again, I will surprise him.

After the visitors left, Aunt Jane was quite cross with her niece.

"It is not proper to talk so intently in company with a man you barely know," she said. "I am distressed with you, Honor. It was rude to leave us with his cousin's wife like that. I am quite worn out with being polite to such a foreigner. Has Mr. DiRoma turned your head with that strange dress he gave you?"

Honor looked at me in dismay.

"Aunt Jane," I said, "let me freshen the teapot and give you another cup. You had hardly anything while our visitors were here. Did I tell you that I wrote to thank my brother for my earrings? Only I have a problem I did not tell him. He forgot that my ears are not pierced. Can you do it for me? It takes an artist's eye to be sure the earrings will hang evenly."

"I have a needle," Honor says.

Between us we turn the subject. It costs me the pain of having the earrings inserted, of course, but I wanted that anyway.

"Wipe your ears around the wires each night and morning with spirits," Aunt Jane instructs me. "Do not remove the earrings until the holes are quite healed. Tonight, be sure to wrap a cloth about your head so as not to get blood on your pillow."

She seems to have forgotten her anger at Honor.

While we were preparing for bed, Honor mentioned the subject again. "What is wrong?" she asks me. "She knows I care for Mr. DiRoma, that I am not light-minded."

"I think she is afraid," I say. "Perhaps you and Mr. DiRoma must be sure she knows that she will not be left alone if you marry."

"But he has not spoken of such things," Honor says.

"Not yet," I say, and we have an intimate talk about love and how handsome Mr. DiRoma is before I say my prayers.

That was last Sunday. This morning Mr. DiRoma made the ice delivery at Fourth Street again. I walked outside with him to give a carrot to his horse. It is a huge animal but placid in its nature, as it must be for the noise and confusion of the city streets. I thanked Mr. DiRoma again for his gifts and for bringing Daniel's letter.

"I was glad to see you all at Elizabeth Street," Mr. DiRoma said. "But Miss Jane Corbett seemed uneasy with me when I said good-bye. Is everything all right?"

"We have only a moment, so I will be direct," I say. "Are you courting Honor?"

The horse has taken its carrot and bumps against my arm to get my attention for more. I take the harness and pull its head down.

"Yes," Guido DiRoma says. "Yes, Miss Mina. You see the direction my ship sails. I like the spirit of New York, and I like this New York daughter."

"Then go a little slowly," I say. "Talk to Aunt Jane more than to Honor next time you visit. Be sure Miss Jane Corbett knows that you will not be between her and her niece, who is all she has to love in the world."

"Thank you, Miss Mina," Mr. DiRoma says. "I see the wisdom."

"How is Mr. Serle? Did you have your talk?" I ask, petting the horse. He is getting restless. There are no more treats, and it is time to move on with his work.

"The man is a fool," he says.

Mr. DiRoma sounds angry.

"A fool?" I ask.

"He talks of marriage soon. This Madame Moses has an

engagement at the Havana Opera next spring. They will go to Cuba and then to Europe for her work, I believe."

"But why is that being a fool?" I ask. My heart hurts. "If he loves her?"

"The woman is beautiful," Guido concedes, "but she wants an audience of thousands to adore her, not one poor husband. She will chew *Beniamino* up and spit him out."

"I am sad for him, then," I say. "He deserves love."

I know I must go in, not stand about in Fourth Street talking of Mr. Serle.

"Well, Mina *di mièle,* we cannot save him from himself," Mr. DiRoma says.

"What does it mean, *di mièle?*" I ask. "You said it before."

Guido DiRoma looks uncertain.

"I forget the English," he says. "Now I must go before all this ice melts. Thank you for your good advice about Miss Aunt Jane Corbett."

I think I will ask the cousin's wife what *di mièle* means when I see her next. I do not wish to think about Mr. Serle.

TUESDAY, DECEMBER 31, 1850

It is the end of my second year in America.

Guido DiRoma called on Honor and Aunt Jane again. His cousin and the cousin's wife came too. Honor and I exchanged language lessons with the wife, while the husband and Mr. DiRoma made a fuss over Aunt Jane. It went very well, Honor and I think.

I had a busy Christmas season. The Westervelts had friends to stay and gave a dinner party for ten and then—a different night—an evening party. A *soirée,* Mrs. Westervelt and Marie called it. Mrs. Westervelt takes French lessons with a tutor now. There was music at the party. After I fed the musicians supper in the kitchen, they sang an Irish air, "Love's Young Dream," to thank me.

I received a letter from Daniel yesterday with Christmas and New Year's wishes. He had my packet in time for his Christmas celebration. That I am well and contented gave him heart for his work, he said. I think I will ask him again whether I might journey to California to join him. I have enough money now to travel so far.

I set my pen down for a while and have just picked it up again. I looked back through my book to see if I have changed in two years. It is hard for me to see, but I think perhaps I am more sober, more content to be private in myself than I was last spring. I seemed to write only about Mr. Serle then.

I have left out so much of my life. I intend to keep a record of menus and new recipes, but then I forget when I sit to write. I forget also to record the changing rich assortment of foods in the markets, the many people I meet and their ways. Last month we hired Bridget's sister Margaret to come to help in the house and the kitchen. She and Bridget share a room. Marie has her own room now, which seems to please her, although she often seems bitter and unhappy still. The Westervelts do not appear contented, but the atmosphere in the kitchen and here on the fifth floor is pleasant enough. There are so many kind people at the market too. Young Mr. Woodcock, the butcher's handsome son, hurries to serve me at the butcher's stall and then is tongue-tied when I comment on the weather or the choice of meats.

I see I never wrote about the day Mrs. Westervelt actually asked for a particular dish—a calf's head, because she heard that it is genteel at a dinner party. When it was delivered and I unwrapped the brown paper, I burst into tears. Bridget had to help me clean and prepare it because I could not bear to look at the poor thing and kept trying to work with my eyes closed.

I never wrote about the Sunday in October when Honor and Aunt Jane and I wrapped up warm and took the ferry back and forth across the river so that we could admire the blazing red and yellow autumn colors of the trees up the New Jersey shore.

Life pours its bounty and its beauty as well as its sadness over us every day.

At about three o'clock yesterday, the bell rang for Marie, who was in the kitchen polishing silver. She rinsed her hands and went up. When she came down again, her lips were pressed tight together, and she had an angry look in her dark eyes.

"What is the trouble?" I asked her.

"Madame wants tea sent up in half an hour," she said, "and I am to put on a clean apron and be upstairs to open the door. She is expecting a guest."

That sounded ordinary enough to me. Mrs. Westervelt rarely seems to think that advance notice of guests for tea is necessary.

"I have cake left from yesterday," I say. "Did she say how many guests she expects? Did she say black tea or green?"

"Just one guest," Marie says. And then she shakes her head. "She is careless," she says. "Look what I picked up in the hall where she dropped it." She holds out a folded note to me. "Look at this," she says.

The letter is in a bold hand. *My darling Julia, your kiss yesterday*— it begins.

"I cannot read this," I say, handing it back.

"What is it?" Bridget, all agog with curiosity, is wiping her hands on her apron.

"It is not our business," I say, and Marie sulkily puts the letter in her pocket.

"It will be our business when Mr. Westervelt finds out his wife is unfaithful to him and the house is broken up," Marie says. And then she bursts out, "It is not right that some women have no one, and this rich whore thinks she is entitled to two men."

Poor Marie.

"How will Mr. Westervelt know of his wife's behavior?" I ask.

Marie's face contracts itself into deeper lines of anger. "She dropped her letter in the hall," she says. "I might drop it somewhere else."

"Be careful," I say. "No one loves a messenger who brings bad news."

Bridget nods and goes back to her work. "Come, Margaret," she admonishes her sister. "The turnips must be scrubbed ready when Miss Mina wants them for her stew."

"I will do as I think best and not tell you," Marie says.

"I do not wish to know," I reply.

Marie is angry. Julia Westervelt is unfaithful to her husband. Storm threatens to break over our heads at any moment. I wonder if it is myself or some care for Mr. Westervelt that I am thinking of. His gray eyes looked sad the night I spoke with him.

I do not know what Marie did exactly, but she did something. After breakfast, when Jasper Westervelt had left for the day and the daughter was gone out to her music lesson, Bridget and I heard Mr. and Mrs. Westervelt arguing in his study. As their voices rose, the sound carried clearly down the stairs.

"Paul Forrest is barred from this house, Julia," we heard him say in an angry voice.

"You are impossible, Seton," we heard the lady cry. "You are such a hypocrite."

"And whose fault is it that I despise my home?" he shouted.

"You never loved me," Mrs. Westervelt accused him. "You destroyed our marriage before it began."

"Enough," he said. "For twenty-two years you have thrown this accusation at me. For twenty-two years I have been faithful. Now you betray me with your pet monkey Paul Forrest. You are not a fit mother."

"Get out!" she screamed. "Get out of my house. And don't forget it is my house."

"Forget!" he shouted in a rage. "You remind me every time you have a lie to hide."

We heard her shriek and burst into a storm of weeping. We heard his footsteps in the hall, and then the front door closed hard. Bridget and I looked at each other silently. The dumbwaiter whirred, bringing the breakfast dishes. Marie came down the stairs.

"Did you hear them?" she said with satisfaction. "He has found out where she goes on Tuesday nights and whom she entertains alone in her sitting room."

"Is this house really hers?" I ask.

"Oh yes," Marie tells me. "The house and the money is all hers. He works in her uncle's firm too. He will have to sacrifice everything to be free of her."

After Marie goes upstairs for her morning work, Bridget and I talk with dismay about what may happen. Bridget asked if we can look for work together if we lose our places here. She seems very confident that I will have opportunities.

To finish the dismal day, I encountered Jasper Westervelt on the street in the late afternoon. I had been to the chemist's to purchase rose water and oil of sweet almonds. The bottles of hand lotion are low, and at this time of year we most need soothing creams for our hands and feet too. I encountered Jasper going away from the house as I returned, bundled in cloak and hood and woolen gloves against the cold. He lifted his hat to me in a gentlemanly way and turned to walk beside me. Of course, there was nothing I could have done but run to avoid him, and that seemed beyond foolish.

"I trust you are in health, Mrs. Pigot," he said politely.

"I am well," I said. "Thank you for your respect these past months."

I hoped my words would make a warning of the behavior I expected from him in this chance encounter.

"I need to ask you a question," he said in a low voice.

I think I sighed. He persists in wanting something from me.

"Ask, then," I said. "I make no promise to answer."

"What is the relation between you and my father?" he asked.

His question shocked me. I swallowed and tried to speak firmly.

"Mr. Westervelt employs me as cook to his household," I say.

"But there is something else—" Jasper Westervelt begins. "My mother said—"

He breaks off what he was about to say and raises his hat to a woman who glances at us with curiosity as she passes. Jasper looks very unhappy. I almost feel sorry for him with his sad-eyed father and selfish, unfaithful mother. I wonder if that is what he is trying to persuade me to talk about with him.

"There is nothing else that pertains to me," I say firmly. "You must ask your parents if there are family matters you wish to know."

"I thought you might help me," he says. "You and my father have some friend in common."

He looks sly, but his voice sounds humble. Perhaps I misjudge him because I dislike his looks.

"I am sorry, but I cannot help you," I say, more kindly than I intended. "I know nothing of your parents' lives except that your father likes shad roe. And now I must hurry. I am behind in my work today."

Of course, that I know nothing of his parents is an untruth. I know that Aunt Jane knew his mother. I suspect—although I would never think it proper to say so to Jasper—that his father's concern for Jane Corbett's well-being and her blushes when she hears his name suggest there was a close, even an intimate, friendship between them once. Also, I read the beginning of the note that Marie picked up. Perhaps that is the punishment for prying— one is pushed into a lie or else must reveal one's breach of another's privacy. I feel sad for Jasper Westervelt and annoyed at myself that I am in a dishonest position.

MONDAY, FEBRUARY 17, 1851

I learned from Guido DiRoma's cousin's wife that *mièle* means *honey* and that my name, Mina, means *mine*—not *mine* as belonging to me but *mine* like a gold mine. I suppose it is not proper for Mr. DiRoma to call me "Mina *di mièle*," and that is why he would not tell me what it meant. I wonder if he had not met me with Mr. Serle whether he would have chosen me instead of Honor. I cannot wonder much. The thought comes into my mind because I feel lonely. Guido DiRoma and Honor Corbett are so well suited. I hope they will feel that Aunt Jane is ready for change, and marry soon.

The newsboys are crying good news in the streets. The ship the *Atlantic* that everyone believed lost on her crossing from Europe is safe. I said a quiet prayer of thanks before I sent up dinner.

FRIDAY, APRIL 4, 1851

The Westervelts have made up their differences, it seems. She no longer goes out on Tuesday nights and there has been no more shouting these past weeks. This morning I walked out to the Tompkins Market to fetch the duck galantine that I ordered from Mr. Torrilhon for a small dinner party tonight. I went myself to ask how his poor invalid wife is faring and also to see if there are fresh greens coming in from the country. Mr. Larkins promised to keep a bunch of sorrel for me if he could obtain it. The shad are running already, and I hoped to please Mr. Westervelt with shad roe with a sorrel sauce.

Mr. Serle stood talking to Mr. Larkins when I turned into the aisle of produce stalls. My heart turned over in my breast to see him, slim and dark, his hat in his hand. Sunlight from a gap in the roof above Mr. Larkins's stall lights the rough curls at his forehead.

"Here she is," Mr. Larkins said. "And looking her bright self—she is like a flame that lends warmth and light to my dull mornings."

I was surprised that he would say such a thing. In the year and more since I have traded with him, he never spoke so. I think I blushed.

"She is a bright vision, indeed," Mr. Serle says.

He smiles at me as if it has not been seven long months since last we met. I do not know what to say to him. He must feel strong enough to be a friend or he would not be here, I think with hope.

"Are you well, my dear?" Mr. Serle asks me as Mr. Larkins goes to attend another customer. His manner is quiet, courteous. Perhaps he is trying to be an uncle now.

"Yes," I say. "I have not seen you since September at Mr. Barnum's Museum. I hope you are in health." I wonder if he is married. Does politeness require that I ask after the health of Madame Serle also?

Mr. Serle shrugs. "I find the winters hard," he says, "but I am well enough."

"You are working in New York?" I ask.

I feel a longing in my heart as I say it. I should so like to know that he is still near.

"I have been to the cities of Philadelphia and Baltimore since last I saw you," he says. "I will stay in New York now. I work on private parties for the Delmonicos again."

"That is different than I thought," I tell him. "Mr. DiRoma told me you were going to Cuba. He told me in December that you would be married soon."

"Guido said so?"

"He is your friend. I thought he would know," I say.

Mr. Serle flushes red under the olive of his skin. "He is mistaken."

"Oh," I say.

There is a pause, and then I cannot help returning to the subject that interests me.

"So you are not married yet?" I ask.

"No."

Mr. Serle does not look at me. He studies some early imported asparagus laid out on a tray. He stares as if it is a rare botanical specimen at Mr. Barnum's Museum.

"The lady must be disappointed," I tell him.

Now he looks at me direct.

"She is very angry," he says.

I wonder if she threw something at him, but I do not dare to go so far as to ask.

"Long engagements suit some people better than others," I remark.

"And you?" Mr. Serle asks. "Are you engaged?"

"No," I say.

"Mr. Larkins tells me you refused introductions to several rising young men," Mr. Serle says. "I hear Mr. Woodcock the butcher was hopeful that you would like his son."

I shrug and, in my turn, study the asparagus. I think my cheeks are red, but it is, after all, a chilly spring morning, threatening rain at one moment and then, suddenly, clearing to sun again. Perhaps I am the one not strong enough for friendship now. I must calm my heart.

"At the Columbia House Hotel, I once overheard a woman say, 'Liberty is a better husband than love,' " I answer.

When I look up at Mr. Serle, he is staring at me. Perhaps he is surprised that I am not crying or telling him I need him to solve a problem. But there is a hurt, not surprise, in his face.

"You should marry, *cara,*" he says in a low voice. "You should marry. You are made for love."

I stare at him, speechless. Have I heard right? I must have misheard, or he has thought better of his words, for he looks at me now with a kind of coldness.

"I have a favor to ask of you," Mr. Serle says.

"A favor?" I ask.

Anger fans a flame in the ashes of my heart. He will not allow love, he engaged himself to a woman just for her religion and her outer beauty, and now he returns to trouble me.

"I would like to bring Anna and her daughter to call on you," he says. "Stellina asks for you whenever she sees me." He has flushed red again, as he does when emotion moves him. "It distresses Anna." He pauses. "Even though she knows she owes you gratitude for saving her daughter on the ship."

"She still believes her brother's fantasy that I was your mistress?" I ask. I feel impatience now as well as anger. He made his life; he should accept it.

"The market is not the best place to talk of these things." Mr. Serle regards the asparagus again, not me.

"I do not wish to talk of these things at all," I say. "How will calling on me help anything? And it would have to be at the Corbetts'. Surely I cannot entertain a lady like Madame Moses in the Westervelts' kitchen."

"I will not give up my friends," Mr. Serle says. "If she could know you better, she would understand."

He holds his hat at his breast like a shield—as he did when he first saw me in a woman's dress. I almost feel sorry for him. I do not think Madame Moses will understand any more than if he explained to her that he wants two wives.

"We might come to the Miss Corbetts' this Sunday," Mr. Serle urges. He is intent on his own plan for me. "I remember the tranquillity of your life there. Guido tells me it is still the same. It would be good for Anna to see that."

I look at him in puzzlement. He only saw the Corbetts' rooms once. He too has his fantasies, I think.

"Honor has a great deal of work," I tell him. "She asked Mr. DiRoma not to call this week. I promised to help her next Sunday and the week after also. She has commissions for dresses and bonnets for Easter and one from a Jewish woman—there is a festival for your religion soon, she says."

"*Pesach,*" Mr. Serle says. "When might we call?"

"Not Easter," I say. "I will work that day. The Westervelts have guests staying."

"How many guests?" Mr. Serle looks suspicious.

His expression makes me smile despite myself. His nature is to protect, and I must love that in him.

"Just one couple and their daughter from Massachusetts," I answer him. "Mrs. Westervelt is very careful now to tell me how many guests are expected."

"Good." Mr. Serle speaks with satisfaction. "When can I call?"

He is inexorable. I feel his burning will, which consumes my excuses like kindling in a blaze.

"I will go to the Corbetts' the Sunday after Easter," I concede.

"Sunday, April twenty-seventh." Mr. Serle settles his hat on his head and takes out his pocket notebook. "I am writing it down."

"Yes," I say.

"Until the twenty-seventh."

Mr. Serle returns his notebook to his pocket.

"Good-bye," I say. He walks away through the market stalls and I stand still, watching him. I feel exhausted. When he is out of sight, I rest a moment, contemplating the heaped greens and browns of Mr. Larkins's vegetables and quieting the mix of love and anger and pity in my breast. Then I make my way to see Mr. Torrilhon and finish my purchases.

PART FIVE

THE ERIE CANAL

Almost ten months are gone. Today is January 16 of 1852. The day I saw Mr. Serle and wrote in my book was April 4 of last year. Even when Honor sent my trunk with my things in the fall, I could not bear to look at my journal. I finally opened it tonight. Now, on this winter evening in the village of Uncas Falls with the fire blazing in the hearth, the kitchen quiet, and the child asleep, I dare to think about my life again.

I feel confusion when I try to remember what happened and when. I cannot recollect exact dates. I think I must just set down events without worrying about what day was which. The truth of things is not in the calendar but in the feeling they leave in the heart.

I return to early April of last year. I saw Mr. Serle in Tompkins Market. I remember a confusion of hope and despair as

I watched him walk away among the produce stalls. He did not end his engagement, but he delayed his marriage to Madame Moses. He found the courage to return to me as a friend. I live still in his life, his heart.

The week following, the Westervelts began to quarrel again. Marie said that he found out she was still meeting her lover, Mr. Forrest, despite her sworn promises. Perhaps Marie informed on her to Mr. Westervelt. Marie certainly knew Mrs. Westervelt's comings and goings; she claimed that she could always tell from her choice of clothing just what her purpose was when she went out.

The Westervelts were careful at first not to quarrel openly, but that changed quickly. We heard shouting and tears at all hours. Marie reported that even with their guests from Massachusetts present, they were sharp with each other at the table. By then, Bridget and I had given up telling Marie not to gossip. We were concerned about our jobs. I knew I did not wish to work for Mrs. Westervelt if her husband left. She has no palate and no sense of the balance necessary to make a meal. But finding a new household seemed a difficult change to make when I was so used to the kitchen and loved it. Besides, the thought of studying the advertisements with their *No Irish* and *Protestants only* darkened my heart.

Things became worse the Monday before Easter. I returned from the market and set my basket of salad greens on the table. I had been thinking about spring and wondering what the visit of Benjamin Serle and Anna Moses would be like. Honor said she thought it just like a man to expect the women he could not choose between to agree over him. I bought a bunch of red tulips at the market for pleasure of them. I heard a noise and thought Bridget was in the pantry.

"Bridget," I called, "I found radishes in the market today."

"Mrs. Pigot?" the person said.

It was not Bridget but Jasper Westervelt who came out of the pantry.

"What are you doing?" I asked, annoyed.

"I was looking for a piece of meat and bread," he said. "I do not wish to wait for breakfast with my parents and their guests. It is too unpleasant."

He looked very sad and bedraggled with his hair uncombed. I felt sorry for him.

"Sit at the table here," I said, "and I will give you some ham and eggs and toast. I must just hang up my shawl, set my flowers in water, and put my apron on."

"Thank you, Mrs. Pigot," he said.

He sat and stared about him. Bridget had left the coffee from our breakfast at the back of the range. I took a holder and pushed the pot over the heat to warm again.

"Will you have your eggs boiled or fried?" I asked.

He was lost in some private dream, and I had to repeat the question.

"Oh? Fried," he said.

Young Margaret came in then. She fetched eggs and butter from the pantry for me. I had the breakfast for six people upstairs to begin as well as feeding Jasper Westervelt. Bridget too came in almost immediately. Her face had a fresh look to it. I think she might have been at the alleyway door talking to Michael, who delivers our wood. She seemed surprised to see Jasper Westervelt sitting at the kitchen table with his place laid before him and a mug of coffee, but she said nothing.

We all went about our tasks, of course. I served young Mr. Westervelt his food. As I began to slice ham for the breakfast upstairs, he ate silently, watching me. I had almost forgotten him in the bustle of setting pots on the range, putting muffins in to bake, and frying sardines, when he spoke.

"Are you related to my father?" he said in a low voice.

"What?" I said, pushing the pan of sardines to the back of the fire to keep warm.

He looked about the kitchen with an expression almost of shame on his face. Bridget and Margaret were busy at the sink with the water running. Marie was upstairs setting the breakfast table. He spoke a little louder and repeated his question.

"I thought I did not hear you rightly," I said. "Of course I am not related to your father. I never heard of him until I came to this house a year ago January. I do not understand why you persist in asking me foolish questions."

"My mother says—" he began, then stopped himself as Bridget left the sink and came toward the range with a clean frying pan.

"Thank you, Mrs. Pigot," he said in a clear tone. "I appreciate your giving me an early breakfast without due notice."

He set his napkin on the table, stood, made a sort of bow to me, and left.

"Well," Bridget says, "you must be glad to see the back of him. Why was he here?"

"He did not wish to listen to his parents quarrel at the breakfast table," I reply.

"I did not know he was such a fragile flower," Bridget says.

I asked Margaret to wash the radishes and set them to cool. They made a spring hors d'oeuvre with the leek soup at dinner that night.

We had a quiet few days of it then. On Thursday night of that same week, the Westervelts and their children and the guests went to Mr. Westervelt's mother's for dinner and the evening. There are no big parties during Holy Week. Last month, Jacob married the German cook two houses down, to my relief, and boards there for all his meals now. We eat more slowly and talk more quietly without him. Marie, Bridget, Margaret, and I had a simple early supper of bean and vegetable soup and bread and cleaned up quickly.

Marie said that she was going to sit and sew with her friend Camille next door. That family is out this evening also. I think Marie was trimming her bonnet fresh for Easter, for she went upstairs and then went out carrying a work basket. Since the Westervelts began quarreling again, Marie seems more cheerful.

As she was out the door, a messenger brought a note for Bridget from her mother. The youngest child is ill. It must be serious, because the mother would not spend the money to summon Bridget otherwise. I asked Bridget if she wished to go for the night.

"Yes," she said. "Margaret and I will be back by breakfast without fail."

I must have looked doubtful, for she cried, "We cannot leave my mother alone tonight if little Matthew is dying."

"No, of course not," I replied. "I was only worrying what the sickness is and if it is safer to keep Margaret here."

"My mother will want to see her," Bridget said.

"I would like to see my mother." Margaret speaks shyly.

Margaret is only twelve years old.

"Then you must go," I told them.

I packed cakes for the children and told Bridget to take the soup that was left from our supper in a jar. I tried to put the thought that the child would die from my mind. The memory of the mother nursing it in this kitchen, and Mr. Serle caressing its little face and smiling at it, made the tears brim in my eyes.

"Go," I tell them, "and send me a note if, God forbid, the child is not better, and you must stay longer than tonight."

"God bless your kind heart," Bridget said.

"I will pray for the child." I gave the basket to Bridget.

I confess my thought was selfish too. If they did not return in the morning, I did not know how Marie and I could serve seven people and keep the kitchen clean too. When they were gone, I gave my worktable a good scrubbing to calm myself. The tulips I bought Monday were going over, but I set the pitcher back on the table anyway for the last flaming brightness of them. Then I sat, touched the ring at my breast as I always do, and said a quiet prayer for the soul of the child and for all those that I love.

The day was warm earlier, but the night air had cooled the kitchen. I remember thinking I would lock up and go upstairs to write in my book. As I rose to close the windows, I heard a step in the areaway. Perhaps it is Mr. Serle come to find me, I thought, hope making sparks in my heart like the fiery color of the tulips, but no one knocked. Instead, the outside door was opened and closed again. It was Jasper Westervelt.

I was surprised to see him and also exasperated.

"What do *you* want?" I exclaimed.

He came in and closed the door between the passage and the kitchen. He set the bottle he was holding onto the table.

"Please, bring some ice," he said. "We will have a glass of champagne together and talk like civilized people."

"No," I said coldly.

All the pity for him that I felt in the morning was gone like a wave that lifts itself for a moment only and then disappears again into the sea.

"I am going upstairs to talk to Bridget," I lied.

"No, you are not," he said. He smiled in satisfaction, his little eyes bright with his pleasure at himself "I sent a note that her mother wants her and the little girl. I watched them leave just now. By the time they get to her home, it will be too late to return tonight. And I know that Marie is out too. You are going to talk to me."

I am dizzy with anger.

"You caused Bridget and Margaret pain for your own selfish purpose?" I demand.

He does not answer me but pulls out a chair and sits himself as if he will not move again. He is between me and the door. Perhaps it will be better to hear him out and have done with it. Still, I must protect myself. I remember when I was rolling pastry, and Jasper pinned my arms from behind.

I think of what Mr. Serle used to do as he ordered his kitchen at the end of the day. He laid his tools on a clean cloth ready for the morning. He honed his knives. I do that too. Of course, the knives. I will keep a knife in my hand. I look over my knives laid neatly on their cloth. I take the whetstone from the drawer. I can hone knives all night if need be.

"What are you doing?" he asks.

"I am sharpening my knives," I say. "I must be prepared for my work tomorrow."

"Oh," he says. He looks disconcerted. "What about the champagne?"

"I do not drink spirits," I tell him.

"But I want us to have a talk as friends," he says.

"We are not friends. I will not pretend we are," I say. "But I will drink some tea."

He looks very pleased.

"I will forget the wine and join you," he says.

That seems safer to me. It cannot be wise for him to be drinking a bottle of champagne by himself. I have a moment's work to stir the fire, set the kettle on the boil again, and brew the tea. He is silent while I make the preparations.

"Are you not supposed to be at dinner with your grandmother?" I ask him as I pour out the cups and set his before him.

"I pleaded a headache and came home," he says. "Is there sugar for the tea?"

"Of course," I say, rising and going to the pantry for the sugar bowl and to the drawer of the cabinet for two spoons.

"Let me help you," he says quickly when I set the things down and seat myself again.

Before I can say no, he has heaped two spoonfuls of sugar in my cup.

"What are you doing?" I exclaim.

"I am sorry," he says. "I thought you must like it sweet. Most Irish do."

"I am not most Irish," I say.

I think of pouring out the tea and making fresh, but I sigh and let it pass. I wish this interview to be over as soon as may be.

"Well, health," Jasper Westervelt says and drinks his tea.

"Health," I respond. The tea is so sweet that the only taste of it is sugar. "What is it you wish to ask me?" I drink again and pick up a knife to hone.

"Do you have to do that while we talk?" he asks. "I would like your attention."

He reaches out to set the pitcher of tulips to the side, so there is nothing but the knives on the table between us. A red petal falls, a curved boat of color sailing on the white table.

I sigh and set the knife down by my hand.

"You have my attention," I tell him. "What is it you wish to talk of?"

"Who are the Corbetts?" he asks me.

"They are two women," I say. "Miss Jane Corbett and her orphaned niece Miss Honor Corbett. And no, I am not related to them. I have known them for two and a half years. That is all."

"Are they society women?" Jasper Westervelt asks.

"Do Irish cooks visit with society women on their Sundays of rest?"

Really, he seems foolish.

"My mother knows a Jane Corbett," he says. "When she quarrels with my father, she says, 'You wish you married Jane Corbett, don't you? You regret her still.' "

He repeats the words his mother said with an intensity of feeling. I can hear the echo of her desperate tones in his sad voice. Julia Westervelt shouted at her husband that he destroyed their marriage before it began. I drink my tea slowly, thinking. The woman may be a fool, but her jealous anger sounds real. It must be right that Aunt Jane and Seton Westervelt had an intimate friendship twenty-two years ago. I think of Honor's picture of her dead parents. Her father was Aunt Jane's brother. It must have been terrible for Aunt Jane if she loved Mr. Westervelt and lost both his love and her brother who would have protected her at the same time.

I drink more of the cloyingly sweet tea and try to decide what I can say that is not mere gossip about Aunt Jane's sadness and yet satisfies this prying miserable boy. Even to persuade Jasper to leave me alone, I will not use the private feelings of others.

"Miss Jane Corbett told me she knew your mother when they were schoolgirls," I say. "But Miss Corbett is no society lady now. She teaches painting to young women and tints plates for a publisher to earn her bread. She mentioned your mother just twice in the years I have known her."

They knew each other twenty-two years ago, I realize suddenly—and that means Honor—and Aunt Jane lost her faith. *No!* I think, pushing the understanding away. I will never discuss such a suspicion with a puppy like Jasper Westervelt. I have said enough.

There is a long pause. As soon as I finish my tea, I will stop this talk. I drink and then pick up the knife I set down before. It is my favorite paring knife, and the edge does look a little ragged. I am about to take the whetstone when Jasper speaks at last.

"Are you my father's mistress?" he asks.

He seems to be speaking very slowly, and yet his voice is muffled, as if he is moving away from me. I feel a little strange. His question shocks me.

"What?" I say. "Your father's what?"

My voice seems to be coming from somewhere else, not from my mouth. Perhaps the soup I ate at supper was not good and I am about to be ill.

"My father's mistress," he says, drawing the words out so I almost see them forming in the air.

"Of course not," I answer.

I have something in my hand. A knife. How did it get there?

"You must tell me the truth," he says.

Everything is changing shape in the kitchen. Jasper Westervelt is staring at me. His close-set eyes are black pinholes in his face. They seem to be about to join to become one eye. I watch, amazed, waiting for it to happen. His hand, which is large and circled about by a white shirtsleeve, pushes a cup toward me. There is a spot of blood—no, a tulip petal—on the table.

"Drink and tell me the truth," comes his slow voice, drawling.

Truth, I think. What a remarkable word! It is like *teeth* but different. Are my teeth biting the truth? I want to laugh. Something is wrong with my head.

"What did you put in the tea?"

I must command myself and this boy to stay safe.

"Nothing," he says. "Are you my father's mistress?"

The words roll into dust balls in the corner of the kitchen, freeze in the ice chest, sizzle like spit on the range. The table at which we sit is growing longer and wider. The red flowers reach to grasp our thoughts. Jasper Westervelt is a white death's-head with tiny black holes for eyes and gray lips drawn over white teeth. I must escape.

I am going to stand, I think. I have a knife in my right hand.

I will hold the table with my left hand so as not to fall. When I try to stand, I stagger.

"What did you put in the tea?" I cry.

"It is nothing," comes the slow, strangled voice. "Just answer me."

"What is it?"

My own voice echoes in my head, which is hollow now. He is going to kill me.

"What is wrong with you?"

Fear clouds the room. It feels like running one's face unexpectedly into a spiderweb or a shower of dying flowers.

"My friend said it is harmless. It makes people tell the truth."

Truth. The word grows like a weed from his mouth. It is tangling itself about me like a fat snake. My chest hurts so. I cannot breathe. I will go and open the window. I must have air.

"What is wrong? Where are you going?"

Something is here. An evil thing is binding itself about my arm like a strangling vine, like a snake winding itself in coils. I have a weapon in my right hand. Mr. Serle gave it to me. I strike like a snake. I will cut the coiling weed away from my arm.

Screaming. The sound echoes until my ears pain me. If my head were not hollowed out like the calf's skull emptied of brains, it would not hurt so much. I must stop the screaming. I strike again. The screaming is worse now, and then, suddenly, fades and is gone. Silence grows like weeds.

I am having a dream. In my dream Jasper Westervelt has pulled up my skirt. His hand pushes between my legs to tear my drawers. His face is pressing closer and closer to mine. His two little eyes are merged into one black hole in the center of his forehead, and his mouth is large and pink and round like the rubber force cup Bridget uses to clear the sink when it clogs. If I can stab out his eye, I will be safe. He will not be able to see to find me. I raise my arm to strike. Now he is no longer a man but a one-eyed snake coiled about my waist. His head weaves back and forth, back and forth on the twining stalk of his neck. When I try to strike him, I miss and stab myself. There is blood on my leg and on my hand. I am dying. I have been tricked by the snake into killing myself.

"I will not die."

My voice echoes in the kitchen. I raise my arm. I have a beautiful knife.

Mr. Serle whispers in my ear. "You must cut; first separate the parts and then bring all the flavors together into one."

I strike. My blade plunges into the eye of the snake. Now I can sleep in safety.

Screaming. I am lying on the floor. The table leg rises above me as the cliffs rise along the Hudson River. I am turned to ice. My head hurts. The light and the sound will hurt me if I open my eyes. The snake has Bridget's voice now. A little girl is crying. I forget her name.

"Don't cry," I want to tell her. "Don't cry. I am saved."

"Blessed God, you are here," the snake using Bridget's voice says.

But the snake is dead. Really, it might be Bridget returned to herself. The dream recedes a little. I am in the kitchen, which is very cold. Someone speaks in a low voice.

"*Dio in cièlo,*" he says. "*Madònna mia. Che còsa è fatto qui? Dio in cièlo. È morta. È morta.*"

"Guido?" I ask. My lips are numb with cold.

"*Grazie a Dio,*" the voice says. "*Vive. Vive.* Miss Mina Pigot, Mina *carissima,* can you speak to me? *Sono* Guido. Speak to me."

"He gave me something in the tea," I say. "I think I killed him."

"Who?" Guido asks. "Who was here?"

I begin to shake with cold.

"Is he dead?" I ask.

The voice that is Guido speaks from very far away. "No one is here except me and Bridget and Margaret," he says. "You have a knife in your hand. Will you give it to me?"

"No," I whisper. "No. I need it."

The faraway voice says, "Think, Guido, think."

Something happens—only I am not sure what. There is movement, and a voice that might be Guido is speaking, and Bridget's voice sings softly to me or perhaps to the crying little girl. I dream of being on a ship. The ship rocks in the waves. There is a smell of straw and horses that is very comforting. I am cold, so cold.

When I awaken, I am lying on a bed with a blanket wrapped about me. Aunt Jane is sitting beside me. She has a basin and a sponge. She is washing my left arm with warm water. My right arm and hand are wrapped about with a piece of old canvas.

"Where am I?" I ask.

"Thank God!" Aunt Jane says. "You are safe in my bedroom on Elizabeth Street, my darling," she says. Then, "Guido!" she calls, "Guido! She is awake. Come in!"

How strange, I think, Aunt Jane never said anything but *Mr. DiRoma* before. And she is inviting a man into her bedroom. This is very improper.

"What is wrong with my right arm?" I ask them.

"You are holding a knife, *cara*," Guido tells me in a low voice. "You would not let it go. I was afraid you would hurt yourself—or me—with it when I carried you to the cart to bring you here."

"Oh!" I say.

The ceiling of the room is turning above my head.

"You are safe, Mina," Aunt Jane says anxiously. "Will you let go of the knife?"

"Yes," I say. "I think so."

Gently, Aunt Jane takes the piece of canvas from around my arm.

"Give the knife to Guido." She speaks softly, as one would persuade a child to take a poisonous berry from its mouth.

"My hand hurts," I say in surprise.

I cannot seem to release the knife. Guido rubs my thumb and fingers tenderly.

"Let it go," he says. "Let the evil go from you."

Aunt Jane massages my arm and shoulder and Guido my

hand. I sigh and lean my head to Aunt Jane's breast. When, at last, the knife drops from my fingers, Guido takes it away. Aunt Jane bathes my face and arms with warm water. There is a long cut on my left arm that she binds with a clean cloth.

"Can you tell us what happened?" Aunt Jane asks.

Her voice is drawling, slow and far away in the distance now.

When I open my eyes again, Aunt Jane and Guido are both sitting by me. Their faces are round and bright like two full moons. The room holds steady for a moment and then begins to shift. I shiver in the cold.

"I am poisoned," I say.

"Who did this?" Guido's voice is a judge and executioner. "I will kill him."

"Jasper Westervelt put something in the tea," I tell them.

My words make ugly lumps of ice in the soft air of Aunt Jane's bedroom, which smells of lilac bath powder.

"I killed him."

"Should I give her an emetic, do you think?" Aunt Jane asks anxiously of Guido.

"Wait," he says. "Did you see what he put in the tea?" he asks me.

I try to think. I went to the pantry for the sugar, but, really, I wanted to go upstairs.

"My trunk!" I cry. "Where is my trunk with my brother's letters and my brooch that Mr. Serle gave me? He will steal from me."

I began to cry then, fat tears that ran hot down my frozen face.

"I want my trunk," I wail like a spoiled child, and even Aunt Jane's arm about me and Guido's soothing words will not console me.

I am not sure what happened then. I slept, I think, and had terrible dreams again of snakes, giant weeds, tulips dripping blood, and Jasper Westervelt with one eye in the middle of his face and hands with glowing fire pokers for fingers. I was not cold now, but stifling hot. The tulips caught fire. The kitchen burst into flames. When I awoke bathed in sweat, Honor sat beside me, hemming a piece of sky-blue silk. The world steadied itself.

"Honor?" I say.

She sets her work aside and strokes my hand. "How are you feeling, Mina?"

"I am very hot," I say. "There is not enough air."

Honor unwraps me from the pile of blankets and helps me to sit up. She brings water to bathe my face and arms. She wraps my cut arm in a fresh bandage. The bleeding stained through the first one. She helps me out of my wash dress. The neck is torn. There is a great slit in the skirt and in my petticoat too. The petticoat and my drawers have bloodstains on them from a wound on my leg. Honor washes that and says it does not seem deep and has stopped bleeding. She brings me her flannel wrapper to put on and has me lie down again with just one blanket. Then she opens the window wide to refresh the room.

"Would you like a drink of water?" she asks.

"Yes," I whisper. Now I am shivering with cold again.

Honor brings me water and helps me hold the cup, because my hands are shaking. She spreads another blanket over me and closes the window. When Aunt Jane and Guido return, Honor is sewing again, and I am dozing in a dream of red boats sailing above the blades of silver knives, visible in clear water under them.

Guido sets my trunk down with a thump. He comes and takes my hand.

"You look better, *carina*," he says. "Not so white and gray like death. I am glad."

"Oh, Guido," I say and begin to weep again.

He pats my hand. "All will be well, *carina*," he says. "No one is dead. Aunt Jane will tell you everything. I must go to my work."

"Thank you," I say. "Thank you."

I hear Honor's and Guido's voices as she sees him to the door. Their voices climb and fall like ocean waves, lapping against a ship. I am floating on their voices. They sound serious and yet not sad. I am not going to die. They are happy for me and for themselves. Honor comes back to say she is going to build the fire and heat soup for us all. It is almost evening. Aunt Jane is sitting where Honor was. She holds my hand.

"He calls you Aunt Jane now," I say.

She smiles at me. "He is a kind man," she says. "He deserves Honor's trust."

"Thank you for my trunk," I say.

"I have your wages for you and a good character from Seton Westervelt," she says.

Her face turns bright pink. She sets a packet on the bed by my hand.

"Wages?" I ask.

I will never go back to Fourth Street. I feel such confusion. Jasper Westervelt has stolen my life from me. I have lost my place. I can never walk out to the Tompkins Market again, never be surprised to see Mr. Serle talking to Mr. Larkins.

Aunt Jane tells me the story quietly. They went to Fourth Street, she and Guido. Aunt Jane went to the front door and asked to see Mr. or Mrs. Westervelt. Of course, it was Marie she spoke to, who went away and then returned to tell her that Mr. Westervelt was gone to his offices and that Mrs. Westervelt would not see a visitor. Marie seemed very cold and did not ask about me, even though Aunt Jane mentioned she was come on business about Miss Pigot.

Meanwhile, Guido went to the basement door and talked to Bridget, who was so glad to see him and have news of me that she threw her arms about him. Bridget took Guido upstairs for the trunk and made sure that everything of mine was packed away in it. Guido said she cried for me. Bridget told Guido that Jasper Westervelt was ill and that the doctor had come and left. She sent up soup and boiled eggs and toast. The tray came back with everything eaten. She did not think he could be dying.

"Guido and I conferred then," Aunt Jane says. "We wanted to know what drug he gave you. It might require an antidote. We believed also that Jasper's evil should be spoken of. We went to Mr. Westervelt's place of business and demanded to see him."

"Oh," I say sadly. Even after twenty-two years Aunt Jane

knew where Seton Westervelt spent his days. I was right to think he broke her heart.

Aunt Jane's face is pink again, and her eyes do not meet mine, but she speaks with determination.

"When we arrived at his office, he saw us immediately," she says. "I told him of your state. All of us returned to Fourth Street."

"Did you see Jasper?" I whisper.

I wish Aunt Jane would tell me what happened to Jasper. I hear a screaming in my ears when I try to think of him.

"We saw Jasper," Aunt Jane says in a grim voice.

I flinch. What did she see?

"His father made Jasper come down to the parlor to us," Aunt Jane says. "He has knife wounds down the side of his face and on his shoulder. I hope he will carry the scar on his face for the rest of his life. He told his parents he was attacked on the street as he returned from his grandmother's house. He never mentioned you, alone and perhaps dying in the kitchen.

"With that fool Julia, his mother, weeping and complaining all the while, his father questioned him harshly. He gave you the drug hasheesh. Like laudanum, it helps sleep and brings strange dreams. Jasper had an idea that it would make you tell the truth that you are his father's paramour. He spilled out everything. His mother told him that his father is a hypocrite, because he has a lover too—the cook. Seton was furious. Guido had to prevent his striking the boy. I should have preferred to strike Julia myself."

I did not kill Jasper, I tell myself. I have that for comfort.

"Seton has sent your wages and extra for your pain," Aunt Jane tells me. "He was very insistent that you also have a letter from him attesting to your honesty and skill. He said over and over again that we must carry his apologies to you for his son's shameful actions. He expresses great respect for you."

"I did not find him a bad man," I say.

"I should never have let you take work with the Westervelts," Aunt Jane tells me. "I had a bad feeling about it."

"But I loved the kitchen," I say.

I cannot go back to the kitchen that I made my own place. What will become of me?

Aunt Jane begins to weep. She sits with her handkerchief knotted in her hands, letting the tears trickle on her cheeks. I reach to touch her hand. My head swims.

"I am sorry," I say. "I have made pain in your life."

"Oh no," she says. "In twenty-two years I saw him just three times, passing in the street. Always I wondered what he thinks and feels. Today at last we spoke. He behaved like a gentleman. Today eased my pain."

"But why are you crying, then?" I ask.

"It is just feeling overflowing," Aunt Jane says. "I am so grateful that he gave me Honor. Poor Seton. Julia has no love to give him and no virtue, and his son has shamed him. I can feel sorry for him now."

"He gave you Honor?" Have I heard right? Aunt Jane has confessed her truth.

"What have I said?" She looks at me in horror.

There is a silence, and then she swallows hard and takes my hand.

"Oh, Mina. I spoke without thinking. Seton does not know, nor Honor either. You are the only one except my poor dead mother I ever said it to. You must never tell."

"No, no," I say. "I will not tell your secret."

I feel dizzy. Little ribbons of thought—what Aunt Jane said months ago and the understanding I pushed from me as I drank the sugary, dangerous tea—waver in my head.

"Mr. Westervelt is why you lost your faith?"

Aunt Jane nods. "He loved me, he said. We were secretly engaged, because we had no money to marry and his mother disapproved. He was so poor, he told me, and his mother was ill and urged him to marry the niece of the man who employed him. I did not know—I did not realize I was—well, his engagement to Julia Archer was announced, and I did not speak. I felt such shame. It was a terrible time," she says, "yet how can I regret it now?"

She lets go my hand and wipes her face with her handkerchief. I am not strong enough to bear this secret and keep it from Honor. I do not want this. My mind is not my own anymore. My head aches.

"I will sleep," I say. "Please sit with me. I am afraid of the dreams."

"Aren't you hungry for some soup?" Aunt Jane asks.

"I am too tired just now," I say.

When I awaken from a dream of my dear dead sister, Eliza, holding a green ribbon in her hand, I have my night shift on, and Honor is sleeping beside me in the bed. My head is clearer. The morning is cool, but I am not shivering anymore. I find that I can stand and bathe myself and dress. The bandage wrapped about my arm looks clean. No blood stains through it. I go down to the privy. I hold to the railing carefully, for I feel a little dizzy on the stairs. The privy smells evil and so do I. My body is clearing itself of the poison, I think with hope. Perhaps it is a good sign even though unpleasant.

Honor is awake when I come upstairs again.

"You are up, Mina?" she says in a sleepy voice. "Are you well enough?"

"My head aches, and I am very thirsty," I tell her.

"I think you must eat." Honor gets up and puts her slippers on as she speaks. "You had nothing but a little water yesterday. Come to the other room."

"I am not hungry, only thirsty," I say.

"Nevertheless, you must eat," Honor tells me. "Aunt Jane worried that we should give you cayenne pepper and an emetic for the poison. I thought it better just to let you sleep. I think your headache now is hunger."

She puts on her wrapper. In her workroom, she rakes the embers in the stove to life, adds wood, and sets the kettle on. I find the bread, the crock of butter, and the eggs. We move quietly, speaking low, for Aunt Jane is still asleep in Honor's room.

When we are seated at the table, Honor leans to me. "I soaked the blood from your drawers and petticoat yesterday," she says. "They are clean. Shall I repair them?"

I shake my head no. "I will do it," I say. "Was there much blood?"

Honor in her turn shakes her head. "There was only one small spot on the leg of the drawers and another even smaller on the petticoat," she tells me. She takes a quick breath and speaks in a whispering rush. "He did not violate you, I think. The drawers would have been torn. There would have been more blood elsewhere."

I stare at her. How did she know? How did she know I fear what happened when I was lying on the floor, caught in the terror of the dreams the drug made in me?

"You spoke in your sleep last night," Honor answers my unspoken question. "You cried, 'Jasper, stop!' "

"I did?" I remember a dream of Jasper, but I do not know when it was. His hand groped between my legs, I think suddenly. I shudder at the memory of the feeling.

Honor butters toast for me and cuts it in thin strips. I study her. Does she look like Seton Westervelt? I am glad that she does not resemble Jasper Westervelt. Her eyes are set apart, not close, and her ears are neat and small. Only her rounded chin might be a little the same. It is terrible that he must be her half-brother. I will never tell. Her gray eyes are very like her father's, I think. She looks up and sees me staring.

"Eat, Mina," Honor says, pushing my plate closer to me.

I try. I eat half a piece of toast. I drink two cups of water. Honor makes coffee for us. I am glad she does not ask if I wish tea. I will never want it again.

"You said something else in your dreams," Honor says.

"I did?"

I think Honor wants to tell me what I said, but she is silent again.

"What did I say?" I ask at last.

"You cried for Mr. Serle to help you," she says. "You called his name. Would you like to send a note to him? Would you like to see him today or tomorrow?"

"I cannot," I tell her. "I cannot see him."

"Are you sure?" Honor looks at me doubtfully. "He is your friend. Guido will tell him you are not well, and he will worry."

"I cannot see him yet. I cannot ask him to come. You have work to do."

It is not just Honor's work, I admit to myself. I am too ashamed and angry to see him. Jasper Westervelt betrayed me. He stole my mind and hurt my body. But Mr. Serle did worse—he wounded my soul. I never tempted him. I asked only friendship from him, and he chose his religion and Madame Moses and threw away an innocent love.

"It is true that I have commissions to finish," Honor is saying. "I have two women coming today. For one I must just press her skirt and sew silk flowers to her new bonnet, but for the other I have hemming still not done. Even so, you can talk with Mr. Serle in Aunt Jane's studio. You must think of your own comfort, not my work."

"No!" I say. "I do not want him here. I will go out to church now, before there are many people about," I tell Honor. "I need to pray in a church. Then I will return and sew for you. I am better being very quiet."

"Are you all right alone?" Honor asks me.

I assure her that I am. Her customers depend on receiving their Easter dresses today.

The morning light makes my eyes squint. When I walk, sometimes I am all right, and then sometimes I feel as I did when I first landed from the ship across the ocean. I will go to St. Patrick's, I think. Tompkins Square and Saint Bridget's are too far away.

The church is more crowded than I expect. There is an early Mass. I am too late to go to confession before the service. I will have to come back in the afternoon. On the Saturday before Easter there are many faithful wishing to shrive their souls. I slip into a back bench, kneel, and join the prayer. It is comforting at first, only I cannot seem to keep my mind on worship. I keep drifting away into remembering the kitchen at Fourth Street, a pitcher of dying tulips, Mr. Serle's face tilted as he considers a problem, his eyelids hooding his dark eyes and a glass of lemonade, golden with a spray of green mint leaves, before him on a scrubbed table.

The music swells. The sound fills the church, making my head echo. The memory of my brother kneeling beside me fills my mind. If I turn my head, I will see him. Horror floods me. Perhaps this is a sign he is dead and his soul has come to warn me. I have the feeling of being unable to breathe. Hastily, I rise, cross myself, and hurry from the church. As I pass down the steps, a man coming up starts and puts out his hand as if he will stop me. It is Mr. Branton. I should never have come here. I pick up my skirts and run.

People bustle about on the streets. I do not want to go to Broadway and so turn into Crosby Street. I pass the house of Herr Meyer's brother, where Daniel and I attended the musicale years ago. I listen outside the house. An upstairs window is open. Someone is playing on the piano. I have heard this music before. I can hear Herr Meyer's voice in my head. It is a song, I know, but without words to it. The notes come tumbling past the curtains and fall about me in confusion on the street. I feel very strange again. I will go back to Elizabeth Street, where it is quiet.

I must turn at the next corner to go home. I come to a building whose doors to the street stand open. There are granite steps leading up to the doors. I can see that inside is a vestibule. A man wearing a hat and a great white shawl with fringes hanging down passes across the hall. He is carrying a book in his hand. He stands in the doorway. Another man comes to join him. They are getting air, I think. It must be stuffy inside the room they came from. The sound of a man praying loudly comes from the inner place. I know the rhythm of these words. This is Mr. Serle's church, I think in surprise. Only he does not call it that. I search in my slow, muddled head for the word. *Synagogue,* I remember triumphantly, that is the word he says.

I hear the single voice call out in the synagogue and then the voices of many people together. Only they are not quite together. It is all one, and then a voice rises above the others or says a word suddenly clear and alone, separated from the hurrying flow of sound. The volume of it builds and runs away in little ripples of speech. It makes a strange chanting. I wonder if Mr. Serle's voice is among those I hear. What is it like within this place? I wonder. Is it dark or bright?

The two men speaking to each other in the open vestibule of the house stare at me. One speaks to the other, who shrugs and turns away to go back inside. The voices are chanting louder now. They are one great sound raised to God. It is like the organ at Saint Patrick's, I think, and the people singing there. All over the city prayers are rising up like smoke toward God. I wish the sounds did not hurt my ears and echo in my head. It might be very beautiful.

The man who did not go inside comes to the steps.

"Do you wish to go in, miss?" he asks. "I will show you to the ladies' gallery if you like."

"Thank you," I reply as politely as I can. "I heard the prayer and paused to listen. I must go now."

I make my way slowly to Elizabeth Street. I cannot be standing outside the synagogue when the service is over. It would not be proper. They might think I came to stare or wanted something.

From the hallway I can hear Honor speaking in her workroom. One of the women must be here already for her dress and bonnet. I go into Aunt Jane's empty studio. She sees a student at the girl's home on Saturday, I remember. In the bedroom, I straighten the bed, fold my night shift. Honor has left my petticoat, drawers, and chemise neatly on a chair. The packet of money and Mr. Westervelt's letter lie on top of them. I open my trunk to put the things out of sight. I move mechanically. Nothing is real.

My valise was lying on the floor beside the trunk. I had to set it out to find clean clothes this morning. Bridget must have crammed my things together in great haste. Or perhaps I jumbled everything myself in my fumbling about when I dressed earlier. At this distance in time, I do not remember clearly what I did or how I thought. My body was no longer shivering with cold, but my mind was still frozen somehow. I found the green ribbon Mr. Serle gave me and his handkerchief with my tears in it and sat on the edge of the bed for a long time, holding them both, unable to cry or think or even feel properly. This is love, I thought. This terrible icy pain is love.

It came to me then in my confused despair that it would be better for everyone if I left them. Truly, looking back, Jasper Westervelt did steal my mind from me for a time. Mr. Serle will not suffer, I thought. I will help him by going away. He will not have to choose between love and his people. And Madame Moses will be glad that I am gone; her love for him will be surer. That will be my gift to him and to myself—I will never have to be polite to them again. Aunt Jane will not be embarrassed by the impossibility of my ever being a lady or worry that I cannot keep her secret. I suppose I hesitated at Honor—but then I thought that she had Guido. Why should they need me anymore?

I will find my brother, I thought. He will know what I should do. A sort of dreadful energy took me. I crammed the valise full then with summer clothes, my brooch, my green ribbon, and my mother's sea-ruined prayer book. I remembered to put my money and gold dust in at the last. I cannot have been completely mad. The valise would barely close. I wore my blue and white dress, my shawl, my gloves, my bonnet, and my earrings. I found a sheet of drawing paper and a stick of crayon in Aunt Jane's studio. I wrote a note:

Dear Aunt Jane and Honor,

Thank you for all your help to me. I am going to find my brother in California.

Love, Mina

Carrying my valise in my right hand because my left arm ached a little, I walked away down the steps and along Spring Street to Broadway. My head hurt, and I pulled my shawl up over my bonnet to shield my face. I do not want anyone to see me, I thought.

I was so muddled that I could not think which way was to the dock. I found a cab at a stand on Broadway and told the driver to take me to the Hudson River boat line. He had a kind face and looked quite sober. I recall that I thought I was being very clever not to look weak and foolish by asking the way to the boat.

The journey on the water brought me a few hours of peace. I sat in the ladies' lounge and on the outside deck for a time. It was crowded everywhere with people going to their families for the Easter Sunday holiday. There was food served in the lounge. It was rather coarse food, fried beefsteaks and sliced salt ham mainly, but a small piece of meat, some bread, a little cider, and the fresh air of the river made me feel more comfortable. I drew up my courage to speak with a stout, motherly woman traveling with her grown daughter. I heard them complaining that their favorite hotel in Albany was burned down and they must plan to settle for second best.

I told them lies about how I was a young wife whose husband had gone ahead to Michigan to buy a farm in country that is being developed. It gave me relief to tell the lies. I am someone else now, I thought, someone who might feel the hope of a journey toward love, not the pain of fleeing shame and sorrow. I asked about a respectable hotel. When the steamboat docked at the city after nightfall, the two women kindly took me with them to their hotel in the carriage they hired. I felt grateful to be spared making inquiries and being on the street by myself.

The hotel did not seem second best to me but rather grand. I did not care really. My mind was still frozen. I could have been a puppet figure, moving my arms and legs from strings. The ladies asked if I would take supper with them, but I said the truth at last. I had lately been ill and was very tired. I went to bed.

I dreamed in the night. I stood in the garden of a great brick house. Red tulips bloomed in rows beside gravel walks. The house rose high above me with windows lit by lamps within. I walked along a gravel path, looking for the door. I walked and walked. I found a porch with steps up. I found an areaway with steps down. Nowhere could I find a door. At last, after I walked many times completely around the place, I began to pull at the bricks of the wall. There must be a hidden, secret way to enter.

Just as I thought a brick moved under my hand, I was thrust back rudely. The tulips had grown tall into red-coated soldiers. I knelt on the gravel before them, folding my hands before me in prayer. Let me in, I begged in the silent voice of dreaming. The tulip soldiers did not answer. They had no mouths to speak.

On my knees, I gazed up at the bright windows. I could see inside now. In a room Mr. Serle and Madame Moses stood, posed like a picture in a frame. He wore his dark suit and gleaming white shirt. Jewels glittered at her ears and on her white fingers. I could see she was singing him a song even though I could hear nothing. As I watched, Mr. Serle turned his face toward the window. His dark eyes gleamed and his lips curved. His hand, circled about by the white of his shirt cuff, reached to me. I stretched my hand to touch him. The glass pane between us wavered, rippling like the surface of water in the wind. I could see his face and his hand wavering too as if sinking away from me in a deep pool. I awoke with a start.

Church bells were ringing for morning services. It was broad daylight on Easter morning. I am in Albany, New York, I told myself. I am on my way to California to join my brother. My mind must have been working a little more clearly by then because I remember having doubts about the wisdom of the journey. I counted up my money and wondered if it would be enough. I will want some warmer clothing, I thought. It might take several months to cross the plains, and the mountains will be high and snow covered. And then, muddled again, I decided I would just begin and find honest work along the way as I could. I did not allow myself to think what I would do if there was no honest work.

I did not wish to eat alone in the hotel dining room. My arm ached a little but no blood oozed from the cut when I checked it, so I rewrapped the bandage. I smoothed my hair, put on my bonnet, took my bag, and went down to pay for my room. It was a beautiful morning, clear and warm. With my valise in my hand, I did not think I should go into a church among all the people dressed in their new spring finery. Instead, I walked down to the river. I will find the boats that go west on the canal, I thought, and arrange my passage; then I will decide about church. I found a cake shop open and bought a bun and a mug of dreadful, burned-tasting coffee.

It was good I had something to hearten me, for I had a weary walk of it before I found the canal and the boats. Few people were about, and I went many steps out of my way before I asked directions of an elderly couple who sat on a bench together, gazing at the river. I had set off in the wrong direction; the great basin, where the lineboats that carry cargo from New York to Buffalo and back again tie up in tiers, lies to the north side of the city, not the south. When I found the place at last, another problem faced me. The packet boats that take passengers do not begin at Albany. It is necessary to take the train to a city farther west—Schenectady, a strange name.

A boy fishing from the bank explained my mistake to me. I must have looked as tired and dismayed as I felt, for he said, "Do not cry, miss. You need not go back to the train station. Many of the lineboats take on passengers. It is not so quick as a packet, but it is much cheaper. Walk along the path here and ask."

I walk slowly in the direction he indicates. My bag is heavy in my right hand, but shifting it to the left hand makes my cut arm ache more. The day is warm now for my shawl, but I do not think it would be respectable to take it off. I see that the boats are long, low barges. They have no windows along the sides of them, but only at the front, the bow, and at the back. Some of the boats are piled up with barrels lashed to the tops, others ride higher in the water. The lighter ones must be waiting to be loaded.

All is very quiet. Perhaps it is because of the holy day. The only person now in sight is a man sitting on the bow deck of a lineboat with his feet propped up on the rail.

"Good morning," I say.

I must be bold, I think, if I am to care for myself and make my journey.

"Good morning, Daniel," the man says in a hoarse voice. He lowers his feet, spits over the rail, and stares at me in a bewildered way.

This man is Flint, the sailor from the *Victoria*. He had some connection in Albany, I remember uncertainly.

"Good morning, Flint," I say. I should feel amazed to find someone I know, I tell myself. Only, if Jasper Westervelt can give me a drug that takes my thoughts and puts terrible dreams in their place, anything could happen. The frozenness was in me still, draining surprise and gladness from the world as bleach takes color from a cloth.

Flint is the same. His hoarse speech, the small gold anchor in his ear, his sad air of confusion. His scar, fresh looking on the ship, is a dead white stripe above his eyebrows, which are knit in puzzlement.

"You remember me, Flint?" I ask.

"I remember your bright hair and kind voice," he says.

"But I am a girl now, not a boy," I point out to him.

"All right," he says.

"I was Daniel on the *Victoria* when we came to America," I say. "Now I am Mina."

"Yes, Miss Mina," he replies. "Where are you going this time?"

He has enough wits about him to ask me a sensible question, even though he does not notice the difference between a boy in trousers and a girl in skirts.

"I am going to California," I say. "I have a brother there. I am looking for passage to the west. Or I will work for passage."

"Yes, Miss Mina," Flint says.

There is a silence. I set my bag down beside me to rest my arm. I suppose we are both thinking. I am wondering if it is safe to ask Flint for help and wondering at myself that I do not really care what is safe or not. I cannot guess at all at Flint's thought.

"I remember the wooden chain you gave me," I tell him.

Flint looks puzzled still. When he thinks, he is like a small child laboring over his copybook. His brow wrinkles so the white of the scar folds in, and his face knots up as if that will help a thought to come. After a moment, his brow clears, and he smiles. He has lost teeth since we were on the ship *Victoria*.

"I will take you to Buffalo on my lineboat," he says. He makes the offer with pride. "I am the captain. You know a ship. You can be crew and cook. I wondered what to do."

"Yes," I say. "I can cook for you. What work does the crew do?"

"There are the horses to guide and care for," he says. "They have to be taken around the locks. And there is the kitchen to keep."

"Horses?" I ask. "I can care for horses?"

Flint nods. He seems not to find anything strange in our

conversation at all. "There are two horses," he says, as if reciting a lesson. "If I travel night and day, I must change horses at the livery stables along the way for a fee. If I travel only in the day, I keep my own two horses. I wish to sleep at night. I bought the horses yesterday. They are at the stable, waiting for me."

"Have you fed them?" I demand. Horses seem more interesting than people to my numb mind. "Have you groomed them?"

Flint looks confused. I pick up my bag.

"Come," I say. "You must show me where I can sleep on the lineboat. We will go look at the horses. I will help you."

That is how I came to travel west on a lineboat with Flint. That Easter Day, he showed me the boat. There are two cabins, one at the bow with two beds built into the sides of the boat, and one at the stern. The cargo area is in between. To go from one cabin to the other, one must climb up to the flat rooftop of the lineboat and cross it. The stern cabin is the larger, with a cookstove and table for meals and then, beyond that, two beds built over storage cupboards. I take the stern cabin and put my bag away. Flint will sleep in the bow, just as he did on the *Victoria*. He still chews his tobacco, but he promised that he will never do so inside the cabins. That was my condition for cooking for him. I could not bear the smell and dirt.

After we looked over the boat together, we went to see the horses. Flint had not done so badly. Both animals seemed a good size for towing a barge, and sound in the legs and lungs so far as I could tell. Whether they have the stamina for hours on the towpath every day, I cannot judge until we all are working together. The stableman seemed not too rough and answered my questions about the canal and feed for the animals readily enough.

The horses were boarded at the livery stable until the lineboat was ready. We were taking furniture from the workshops of New York all the way to Buffalo. In the event, we did not leave for two days. Flint seemed not to have noticed that there was nothing to eat on the boat and nothing to cook it in or serve it on either. I needed to find stores and buy pots, dishes, and pantry staples.

Flint gave me some money for the supplies, and I used some of my own also. I purchased one good cooking knife. I thought about a paring knife also and examined the choices. Finally, I bought instead a folding knife like the one Mr. Serle carries. It will be useful for small chores, and I can keep it in my pocket with my housewife all the time. I will feel safer to have a knife ready when I need it. I bought a whetstone too. A tool that is not clean and cared for is useless.

By observing the boats around us and asking questions, I soon understood that Flint and I will have a hard time of it with just the two of us operating our boat. There must be a helmsman steering and someone riding or leading the horses. At the locks there are other tasks. Someone must release the towrope and secure the boat so it does not wreck itself against the stone walls of the lock as the water rushes in or out.

"Should you look for another crew?" I asked Flint hesitantly as I set oatmeal and coffee for our breakfast on the table in the stern cabin on Tuesday morning.

"I asked Phil to come with me, but he would not leave Zip," Flint told me. He poured almost the whole pint of cream into his bowl and picked up his spoon to eat.

"Who is Phil?" I asked. "Is Zip a person or a place?" It was like feeling about in the dark to talk to Flint.

"But you know Phil," Flint told me. He knit his brow in puzzlement. "Phil was on the boat across the ocean. I saw you talk to Phil in New York."

"Phil?" I try to remember. "Oh my," I say.

Phil must be Phoebe from the boat. The girl selling flowers called her Phil.

"I saw Phil and you and a woman with tracts on the street in the city," I say to Flint. "It was night and raining."

"Yes," Flint says. He is busy eating.

"Is Zip the woman with the tracts?" I ask.

I taste the oatmeal in my bowl. It is hard to be interested in the food or the conversation. Either we need another person to work on the boat or we do not. Flint has eaten all his oatmeal and is licking the spoon.

"Mrs. Zipporah James," he says. "My wife. Is there any more oatmeal?"

"Here, eat the rest of mine." I push the bowl in front of him. "Your wife?" I am startled almost into curiosity.

"I married her at Uncas Falls," he says, "before I went to the war and was killed."

"But you are alive, Flint," I say. "I see you."

He shakes his head and then looks as if the motion hurt him. "I am the ghost of myself," he says.

This may be the truest thing he has ever said to me.

"Yes," I say sadly. "Yes, I think you must be. I feel the same about myself today. But what about a third person on the boat?"

Flint has finished the rest of my oatmeal and is licking his spoon again.

"I don't want people we do not know on the boat," he says and then gets up.

And that is the end of the conversation. He goes out without speaking further, leaving me to wash the few dishes and clean the kitchen. I do not care really. It will be quieter with just two of us, and I want so to be quiet. Flint is strange, but he rarely asks questions. He does not make me think when I do not wish to.

Well, then, here I am. Flint is the captain. He will steer the boat. I will ride the horses on the towpath. I buy a boy's pants and shirt. I purchase two hats, one a cloth cap and the other shady straw for the hot weather. We set out under the bridge that crosses the entry to the boat basin and then up the canal toward West Troy. Between the two of us and the horses, we are under way. The work is not easy, but we manage.

Once we were started on our journey, I felt calmer. I must write a letter to Honor and Aunt Jane to say I am traveling and safe, I thought. As soon as we made our first stop, I went into the shop by the canal to buy bread and cheese. I should ask for paper and ink, I told myself. They will surely have such things. The place was not very large, and as I waited my turn to be served, I saw that—as in many such simple stores—they had recently papered the walls with newspapers.

The newspaper was a *Tribune* from New York. I could see the sheet with the date for the tenth of April. I read the headlines idly. South Carolina may secede. Something is wrong with the finances of Turkey. There is dissatisfaction and confusion at the World's Fair in London. There were marriages and deaths followed by notice of prices for ashes, cotton, and flour. There is much concern about the Fugitive Slave Law.

Above the store's sacks of cornmeal and wheat flour, I saw a notice under *Amusements* with a name I recognized. Madame Anna Moses, the world-renowned soprano, and the virtuoso pianist Herr Sadick Meyer are giving a concert. I remembered sitting in the musicale in the house on Crosby Street, listening with Daniel and Mr. Serle on either side of me, and my heart turned over in my breast. She is like Jasper Westervelt, I thought, remembering her insulting words and her brother's toying with me like a tabby with a mouse. I am a nothing to such people.

"Yes, miss," the man at the counter said to me.

I bought the bread and cheese I came in for and left quickly. What would I say in a letter? I thought. They are all better without me. I had had little appetite since Albany, and after that day I had even less. My wash dresses, which fitted neatly when I left the city, soon felt slack about me. I should eat, I knew, but when I forced myself, I felt nausea rise after a few mouthfuls. It was more satisfying to see Flint eat with pleasure whatever I set before him.

By the time we have been going west for a few days, I have found a routine. We rise and eat breakfast. I make a basket of sandwiches and fill a stone jar with cold tea for Flint. Then, for hours, I am a boy on a horse, my braid of hair well tucked up out of sight. I have other tasks too. When the boat must be weighed and a toll paid on our cargo at the weigh lock in West Troy, I have to go aboard and help Flint find his bill of lading and clearance papers because he has forgotten where he put them for safety.

In the first days on the "flight of five," the five locks that come almost like a stairs at the start of the canal, I learn the procedure of locking up, which is what they call rising in the lock to a higher level of the canal. When the slope of the land and the river go downward and the canal lock lowers the boat, they call it locking down. It is simple enough. I am glad to stay with the horses. It makes me uneasy to see the rushing force of the water against the great lock gates and the tilting, bobbing boat, like one bubble among many breaking bubbles, rising on the flood.

At night we tie the boat at the bank, water, feed, and groom the horses, and make a supper with what I can buy at one of the little canal stores or what I have laid by. I wash and change back into female clothing to cook. I suppose someone who did not observe us closely might think three people worked on our lineboat: Flint, a red-haired woman, and a boy who wears a hat always.

Generally the life is quiet. I became used to the rhythm of riding and the signs that meant to be alert for a passing boat. At the locks there were people to talk to if one wished it: French from Canada, Indians selling sweet-grass baskets, Germans going west to farm, Irish, Dutch, Yankees, Africans. I saw a Chinaman once. I think if I had not felt ill, I might have found the people interesting though rough spoken and that first journey beautiful. Near the village of Little Falls, the Mohawk River rushes east through a great glen with hills rising about it. I saw the romantic beauty of it with my eyes, but it did not touch my heart.

After several days—I am not sure how long—I fell ill. I had been heavy and tired all the morning, as I am when my monthly bleeding comes. Only, as the feeling began, it seemed different. I thought about it as I rode Trey, the second horse, along the bank. The first horse is Pompey. He is very steady and knows the path. Trey is more easily startled, which is why I ride him and let Pompey lead the tandem. It came to me that perhaps Jasper Westervelt did violate me while I lay on the floor at Fourth Street. Bridget told me once when Mrs. Westervelt sent her breakfast down untouched that women who are with child are often ill in the morning at the start. The thought frightened me.

The day was warm. The lineboat glided noiselessly past green meadows and willow trees overhanging the water on the opposite bank from the towpath. My head was light, and as noon came I developed a terrible cramp in my side. I felt a thirst. The train line, the high road, and the canal all ran near each other in that place. The sharp whistle of a locomotive sounded sudden and very close. Trey tossed his head and then balked. I controlled him but barely. Something is wrong, I thought. My leg is wet.

I fainted then and fell from the horse. When I came to myself again, I was lying on the towpath. Flint was kneeling over me, bathing my face with water and weeping.

I lay in the cabin after that, feverish and bleeding more heavily than ever in my life with my courses. I had cramping pains such as I never had before. My right arm hurt too where I twisted it under me as I fell. Poor Flint. He tied the boat at the bank and stoked the stove until the stern cabin was an inferno of heat. He seemed to think I was cold, although he did not ask me. He tried to give me tea, which I refused, and he went to the store along the canal for bread and brandy. I tried to eat bread and cheese and vomited. I drank a little brandy and water. That stayed down but made my head ache. In the second day, after a night of terror-ridden dreams, I began to weep with fear.

"I am dying, Flint," I cried. "What will I do?"

He stared at me, his forehead with its white scar wrinkled into sea waves and his mouth hung open in the very image of anxiety.

"I will get Lydia Mary," he exclaimed at last.

I heard his step on the deck, and then the boat swayed down and up again. He must have jumped to the bank, I thought. I closed my eyes and tried to pray. I could feel the blood seeping through the rags into the bed under me. Later, I heard Flint's voice on the bank.

"This way, Miss Lydia," he said.

"Thank you, Flint," replied a young-sounding woman's voice.

The boat moved in the water. Feet trod the deck above my head. The light in the cabin was blocked by figures in the door. A woman stood by me, looking down. I could not make out her face in the dim light. Even though the day was warm and the cabin sweltering, she wore a greatcoat and a broad-brimmed hat.

"Who are you?" I asked.

"I am Doctor Lydia Mary Walker," she said. "I am a graduate of the Syracuse Medical College. Flint tells me you are Miss Mina."

"Yes," I say. "I am Mina Pigot."

"Flint!" This woman looks back to where he is hovering like a great ungainly bird by the cabin door. "Flint, go out to the store and buy five yards of new muslin."

"Yes, Miss Lydia," he responds, and the boat sways as he goes to the land.

"You know Flint?" I ask.

"I grew up in Uncas Falls with Flint and Zipporah, his wife," she says briskly. "I am in Utica now. Did you know you are very near the town of Utica?"

She takes her hat off and puts it on the cabin table.

"No." I close my eyes for a moment, trying to remember our journey. "I am not sure where we are."

"Flint said you are dying," the doctor says. "Tell me what is wrong."

I tell her about the bleeding, about the pains in my stomach, about the hasheesh, about the knife. Tears run down my face. I cannot stop. Doctor Lydia Mary Walker does not comment. She listens. She takes my wrist between her fingers. She looks at the red line of the wound on my left arm. She moves my right arm to be sure it is not broken. At last, when I fall silent, she brings a clean dishclout and a basin of water. She bathes my face.

"I need to move you to see how much blood you have lost," she says. "I will sacrifice one of your dishcloths to make a pad for you on this chair."

With her help, I move from the bed to the chair. I feel weak and dizzy, but I do not faint. Now that I am sitting, I can see the woman's face. She is a small person inside all her clothes. Her face is round and plump cheeked. Her hair is drawn up into a rather scanty-looking coil about the crown of her head, and she has sparse ringlets at her temples. Her eyebrows, which are dark and thick and almost meet above her nose, seem more luxuriant than her hair. She has bright brown eyes and small plump hands. Like Honor's hands, I think, with a shock of memory.

"This is not so bad," the doctor is saying. "Can I examine you, my dear?" she asks.

"Examine me?" I feel myself begin to tremble. Tears slide on my cheeks again.

Doctor Walker looks at me sharply. She takes my wrist in her plump fingers again. She shakes her head.

"I will help you clean yourself," she says. "I am going to have Flint return with me and fetch beef tea for you and mint syrup to soothe your stomach. I do not think you are dying. But you seem starving and frightened."

She says little else but goes to throw the bucket over and fetch water, which she warms on the stove. She helps me wash. When Flint returns with the muslin, she makes my bed fresh for me with the new cloth for sheeting and tears off the end of the old sheet for more rags. She finds my night shift in the cupboard. I suppose she sees me as I take off the shirt I was wearing when I fell from the horse and put the night shift on, but she does not stare. When I am ready, she has me drink some cool water. When she stands by me this time, I can see that she wears not skirts but full trousers under her coat.

"Well," she says. "We will see. Flint will come with me to fetch soup for you and food for himself too. He will be back directly. I will come by again tomorrow."

"Thank you," I tell her.

I feel grateful that she made me comfortable and cleaner. The cramp inside me eases.

Flint kept the lineboat tied up in the same place for another night, of course. He cannot move without finding someone to guide the horses while he steers. Doctor Lydia Mary Walker came to see me again in the afternoon. Even though the day was warmer than the day before, she still wore her full trousers, white shirt, and knitted wool vest, and the canvas greatcoat to her ankles over all.

"Are you better?" she asked me. "Have you eaten?"

"Yes," I told her. "Flint brought me the beef tea. I drank a cup last night and one this morning. Thank you."

"Has the bleeding lessened?" she wanted to know.

I nodded yes. "Almost completely. There was just a little this morning," I said.

"May I look at you?" she asked me.

"Look at me?" I felt frightened again.

She took my hand gently in hers.

"Your skin is cool today," she said. "Your color is pale but almost normal for you, I think. The bleeding that so perturbed you has stopped. From what you told me yesterday, you might have been"—she pauses—"you might have been violated. It may be that you conceived and miscarried. It is also possible that you suffered a blow you do not remember. The bleeding might have been an aftereffect of that. Or perhaps this is just a mischance of nature." She sighed. "We know so little, my dear. If I could look at you and touch you, I might learn more. Or I might not. I would like to learn more."

"What would you do?" I ask suspiciously.

"Let me see." She looked about the cabin. "I would draw the blinds for privacy and lock the door. I would light the lamp. I would have you raise your shift above your breasts. Sometimes a women's breasts begin to swell and the nipples darken if she is with child. Then I would ask you to lift your knees to allow me to look between your legs and press on your belly. I would be touching you to feel if there is swelling inside you that could have caused bleeding."

"Are your hands clean?" I ask.

Miss Walker laughs. Her dark eyebrows lift and her face lightens.

"You are an intelligent young woman," she says. There is a kind of joy in her voice that I like. "I would wash my hands very carefully both before and after I touched you."

I think about it.

"I should like to know what happened to me," I say. "Perhaps then I will not be so afraid. If you look at me, will you be able to tell me what happened?"

"Honestly, I may not know," Miss Walker replies. "I shall tell you what I am doing as I proceed. I will not tell you what I think or infer until after."

She is true to her word in every way. She is quick and decisive in her movements, and although I feel awkward and strange, I do not feel shamed by what she does. Afterward, she helps me to pull down my shift and to sit up. Then, as she said she would, she washes her hands again. She unlocks the door and brings me a dipper of cold water from the barrel.

"Did you find out what happened to me?" I ask.

"You are a good patient," she says. "I wish all women could be as sensible and brave as you."

"I was brave?" I ask.

Miss Walker laughs and pats my hand kindly.

"I think this was a mischance of nature," she says. "What happened to you upset you very much. You said the hasheesh made you ill for several days. I felt no swelling or tumor. I saw no signs of the changes of pregnancy. I believe you are a virgin."

"Oh," I say. "Are you sure?"

"Every woman is made a little differently," Miss Walker tells me. "You have the signs of virginity but not so completely as some women do. You work hard. You are accustomed to ride horses astride. Many medical men think that has an effect. But what do men know? It may be just how you are. Your marriage night will be happier for you than it is for some women whose first experience is only pain."

"You think I am all right?" I feel anxious that she talks of marriage nights.

"I believe you are an untouched young woman. I would swear to a judge that you did not miscarry. Can you be content with that?"

"I will have to be," I tell her.

I feel despair and anger. Jasper Westervelt makes me feel this way. I fought him, and I fled, but he has followed me.

Miss Walker looks at me. Concern gleams in her bright eyes.

"There is violation of the mind as well as of the body," she says.

I nod yes. I feel violated even if I am untouched in my sex.

"I believe you have a choice before you, my dear," Miss Walker says in her considering way. "One path is the road of regrets, bitterness, tears. It is smooth and broad and easy enough to set one's foot along. Follow that path and you will return soon enough to where it began. The other way is harder. It means forgiveness, trust renewed. That path is worth the journey."

I sigh then. "I know," I say.

Miss Walker changes her tone abruptly. "I have an order for you," she says briskly. "Doctor to patient."

"Yes?" I must sound surprised.

"You will get up tomorrow, and you will eat," she says. "Flint tells me you are a fine cook. Why are you starving yourself?"

I cannot pretend with this woman.

"I am so sad," I say. "The world has lost its color and its savor. Before I could not eat when there was too much. I thought of the starving people I left in my home country and felt their hunger in my heart. Now it is more than that. Even if I tell myself to eat, nothing tastes right to me."

"Then you must eat just to eat or choose to die," this strangely dressed woman doctor tells me.

She writes a list for me. It is as if she is writing a direction for the chemist to make up a medicine. Bread, meat or egg, cheese or milk, fruit, greens. Five portions. I must have something of each every day no matter what, no matter if it is just a little.

"Promise me," she says, putting the piece of paper with the direction into my hand.

"I promise," I say.

"Where are you going?" Lydia Mary Walker asks. "Why are you traveling with Flint?"

"I am the cook and crew on the boat," I say. "Flint is helping me start my journey to join my brother in California."

"California?" Doctor Lydia Mary Walker looks at me with grave concern.

"Yes," I say.

"No," she responds, "you are not strong enough. You must go back and forth on the canal at least once more and gain flesh and health. If you go now, you will die on the plains or in the desert. Your body has no resources against privation."

"But I must go to my brother," I say in despair. "I have no one else in the world."

"And what will he have if you are dead?" she asks me.

I stare at her.

"Go back," she says. "You said the names Miss Corbett, Bridget, and Guido to me yesterday. They all helped you. Write to them. Go back to them. Write to your brother. You have asked too much of yourself these past weeks. Wait, build your strength, and then perhaps you will go to California."

I nod. I remember that I have money in a bank in New York City to pay for travel. I wonder why I forgot. My mind has been clouded. Maybe Bridget will go with me to California if I ask her. Memory burns up like a flame in me. I will not be the madwoman I saw by the train line, with her dress all torn and the men holding her arms. I will not choose to die.

"I will wait," I promise. "I will eat and grow strong."

"Good," she says. "Insist that Flint give you money for food of good quality. He is not poor."

She writes her name and street in Utica on another piece of paper. "If you need help, you can find me here," she says, "or just call for a visit when you are passing on your return journey. You can tell me your impressions of the great falls at Niagara."

We stayed tied up near Utica two more days, until both my aching arms were better. I drank the mint syrup in water and followed the doctor's direction as best I could. As soon as I felt strong enough to ride again, we set out.

"Time is money on the canal," Flint said, but he did not say it as if it mattered much to him.

Perhaps it was the voice of the black-clad, stern-looking wife I saw in New York that rainy night who spoke in his head of work and necessity. Certainly we did not push as fast as many of the freighters did. Flint showed no disposition to it. He would stop sometimes in mid-afternoon if we were near a village and shops.

He would call to ask me what we would eat for our dinner and whether I needed to buy supplies. While I shopped and cooked, he liked to sit on the little stern deck of the boat, chewing his tobacco and staring at the water.

The packet boats make the trip from Schenectady to Buffalo in six days, hurrying always day and night, changing horses at the livery stables every fifteen miles or so. With my illness, our travel in daylight only, a two-day wait at the weigh lock in Syracuse because the mechanism was under repair, and an afternoon and a morning lost when Pompey threw a shoe and the farrier could not be found at Brockport, it took us almost a month to reach Buffalo.

They say that one can hear the roar of the great falls of Niagara from miles away. I did not find it so. Perhaps the sounds of the canal traffic, of the factories that are building everywhere, and of the hodgepodge busy city of Buffalo hide the noise of the water now. Perhaps when the country was all wilderness, travelers would know they were approaching the marvel. Nowadays, with the country improved and improving everywhere, nature is pushed aside. It does not call to welcome us as it once did.

So it happened that I did not know how close we were to the great waterfalls until we were waiting to unload our cargo at Buffalo.

"When are you going to see Niagara Falls?" Flint asked me in his hoarse voice.

He was eating beef hash and eggs for his breakfast, mopping up the yolks with chunks of bread. I never saw anyone eat with such relish as Flint did. I might have given up and starved to death in those weeks if there had not been Flint asking always what the next meal would be, eating every crumb, licking his fork and knife and spoon, and thanking me.

"I had not thought about the falls," I said. "Are they near?"

"You must ride Trey and take some food and go to sit and look," he told me. "It will be good for your soul."

"Oh," I said.

I sat and stared at him over my cup of coffee with milk and sugar. I wonder at the jumble of bits and pieces of life that is Flint's mind.

"Yes," he said. "You will go and spend the day. We will be un-loaded today. Tomorrow we take on grain and wines from Ohio, and you can buy supplies for your cooking. Then we start east."

"Can you tell me the road?" I ask him, and he does.

I arrived at the falls in the late morning. Of course, I wore my lad's clothing and my straw hat for the journey. I rode Trey out of the city and along through the fields and farmlands beside the tranquil river. When the river began to ripple and change as it tumbled and frothed into rapids, I heard the rumor of water in the distance. I saw the clouds of mist that rise perpetually over the falls and the rays of the sun striking light across them.

I found a place to tie the horse where he could have the shade of a small ash grove and also reach grass to crop. There was an-other horse tethered nearby, so I thought it must be all right. Not far away was the plateau where two sets of stairs descend, one to the ferry that crosses to and fro in the river, and the other to the foot of the American waterfall. I chose to go down to the falls. I did not think I had time for the ferry, nor did I wish to leave Trey in a strange place for long.

The stairs were very steep and, at the bottom, slippery and grown with green moss from the continual spray thrown up by the great cataract. There were parties of ladies and gentlemen and children coming and going, exclaiming at the sights or silent in awe. One dark-clad man stood off to the side looking intently into a small red leather-covered book. His lips moved as if he might be praying, or perhaps he was reading the words of some poet or travel writer inspired by the view before us. I had the feel of watching people partaking in a ritual of some new church.

An artist had set up a little folding stool and easel and was busy painting in watercolors, looking up and down from the falling water to his paper. Several of the people who came down would look at the view and then go to stand behind the man and make comments on his work. I thought it very strange and dis-courteous, but he paid them no mind and daubed away with en-ergy. He looked a rather cheerful person in his open-necked shirt, loose canvas coat, and summer straw hat pushed back on his head so that his brown hair and sun-warmed face showed.

I found a rock away from the foot of the stairs where I could sit and contemplate without having travelers crossing always in front of me. The cataract made a column, silver and emerald, down the great cliff above me and buried itself in the turbulent river before my feet. Mist hung like smoke above the water. As I sat, lost in the midst of such grandeur, I had a vision of the country beyond me to the west, a vast place of land and lakes, pouring itself, emptying itself, and yet an endless, an eternal, surge of sound and water. What strength must lie above the falls! How many miles of lakes and rivers must exist to create this ever-flowing cascade, this illimitable abundance of the great substance of life! I think, as I look back from the snug, firelit kitchen where I write in Uncas Falls tonight, that in some depth of my mind I knew then that I would not travel to California soon. I did not have the strength in me to push against such power.

I sat there a long time, staring at the water, the rocks, the plants clinging to their places in the cliffs, the sky. As the sun climbed past noon, the visitors went away up the stairs to their dinners. I had a strange feeling. What is it? I thought. And then I knew that I was hungry. I wanted to eat. I took out my packet of food to see what I had brought. A sandwich of ham and cheese, a boiled egg, an orange.

I held the hard-boiled egg on the flat palm of my hand. It is an amazing work of nature, I thought. Beyond me is the might of the falling water, the spray and rainbows, the destruction and chaos. The egg is small and smooth and mysterious. Anything could be born from an egg. Which creation of God is truly more powerful? I wondered.

"What are you thinking?" a man's voice asked.

"I was wondering if we are inside the egg of the universe," I said, and then looked up. "Oh!"

The artist who was painting at his little easel when I arrived sat close to me now. He had a pad on his knee for sketching and his crayon in his hand, which was filthy with the reddish stain of the stuff.

"How do you do, young man?" He nodded to me politely. "My apologies for startling you."

Now I could see that his countenance was indeed open and cheerful. He had brown eyes, a straight small nose, and a general appearance of alertness and vigor. There was something in the line of his jaw and the humorous set of his mouth that made me think of Mr. Serle. He seemed to be staring at me expectantly.

"You look hungry," I said.

He sighed in a great gust. "I was hoping you would ask," he said. "I am starving."

"I will share with you," I told him, "only I forgot to bring drink, and I have nothing with which to dip water from the river."

"I have a cup I use for my watercolors," he said comfortably. "I will just wash it."

"All right," I replied. "Don't fall in. The rocks look treacherous, and I think the water might carry you all the way to the great Atlantic Ocean before you came to the surface of it again."

I took my knife out, opened it, and divided the sandwich in half. I peeled the egg and divided that too. The young man came back with his tin cup brimming full of water. It looked as if he had tried to wash his hands.

"You peeled and cut the egg," he said in a disappointed voice as he sat on a low rock beside me.

"Why would I not?" I asked. "Do you eat eggshells?"

"No," he answered, "I wanted to sketch it in your hand."

"Well, you cannot eat it and have it to draw too," I told him. "You said you are starving."

"I did, and I am," he replied. He put his half egg in his mouth.

We ate and drank from the water cup in silence. It did not take long for the sandwich to disappear. I cut the orange into sections, and we ate those down to the rinds.

"Watch this," the young man said.

He inserted a section of orange peel into his mouth and showed me a dreadful orange grin. I laughed at his silliness. It felt such a long time since I laughed. Then I remembered that my brother did the same to tease me once, and tears brimmed in my eyes.

"Are you all right?" The young man was looking at me curiously.

"Oh yes," I said. "Do you make pictures to sell?"

He sighed even more gustily than before.

"Yes, I make pictures to sell," he told me.

"Travelers here must like to have reminders of the beauty of the place."

"Yes, they do," he answered. "At the hotels I sold several watercolors illustrating the landscape. I wish my heart were in such things."

"What do you like to do?" I asked.

"I'll show you." He opened his sketchbook.

I was amazed as he turned the pages. There were views of farmlands, hayricks, and hills. There were many sketches of Niagara; he had seen the great cascades from all directions and recorded the heart-shaped leaves of a tiny plant bathed in wet as well as a kind of map of the whole, imagined as a bird would see it flying over.

Almost always, though, he had drawn people. There were men working in the farm fields, women at their kitchen doors, tourists pointing, openmouthed. The landscape was background for him, I could see. It was humans that came alive under his hand. His talent lies in the way a line of chalk captures the turn of a child's head looking up to see its mother, or how a work-worn hand grasps a rake. He had drawn me sitting on a rock with my hands clasped about my knees and the waterfall behind me. It was a rough, not a polished picture, but I could see in the lines of the thing that the figure is alert to the power of the water beyond and yet quiet inwardly. The last sketch in his book was the beginning of a hand—and an egg.

When I mentioned my thoughts, he looked pleased and abashed too.

"You understand me very well," he said.

"You must follow your gifts," I told him. "It is better so."

He looked at me with his curious nature all alive in his face.

"I must go," I said. "I left my horse above. I must return to Buffalo before evening."

"I am going that way too," he declared. "Let us ride together."

I hesitated and reached up to pull my hat more securely about my ears.

He must have seen the uncertainty in me, for he said quickly, "I am very harmless. I would not intrude on any fellow who does not want company."

"It is all right," I say. I have my knife in my pocket, after all.

He packs up his artist things. I admire that it all makes a neat bundle that he can sling on his shoulder. We make our way up the steep staircase. Climbing away from the water feels like going back to a world of ordinary objects. The air is looser up above, not compacted and made heavy by the weight of water pressing down as it seemed at the foot of the falls. Trey nickers; he is glad to see me.

The young man approaches his horse with diffidence and has difficulty securing his bundle, but he declines my help when I offer it. The ride back is pleasant. My companion chats enthusiastically about the summer sketching trip he is making. In the winters he lives in Brooklyn across the river from New York City. He has a studio for painting in his father's house. He is happy because he already covered half his expenses for his journey with the pictures he sold in Niagara. He points out the bridge to Goat Island, houses that have pleasing shapes, a group of gnarled oak trees like old men talking, the way the afternoon light strikes the windows of a house making a blind face. He wants me to see everything. It is enough that I say yes and yes again to show that I am giving my attention.

At the outskirts of the city where there is a choice of roads, we stop the horses.

"Will you join me for dinner?" he asks. He sounds hesitant. "I find our American fare for travelers poor and coarse indeed in such places as I can afford, but I took your lunch. I owe you payment."

"No," I say. "You will come to supper with Flint and me. Why eat traveler's poor victuals when you can eat good food?"

"Really?" He is brimming with enthusiasm again. "It is not too much?"

"It will be good for us," I say. "We have never had company on the lineboat yet."

"A boat?" He is all questioning energy.

"Come," I say. "I will show you the way, and then you will go to your hotel to refresh yourself. There will be a surprise for you when you come back again."

Well, he seemed surprised indeed when he came back and found me in my woman's dress and apron, cooking our meal.

"I know you by your eyes and your voice," he said. "But I have not the artist's eye I thought I had. How could I mistake you for a boy?"

"We see what we expect to see," Flint says, and he is right for all that he sounds uncertain as he says it.

Our guest asked for a tour of the lineboat, and Flint showed him about while I set the table. The tour seemed to be a success, and the meal went well also. It was a cool night by the water with a light breeze from the great expanse of Lake Erie. I cooked a chicken stew with new carrots, spring onions, and cornmeal dumplings, a lettuce salad, and maple sugar cream. Flint and our guest ate enthusiastically. At the end I set out a bowl of oranges and nuts for the two men and rose to begin cleaning things away.

"I will help you—" Our guest struck his hand to his head dramatically. "I want to say your name, but I do not know it."

"She is Daniel when she rides, and Miss Mina when she cooks," Flint said. He had cracked a walnut and was intent on prying out the meat.

I looked at Flint and shook my head.

"I will call you Miss Mina, if I may?" the man said. "And I am Maurice Clemens." He paused and smiled. "Perhaps you will call me Mr. Maurice."

"Certainly, Mr. Maurice," I answered.

"Well, Miss Mina," Maurice Clemens said, "if you will lend me an apron, I will wash your dishes. I seem to be falling further and further behind in what I owe you."

"I have just one clean apron tonight, and I am wearing it," I tell him, "so I will wash and you will dry the dishes."

When all was done and put away except for the mess of nutshells Flint had made at the table, I put the kettle to boil for tea. We sat down again.

"May I?" Mr. Maurice asked, taking a small sketchbook from his coat pocket.

We talked around the table of Mr. Clemens's travels in America, and mine across the ocean from England. I made black tea for the two men and mint tea from syrup for myself. All the while the artist's hand was busy drawing, which distracted me at first but, talking of the storm at sea, I ceased to notice it.

"Remember, Flint?" I said. "You hit your head on the capstan and you were ill."

"I think I remember," he said slowly and uncertainly. He did not want to talk of his sailing when Mr. Maurice asked him, but after I spoke of the green beauty of my village in Ireland, he told us a little of growing up in Uncas Falls, where he was happy as a boy.

When the tea is done, it is time for the guest to go. He shakes our hands and thanks us over and over.

"If you are here for a few more days, I could visit with you again," he says longingly. "This evening reminds me of the disadvantages of being a solitary traveler."

"We leave tomorrow to go east," Flint says. He sounds like a captain or a different person suddenly. "You can come with us on the canal for a week. If you pay something for your food and help me with the ropes at the locks, we will be glad to have your company. Miss Mina needs cheering up."

"Flint!" I say. I think my mouth opens in an *O* of surprise.

Maurice Clemens brought his things down from the hotel the next morning and moved into the bow cabin with Flint. On the wharf nearby, a group of immigrants were transferring their motley assortment of goods from a lineboat to a lake freighter bound out for new settlements in Michigan, and Mr. Clemens wandered off to sketch them. When he returned, he was very excited to watch how our boat was loaded with grain by swinging the barrels out from a mast on the shore. There was a strange moment when the barrels were done and the men began to lash the demijohns of wine along the top rails of the boat.

"I should never have said yes to wine," Flint wailed, staring at the bottles in their wickerwork casings. He was holding his head as if it hurt. "Zip will be angry at me."

"Why?" I asked him quietly. "Why are you upset, Flint?"

"She will think I broke the Pledge," he cried. "But she will be angry too if we lose money on the journey."

"I will explain to her," I told him. "I will tell her you did not drink a drop of the wines. You had to take the load for the good profit it offers."

"All right," he said, quieting like a comforted child.

I was very glad through the first days of the journey east from Buffalo to have another pair of hands for the work. There is a long, deep cut between Buffalo and Lockport where the tow-path runs along a ledge in the cut itself, not on a bank above it. I had been frightened going west that the towrope would snag and the horses and I would be dragged from the path to hurtle into the water below with no way up. With Maurice Clemens on the boat to trip the release for the towrope if there was need and to help Flint, I was more at ease guiding the horses.

Seeing the busy canal in his sketches and hearing Mr. Maurice's endless questions, I began to feel the pull of the bubbling life about me and to attend to its curious quirks. Not that all was happiness. Often, I awoke in the dark with Jasper Westervelt's face leering tulip-red into mine and could not fall into sleep again. Many days I dreamed my way along on Trey's back, forgetting the present in the dull sadness of the past. When I felt no appetite, I had to think of Doctor Lydia Mary Walker's list to be sure that I had put enough for strength inside me. But, even had I wished to, it would have been hard to resist Flint's pleasure in eating and Mr. Maurice's joy in seeing. I was drawn along by them.

At the canal shops, whose front doors face the water, I began to recognize and greet some of the women and their children. I came to know Celeste, who traveled with her husband and two children at much the same pace as Flint and I. It was good to have a woman to talk to about ordinary problems such as methods for cooking salt fish or how to get stains out of a shirt. Mr. Maurice's things were always marked with paint or chalk or crayon.

Maurice Clemens woke questions in me with his talk. He helped me to understand Flint better. One evening after a dull and heavy day, rain had come on. We ate a quiet meal. I built the fire in the stove for cooking and then kept it high to take the damp chill from the cabin. Maurice asked Flint about the building of the aqueducts that can carry whole rivers across the canal. While we were stopped to exchange our load of grain for barrels of flour, he had been very excited to draw diagrams and sketches of the stonework where the Genesee River crosses at Rochester. He kept wanting to know when we would see another aqueduct.

"I do not know," Flint said. "My head will break in a minute if you make me think too much. Since the war, I am only a ghost, you know."

Maurice was quiet then. He drank some cider from his glass and studied Flint, who had lowered his face to his dish and was eating his second helping of new potatoes made the way he likes them, boiled and broken up in milk and butter.

"What war were you in, Flint?" I asked.

"The Mexican War," Flint said without looking up. "First Regiment of New York Volunteers. Twelve hundred of us went out. Two hundred and sixty returned."

"My God," Maurice says, and passes his hand over his face as if one could wipe away the thought of so much death.

Flint looks up now, his face contorted with feeling. The cabin seems filled to bursting with rage. I am afraid to speak. Like a needle in a boil, the wrong word will release poison on us, which can kill or cure.

"We pulled the guns with ropes," he said. "We were mules, not men. At Mexico City we took Molina del Rey and then was Chapultepec. The gun exploded. John next to me was killed. His head rolled backward from his body."

I can see Maurice's right hand under the table. He has no pad or crayon, and yet his finger is moving against his leg, as if to draw is the only way he can listen.

"I am glad you lived, Flint," I say quietly.

"No!" Flint cries. "I was killed. See! See!"

He stands and rips at his clothing. His chest and his belly are a maze of scars, and something else is wrong. Something—

I think for a moment I might vomit. Flint's groin is a great lump of scarred and distorted flesh, and where his manhood should be is a sad rag of tissue and nothing else. I turn my head and tears brim in my eyes. I bite my lip to stop the sadness with a different pain. I must not be shocked, I think. I must not make it worse for him.

Maurice's face is a mask of horror, mirroring Flint's.

"My God!" Maurice says.

"How old were you?" I ask. I think it might be good for Flint to talk, to hold him to the world, to know we can accept his pain with him.

"I was nineteen," Flint says. "I married Zip. We quarreled, and she said I was not a man enough. I ran away to war to be a man. I saw men dig their own graves and be hanged as traitors. I killed a man with my bayonet in a cornfield. Then I was killed myself."

"My God!" Maurice repeats.

"The gun exploded," Flint says again. "John next to me was killed. His head rolled back, and then they put it on my body by mistake when I was ill."

Poor Flint. I touch the rosary in my pocket. His body is beyond help, but I will pray to God to heal his mind and give him comfort.

"I went to be a man! I went to be a man!" he shouts.

Flint sat then, laid his head down on the table, and cried hoarse, racking sobs. Maurice put his hand on his shoulder and left it there. We all sat quiet for a long time until the fire burned down in the stove and the cabin grew chill. Maurice roused Flint gently and helped him pull his clothes about him. I offered tea, but

Flint shook his head no. I heard their heavy steps across the roof deck as they went to their beds. I warmed water then and washed the dishes. It was late, but I needed the work to calm me.

In the morning, no one mentioned anything. The days floated by again as usual.

After Syracuse, I could see Maurice Clemens growing increasingly restless. I think he had grasped the workings of the canal and seen the variety of people on it. He knew how the packets pass us with their roof decks crowded and heard the gay blast of their horns that tell everyone to duck down for a bridge.

"I think I might go north next," he told us at supper. "I should make sketches in the Adirondack Mountains. I hear the scenery is wildly romantic and sublime."

"I wonder at you," I commented. "You would use your talent as well drawing the variety of people in New York City. What is this yearning for wilderness?"

"It sells, Miss Mina, it sells," he said in a hollow voice. And then he laughed. "City people want to taste the thrill of wilderness after a day in a dull office just as they want the sweetness of sugar to lighten a heavy meal. I can sell sugar. Why not?"

"So long as you do not drown your best talents in syrup," I told him.

"We will see," he said. "I have a letter from the Academy of Design trustees. A gentleman—*S. Meyer,* he signs himself—tells me I may submit three works for the winter exhibition."

He looks at me sharply. "You know this gentleman," he says.

Maurice knows life by seeing it. It is useless to lie to him, because some small movement in me has already told him that I recognized Herr Sadick Meyer's name.

"I met him on my journey to America," I say. I wish to push the memory of Herr Meyer and his sly ways from my thought. In the sparkling warmth of a summer day, I will not think of his stirring trouble between Mr. Serle and me. Or of his beautiful sister and her songs.

Maurice Clemens must see my withdrawing, for he nods and does not ask further questions. "I hope S. Meyer and his colleagues like my work," he says.

"You will succeed," I assure him.

The next day Maurice Clemens left us to roam north of the canal and sketch at Trenton Falls and in the Adirondack Mountains. He talked to me after I had given him his breakfast.

"I will miss these summer days on the water with you and Flint," he said.

"We will miss you too," I told him. "You have been good for us with your cheerful ways."

"I am only a poor artist," he said. "I cannot offer a wife anything yet. But in a few years—" He stopped.

"I am sure you will have success with your pictures," I said.

"If I do, will you consider—" He stopped again.

I must have looked puzzled.

"If I could offer you a home, would you marry me, Miss Mina?" he asked, returning to his direct way.

I shake my head. "No," I say. "I think you are a good man, and a fine artist, but this is a summer daydream you are having. I am not the wife to suit you."

"I think you are," he says in a rather argumentative tone. "You are a pleasure to look at and to draw. You are an excellent cook. You are resourceful and thrifty. You are quiet, kind, and companionable. What more could a man want?"

I laugh at him. "You can hire a housekeeper who fills your requirements," I tell him. "A sensible housekeeper and a faithful dog, and you will have what you describe."

He laughs then too. "You know what it is to love someone, I think," he says, growing serious again, "and the someone is not me, not yet."

A thought of Mr. Serle, gazing across a table at me as I weep, rises unbidden in my mind. I push the picture away and turn to set the kettle on the fire. I need hot water for the dishes. When Maurice Clemens leaves us an hour later, he takes my hand cordially.

"You must think about my proposal," he says. "This boy-girl life is not good enough for you."

He reaches his arm about me suddenly and kisses me full on the mouth for a long moment.

"Oh!" I say. I feel breathless and confused. It is not an unpleasant confusion.

"Oh?" He takes me by both shoulders and looks into my eyes. "Oh? That is my reward for offering you my heart?"

His laughing face tells me that he is not truly hurt.

"I wish you well on your journey," I tell him. "Try not to propose to every competent cook you meet. You might have a harem following you back to New York."

"You are not going to escape me so easily," Maurice tells me. "I am going to write to you in care of the harbormaster at Albany. I will see you there before the summer is over. Be sure to ask for my letter."

Then he releases me, jumps to the bank, pumps the hand of Flint, who is with the horses, pats Pompey on the nose, waves to us all, slings his bag and sketching things to his shoulder, and goes tramping away down the towpath to where the road leads toward the village of Rome.

Well! I think, my heart slowing to a more normal pace, Maurice Clemens is an interesting young man. I go to wash my face and smooth my hair before I join Flint to hitch the horses for the day's work. After a long sleep, I am suddenly awake in a new-born world.

It was perhaps the honest playful talk, perhaps the kiss, perhaps understanding something of Flint's sorrow, which is so much beyond mine, but I felt change inside me after the time with Maurice Clemens. His nature is like sunlight playing on running water, quick, ever-shifting, joyful.

At the next opportunity, I bought paper and pen and ink and wrote to Honor and Aunt Jane. I told them I missed them. I told them I was traveling and recovering myself in body and mind. I told them I was sorry for any pain I caused them. I said that I would write again as soon as I could and that I expected to return to New York in a few months to find work for the winter.

After Maurice left us, we made good time locking down after Utica to Albany again. I wrote again to Honor from Albany. I wrote less of my sins and more of seeing Niagara Falls and the sights of the canal. I told them of meeting a cheerful artist, Maurice Clemens, who hoped to exhibit his paintings in New York. I hesitated and then decided not to mention that he lived on the lineboat with us. They might not understand my unladylike behavior in living with two men on a boat, even though I felt perfectly proper in myself.

At the end of the letter, after I had written my love and gratitude again to Aunt Jane and Honor herself, I added a message to Guido DiRoma to thank him for carrying me away from the Westervelts' house when I was drugged. I thought for a long time after that. I will be happier if I say my truth, I thought. *Please give my good wishes to Mr. Serle,* I wrote. *I hope he still sees his friends. And if you know, tell me when he marries. I pray for the good health and happiness of all who have helped me make my life.* I cannot say more. My hand writes my wish not to lose all connection to him, but my heart still holds a hurt.

The next day Flint and I set out west again with another load of furniture. We are a shuttle in the loom of America, weaving the fabric that makes our country.

It happened in hot weather. It was late June or early July by then. I had lost the count of days completely. We were on our way west, nearing Utica again, and I thought of Doctor Lydia Mary Walker's invitation to me to call on her. I should do it, I thought. I can learn from her. She must know about herbs and medicines. Perhaps she can tell me if there is something I can do to help Flint clear his clouded mind. I made up my mind to see Miss Walker, only I wished to take her something as a thanking gift.

I was thinking about it when we stopped in the line waiting to lock up. There was a great clot of freighters and a packet already before us. A mechanism in the westward lock was broken. The word came back that the blacksmith was coming. He was needed to forge a part. We would not move before nightfall. Some people took the opportunity to bathe in the river. My friend

Celeste on the next lineboat called to me. Did I wish to walk up to the store in the village with her? I called back that I could not. I had laundry.

I did my work quickly. I soon had the sheets and other things strung up to dry in lines across the little stern deck. Flint was grooming the horses. He looked very content. He talks to the animals more often now, which seems to soothe him. I wandered away a little to see what was near us in the countryside. The wild raspberries along the canal banks gave me an idea to take Miss Walker fresh berries or perhaps cook them into jam for her. The bushes looked heavy with ripe fruit.

The picking took me up a bank. I could hear the murmur of the river and the boat life, still but overlaid with the sound of insects shrilling and the song of birds. Sweat gathered on my forehead under the edge of my straw hat. I came to an open place where there had once been a house. I could see the shape of the cellar hole, the burned timbers fallen into it, and the stones of the foundation. A lilac bush grew by the threshold that still showed among the meadow weeds and rambling raspberry canes growing up over it.

I bent to pick and heard a moaning sound. The woman lay behind the old foundation wall where the stones stood knee high still. She was half sitting, propped against the rough wall. I could see immediately that she was in labor. Her belly swelled under her stained skirt. I set my basket aside and knelt beside her. She did not seem to feel my presence until I touched her hand.

"I am here," I said. "I will get help for you."

She turned her head to me. She has dying eyes, I thought with a shock, remembering my mother in her illness and John Deegan on the steps of the house in Elizabeth Street. She will be gone in a few hours at most. To stand before the mystery carries the soul beyond sorrow into awe.

"I am going to call for help," I said, "and then I will return."

I went to the top of the bank I had climbed and shouted for Flint. When he came shambling up, looking puzzled, with the currycomb still in his hand, I told him he must take Trey and go for Doctor Lydia Mary Walker immediately.

"Tell her it is a woman giving birth," I say. "Tell her I think the woman is dying. Do you understand, Flint?"

Flint looks at me with tears in his eyes. "I will go as quick as can be," he tells me.

"You are a good man, Flint," I say. "Now hurry. And if you see Celeste on her way from the store, send her to me."

I go back to the woman and kneel by her again. Her lips are dry and cracked, her hair a matted tangle. She breathes in long, slow, sighing gasps. I touch her belly tentatively and feel a little jerk of movement. Perhaps the child is still alive within her, wanting to be born. This is beyond my knowledge.

I can only try to ease her until help comes. I look about to see if there is water. A tin cup is near her hand on the ground, but it holds a spoonful of water only. I lave her lips with what there is and then take her cold hand in mine.

"I am Mina," I say. "I have sent for help."

She turns her head a little to look at me. Her lips part as if she would speak, but only sighing breaths come. And then her hand tightens on mine. She cries in the low moan of pain I heard before. I see her body arch with the force of the child seeking its light. I should cut her skirt away and try to help it, I think.

Celeste comes running. "Poor thing," she says. "Here, Mina. Let us lift her up a little and get her skirts back. It may be I can see why the child is not coming."

I take my knife and slit the skirt. Underneath, her ragged skirt and petticoat are stiff with drying blood, and then freshly wet on top of that. I have never seen so much blood. I see that the blood that frightened me when I was ill was nothing at all compared to this.

Celeste is feeling the woman's belly and trying to see between her legs.

"Oh God," she says. "The baby is turned wrong. I see an arm, I think."

"What can we do?" I ask Celeste.

I feel despair. The woman's hand lies lax and cool in mine. Her face is white as moonlight on water.

"Hold her," Celeste tells me. "Hold her. I will try to turn the child."

I put my arms about the woman and hold her tight. She turns her face into my shoulder just a little. She lives still.

"Pray," I whisper at her ear. "We will both pray."

The woman makes a sound. She is trying to speak.

"What?" I ask her. "Tell me if you can."

She is saying a name, I think. Thomas, it sounds like. Something with a T to begin it. Her voice is cracked from thirst. I wish I had more water for her.

"Thomas?" I ask her doubtfully.

She stiffens herself and tries again. *Tobias,* I think she says.

"Tobias?" I question, and she nods just enough that I can feel the tremor of movement.

Someone is here. I feel it. The woman gazes beyond me with her dying eyes. I turn my head to follow her gaze. There is a great white dog standing by a tangle of bushes across the clearing. It is as if by saying the name Tobias, she summoned it. I have never seen such an animal. Its shoulder will come to my waist, I think. Perhaps this is Tobias.

"Tobias!" I call.

The dog regards me steadily, and then it turns and stares into the bushes. It gives one deep bark. I feel the woman relax in my arms and then stiffen herself again. Celeste is reaching in to push at the baby. I can see that she has blood on her arms and dress now.

The woman cries loud in pain. She cannot bite it off into a moan this time. The dog barks again. There is a movement and a rustling in the bushes. A child crawls out. His clothing is gray with dirt and his feet are bare. He is dirty, scratched, thin as a little splinter of wood.

"Mama," he cries in a thin wail. "Mama!" and comes running across the clearing with the dog following.

I put out one arm to him and pull him in. I do not want him to see the blood if I can spare him. He shivers in my embrace, skin and bone. Now that the dog is closer, I can see that he too is starved and dirty. As if he does not wish to frighten me, the animal lies down an arm's length away from us and sets his head on his paws. His brown eyes have a depth to them as he regards us, unblinking.

Suddenly the place has more people in it. The doctor has come, and others too. Celeste gives over her place to Miss Lydia. A woman I do not know comes to support the laboring woman. I hold the child only now.

Doctor Lydia Mary Walker looks up at me.

"Take the child away, Miss Mina," she says. "Let him kiss his mother and then take him and the dog to your boat. Feed them a little at a time. Don't let them have too much all at once. And bathe them. We will send for you."

I am not sure if it is the dog or the child that is Tobias.

"Tobias?" I say, and the child moves in my arm. "Your mother is ill," I say softly. "These people are helping her. Kiss her and come with me. I will care for you."

"Mama?" the child says in a tiny, whispering voice.

"Tobias," she whispers.

Someone brought clean water, and she swallowed a little. Her voice is clearer. Perhaps the sure hands of Doctor Lydia Mary Walker are giving her strength also.

"Kiss your mother," I say. "She loves you."

The child kisses the woman, and then I too lean and kiss her bloodless cheek.

"I will care for Tobias," I tell her, holding him in the circle of my arm. "Be easy in your mind. These are good people to help you."

Her eyes are closed now. I am not sure she hears me.

"Come," I say to the child.

I lift him, and with the dog following even though I have not spoken to it, we make our slow way down to the canal and the shelter of the boat.

When Celeste came to tell me that the woman was dead and the child within her also, Tobias and the dog were asleep together on the bed across from mine in the stern cabin. I fed them both with bowls of toasted bread sopped in warm milk with maple sugar. I heated water on the stove and washed them. The child whimpered a little from the water and soap on his raw, scratched skin but did not cry out loud or say a word. I found my jar of hand lotion and soothed it all over him.

Like the child, the dog was very patient and quiet. I was a little afraid because he was so big, but then I felt so sorry for the eager way he lapped the food I offered and for his thin flanks and fleshless ribs under his matted fur. Tobias stayed close at my leg, holding my skirt as I washed and then tried to comb the dog.

"What is the dog's name?" I asked.

The child flinched in fear and did not answer. I thought of how he whispered *Mama* to his mother and her whispering voice in return. I lowered my own voice almost to inaudibility to ask again, "Does the dog have a name?" and bent to the child.

The dog turned its head and nudged at Tobias's hand.

"Rafe," Tobias breathed.

"Rafe is a good dog," I said as softly as I could, "and you are a good child."

The child was taught to be quiet. He is a baby bird that must fear predators.

I took the dry laundry down from the lines. I buttoned Tobias into my unironed boy's shirt and folded back the sleeves until his little hands were visible. I washed the child's filthy clothing. The pants were nothing special, but someone had made the shirt beautifully. Even Honor would approve it. I had chops for our supper. I took one, fried it, and divided it with a small piece for Tobias and a larger portion for the dog. After he had eaten again, Tobias yawned widely.

I spread my clean sheet and laid out my shawl for a blanket. The child came willingly when I took his hand and led him. He would have to sleep without a nightshirt until I could make one. I had lifted him in and smoothed the shawl over him when the dog climbed up beside him.

"Rafe?" I said, startled.

He is a huge dog. His shoulder does indeed stand at my hip.

Now that he was cleaner, I could see that his fur was white all over except for feathers of brown and gray along his flanks and legs. He has a noble head, if one can say that of a dog. His brown eyes looked at me inscrutably as he lay beside Tobias. There is room for both of us, he might be saying, and the child needs me tonight. As if to affirm that truth, Tobias reached his hand to touch Rafe's head and sighed.

I bent to kiss Tobias. "Good night, Tobias," I said. "I will be near."

He looked up at me sleepily. What a beautiful child, I thought. He has large eyes like his mother's, only his are not soft brown but clear, bright hazel with a black fringe of lashes. His brown hair curls on his forehead and about his ears. His skin is olive. He is so thin and cut about by weeds and branches that my heart hurts to see it. He looked at me solemnly for a moment, and then his eyes closed. Just afterward the dog's did too.

I went quietly to set the table and build the fire to cook Flint's supper and mine. Soon Celeste called my name from the canal bank. I went out to the deck, and she told me the news.

"Will you come aboard and have some food?" I asked her.

"No," she said. "I must go to my man and my children. Flint said to tell you he is coming very soon."

"Where is the woman?" I asked.

"The doctor tended her there in the field," Celeste said. "Finally, the woman was too weak to labor. Doctor Walker had the men make a litter and carry her to her surgery. She thought she might save the child. But it was too late."

I hear Celeste sigh in the darkness. "The undertaker will see her buried tomorrow. We took a collection."

"I must help with that," I said.

"Doctor Walker asks you to bring the child tomorrow morning," Celeste told me.

"I will," I said.

"Miss Mina?" It was Flint coming.

Celeste went to her boat and waiting family, and poor Flint

came in for his supper. He was weeping when I saw him in the lamplight of the cabin.

"She died, Miss Mina, she died," he told me.

It took me a long time to soothe him and to persuade him to eat. What helped at last was that I took up the lamp and showed him the child and the dog sleeping peacefully together. Then Flint sat at the table while I fried the chops. When all was ready, he suddenly ate with appetite.

"Can we keep them on the boat until we know if he has family?" I asked as we sat at the table.

Flint looked at me as if I had questioned that an egg is an egg.

"Of course," he said.

In the morning, after I dressed Tobias in his washed and mended clothing, Flint and I took him to Doctor Walker. Tobias was very docile and quiet and the dog was too, so long as they stayed together. When Flint wanted the dog to wait in the yard outside the doctor's house, Rafe did not growl or threaten, only pushed past Flint impatiently and entered beside Tobias.

Doctor Lydia Mary Walker thought Tobias to be four or five years old. The child would not answer questions. He hung his head and clutched my skirts when we spoke to him. I got just one whispered no from him when I knelt to ask him if he knew the name of the place where he and his mama were going.

"Let him be," the doctor told me. "Let time ease him. Feed him, treat him gently, and see if he will tell you more."

"There were no papers or money sewn somewhere in the mother's clothing?" I asked. "She had no bag of things?"

I remembered how my brother and I prepared so carefully for our journey from our home. I remembered with a pang of sadness my brother's riding boots.

"There was nothing," Miss Lydia said. "Perhaps she lost a bag on the way. Perhaps they were escaping slavery, and she thought it dangerous to carry anything."

I had not thought of such a thing.

"The child does not look African," I said.

"No, he does not," Miss Lydia replied. "Nor does the mother, but there are many mixed-race peoples, and we are on the route north to the safety of Canada. Who knows?"

"Will he be safe from the bounty men?" I asked.

Maurice Clemens and a captain of one of the other lineboats discussed the Fugitive Slave Law passionately one night. Bounty men looking for escaped slaves were in Rochester this past month. There is much anger about it in the country hereabouts.

"You will care for him?" the doctor asks. "It is that or the orphanage."

"No!" Flint says. "No orphanage!"

He has been watching silently all the while.

"There is nothing of his past for him to keep?" I ask.

Miss Lydia gives me a small packet.

"His mother wore two tortoiseshell combs to pin up her braid," she said. "I took those and cut a lock of her hair. It is all we can do for him."

I put the packet in my pocket and took Tobias to say good-bye to his mother. We saw the woman and baby buried in the common graveyard. When the undertaker asked about a marker, I gave him money for a board.

"What will I put on it?" he asked.

"Say *Here Lies Tobias's Mother,* and the date she died," I told him.

When we went back to the canal afterward, Flint and I asked up and down the boats for information. No one knew who the woman might be. No one had seen her, and surely, they said, pointing to the great dog, a person would remember *that,* if not the woman herself.

We continued west the next day. We had our business to keep, and the canal demands movement always. There was, however, change beyond having the child and dog on our boat. I saw immediately that I could not tend Tobias and ride all day. Flint suggested taking him with me on Trey, but I said no. To make the child sit before me without moving for hours would be a cruelty even if it were possible to do. I pointed out that most freighters carried a captain and two crew as well as the cook. We had economized long enough.

We hired a driver, Joseph, a boy of about fifteen or so, a bright, sensible lad who needed work to help his widowed mother and to pay for his own schooling in the winter months. I had him show me that he knew how to curry and to harness the horses. Flint asked him how he would check that the horses were not sore or hurt. I was pleased that Flint thought of it. I never know what will stay in his head and what pass out of it. His mind seems a colander in which the holes are different sizes, depending on the moment.

It was very different now to keep the boat and tend the child. I think my cooking improved since I had more time to plan and work throughout the day. I made stews, cakes, and dropped biscuits. Flint ate more than ever, and very soon Joseph, Tobias, and Rafe were not far behind in appetite.

Tobias became very agitated the first day as we set out. He stayed so close to me and held my skirt so that I tripped over him when I turned quickly. I feared I would drop boiling water on his head as I worked. The dog too paced back and forth in the confines of the cabin, but when we came to a lock and I urged the animal to jump to the bank, he would not go until we all went to the land.

At last, I sat and put my arms about Tobias.

"What is wrong?" I whispered to him.

"Are we going back to Grandmama?" he whispered in my ear.

"Can you tell me where Grandmama lives?" I asked.

He shook his head and looked frightened.

"We cannot go to her," I said quietly. "We are going west to the city of Buffalo, which lies beside a vast lake called Lake Erie. At Buffalo we will turn the boat around and come east again."

He stared into my face but said nothing. At first, I did not know how best to help him. Over the days, I found that if I talked to him in a quiet voice without expecting an answer, it calmed him. I quickly made a habit of saying what I was doing and what I saw.

"I am making slapjacks for breakfast," I would say. "First I take an egg and milk and then I beat in cornmeal." Or, as I sat on the stern deck sewing for him, "Look at the ducks on the water. See how they make ripples as they swim." And, "I am making a nightshirt for you, Tobias. My friend Honor taught me to make a neat seam this way." Or when a packet went by, "Smell the cooking smells this morning. The ladies and gentlemen are going to have beefsteaks fried in butter and strong coffee for their breakfasts."

I thought it might be good for him to have small tasks while I was working. He seemed very frightened when I put a handful of peas in front to him and showed him how to shell them into the basin. His hand shook. When he picked up a pod and opened it, the peas fell out and rolled to the floor. I was shocked then that he put both hands above his head as if he expected a blow. The dog, which had been lying near, stood and came toward me.

"Tobias," I said very softly. "Let us sit and do this work together. See? We hold our hands over the basin so the peas fall into it."

He brought his arms slowly to the table. The dog lay down again. I shelled the peas with Tobias and talked of how the pods are little boats and the peas the passengers inside. We are like peas and our lineboat is our pod, I said. The child nodded solemnly. He has not laughed or even smiled yet.

I did not like to be on the boat in the locks. The turbulent rush of the water made me uneasy. I especially did not like the feeling of being confined when the water level fell and the stone walls rose overhead as the boat locked down. When I could, I would take Tobias and Rafe and we would walk around the lock on the path. Sometimes my work or Flint's need for help with the ropes kept me on board.

The first time it happened that we were in the boat when we locked down, Tobias rushed to me in terror and pressed himself against my legs.

"I do not like it either, Tobias," I said. "What can we do to help us feel better?"

"We could hug Rafe," he whispered.

I was amazed that he had answered me at all.

"Yes," I said. "We will sit on the floor with Rafe and stroke him. That might help."

After that, Tobias began to talk a little more. By the time we were turned back east from Buffalo, he seemed almost at ease. One afternoon on a quiet stretch of water, I asked him about his whispering.

"Did your mama want you to whisper when you were traveling?" I asked.

He nodded yes, and his frightened look came over him.

"It is all right," I said. "Your mama was wise. But being in the boat is not quite like traveling on the land. We talk as we wish. You can whisper, or you can talk to me and Flint and Joseph just as we talk to each other."

He nodded. That night at supper, he whispered in my ear if he could give Rafe his eggplant from his plate. I asked him why.

"I don't like eggplant," he said in a voice that, while not very loud, was not a whisper either.

"I'll eat it," said Flint and Joseph at the same time.

"We will divide the eggplant between Flint and Joseph," I said. "I will give Rafe the soup bone to chew out on the deck. I think he will like that better than eggplant."

That night after everything was cleaned away and Tobias, with Rafe lying beside him, was tucked into his bed between his own clean sheets, I remembered that I intended to go west to California once. It is only weeks ago but it seems years. We were in Buffalo, and I did not think of it at all.

As I lay in my bed in the cabin, I felt the gentle rocking of the boat. A night bird called on the water. I heard Tobias murmur in his sleep, and then the dog sighed and all was quiet again.

I thought of Maurice Clemens, and his keen eye for beauty and cheerful interest in our human world. I thought of Honor, with her easy ways and busy hands. I thought of Mr. Serle, kind and calm in the center of every storm. If I can show Tobias these people through myself, he will grow wise and be strong.

There are so many layers of memory to my life now, I thought. I wonder sadly if my brother thinks of me ever in his life in far-off California, if Mr. Serle is married and happy, if Honor and Aunt Jane are angry at me or regret my absence, if Maurice Clemens will be rich and famous, if Flint will recover his mind, if I will have the strength to keep Tobias well and safe. I sigh in fear. And then I hear a little answering sigh. Perhaps it is the dog again, I think; perhaps it is an angel's breath. I kiss the ring on my finger. My mother in heaven loves me. I drift into sleep.

PART SIX

UNCAS FALLS

SOMETIME IN JULY WE arrived at Albany again. After the load of flour was delivered, I went to inquire at the harbor-master's office if there were letters for me. Honor had written to me, and Maurice Clemens had too. Honor's letter was kind.

> My dearest, darling Mina,
>
> Aunt Jane and I cried when your letter came and kissed each other because we could not kiss you. We are very relieved to know that you are well and safe. Because you are safe, we find that we can forgive you. Yes, there was pain and sadness for us in knowing that you could not find comfort in remaining with us. Your explanation does much to help us understand.

Guido, of course, is also happy to know you are recovering from your ordeal. I suppose you knew that Mr. Serle was to visit here on Sunday the 27th of April, although you never told us. In the event, Mr. Serle, Madame Moses, the child Stellina, and Herr Meyer too all arrived to surprise us. Mr. Serle was terribly upset not to find you, but Aunt Jane did not think it proper to discuss why you were not here. At last, I asked Guido to take Mr. Serle aside to explain, and then I took the liberty of showing him your note. I feared for a moment he might faint. He turned red, and then his face went ashen. He has called several times to ask if we have heard of you. I will be glad to tell him of your message—indeed, before I began this letter, I posted a note asking him to call to hear your news.

The rest of the visit might have been considered somewhat comic if our worry about you had not been foremost. There was nothing to eat, of course, or nothing that you would have considered sufficient, and then, in her distress, Aunt Jane spilled tea on Herr Meyer. My Guido and Mr. Serle and Madame Moses had some sort of argument in Italian while the brother stroked his beard and . . .

Well, I will not copy it all out, for the rest was about Madame Moses's dress, little Stellina's bewilderment, and that Aunt Jane thinks it proper etiquette to return the call, which Honor gravely doubts. I will reply to Honor in a day or two when I am more settled. If she is going to share my news with Mr. Serle, I must think about what to say. The visit sounded sadly confused, not comic, to me, perhaps because I know its foolish purpose was to show I was not Mr. Serle's mistress—nor does he love me—and I feel anger still.

Maurice Clemens's letter was purely his cheerful self. *Dear Miss Mina Pigot,* he wrote in his decisive hand, *I now am in Albany until September fulfilling a commission to paint a landscape mural in the dining room of a gentleman's house. I count on you to invite me for a pleasant meal with you and Flint as soon as your lineboat is tied up. I need strength for my work. Yours faith-fully, Maurice Clemens.* Under his signature he printed the direction to reach him. Of course, I wrote a note to Mr. Clemens to invite him to eat with us.

With the lineboat unloaded and Flint planning to take on furniture again to go west, I had to decide what to do. After some hesitation, I told Flint that I could not stay with him. I liked the varied travel on the canal for myself, I said, but it was too much for Tobias. The journey west frightened him. He was much better since we turned east. He needed to be settled in one place to recover himself. Flint looked sad, but he did not object. I think he understood. He told me that we must take the papers and make our report to his wife, who owns the lineboat.

"Zip will know what to do. She is a fine manager," he told me. "Almost as good a manager as you, Miss Mina."

When Maurice Clemens arrived for supper, he was startled to find Tobias, Rafe, and Joseph with us. The whole story of the changes since we saw him had to be explained. He seemed a little shy of Tobias, although he engaged Joseph in conversation about his studies in his usual easy manner.

"Are you returning to Buffalo?" Mr. Maurice asked me. "The thought of travel in this fine weather makes me restless. I wish I were not tied to my work here."

"Tobias and I will not go west again this year," I replied.

"But where will you go, Miss Mina?" Flint exclaimed, as if hearing the news for the first time. He held out his plate for another slice of boiled tongue with mustard and caper sauce.

"I might rent a cottage in the country near here or else go to my friends in New York for advice," I said.

After our meal, Flint and Joseph walked into town. Joseph wanted to see the sights and shops of a real city, and Flint seemed glad to amble off with him. I put Tobias to bed with Rafe to watch him as usual, and then Maurice Clemens and I sat on the stern deck of the lineboat and talked for a time of travel and his work.

"I have met your friend Mr. S. Meyer," he tells me.

"He is not my friend," I say stiffly—but curiosity has the better of me. "How did you meet him?"

"He knows the man whose dining room I am decorating. He was here in Albany last week to visit."

"I am glad I missed him," I say.

"I am glad I did not," Maurice returns. "He admired my mural and bought several sketches of Niagara Falls"—he pauses as some thought strikes him—"and other subjects. He assures me that my work will be accepted for the Academy of Design winter show."

"What good news," I say. I hope Mr. Maurice will not question me further about Herr Meyer. The thought of him, fingering his beard and making fantasies, annoys me.

Maurice must see the feeling in me. He changes the subject.

"Flint seems better, more at ease in himself than when I last saw him," he said. "You have cared for him kindly, Miss Mina."

"I wish I could see my way to do more," I replied. "I wish I knew what it might be."

Maurice Clemens has been sketching as usual even as the daylight faded and the stars kindled in the sky above us. Now he sets aside his book and crayon. "Come here," he says and pulls me to him in his chair. "I have been thinking of this every moment since I saw you again."

He folds his arms about me and kisses me. He kisses me for a very, very long time. With his mouth on mine, he pushes his hands into my hair until it begins to tumble about my shoulders. He strokes his hands down my back and about my waist. His hand moves up to trace the shape of my breast through the thin cotton layers of my dress and chemise.

I am bewildered by my strange feelings. The pull of life in me, the shame I felt when I dreamed that Jasper Westervelt groped between my legs, the joy of Maurice's arms about me and his mouth on mine. I am an apple tree in spring bud. This is more than thought or feeling. I am afraid and yet not quite ready to struggle. Like running with John Deegan, this is a new and dangerous experience to be savored, but with caution.

This is what Mr. Serle feels when he is tempted, I think. I never imagined it. How foolish I have been. And truly a child—he was right to call me that. Questions well up in me. Why did I not understand the pull and power of this feeling before? Why was Mr. Serle afraid to show me what he knew? Does he give himself up completely to this force when he is with Anna Moses? Or does he see himself in her arms and wonder at himself as I do now with Maurice?

Maurice stops kissing me suddenly. "You are not here with me," he asserts. "Where are you?"

"Oh!" I exclaim. "How did you know?"

I regain my chair. The boat rocks gently.

"Thank you," he says. "Thank you for indulging me for a moment. You are still in love with that other fellow, I see. I suppose I will have to find you again in a month or two and kiss you some more to learn if you have forgotten him yet. It seems a rather new and difficult method of courting, but if you can stand it, I will do my best to adapt."

I am regaining my composure now. I am glad he cannot see my hot face clearly in the dim light that comes from the cabin, where the lamp is lit upon the table. I must resist him, and yet—he has guided me out of a dark woods. How strange, I think, it is as if my body spoke to my mind and heart. Understanding has stepped from shadow to the light.

"That is the end of kissing," I say. "I will not mislead you. I hope I have not, nor caused pain."

"Not much," he says. "I will survive. And tonight's kiss was very nice—worthy of a place in any aspiring lover's collection."

"Do you truly take life so easily?" I ask.

I cannot make out his expression, but when he speaks, his voice sounds contented and relaxed.

"It is a kaleidoscope world, Miss Mina," he says. "I find a beautiful pattern and admire it. I turn the brass tube, and the pieces form themselves into new and equally lovely universes. I like the next pattern as well as the last one because there is beauty everywhere."

"You are fortune's child," I say, pinning up my hair.

He does not answer that but takes his drawing pad and tilts it to the light and writes his address in Brooklyn.

"If you take a cottage near here, you can invite me to dinner. If you return to New York, write me at this address," he says. "I would like to paint you."

When Flint and Joseph return and he leaves a few moments later, we say good-bye formally.

The next morning, I dressed Tobias and myself neatly. I had bought Tobias shoes at Syracuse, but he wore them only once before. He looked down at his feet suspiciously after I put the shoes on him and then went to show them to the dog, who was lying on the stern deck.

"Look, Rafe," I heard him say. "We have shoes. Mama promised we would have shoes."

My heart twisted in my breast. The child does not forget his poor dead mother. I went out to him and knelt beside him. "Your mama told you truth," I said gently. "Is there any other word of hers I can help come true?"

Rafe pushed my hand with his great head as if the answer might be yes, but Tobias only stared wide-eyed at me for a moment and then reached out his hand to touch his shoes.

I put on my bonnet and gloves, which I had not worn since Easter Day when I found Flint. Tobias and Rafe both looked at me with surprise when I joined them, ready to go to meet Mrs. James. Flint wore a coat that I had never seen before and found his hat. He looked more a man of business than a sailor suddenly. We left Joseph at the boat to study his Latin grammar book and tend the horses.

Zipporah James lives with Phoebe, who is Mr. Phil now, in a small, neat house on the Clarksville Road leading out of the city of Albany. It was a dusty walk on a hot day. When we arrived, Flint knocked on the door as a visitor would. An elderly woman in a black dress and a maid's blue morning apron came to let us in.

"Why, Mr. Flint!" she exclaimed. "Come in! Come in!"

"Hello, Mercy," Flint said shyly. "I hope you are keeping well?"

"Very well, Mr. Flint," Mercy told him. "Miss Zip will be surprised to see you."

"Who is here, Mercy?" a harsh voice called from the back of the house. "What are you doing chattering in the hall?"

"Mr. Flint is here," Mercy called back without ceremony, "with a young woman and her child and her dog."

"What has he done now!" exclaimed the voice, exasperated.

Mrs. James came into the hall, followed by Phoebe, wearing boy's clothes still. When I saw Zipporah James that rainy night in New York, I thought her a middle-aged woman, much older than Flint. Now that I see her in her house without her poke bonnet and in daylight, I see that she is young. Her skin is smooth, her dark-brown hair glossy, her figure erect. And yet there is a hardness to her eyes and a stiffness in her—a way of carrying herself as if her bones might hurt—that make her seem old. Where Flint is soft looking, uncertain, and kind as best he can be, his wife is all angles and anger.

Mrs. James looks us over.

"Get that dog out of the house," she says sharply.

Rafe sits on his haunches and looks at her with his red tongue hanging out. He might be thinking of eating her, he might be laughing at her.

"Perhaps Mercy could take the child and the dog to the kitchen for a cool drink while we talk," I say mildly.

"Who is this person?" Flint's wife asks him. "And what do you want, turning up like a bad penny when we are busy?"

She sounds very rude, but I think that Flint's wound must be her wound and her pain too. Poor Flint looks at her with a mix of terror and some other feeling—love perhaps, or a need for love. He seems to have lost his speech.

"I am Mina Pigot," I tell Zipporah James. "I know Phoe—that is, Phil from the boat to America almost three years past."

Mrs. James waves her hand dismissively to Mercy.

"Take the child and dog away," she says as if she just thought of the idea. "What is your business?" she demands.

Flint finds his tongue. "Miss Mina fed me and drove the horses for the boat," he says. "Now she must care for the poor orphan child. I will give her my farm in Uncas Falls so she can live. I thought I should tell you, Zip."

I think my mouth gapes open. He has not said a murmur to me of such a thing.

"I wish a place to live, it is true," I say.

I am not sure what Flint means by *give*.

Mrs. James's eyes narrow as she looks from Flint to me and back again.

"Mr. Phil," she says abruptly to Phoebe, "is this woman honest?"

"Oh yes," Phoebe answers in a careless way. "Very."

We all stand about in the hall then as Zipporah James berates her husband. The farm is his, but she has rights to use it, she claims. She is a great debater, or would be if anyone had the energy to argue against her. Mercy never takes the child for a drink but stands and listens. To a seemingly endless lecture by Mrs. James about presumption and misplaced trust and foolish kindness, Flint gives no excuses but stubbornly repeats again and again, "They must have a good place to live."

I am about to tell Flint that it is all right, I will rent a cottage, when Phoebe intervenes to say, "Give over, Miss Zip. He has made up his mind."

"What there is of it," Zipporah James spits.

The insult to Flint upsets me. Now I feel stubborn too. Flint should do what makes him happy.

"I do not want this farm *given* to me," I say. "But I accept Mr. James's kind offer to live there."

In the end, it is Phoebe and I who decide what must be done. Tobias and I will go to the farm in Uncas Falls. The farm will be run as usual, with extra produce sent to Mrs. James. What I grow or preserve myself will belong to me. I will live free in exchange for cooking for the farmhand, who maintains the place, and for a Mr. Silas King, who ministers to a chapel in the village and also works for Mrs. James. Mr. Henry Carlton—he is Mrs. James's brother—and his wife, who are proprietors of the general store, will help us settle in the house. Flint is going to sell the lineboat and give me my wages for the canal. He will purchase a cart and harness. I can drive Trey and Pompey to the farm. The farmhand has had to lease horses for his work and can use them.

"Well," Mrs. James says sullenly. "I hope you are a sensible manager. Mr. Phil and I will visit in a few months and observe how you get on."

"Certainly," I say. "And now the child must have a drink before we return to the boat. While Mercy is giving him something, you can settle the lineboat accounts with Mr. James and write me a note to Mr. and Mrs. Carlton introducing us."

Zipporah James thins her mouth to two pencil lines and narrows her eyes at me, but she does as I ask. After she has written the note, she gives us each a tract from the pile on her hall table.

"Sinners must remember the way of the Lord!" she exclaims, making Tobias flinch. She stares at Flint. "I do not want to see you ever again."

She makes a motion with her hand as if to brush away an insect. Flint looks at her sadly and shambles to the door.

"Good-bye, Miss Mina," Phoebe says. She winks at me. "We will see you in Uncas Falls."

Flint is silent until, halfway to the boat basin, he looks down at Tobias clinging to my hand and dragging his tired feet in the dust. He asks Tobias if he would like to ride on his shoulders. Tobias is excited. I worry that he will fall, but when I see him clutching Flint's hair and smiling, I feel more cheerful and ask if he likes the view high up.

It is a relief to leave the clenched fist that is Zipporah James and go back to the lineboat. Joseph uses the afternoon to find a new place as a driver. I go out to buy a second valise to pack my clothes and Tobias's and the kitchen things I bought myself. Flint tells me to take everything since the boat is to be sold, so I buy a tin trunk too. That night I make a big meal with Flint's favorite potatoes, beefsteaks as Joseph likes them, and ginger cakes for Tobias.

In the morning Flint and I purchase the cart and harness. We say good-bye to Joseph. He looks sad and then cheerful as he talks of going west and seeing his mother.

"Where will you go, Flint?" I ask when Joseph has left us.

"Perhaps the sea again," he tells me. "Perhaps California and the gold fields. Is Australia far?"

He sounds very vague again. I think that he was better when we were on the canal. Seeing his wife made sorrow for him.

"Perhaps you will see my brother in San Francisco," I say. "Tell him I love him if you find him."

"Will you give me a lock of your hair?" Flint asks.

To my surprise, he looks at me direct now, like a man, not a confused ghost.

"Of course," I say. "I have the chain you made me and memories of our good months of work. A lock of hair is not much in exchange."

"It will keep me warm with its brightness," Flint says when I give him the red curl tied with a thread.

"And you will know my brother because his hair is the same color," I say.

"I am going to California." Flint smiles suddenly. "It is far enough away from Zip and her horror of me."

I hope it might indeed be far enough, but I do not say so.

"I will pray for you," I tell him. "Thank you for all your help to me."

"Well, give us a kiss, then," he says in the old way he had when I first met him.

I kiss his cheek and hold up Tobias to kiss him too. Flint hoists his bag to his shoulder and turns away on the road toward Albany.

"Good-bye, Flint!" chirps Tobias.

"Good-bye, Flint," I call to him.

We climb into the cart. Rafe barks once. Flint waves his hand. We wave back. Then I shake the reins, the horses move forward, and soon we are on the turnpike going west.

Our journey to Uncas Falls took us the better part of a day from Albany on the road. When we came at last to the village, Tobias was asleep in the cart, and the lake was shimmering golden silk in the reflected sunset. Uncas Lake stretches northeast and south-west for about twelve miles, but it is narrow across—perhaps a half mile at the widest point. Low, wooded hills surround it. Coming on the road from the north, I could see higher mountains beyond, blue in the distance to the east and south. The village of Uncas Falls lies halfway down the western side of the lake, where Uncas Creek flows into it. Sawyerville is a larger town at the very southern end of the lake.

I found the Carltons without difficulty. Their store is the front half of their house, facing the road. They live behind on the lake side with their two children. I was a little afraid that they would be stiff and angry like Zipporah James, but they turned out to be pleasant folk. Mr. Henry Carlton and his sister Zipporah resemble each other in their brown coloring and sharp-cut features. He is tall and angular, but his expression is genial in the American businesslike way. Mrs. Carlton, Georgina, is a twit-tering, friendly soul, small in stature and quick moving. Indeed, the Carltons are like a mismatched pair of birds, a hawk and a house wren.

Tobias and I were both a little overwhelmed by their house. The family lives in rooms behind the store and upstairs above it. The extra goods that have not yet been set out for sale are every-where. There are barrels and casks and crates piled in the corners. In addition to being a storekeeper, Henry Carlton is Postmaster, Jus-tice of the Peace for Uncas Falls, and an amateur botanist. Where his sister seems clenched, he is generous and open—although they share a quality of intensity. He is cataloging the trees of Uncas County. He wanted to demonstrate his special botanical press and show me his books with samples of leaves and bark, maps, and ta-bles of growth, but Mrs. Carlton took pity on me.

"Another time, Henry," she said. "The poor things are ex-hausted tonight. You can bore Miss Pigot tomorrow."

We were grateful to be welcomed and fed and given a bed, even if we had to share the room with braids of onions hung up to dry from hooks in the ceiling. In the morning, we will go to Flint's house—both Mr. and Mrs. Carlton called it Flint's house—and meet Eben Brouwer, the hired man.

The morning was lovely, fresh, and sparkling with light on the rippling lake and on the dew-wet goldenrod in the meadowland along the road. Flint's house sits on the hillside above the road on the north side of the village. We passed the lane leading up to it as we came into Uncas Falls.

I do not know if a house can stand and still die. As we rode with Henry Carlton up the lane and past the farm pond, the solidly built, two-story stone house turned its blind stare down at us, its windows blank pewter plates of reflected morning sun. It was not just that no smoke rose from the chimneys nor livestock stirred in the yard—there was no sign of life at all. No open window with a curtain wafting, no pot of herbs on the doorstep by the kitchen, no laundry snapping on a line, no hay rake or hoe left leaning against the barn. The lane itself was grass grown and wild.

The house inside had the same feel of absence. It smelled of dust and mice. For all that, I thought it a beautiful place. The main part has a porch across the front with French doors leading onto it. An ell—which also has a porch—to the right of the main house is a summer kitchen with an attic floor above it. That ell was the original small farmhouse, Henry Carlton says. What is now the main house was built later. The length of the house and the porches face south and east to the morning sun and the lake. The barn is attached to the ell. In the winter, it is possible to tend the animals without going outside at all.

It is not necessary to go outside for water either. The house has a cistern in the cellar and hand pumps at sinks in both the main house and in the ell. There is a clear, good spring of water on the hill above the house. A wooden pipe leads down to the cistern, and an overflow outlet takes water out of the house again and downhill to a farm pond. From the pond the water trickles in a little stream to the lake. The water runs all winter except in the very worst of the cold, and then the cellar reservoir is enough to supply our needs.

Henry Carlton tells me that the main house was built by an

Irishman, a mason who learned his trade building the Erie Canal. Flint's father bought it from him, and Flint grew up here. Flint married Zipporah, and they lived in the house with Flint's parents until the mother died and Flint went to the Mexican War.

Henry Carlton hesitated in his story then.

I said, "Flint was wounded grievously. His body and his mind are both affected."

Mr. Carlton nodded. "When he returned in the winter of forty-eight, he was mad with grief, and drinking whatever spirits he could find. Zip fled to New York and retreated into her work for Temperance. Flint's father died that spring. Flint disappeared after we buried him."

"It is a great sadness," I say. "Flint has been kind to us."

Mr. Carlton looked at me with curiosity in his narrowed eyes, but he did not question me. He is very courteous in that way. I think it is a country habit.

The house inside was furnished with bedsteads, tables, chairs. There was blue and white china in the cupboard. There were a few pots as well as the andirons, spider, and cranes in the kitchen fireplace—indeed in both kitchen fireplaces, for there are two, in the main house and in the ell, which is used as a summer kitchen. Dust lay everywhere and old cobwebs hung in the ceiling corners. In the parlor, the sun had bleached the wallpaper, a pretty pattern of two shades of blue on a cream background, to a ghost of itself. In the other front room, which I had thought would be the room for dining, was a bedstead and a chest of drawers. Someone had closed the shutters there and the wallpaper, the same blue dianthus as in the parlor, still looked fresh with its sprigs and blossoms blue and cream, not grayed and yellowed.

We found Eben Brouwer, the hired man, just outside the barn. He is a weather-beaten old man, sun-browned, spare and rope-muscled, and very soft-spoken. Tobias seemed to find comfort with him almost immediately. When I turned from speaking with Mr. Carlton about whether he delivered supplies or if I should come down in the cart, Tobias was earnestly introducing Mr. Brouwer to Trey and Pompey and Rafe.

"How d' you do, Miss Mina?" Mr. Brouwer said to me, tipping

his straw hat back a little from his face with one finger. "Are you thinking of a cow? Your son will want milk."

"Yes," I said. "A cow and hens surely, and geese perhaps. Will you advise me?"

Well, that was the beginning of a season of work. In the past, Eben and Mr. Silas King slept in the attic over the ell until the weather turned. Then they went to board in the village for the winter. Eben supported himself when no farm labor was needed by working with the blacksmith in Uncas Falls. He makes shoes for people too. Now, with animals to care for, wood—cords and cords of wood—to cut and carry, and ashes to take out, as well as other work, he will stay at the house with us and go down to his jobs in the village as there is need and as he has time.

"There is less call for boots hereabouts these past few years, Miss Mina," he told me once. "The new factories will put all of us out of our work soon."

Tobias and I will sleep in the front bedroom on the first floor of the main house. Eben will be in a smaller bedroom on the other side of the kitchen for the winter. I have hired Lily Turner, a childless widow who lives just down the hill, to help. Despite her delicate-sounding name, she is a strapping woman, who takes a pride in her strength for work. She is shy and slow to learn, I discover, but good-natured—even though she tells me one morning in a burst of honesty that she finds some of my ways very foreign. *Frenchified,* she calls my use of a larding needle and my making sauces for vegetables, and then admits, as if conceding a weakness of character, that the food tastes good. Lily eats her meals with us but sleeps at home with her elderly parents. They need her to help keep the fire in the cold weather and to start their breakfasts, she says.

All through the end of summer and into the fall we cleaned, repaired, and refurbished the house. I began to stock the pantry and the cellars against the cold weather. The gardens are in ruins from neglect, but Eben, Lily, and I made a start on restoring them. There were tomatoes and pumpkins that had seeded themselves, and apple trees. We fertilized the asparagus bed and marked it so we would not dig it up by mistake later. I have planted a hop vine by the barn. If my yeast dies, I will have what is needful for a starter. I had a moment's fantasy that Mr. Serle might visit someday and show me how to make beer, but I pushed the foolish thought away. The terrible nightmares of flaming tulips have faded, and I have begun to dream of him again, holding me. I started an herb garden with slips that Georgina Carlton gave me. Sorrel, thyme, and mint will grow in the spring. Eben repaired the coop for the hens in the barn and made a door to an outside pen so they can sun themselves in warm weather.

Georgina Carlton gave me a setting Poland hen and a clutch of eggs. Henry Carlton helped Eben find a good cow. We bought ducks and geese also. I am undecided about a pig just now. Lily told me where the best places for blackberrying and nut gathering are. Tobias grew almost plump, and then shot up an inch in height from August to October. We made a place on the wall beside the kitchen door to mark his progress. Soon after that, Tobias found an old horn button wedged in a crack in the bedroom floor.

"Does someone want it?" he asked me, holding it on the palm of his hand and gazing at it longingly.

"It is yours, my darling," I told him. "You have found it. You may keep it."

"Thank you, Mother," he whispered.

I looked at him. "You would like to call me Mother?" I asked. He nodded. "Rafe says I should not call you Mama."

"Yes," I tell him. "Mama is for your one and only Mama who carried you under her heart until you were ready to be born. But a mother can also be someone who cares for you and loves you. I will be very happy to be your mother. Thank you, Tobias."

I have taken up my pen again tonight. Tobias is asleep in his bed with Rafe beside him. Eben is here rubbing tallow into the harnesses. He sits by the fire, looking sleepy.

Of course, I wrote to Honor and Aunt Jane the first days we were here to say that I could not come back to the city now. I said

I have taken in an orphan child to care for and that we are living on a farm in the village of Uncas Falls. I asked for news of them and to have my brother's letters if any had arrived.

Honor wrote to me promptly.

My dearest, darling Mina,

We would scold you for not coming back to us immediately if you had not explained that the child you care for needs country life. You must tell us about this child. A boy or girl? How old? If you do not tell us everything, you must be prepared that we will visit to find out your secrets for ourselves.

The two letters that have come from your brother are enclosed in this packet. Your trunk is roped up and ready to send to you as soon as you give directions.

But I must tell you the news here. Guido DiRoma and I are engaged to marry. Are you surprised? Aunt Jane says she is happy, but she is not as happy as we are. We will be married in the spring just as soon as the changes to this house are complete. I have told Benjamin Serle that I owe a great part of my joy to him because he brought my Guido to me. I owe the other part to you because you knew Benjamin who brought Guido—well, you see it is like a children's song. If you think I am become giddy and silly, you are right. I wish you were here for our talks at night and to give me advice on my wedding clothes. . . .

The rest was about fabrics and the fashions and that Guido DiRoma bought the house on Elizabeth Street. They are adding modern plumbing to bring the Croton water in and also gas jets, which Honor dislikes because the light affects how colors appear under it. I was glad she mentioned Mr. Serle. It must mean he has not chosen Madame Moses over his friends. Still, I was disappointed that she did not report what he said when she told him the message in my previous letter. Perhaps in her happiness she forgot something that happened more than a month ago. Honor says that

Mr. DiRoma sends his good wishes to me along with hers and Aunt Jane's love. Well, I thought, their engagement is not a surprise. They are very well suited.

I turned eagerly to my brother's letters. One was written in April and the other in early June. They are both rather short and businesslike. The second one shocked me, though.

We are recovering from the fire of May, Daniel wrote. *It is the worst yet, with much loss of life. My business was set back, but I have an interest in the new construction, so I will recover my losses. I have been a little surprised not to receive one of your worried letters. Maybe you are getting used to the constant reports of destruction here, or maybe your letter is delayed.*

I felt very upset that I did not know his danger. He must think I do not care for him. And yet—he writes always of his business first. He does not tell me of his thoughts and dreams or even of the people he meets. He complains not to have a worried letter, and yet he never asks me of my life but only says pray for me. I wonder if he hopes that I will become a nun and give my life to prayer.

I moped about for a day, being sorry for myself that my brother does not love me as I think he should and feeling shame that I did not know of the fire that might have killed him. Then I sat down and wrote a letter to Daniel. I told him some of what I have written here about why I left the Westervelts. I told him about Tobias and that I am happy living in the country with him. I said that I am glad my brother is alive and that I want to know of his life.

Business, getting and spending, however important, is not the heart of life, I wrote. *I want to know of the people you care about and your dreams. I want to tell you the truth of my soul in my letters. Please tell your truth in yours.*

Of course, I was anxious after the letter was sent. Perhaps Daniel wants to hold to the memory of a little sister who sells cigars in a grand hotel and goes to church and is content. A grown sister—however virtuous in her behavior and her heart—who lives with unmarried men and adopts a child might frighten him.

It is strange. I thought of that young girl I once was all the autumn days. The Corbetts sent my trunk to Albany. Henry Carlton fetched it for me when he had business there in early October. I was glad to have my winter clothing and my books. I set the china mug I carried in my bag from Ireland on the bedroom mantelpiece. I did not even open my journal that Mr. Serle gave me, though. Instead, I bought paper from the Carltons' store. I wrote the story of the spring and summer of 1848 when I left Ireland and worked in England with Mr. Serle. I had to write it, I thought. It gave me hope that I was once that child who found a goodness and a love in spite of sorrow.

When I was finished with the writing, I laid the papers in a box and put the green ribbon that Mr. Serle gave me that sad evening at Fourth Street in with them. Now I am done with the past, I thought.

I must have been wrong, for, with the story of how I came to America recorded and set away, I found myself opening my private book again and writing as I do tonight. I had to write of Jasper Westervelt and the Erie Canal. I had to. My book and my need for it tell me I can never be done with the past. I discover my world as it is slipping away from me. I am trying to reach my hand out to the rain and catch one drop. If I could only hold and know that drop completely, I might know myself. It is impossible. Life drenches me.

I see that I have neglected to tell about Mr. Silas King. Perhaps this is because he comes and goes on his private business, an aside from our daily lives. Like Eben, he is a lean man, but not work-hard. He seems a sort of young-looking old man—the opposite of Flint, who is young and yet worn with sorrow. I think Mr. King is of a style that will desiccate into an appearance of mummified youth. His coloring is brown, but there is a grayness to him. He is a cloudy day always.

Mr. King is a vegetarian. He exists on dried beans, nuts, and grains. He allows himself Dutch cheese once a week but not eggs—that is eating a living thing, he says. Because of him, I often use sunflower-seed oil and flaxseed oil instead of lard. I have made many attempts to bake healthful bread for him. He eats whatever I make with patient silence. Perhaps he does some sort of penance of the flesh he does not speak of. He seems to have decided to do penance also by sleeping in the attic all winter. When he appeared after we had been in the house a week, he knew of us from Zipporah James.

"Since I am to board here, I will keep my place above the summer kitchen," he said in his flat voice. "It will be more convenient."

Convenient for what? I wondered, but I did not question him. He does not invite questions. I soon found that his arrangement was indeed more convenient for me. He has his separate entrance through the ell to his room. When he comes in late at night from his travels, as he often does, he puts his horse in the barn and goes to his bed without our even knowing he is returned until he appears at breakfast the next day.

He does not wish Lily to air his bed or clean his room for him. "Don't go to that part of the house, if you please, Miss Pigot," he said in his austere way when I asked him about cleaning and laundry. "There is no need. I take care of myself."

"You do not wish at least your shirts washed and ironed?" I asked tentatively. I had found a good laundress in the village.

"No," he said curtly and went out, I suppose to talk to Eben about something, for I saw them conferring in the courtyard. The talk ended, Eben tipped his hat to Mr. King, and Mr. King mounted and went off down the lane to the main road.

"What does Mr. King do?" I asked Eben that evening.

Eben had come in to wash at the end of his day's work. Once I understood his needs, I made sure we have hot water and a fresh towel ready for him before supper. There is a small scullery next to the door between the main house kitchen and the summer kitchen that I have organized as a washroom. Eben is very thoughtful about leaving his boots on the mat at the door. In the country with outdoor work and animals, it is a different dirt than in the city, but it is dirt all the same.

"Silas King ministers at the church here and teaches the Sabbath school. He works for Mrs. James elsewhere," Eben said, pausing at the scullery door.

"What sort of work?" I asked.

Eben shrugged. "Beats me," he said as he disappeared into the scullery. He put his head back around the door. "He believes those papers she hands about," he said and then was gone again.

At supper he said to me, "Mr. King and Miss Zip want everyone to take the Pledge. Miss Zip threatened to send me off if I did not agree to teetotal."

"Oh dear," I said. "I cannot manage without you, Eben."

Tobias dropped his fork and looked stricken. "Is Uncle Eben going away?" he whispered to me.

"Uncle Eben?" Eben said.

He looked as if someone had surprised him with a gift to open. I heard Rafe's tail thump on the floor.

"Is it all right?" I asked.

"Of course," he said.

"Miss Zip was not serious about the Pledge and your job, I hope."

"Perhaps she was," he said. "I meant to warn you when I saw you had bought brandy and wine."

"I don't drink it," I said. "It is for keeping mold from preserves and for cooking occasionally."

"Hide it," Eben said. "What they do not see will not distress them. I have some hard cider myself in the cold cellar."

So Eben and I have a secret together. There is a locked cupboard in the dish pantry now with our bottles stored away. It seems foolish to me that it is necessary. How can anyone cook a tough hen without wine? And Eben is not a tippler. He has his bath on Saturday when his work is done, and a glass of cider with his meal if Silas King is not with us. On Sunday, he goes down to church and Sabbath school. Sometimes on Sunday evening he stays in the village and eats his supper with the family that has a pottery. They make pickle crocks and jugs mostly. The wife is his second cousin, Eben says.

Eventually, in October, I learned what Silas King does besides lecture and give out tracts for Temperance. It was a Saturday evening after a lovely autumn day. The slanting sun turned the red maples and the yellow poplar leaves to flame as Tobias and I gathered the last of the chestnuts under the trees along the upper pasture. Tobias smiled to see the squirrels race in the trees, flirt their bushy gray tails, and chatter their annoyance at us for taking their stores. Lily had gone home early, taking beef stew and a bag of honey cakes for herself and her parents with her. Eben was reading his *Times* as he waited for supper. He exclaimed suddenly.

"So that is why Mr. King has not returned," he said.

"I hope it is not bad news," I told him.

I had set Tobias to picking burrs out of Rafe's coat. The dog bounded after a bold squirrel and into weeds before I could call him. The child looked up with frightened eyes.

"No, no, it is good news for Mr. King, I am sure," Eben said.

"What happened?" I asked quietly.

Tobias went back to grooming Rafe.

"A man named Jerry McHenry was taken in Syracuse as a fugitive slave and imprisoned. The Abolitionists rescued him and carried him away to Canada. Now the rescuers are to be prosecuted for riot. Our Mr. King is among them. There is great fuss and furor at the courthouse in Auburn. The Bloomers are all out and parading about the town with gentlemen escorting them."

"What are Bloomers?" I asked.

"Women who wear Bloomer costume—a sort of fancy trousers, I hear," Eben said. "They are all for rights for women and for slaves too."

"Oh," I said.

Doctor Lydia Mary Walker must be a Bloomer.

"I wonder if Mr. King will be back in time for his service to-morrow," Eben said.

He was, for he traveled all night to be in Uncas Falls for Sunday, and then went back again to Auburn to hear the judge's verdict on the rescuers Monday morning. We heard the story at supper Wednesday night when all was over. Mr. King was still elated by the great events. He did not tell the story direct, but instead treated us to a long grace before our meal. He thanked God for the opportunity to serve Him by protecting one of the least of His black children. He thanked God for the men, of whom he was privileged to be one, who had the courage to seize the poor fugitive from his captors. He thanked God for the toll-takers on the roads, who had sped the rescuers on their way and delayed the pursuers. He thanked God for the judge who set the low bail for the arrested rescuers. He thanked God for the men and women who came to cheer the rescuers for their good deeds. He omitted to say thanks for the horses and for the road-builders who made the roads they trod to Canada or thanks for Canada, where black men are free. In the end, it did not seem much like prayer. We listened to Mr. King boast to God.

Eben winked at me halfway through the recital, and I had to put my napkin to my mouth to stifle a laugh. Lily was not so discreet. She shifted in her seat and sighed twice. We heard it all again on Saturday, because Mr. King made the story the subject of his Sunday sermon. He asked us to hear it for practice, and we could not say no.

After he had read to us, he declared with great satisfaction, "This is the best sermon I have ever written. I am going to send a copy to Mrs. James."

His words that the human body may be enslaved, but the human soul never can be, stayed in my thought. I wonder if it is so. Tobias's fear shackles his spirit. Strangely, the picture of John Deegan dancing at the side of Mr. Branton came into my mind. And then I thought of Mrs. James and her hopeless anger at poor Flint. Perhaps there is more than one kind of slavery.

So Mr. King is an Abolitionist, a worker for Temperance, and a vegetarian. I suppose if he escorted a Bloomer lady in Syracuse he is for women's rights too. It seems a lot for one man to worry about. I would be glad if there were no slaves. That seems more important than whether I can vote, but then—if I could vote, I could help elect the antislavery men. The more I think of it, the more complicated it becomes. For me now, it must be enough to care for Tobias and Eben and feed Mr. King a healthful diet, so he can do good works.

Still, Mr. King's words about the spirit reminded me that I

must consider the needs of Tobias's soul as well as those of his body. I have told Eben that I am a Roman Catholic. Eben looked somewhat downcast, I thought, but he made no spoken comment, just nodded.

"I am not a very good Roman Catholic," I said, remembering how on Easter Sunday in Albany I was afraid to go among the congregation with my valise in my hand. I went to confession finally in Syracuse. The priest gave me a penance for my anger at Jasper Westervelt and another for tempting him to be interested in me. I did not even think to argue, but I have not sought a priest since. And yet, I say my prayers and feel comfort.

I cannot explain all this to Eben. We do not know each other well, and it is not his burden anyway. He must sense something of what I feel, however, for he says, "Henry Carlton once said to me, 'The nearer the Church, the further from God.' "

"Yes," I replied, "I think I understand that."

When I come to know Eben better, I will ask him if he shares the common suspicion of what the newspapers call Papists. Of course, he assumed that Tobias too is Roman Catholic.

I wish I could assume it myself, but I cannot. I wonder what is right to teach him. His mama had nothing of religion on her person. I believe she would have kept her rosary or a small cross at least if that was her faith. It is the kind of problem I would like to discuss with Mr. Serle. He would understand my worry about what is proper and just.

At last I decided there could be no objection if I taught Tobias the Psalms. They are beautiful in themselves as well as belonging to both the Jewish and the Christian faith. Even a Mohammedan could respect them. In the parlor here is a small shelf with books, and the King James Bible is one of them. It might have belonged to Flint's mother, for the name in it is *Clarissa James*. Tobias and I began with the Twenty-third Psalm.

On Thanksgiving Day Eben and Tobias and Rafe and I went to the village service at the Congregational Church and then to the Carltons' for our dinner. Mr. King did not join us. After our service in Uncas Falls, he went to meet Mrs. James for a special Temperance lecture in Albany. Georgina Carlton had seemed hesitant whether I would wish to attend church before dinner and mentioned in an excusing sort of way that the service was not very religious. I was in the store to buy a pound of raisins for puddings.

"Some think it too much a Yankee holiday," she said. "Perhaps I am partial, for my grandparents came here from Connecticut." She hesitated for a moment and then said in a trembling voice, "Henry may shock you with his talk after the service. He is an atheist. He comes with me to church on Thanksgiving and Christmas only and complains a good deal afterward. I thought I should warn you."

I reached across the counter to touch her hand. We see each other often and are friends, I hope. "It is all right," I said. "I accept such things, but I am sorry if it troubles you."

Georgina sniffed and smiled timidly at me. "I try to understand him," she said. "His theories are very important to him, and he wants to explain them all. Marriage can be difficult." She sighed, weighed up my purchase, and wrote it carefully in the ledger.

I liked the Thanksgiving service very much. As Justice of the Peace, Henry Carlton read the proclamation for the special holiday from President Fillmore. There were readings from the Bible and American history and hymns. Mr. King led the service and gave a sermon, which was not overly long. Tobias only yawned once. Little Jem Carlton had to be stopped by his mother from kicking the back of the pew in front of him.

At dinner afterward, Henry Carlton did not mention his convictions, only bent his head dutifully when Georgina asked Eben to say a grace before we ate. I brought bread, two pies, and a big pot of pumpkin and chestnut soup. Mr. and Mrs. Turner and Lily brought cucumber pickles and a jug of cider. Georgina Carlton roasted the turkeys and made the rest, except for a box of sweetmeats that the Coovers brought. He is the blacksmith. He and his wife have two boys at home and grown children who have gone west to claim homesteads. The two living Carlton children are Jem, six, and Annie, eight, who shows herself superior to the little boys by helping her mother and chiding Jem and Tobias for making dirt. Tobias is very shy with Jem and Annie. He watches them openmouthed.

After dinner we had recitations and songs. Tobias said his psalm nicely, and the Carlton children sang "Woodsman, Spare That Tree." After other music to Henry Carlton's fiddle and Eben's pennywhistle, we all sang many songs together, ending with "Hail, Columbia." "Firm, united let us be, rallying round our liberty," our voices blended. "As a band of brothers joined, peace and safety we shall find."

Later Eben made popcorn, stripping the kernels from the ears and shaking them in a wire basket over the glowing coals of the fire. Tobias and I watched. I could see the hard yellow kernels swelling in the heat. Suddenly, one kernel split and turned itself inside out into a giant snowflake. And then another and another, into a whole snowdrift, they exploded.

Tobias's eyes were very wide. "Mother! Rafe!" he exclaimed. "Listen! The corn goes pop, pop, pop."

"That is why it is popcorn," Eben told him.

Walking up the hill on the way home, Eben carried a lantern to light our steps. We had Tobias between us, holding our hands. The wind was cold off the lake. The green meadows of summer lay brown and dreary, wanting the decency of snow to shroud their death. As we plodded, still warmed by the warmth and light of the Carltons' crowded kitchen, a beat, as of oars pulling a boat through water, and a strange, deep cry broke the silence. A presence soared across our path, a dark span of great wings and two enormous round yellow eyes, bright in the lantern light.

Tobias clutched even tighter to my hand and made a little whimper of fear.

"What is it?" I breathed. The thing seemed huge—big enough to carry Tobias away in its talons—as it wheeled over us and stroked west toward the pine woods, the feathered edges of its wings just visible in the dim night.

"It is an owl," Eben said. He sounded easy in himself. "A great horned owl by the size and the yellow eyes. You should be glad to see him, Miss Mina. He is hunting mice."

"You are not afraid of him?" The swinging pool of lantern light made the night safer.

"I was not born in the woods to be afeard of an owl," Eben declared.

"Are you all right, Tobias?" I asked.

"I am not afeard," Tobias said stoutly, although his hand trembled in mine, and then, looking up at Eben in awe, "You were born in the woods, Uncle Eben?"

Eben chuckled in his comfortable way. "In a manner of speaking," he said.

As I tucked Tobias into his bed, he looked up at me, his eyes green-brown pools of light within the dark fringes of his eyelashes. "I saw a great owl, Mother," he whispered, "and I ate popcorn.

"Pop, pop," I heard him whisper to himself and Rafe before he fell asleep.

The weather closed in on us early in December, with cold and snow drifting up against the porches by Christmas. Silas King was away in Albany and then returned. Eben shot a deer. We had venison for our Christmas dinner. I made a dish of Indian rice and vegetables and nuts for Mr. King, who said an excessively long grace over it before any of us could eat. Poor Tobias sank lower and lower in his chair until only his bright eyes and tousled head were visible over the table edge.

I preserved the extra deer meat in molasses, saltpeter, salt, pearlash, and cinnamon. It will be a welcome change from the dried beef jerky, salt pork, and salt fish we purchase from the Carltons. Eben says he will shoot rabbits—and squirrels and raccoons too if I wish. I said not squirrels, thinking of how Tobias smiled to see them chattering. And then Lily said she does not care for raccoon; it has a very strong taste. When the lake is frozen hard, there will be ice fishing. We will also fill our ice vault ready for the hot months.

It was a great satisfaction to me to make the house and to lay in supplies for the winter. I suppose it is foolish of me. At

Fourth Street I took such pains to be thrifty and wise—it ended in nothingness. It seems beyond my understanding of myself that I would begin again here. Perhaps it is not so much seeing the jars of blackberry, peach, and pumpkin preserves with brandy-soaked paper in the mouth of each to prevent mold, or the crocks of pickles and brined meat, or the bags of oats, cornmeal, and dried currants hung up where the mice cannot reach them, or the barrels with apples and root vegetables laid in clean sand, or the smoked ham and the two smoked turkeys that Georgina Carlton showed me how to prepare. My hands picked the fruits and vegetables and cleaned the meat. My hands built the fire, set the pots on it, and took them off again. My help, Lily, worked willingly with me. She and my neighbor have given me gifts of time and knowledge. I have thought of the needs of those I care for and anticipated their pleasures. It is the work for itself and the meaning of it—not the shelves of jars—that satisfy me.

Now on a cold night in early February, with the snow a billowing quilt about the house, we are comfortable within. The house that was a dead thing when I first walked through its door has come alive. The animals are safe in the barn. The fire burns clear at our hearth, the lamps are trimmed and shed warm light without smoking. Tobias plays with the letters I wrote for him on squares of pasteboard, stroking them and whispering their names to Rafe. He is learning the alphabet. Eben has brought out his cobbler's bench. He is making me a pair of stout boots for work outdoors. Mr. King frowns over his paper at the other end of the table as he writes his Sunday sermon.

All is serene here. Outside in the moonlight, the wind will be lifting up little sparkling veils of ice crystals over the frozen lake. The hills circle us in their austere winter beauty. Under the ice and snow the spring is waiting. The days are already growing longer, although I sense rather than see the change. In March the ice will crack and melt. The moiré taffeta surface of the lake will reflect the sky again. The trees, divested of their snow cloaks and bonnets, will dress themselves in green, and all will be bathed in sunlight, a glorious picture of nature's grandeur.

Six months ago, I came to this strange place that is yet familiar to me. The length of the lake, the circling hills—I have stepped into a dream. Where is the dreamer in whose dream I live now?

SATURDAY, FEBRUARY 28, 1852

Now I am caught up to myself in my book. The light lengthens every day. I hear the water trickling under the snowbanks. Not that the cold does not hold us still. Every night I heat bricks and wrap them in flannel to warm our beds. Tobias has managed to lose three mittens during the winter, and I have no wool to match the one that remains. I seem to knit for him continuously—and for Eben and myself too. I need warm stockings. My foot, where the pony stepped on me four years ago, still hurts me when the weather is cold and damp.

Mrs. Zipporah James and Mr. Phil, as we must call Phoebe, visited us for a week. They came in early February when the roads were still hard packed with snow and travel by sleigh was easy. I opened the second floor for them and renewed the beds with clean oat straw. Next year I will have goose down. There are two beautiful front bedrooms looking out to the lake with well-drawing fireplaces. The back bedrooms are not usable, being without bedsteads. The two were easy enough guests, for they spent their mornings praying and writing their tracts. They visited Mrs. James's friends in the village most afternoons. The only nuisance was that when she had a moment free from her other business, Zipporah James put her nose into everything. She did not seem to have real interest in the workings of the house and farm; rather, she had opinions about all our concerns and the need to share them. Her opinions were all about our faults.

"You have too much food in your pantry," she said. "It will spoil before you can use it."

To my surprise Georgina Carlton, who had brought Jem up to go sledding with Tobias, interfered. "You should inquire before you comment, Zip," she said with a small tremble in her voice that told me she feared her sister-in-law. "Miss Mina will sell her extra preserves at the store. I have asked her to bring them down to us."

Georgina poked me when Zipporah James turned away to sniff at the hard cheeses ripening on the shelf.

"Close your mouth, Mina," she whispered. "It is true."

So the visit brought me that. I counted out what I thought we would need until the harvests start again and took the rest to the store. The Carltons have already sold ten of the twenty-three jars I took to them. Georgina is very pleased with her idea. I am grateful that she was brave for my sake.

I had just one private talk with Phoebe. She came down early to breakfast one morning before Lily arrived. She wears not boy's clothes as I once did, but a real man's dress with trousers, waistcoat, collared shirt, cravat, and coat. She has a top hat and a greatcoat for outdoors too. When I look at her, I have to remind myself that she is a girl and not more than seventeen. She looks to be a slight, dark-skinned, grown-up man.

"Good morning, Miss Mina," she greeted me. "The coffee smells welcome on this cold morning."

I set the cup for her with the milk and sugar near.

"You are up early," I remarked.

"I wake early," she said. "I have dreams of my mother and cannot sleep again."

Her face looked drawn for a moment, and then she reassembled her confident-appearing smile.

"Have you sought word of her?" I asked. "Can the Abolitionists help you?"

She shook her head. "I have asked," she said. "Two years ago the inquiry was passed back to the South. There is no news."

"Are you content with your life as a boy?" I ask. "Does it keep you safe from the bounty men?"

I am prying, of course, but if I do not ask, I will not learn. Phoebe looks very young suddenly as she smiles.

"I am a free man, not a dependent boy or a weak woman," she says. "I am Mr. Phil. I speak of the evils of strong drink at Temperance meetings. I have spoken twice now to the Abolitionists about my escape from slavery. I am very successful at charming gold from pockets and purses for our causes. Miss Zip taught me to read and write. She depends on me to keep our books and manage our work."

She sounds proud and satisfied. I want to ask her if the freedom to be a man is more important than the freedom of living in an antislavery state. Before we can continue, Zipporah James comes in.

"There you are, Mr. Phil!" she exclaims, as if Phoebe might have been lost somehow. "I thought we were going to say our prayers together before breakfast. You know I dislike changes in our schedule."

Phoebe drinks her coffee before she says, "I was just coming up to you, Miss Zip."

Later that same day, the woman who does the laundry for us sent up her daughter with the week's clean linen. After I told Lily to give the girl a hot drink to warm her walk back home, I went upstairs with fresh towels for the washstands. The doors to the front bedrooms were both closed. I was about to knock at Zipporah James's door when I heard two voices and a sudden squeal of laughter.

"Stop it, Mr. Phil, you are tickling me. Stop it!" cried Zipporah James.

"Make me!" said Phoebe in a teasing way.

I set the towels on the chest in the hall and went quietly back downstairs. I thought of disguises and how, on the ship and again last summer, I wore boy's clothing myself. Where would it lead me if I lived so for three whole years? I wonder. Do we betray ourselves or find ourselves in our choice of clothing? I gazed out the window at the frozen lake and puzzled until Rafe bumped his head at my leg and roused me. Tobias is getting into mischief, I thought, and hurried to the kitchen to prevent his climbing up to stir the stew pot at the fire.

"Well," Eben said as our visitors' sleigh went jingling down the lane with Mr. Phil driving the horse. "Well, I think I will drink a mug of cider with my supper tonight. You kept a tight rein on Zip, Miss Mina. She was not so bad as she can be. She left Tobias alone after that one time when you prevented her from slapping his hand."

I am glad they are gone. No one will strike Tobias if I can stop them. After supper that evening, it is pleasant to sit at the table with Eben and read through the list of seeds the Shakers sell. They have the best quality for garden seeds, Eben says. Tobias looks up from teaching Rafe to spell *dog* with his pasteboard letters and asks us if we will grow popcorn. We are making our plans for when the earth is ready to work again.

When Tobias and Eben were gone to bed, I sat by the dying fire a little time before I banked it. Small red and blue and white flames licked up, dancing their warmth away into the cooling room. The last of the log split itself to show the red heart within the burned shell. Dreaming there, I thought I saw faces in the fire: Flint, Mr. Maurice, Daniel, Aunt Jane, Honor, Guido, Mr. Serle, whose dark eyes smile at me. The warmth makes a companionship of quiet feeling.

WEDNESDAY, MARCH 31, 1852

Honor wrote three days ago to tell me that she and Guido are married. They went to a magistrate, not to a church. Mr. Serle was a witness at the wedding, she says, and, of course, Aunt Jane was there and Guido's cousins. They all had a lunch at the new—or rather, the renewed—house on Elizabeth Street after the ceremony.

Being Honor, she had more to say about the pale blue silk she wore than about her feelings at being a married woman now. I think the pleasure with which she minutely described the lace at the neck of her dress and the gold chain necklace her Guido gave her as a wedding-day present tells me as much of the depth of her happiness as if she had heaped large, vague words of joy on the page. At the end of the letter she added as a kind of afterthought that I might like to know that Mr. Serle is living with them for the present. He was ill this past winter, she wrote, but he is recovering slowly.

I was upset that Honor never mentioned it before. Of course, I had to write immediately, a long letter, saying how happy I am for her and Mr. DiRoma. Instead of making a postscript message to Mr. Serle, I enclosed a note for him. I could not find a way to say that hearing of his illness froze my heart with horror. I do not understand that Madame Moses is not caring for him—but I suppose she must come to cheer him, and Honor just neglected to mention it. When I think of him, anger and longing mix in me still. He must live, he must—so I can reconcile my heart. After I tore up three pieces of paper with wrong beginnings, I wrote, *I am dismayed to hear that you are ill. I wish that I could be there to make beef tea and custards for my friend. I pray every day for your health.* I signed the note, *Yours faithfully, Mina Pigot.* It sounded a little foolish to me when I read it over, but I did not know what else to say to a man who might be married.

SATURDAY, APRIL 10, 1852

I was cutting up old newspapers for the privy when I saw the notice. Last week, Madame Anna Moses, the great soprano *prima donna,* sailed from New York for Havana, Cuba, where she will sing with the Havana Opera Company. From Cuba she might travel to perform in Europe. There is a rumor that crowned heads have expressed the desire to hear her. The music critic of the *Sun* wishes the gifted lady a fond *au revoir. The loss for musical circles in New York and our eastern cities is the gain in good fortune for the* cognoscenti *of Cuba,* he writes.

I stare at the words. I suppose Mr. Serle traveled with her. That must be why he did not reply to my note. It makes me sad to think a friend is gone from reach. I hope the sea voyage improves his health. I understand, I think, that he needs to marry. Madame Moses is of his faith and brings him a child and a brother as well as becoming his wife. And they are educated, musical people— and rich. It must open a new world to him. Even so, I wish I had known and said good-bye and safe journey to him.

The stars in the night sky twinkle their beauty across the

vast universe, and so the news from New York City seems to come to me from a remote distance, another life, which brought me pain and failure. I try to shake the sadness away. I remember Doctor Lydia Mary Walker telling me to renew trust.

I thought about it yesterday when I sorted out my trunk. I purchased a chest of drawers for Tobias's things and so rearranged my own. At the bottom of my trunk, I found an old handkerchief with something knotted in the corner. It was three apple seeds. I ate an apple, I remember, the last day that I was in the orchard of the estate in England.

I asked Eben if he thought the seeds would be good after almost four years.

"Can't tell unless you try 'em," he said in his practical, forthright way.

I soaked the seeds and planted them in small pots of earth as he suggested. Perhaps they will grow, perhaps not. We can but water our hopes and give them air and light.

SUNDAY, APRIL 11, 1852

Easter is returned. A year ago, I fled New York and my friends. How I am grown and how life grows about me! I love Tobias. Caring for him and Eben and this place, where I watch the seasons wane and wax and find a peace, has eased me. Now spring brings a new uncertainty. Buds swell and break. The lilac is in leaf—time to plant lettuce, Eben says—and I yearn for the surging growth of summer.

FRIDAY, MAY 14, 1852

I had a dream last night. It was something I knew and yet did not know. I dreamed it—or something like it—before, I think.

I am lying in my bed in this house by Uncas Lake. I awaken into a soft summer night and, rising, go barefoot through the silent kitchen and out the door. I circle the barn, where the animals shift comfortably in the dark, and climb the path beyond. Yet as I walk through the woods of oak and maple, where the faint note of the wood thrush tantalizes the edge of hearing, the land and the time change about me. I am on a green hillside now. Green, green, green, and soft as velvet to my feet while the sky dawns into Madonna blue above me. I descend across the meadow and see the open door of the cottage where I was born. I am home, I think, and my heart sings in my breast.

It takes a moment for my eyes to adjust to the dark in the house. The quiet wraps its arms about me. Be where your heart is and rest, it tells me. In the stillness I hear a small, familiar sound. My mother sits by the fire in her low rocking chair. She knits and hums a tune to amuse herself.

"Mother!" I cry in my dream. "Mother, I am come home to you."

Her song ceases. Her busy hands rest in her lap. Her kind eyes smile up at me.

"Mina," she says to me. "Mina, joy of my heart, you are always here."

"Mother?" I ask. "Mother, what will I do?"

"Love is all we have, my darling," she says. "Trust love."

I am awake in the dark, my face bathed in tears. I am Mina, and I am something beyond that, which has no name yet.

Well, that is my dream. The weather is warm this week. The pale, tender lettuce is up, and the spinach shows dark green against the wet earth. The pea vines grasp the bottom of the trellis. We will have new green peas with our poached fish on the Fourth of July.

TUESDAY, MAY 25, 1852

Honor and Mr. DiRoma are making a wedding trip to see the wonder of Niagara Falls. They waited until the weather was milder and the improvements to the house on Elizabeth Street were at last complete. If I will have them, they will stop in Uncas

Falls for three nights on their way. They would like to bring Aunt Jane too. At the end of the letter there was a postscript.

I hesitate to add another guest, Mina, Honor wrote, *but may we bring Mr. Serle also? He has been so ill and tired these past months, and your note seemed to hearten him. The change and country air and seeing you might do him good. Besides, Aunt Jane told me just now she very much longs to visit you but does not wish to make the trip to Niagara with us. After the brief time with you, Mr. Serle can escort her back to New York. It will help our plans if you can say yes.*

There is another letter enclosed in Honor's. *Dear Miss Pigot, Thank you for your kind note wishing me health. I have thought of you often in this past year. Mr. and Mrs. DiRoma urge me to come with them to see you. Please be frank if it is an imposition. I will understand. Yours respectfully, Benjamin Serle.*

I sighed after I read it. His style of letter writing is annoyingly the same. And then—rainbow bubbles of joy burst in my heart. I was wrong. Mr. Serle is still here in America. *I have thought of you often in this past year.* The life-giving scent of spring came through the open windows. I heard an agitated squawking and shouts from the barnyard. Tobias and Rafe were teasing the geese again. Of course, I did not refuse Honor's appeal. They will all be here tomorrow.

It is peaceful tonight in the summer kitchen, where I write by the lamp at one end of the long table. Mr. King is away as usual. Eben has gone to his rest. The windows are open to the soft night. A whip-poor-will called from the woods a moment ago, a plaintive sound. The scent of the woods and the bridal-wreath bushes by the house perfumes the air.

My friends are coming from the city. New York. I remember the beauty of the harbor on the cold November evening when we waited for our journey's end. I remember the parades. The man acting George Washington rode a great white horse for the Evacuation Day celebration. I knelt in St. Patrick's beside my brother and felt my people near me. I stood in the churchyard with Mr. Serle, looking at the tombstone of the founding father.

I remember the sounds and the odors of the city too: the cheerful voices of guests departing a dinner, the horses' hoofs on the cobbles, the shrill cries of newsboys with the late editions, and the beseeching calls of hawkers of oranges, nuts, candies. I remember how it smells: dirt and the sea and a fetid odor of all humanity crowded together. Here I have almost forgotten the city's concentration of human stink and salt, heat, and an ineffable sweetness. This house in the country breathes animal smells too, but also woods and fields and gardens—a nourishing savor of its own.

I wonder how my friends and I have changed in a year. I tumbled in the kaleidoscope turns of a wider world and then steadied myself to choose the quiet pattern of a village life. I wonder if they will know me. A poor fluttering moth blundered into the lamp and killed itself. Danger flames everywhere. I touch my mother's ring and pray that safety lies in following the heart. Then I must put out the light and go to bed.

PART SEVEN

THE END OF THE STORY

SATURDAY, JUNE 12, 1852

THIS EVENING THE RAIN pours down as it has all day. It makes a pause for us in our work because the fields and garden are too wet for planting and cultivation. I spent the day doing all the mending and sewing I have been too busy to attend to. Now I am sitting at the table in the summer kitchen with my book. It makes me catch my breath to think of all that has changed since last I wrote.

I felt very anxious as I planned for my visitors. Lily and I cleaned and aired the two upstairs rooms for Honor and Guido and for Aunt Jane, but I did not know what to do with Mr. Serle. I finally thought that I would have to ask Aunt Jane to share my bed and give Mr. Serle her room. Eben solved my problem.

"You will have your visitors in the main house in three days," he said. "Time for me to move back to the attic above the summer kitchen with Mr. King. It keeps the dirt out of the house when there is so much field work."

Once Eben moved his things, I cleaned the room and polished the furniture. The room does not have as wide a view of the lake as the second floor gives, but one can glimpse it. The casement window opens to the scent of the meadows and woods and the sound of Uncas Creek tumbling down the hill to the southwest. Luckily, a peddler came by the next day. As well as purchasing cambric for Tobias's shirts and a blue-figured calico for myself, I bought fabric to make a fresh white counterpane. The day of the visit, I set a bouquet of purple pansies on the table by the bed.

Eben left at dawn to meet the party at Albany. I had a restless day. If Lily and Tobias had not been there to remind me of my tasks and their hunger, I would have forgotten to make the noon meal. I found myself looking out the door every few minutes and worrying that there had been some mischance to the steamboat on the river or to the carriage on the road. At least, I thought, it is a beautiful day for a journey, warm and cloudless. I wondered what Mr. Serle thought of the sublime views along the Hudson River.

As the day waned, Uncas Lake became a rippling sheet of silver, and the willows by the shore glowed green as cats' eyes in the slanting afternoon rays of sun. A cart came up the lane, but it was a Mohawk woman selling baskets and Indian rice. I was so flustered that I bought her largest hamper and also a peck of rice, even though it was last season's and I did not need it.

I thought Eben would be back by six o'clock, but it was close on eight when the carriage rattled into the dooryard. Then, of course, after the quiet day, there was everything at once, kisses, handshakes, Tobias to introduce, conducting everyone to their rooms, a babble of voices and needs.

After I kissed Aunt Jane and Honor, and Guido had both shaken my hand and kissed my cheek, Mr. Serle gave me his hand. I thought how his dark eyes are as mysterious to me as when I saw him last a year ago. I wanted so to know his thoughts.

"You look well, Miss Pigot," he said in his quiet, courteous way.

"And you are well, I hope," I told him. "I like your hat." He wears a broad-brimmed, democratic hat now.

I thought he looked drawn and tired, but he nodded and said he was well enough considering the long day of traveling. I wanted to ask him more, but there was Aunt Jane whispering at my ear to ask which way to the privy, and I had the supper to set out. We ate in the summer kitchen at the big table, which is long enough for everyone. I was at the end to carve the roast chickens. Tobias was on my left. I had hoped that Mr. Serle would sit beside me to the right, but Aunt Jane claimed the seat. At the last minute, Silas King hurried in and sat at the end of the table opposite me.

"Has grace been said?" he asked.

I sighed inwardly. He wants to play the minister now, I thought, which I knew was uncharitable. If there were a priest in Uncas Falls, I would have to admit my smallness and do penance. But still, his graces are very long, and from the look of him he had some triumph with a sick parishioner or a Temperance lecture to tell God and the assembled company about. My guests were all hungry and tired.

"Tobias will say the grace," I said.

Tobias said the simple words I have taught him. He did very well considering the excitement of so many new people all at once. He stumbled at the end. I gave him the word, and we all said *Amen*. I picked up the carving knife.

"You should have put the child to bed before supper, madam," Mr. King said reprovingly from down the table.

I did not bother to answer him. "White meat or dark?" I asked Aunt Jane.

While I was busy serving, Mr. King took it on himself to lead the conversation. He discussed the ice business with Mr. DiRoma. Honor asked about the great building being framed on the lakeshore beyond the village of Uncas Falls toward Sawyerville. Mr. King explained it is a new hotel. The place will offer water treatments for those wishing to strengthen their constitutions as well as country walks, boating, and a clean, simple diet.

"They say that means a good business for sweetshops nearby," Eben offered.

Honor laughed, and Mr. King looked down his nose at her. The conversation turned to the journey then. Everyone ate and spoke of the speed of the steamboats and the beauty of the river. Mr. Serle seemed to have little appetite. There was a remote look to his face. He must have been more ill than Honor told me, I thought.

Supper was soon over. The visitors took their lamps and went to their beds. Guido was yawning. It was the brisk country air, he said. That amused me, for the evening was warm and even close. Summer has come early this year.

I had Tobias, who was yawning too, to settle. He was soon asleep in his cot with Rafe stretched on the floor beside him. I was in my night shift and wrapper, brushing my hair, when I heard a shy tap on the door. I opened it, and there was Aunt Jane, looking nervous.

"Am I disturbing you, Mina?" she asked.

"No, come in," I said softly, "but we must not wake Tobias."

"I just wanted to mention to you privately—" Aunt Jane whispered hesitantly.

"Yes?" I tried to encourage her.

"Seton—that is, Mr. Westervelt—he has had such a difficult time. He—"

There was a light rap at the door and Honor entered.

"Well!" Honor smiled at me. "Has Aunt Jane told you the scandal? Seton Westervelt finally divorced his wife. She has gone to Europe with her lover. The daughter is sent to boarding school, and Jasper has run away to sea."

"Honor!" Aunt Jane exclaimed, forgetting to whisper.

Tobias stirred in his bed.

"Ssh," I hushed them.

"Did Aunt Jane tell you that Seton Westervelt called on her?" Honor said softly.

"No," I say.

"He came once for an evening visit and once for dinner with us," Honor murmurs. "We feel sorry for him that he must live with his invalid mother now. Perhaps that is why Aunt Jane wishes to return so soon, even though I urged her it would be good for Benjamin Serle to stay in the country longer."

There is an edge of anger in Honor's voice. I look at Aunt Jane. I wish I could ask her if she ever had an honest talk with Honor. Probably her downcast eyes and pink cheeks indicate that Honor's directness is embarrassing her. She purses her lips together and does not speak. It eases my mind to think that Jasper is gone.

Honor sighs. "Come, darling," she tells Aunt Jane. "We are keeping Mina awake."

"It would be all right for me," I say quietly, "but Tobias is just fallen asleep."

"I made a dress for you," Honor whispers. "I want you to try it on in the morning."

Honor puts her finger to her lips and shepherds Aunt Jane from the room. Since we cannot talk openly, I am not entirely sorry to see them go. I wonder at Aunt Jane. Her blushes say she loves Seton Westervelt even though his betrayal caused her to lose her faith, she said. But then, she never told him she was with child, so perhaps he cannot be blamed entirely. I do not know how I would feel in such a case. I try to imagine losing my faith. It would be like being swept away over the cliff of Niagara Falls.

Perhaps because I have been thinking upsetting thoughts, I have trouble falling asleep. Saying my prayers helps me, but I lie awake to the world for what seems hours. There are so many people in the house suddenly. The familiar creaks and small night sounds are changed, made larger. Tobias murmurs in his sleep, and Rafe shifts himself. My ears ache with the feeling that, if I listen hard enough, I will hear Mr. Serle breathing in his room at the other side of the house.

At last, I drift into a dream. I am standing by the pebbled shore of Uncas Lake. Small waves lap at my feet. Mist rises from the surface of the green water. A boat is coming through the mist. I see the shape of the hull, then a white sail filled by invisible wind. A man is standing in the boat next to the mast. He holds a rope—only I see it is not a rope but a green ribbon the rich color of meadow grass after a rain.

The boat draws nearer to me. The man wears a white shirt

open at the neck, so I see the strong column of his throat. The damp mist makes his dark hair curl about his temples. He wants me to step into the boat with him and sail across the lake.

I cannot go. The boat is too far away from the shore. I will drown in the lake. Now I am sad for Mr. Serle. I want to give him something to show that I am sorry I cannot go to him. I will take my mother's ring from its place in my chemise, I think, and throw it out to him. It will be a gift of love.

I put my hand into my breast. When I draw it out, I hold not the ring but my own heart. It is beating in my hands like a trapped bird. I am so terribly afraid. I do not dare to look at it. How will I live without my heart?

Rafe is by me, pawing at my skirt. He wants me to put my heart back. He wants me to turn from the shore and climb up to the house above the lake.

"God's will be done," the dog says.

I rose before dawn. The dream wakened me, and I could not fall into sleep again. In the first passing freshness of the day, I scattered grain for the geese and collected the eggs from the hens while Eben milked the cow. The two of us ate a silent breakfast—ham, eggs, coffee, and rhubarb pie for him, coffee with milk and sugar and a piece of toasted bread for me. Mr. King came down as we finished. He is on his way to Utica and will be gone for several days. I asked him to stop and remind Henry Carlton that he promised me a lake fish today. The sun came up saffron, rose, and scarlet from the eastern hills, promising heat.

Since the others were still asleep, I let things be in the main house and spent the early morning scrubbing up the summer kitchen and moving pots and pans and jugs. We will keep the fire here, not in the main house, from today. In the great open room of the summer kitchen, there is space for two tables: a scrubbed pine worktable and the long polished maple dining table set near the casement windows where the cool air comes in.

As I finish setting the jars of spices along their shelf, Mr. Serle enters from the main house.

"The fire is out," he tells me.

"I know," I say. "I will cook in this part of the house all summer. See, I lit the fire here very early this morning. The coffee is hot. What would you like to eat?"

"Nothing now. I will wait for the others." He shivers. "The morning air is cold."

"You need to sit in the sun," I tell him.

He looks so gray and unlike himself. He is no better than he was yesterday. It as if his soul went on a journey and has not returned.

"The sun?" He turns toward the windows, which I have thrown open and where light streams in. It as if he had forgotten that the outdoor world exists.

"You are going to sit in the sun," I tell him, and, taking his arm boldly, I shepherd him to the door. "I will bring you coffee with hot milk and sugar as you like it."

"Thank you," he says when I bring the steaming cup to him on a plate with buttered toast sprinkled with cinnamon and sugar.

He does not eat or drink but sets the plate down beyond him. He is sitting on the bench where I showed him the morning sun strikes in and warms the stone wall of the house. I sit beside him for a moment.

"Honor wrote to me that you were ill this winter," I say. "What was wrong?"

"I had trouble with my lungs again," he says. He is not looking at me but out into the distance at the lake. "It was painful in the cold weather, but I am better since April."

"I prayed for your health," I say.

Mr. Serle nods. He looks so tired. "Thank you."

I can bear it no longer. I take his hand in mine.

"I want you to be well," I say. "I think you need to be out of the city in clear air. I hope you will visit us in Uncas Falls often."

Mr. Serle looks down at our two hands. His hand is browner than mine by nature; I love his long fingers and the strength of his grasp. My own hand is tanned from the sun; there are freckles on the back, and a red place on the thumb where I burned myself two days ago making rhubarb preserves. It is not a ladylike, pale hand.

"Thank you," Mr. Serle says again. "I am sure I will be better soon."

He is looking at the lake again, not at me. I sigh. I release his hand. He does not seem to want to talk to me at all.

"It is a beautiful prospect, isn't it?" I say. "Mr. King read us something from his *Union Magazine* a few weeks ago. A writer said, *It is well to have some water in your neighborhood, to give buoyancy to and float the earth.* I forget the name of the writer, but I think the words are very true."

At last Mr. Serle looks at me.

"A wonderful thought," he says. He almost smiles.

Before I can say anything else of a private nature, Lily comes tramping up the steps.

"Did you collect the eggs yet this morning, Miss Mina?" she asks me.

"Yes," I tell her. "Would you begin your day by setting the breakfast table in the summer kitchen? Drink your coffee before it is cold," I say to Mr. Serle, "and take a walk or come inside to eat more breakfast as you please."

I leave him gazing out at the lake. Breakfast is a bustle of people and talk, but Mr. Serle does not come in to join us. As Aunt Jane and I are clearing the table, I catch a glimpse of him, walking by himself toward the duck pond. I fear I will cry. I will never be able to talk alone with Mr. Serle. It is foolish to cry over a breakfast table with its coffee cups, eggshells, crusts, and jam-sticky knives.

Aunt Jane, Lily, and I clean the kitchen from breakfast while Honor and Guido walk out with Tobias and Rafe to see the farm. When Lily goes up to straighten the guests' rooms, Aunt Jane questions me about my living without another woman in the house. She is worried about the appearance of impropriety, she says. I turn the conversation by asking Aunt Jane if she told Honor about Mr. Westervelt or Mr. Westervelt about Honor.

"He was interested in how old I am and then in Honor's age," I say. "I think he suspects the truth."

Aunt Jane looks horrified that I should mention it.

"Please, Mina, please," she begs me with tears welling in her eyes. "You must not say a word, ever. I cannot bear that Honor should know I have lied to her all these years."

"Honor loves you," I begin, but Aunt Jane begins to cry in earnest. I must stop and console her and reluctantly promise that I will not speak her secret.

When she goes to rinse her eyes, I gaze out the window at the lake. I wonder if my promise is wise. The rippling slate-blue water and the blowing clouds above do not speak to tell me. Like prayer, Nature comforts, but it does not answer questions.

Honor comes in then to show me my dress. When I ask after the men, she shrugs and says they are helping Eben load seed corn in the spreader.

"Guido must be working," she says. "And it is good for Mr. Serle to be outdoors."

Honor made me a dress of green and white silk with full oversleeves, cambric false sleeves, and a chemisette trimmed with real lace. I must try it on. Honor wants to be sure that I am not taller since she last fitted me.

"You are still your slim and elegant self, Mina," she says, "but when I saw you last night, my first thought was that you seem larger somehow, more complete."

"I am not such a child as I was," I say. "And in this beautiful dress, I think I will feel truly a woman."

"You like it?" she asks.

For Honor she sounds almost shy.

"I love it," I tell her. "It is beautiful. I never had a silk dress. It is wonderful to me that the first one I will ever have is made by you, my good friend."

Solemnly, Honor drops the new skirt over my head and ties the strings. Then she helps me into the bodice, which fits very snugly through the waist and body and yet is comfortable; it does not bind. Honor has put light boning in the bodice itself. She did not think she would persuade me to a corset, she tells me. The neck of the dress without the chemisette, which Honor says I may wear only in the day, is not low nor high, but gracefully curved.

"The undersleeves are lawn," Honor says, buttoning them and setting the flare of the bodice sleeves to her satisfaction. "Perfect," she says.

We look at my reflection in the mirror over the bureau. This is a version of me, I think. The young woman with her braid of red hair pinned high at the crown of her head and curls springing out as they will about her face wears a dress that pulls in her waist, raises her bosom, reveals her shoulders. She has a woman's shape. Her full skirts and lacy sleeves would never do to milk the cow or clean and truss the poultry for the spit. I wonder if this is the person my brother, Daniel, hoped I would become. A lady regards me from the mirror. I feel myself as a separate being inside her—she is like a doll who must be brought to life. I cannot say something so confused to Honor. I must thank her.

"You are a magician, Honor," I tell her. "This is beautiful."

"Oh, pshaw," she says, or something like it. "You are a pleasure to dress."

After I change back into my wash dress, I sit with Honor in my bedroom for a few moments. The last touch for the dress is hemming the undersleeves. Honor's needle flashes in the fine lawn, making tiny, neat stitches.

"I have to ask you something," I say.

"Oh?" Honor looks up at me with interest.

I take a deep breath and plunge.

"What is it really like between a man and a woman?"

Honor looks puzzled. "But, Mina, surely you have seen animals—"

"I don't mean that!" I exclaim.

Honor laughs. I must look hurt, because she says, "Forgive me, Mina."

"I know the facts of it," I say. "I mean more than facts. I saw a woman dying in childbirth. How could she give herself to love knowing such danger? Why would she trust love?"

Honor sits silent, and then she tells me men and women help each other in love, which she supposes animals do not do. She says the act of love itself can free us from the prison of our selves—for a moment we believe that we are not alone.

"Love is more powerful than we are," Honor says. "Let love move you, and danger is forgotten. Freedom from fear is love's reward."

Freedom from fear? I sit silent, thinking of it, and then I cannot help myself.

"What is wrong with Mr. Serle?"

"I do not know," Honor says. "He was very ill this winter. I will tell you honestly that the worst night before his fever broke, he said your name. He seemed to confuse you with his dead wife. 'I cannot let Mina drown,' he told me."

"You should have written to me to come," I say.

"I asked him when his mind was clearer again," Honor says. "I urged him to let me send for you, and he said no. He said you have your own life. If Aunt Jane had not wanted an escort back to the city, I do not think we could have persuaded him to make this trip, even though Guido and I could see he wanted to come."

I sigh. "We have been a year apart. I need to talk to him."

Honor studies me.

"If you break his heart, Mina, I will never speak to you again. He is such a good man."

"Oh, Honor," I say. My uncertainty lightens. Honor sees hope for us. "Will you tell him he should not break mine? And I would be lost if you never spoke to me again."

"Good." Honor has finished hemming the undersleeves of my dress. She smooths and folds them. "I would not like to lose you either. My mother and I are so fond of you."

"What?" I am startled. "Did you say 'my mother'?"

"Oh God," Honor says, which sounds strange to me because I know she does not believe in God. "It just slipped out. Of course I meant Aunt Jane. I misspoke."

"But—" I begin.

"A lie," Honor says softly. "A kind lie, but I have always known."

I remember Honor holding a watercolor picture of a delicate-looking woman and a protective man and telling me these are her dead parents. Her head tipped in a considering way as she gazed at their images, and her mouth was set in a curve of sadness. She has the same expression now. My heart constricts with the sorrow of understanding.

"Does she know that you know?" I ask.

Honor actually looks frightened by my question. "You must never, never reveal that you know, Mina. I would die. Her dignity is very dear to me."

"Of course," I say. "I love her, and I love you. You misspoke."

"Thank you," Honor says. "I trust your word."

I stoop and kiss her. Our lies hide us from ourselves as well as from the world. But the garments that clothe our bodies cannot dress our souls.

By late morning the day is hot, very hot. The morning haze has thickened into unseasonable, heavy summer weather.

"It is so oppressive." Honor comes into the summer kitchen, fanning herself with her hand.

Even Aunt Jane has loosened the neck of her dress. Eben comes in for a dipper of water.

"You might take your visitors to the falls," he says. "It is cooler up there."

"The falls?" Guido pounces on the question. "What are the falls?"

"The falls tickle your nose," Tobias says. "It is like soda water."

"About a half hour walk from here, Uncas Creek comes down through a meadow into two waterfalls, one after the other, and then runs away down to the village. We can bathe in the pools below the falls," I explain.

"How lovely," Honor says.

"Would you like to take our lunch up there?" I ask.

"Yes!" Tobias cries. "Say yes, Aunt Honor."

When Mr. Serle comes in, Honor and I are beginning to pack two baskets with ham sandwiches, hard-boiled eggs, cheese, a lettuce, and gingerbread cakes.

"What are you doing?" Mr. Serle asks, looking at the table.

"We are going on a picnic." Honor licks butter from her finger. "I am going to bathe."

Mr. Serle stands by the table. Like Guido, he has taken his coat off. His throat rises from the soft white of his shirt.

"Will you make some chicken sandwiches for us?" I ask him. "There is cold chicken from last night. I think you might prefer not to eat the smoked ham."

When he nods yes, I go to the cold pantry where the ice chest is and bring the chicken.

"You will have to share with Honor for the bread and other things," I tell him.

"Is there time to make an egg sauce?" he asks.

"Yes," I say. "I have to make a drink for us. We have a few minutes yet."

It makes my heart hurt in my chest to watch him work in a kitchen again. I had almost forgotten the pleasure of it. Everything he does is neat and deft. He peels one of the hard-boiled eggs, mashes the yolk, and beats in sweet oil, chopped pickle, and flavorings before I have finished making sugar syrup and slicing lemons for the lemonade. Honor, who is the most exacting woman I know, cuts the bread unevenly compared to the precise, thin slices Mr. Serle makes so quickly.

At last we are ready, with our baskets and two old blankets to spread on the ground. I have found a stone jar to hold the lemonade. Lily will finish the chores and then have the afternoon for herself. Eben comes with us. He had a hot morning of work. The corn is almost all planted.

"What will we wear to bathe?" Honor whispers to me.

"I have two pairs of flannel drawers from the winter, and I have my flannel vest," I tell Honor quietly. "I can lend you drawers. Do you have a chemise or vest to wear?"

I do not like to say, even quietly, in front of everyone that Honor cannot possibly wear one of my vests. She is much ampler in the bosom than I.

"If we bathe in the upper pool, the men can do as they please in the lower pool," I add.

We all know that the men will bathe naked, but it is not necessary to say it. At the last minute, Aunt Jane decides that she too will bring a vest and drawers, so we wait while she goes to find them.

"Where is your hat, Tobias?" I ask him as he seizes Guido's hand to pull him out the door.

"Here it is," Mr. Serle says, picking it up from under a chair.

"Where is your own hat, Mina?" Honor asks me. She wears a broad-brimmed straw hat trimmed with daisies, and carries a parasol too.

My straw hat is on its peg by the door. I wish I had time to comb my hair and arrange myself. Honor and Aunt Jane look so cool and ladylike despite the heat. At least I remembered to take my apron off.

At the falls everyone exclaims at the beauty of the place. The clear water of the creek pours down over the rough rocks and makes eddies in the pools where leaves spin in the froth and are whirled away like miniature boats in miniature maelstroms.

We spread one blanket by the upper falls where a clump of young sugar maples gives some shade. Eben plunges the jar of lemonade up to its neck at the edge of the water and piles rocks to secure it in place. The men take their towels and go down out of sight to the lower pool, which is the deeper one. Tobias wants to follow them, but I say no, he must have his bath first and then he may go down.

Honor and I hang the other blanket as a screen and change into our improvised bathing costumes. When we emerge, Aunt Jane finally decides that she too will change.

While Honor tries the water with one toe and squeals at its iciness, I hang Tobias's clothes on a branch out of the way.

We can hear much shouting and laughter from below. Guido and Eben seem to be urging Mr. Serle to try the water.

"*Coràggio! Coràggio!*" Guido shouts.

I am knee deep in the pool with Tobias splashing like a brown brook trout about me.

"Close your eyes, Tobias, here comes the soap," I tell him.

He is very good until I have him thoroughly soapy, with his hair standing up in white, bubbly tufts, and then he shoots from my slippery hands.

"I am soaped," he cries. "Now I am going to swim with Uncle Eben."

Off he splashes out of the water before I can catch him, and then—with Rafe after him—he tears down the path to the lower falls, his paler buttocks twinkling above the brown of his legs.

"Here I am, Uncle Eben!" we hear his cry.

There is a shout, a deep bark from Rafe—then one enormous splash, more shouts, amid much gurgling laughter.

"Is everyone all right?" Honor calls.

Guido is laughing so hard we cannot make out what he is saying.

"What?" we call. "What happened?"

"Tobias and Rafe ran into Mr. Serle and everyone fell in," Eben shouts. "We were swamped."

Honor and I laugh and submerge ourselves to our necks in the cold water. Aunt Jane joins us gingerly. It is delicious to be cool and to feel the pull and tug of moving water. The sky arches milky blue above our heads. In the west, clouds are beginning to pile themselves one on another. We will have a change in the weather tonight. The sound of water pouring over rock pushes the cares of the world away. It is release and blessing.

Reluctantly, we emerge at last and push damp flesh into constricting clothing. I leave my shoes and stockings off. After lunch Honor and Guido decide that they wish to walk up the hill above us and see the view from the top. I think Aunt Jane found the changing of clothes outdoors and sitting on rocks or the ground itself not very ladylike. She looks tired, and her nose is pink with sun. She and Eben return to the house, taking the baskets with them. There is not much to carry, just dirty dishes and the cloth.

"Will you walk up the hill with us, *Beniamino*?" Guido asks.

Mr. Serle shakes his head. "I will stay here," he says. "I have a book."

"Miss Mina Pigot? Tobias?" Guido and Honor are holding hands and smiling. I do not think they really want company.

"Thank you, no," I tell them. "I was up very early. I will rest before we go back. And Tobias must play quietly while he digests his lunch."

Tobias watches them go up the path.

"I have an Uncle Guido now," Tobias says. "That makes four uncles, Mother."

"Really?" I tease him. "Four? That seems a lot. Are you sure?"

"Yes, four," Tobias insists. "Uncle Henry Carlton and Uncle Eben Brouwer and Uncle Silas King. That is three. And now Uncle Guido DiRoma. So four."

Mr. Serle makes a surprised sound. "Uncle Silas King? I thought he is your father."

Tobias wrinkles his nose. "Uncle Silas is not a father. He goes off to rescue people or to lecture them. Or else he is reading his books and studying to be a vegetable."

"You mean a vegetarian, Tobias," I correct him.

"Oh," Mr. Serle says.

He has flushed red across his cheekbones.

"What did you think?" I ask.

He does not seem able to meet my eyes.

"I thought Tobias was Mr. King's son and that he calls you Mother because you will marry his father."

"No, no," Tobias cries. "She will not marry Uncle Silas. Aunt Georgina Carlton asked her whether she thought of him one day when she was showing her the best way to salt lake fish. She said she never would. She said"—Tobias imitates my voice—" 'He is an honorable man, but love? He might as well be one of these dead fish.' Aunt Georgina laughed and laughed."

"Tobias!" I exclaim. "It is wrong to listen to other people's conversations, and worse to repeat them."

"I am sorry," he whispers.

"You must not do it again," I tell him, and kiss his cheek to show him that he is forgiven.

"Will you come play with me?" he asks beseechingly.

I shake my head. "I am very sleepy, Tobias. I was up hours before you. I am going to rest for a few minutes and talk to my friend. Can you play with Rafe?"

Tobias looks over at Mr. Serle, who has taken a book from his pocket and tipped his broad-brimmed hat far down over his eyes to shade his face. I cannot see his expression.

"Will he play?" Tobias whispers to me.

"Not now, dear," I say. "See, he wants to read."

I settle Tobias's straw hat on his head. He sighs, a tragic gust.

"Come, Rafe," he orders.

They trudge up the path beside the falls, but before they are halfway, Tobias is throwing a stick for Rafe. He disappears and then comes back to the top of the path.

"There are strawberries in the meadow," he calls. "I am going to pick them for you."

"Good!" I call back to him. "Stay away from the creek," I add.

He disappears again. The dog jumps to one of the big boulders that command the height of the waterfall and settles himself with his nose to his paws to watch Tobias. I lie back on the blanket. The sound of tumbling water fills the air. Something smells sweet. I cannot think what it is—the wild strawberries perhaps, or early roses.

"What are you reading?" I ask Mr. Serle.

"It is called *The Scarlet Letter*," he says. "Would you like me to read to you?"

"It will be a waste of breath," I say. "I am so sleepy."

"Rest, then," he says.

He sounds more like himself as I remember him. I thought after more than a year that he is changed, but perhaps it is not so much as I feared. He is my friend, I hope. I close my eyes, and the light dances against my lids. The world is golden light. I open my eyes a little.

"Is it an American novel?" I ask.

"Yes, it is very American," he says. "Are you awake?"

"Not really," I say. "What is it?"

"You are not going to marry this Mr. Silas King?" he asks. "Is the child right?"

"Of course I am not going to marry Silas King," I say, closing my eyes and then opening them again. "He is a very virtuous and a very dreary man. Besides, he is a vegetarian. Did you ever bake palatable graham bread?"

"No," Mr. Serle says. "But if I loved someone, I might try." He has set down his book and pulled a blade of grass, which he is winding about his finger.

"I must ask you something," I say.

"Yes?" he replies, bending his head to me.

"Have you married yet? Are you engaged still?"

My questions make him smile. "No and no," he says.

"I see," I say. The glancing light from the water dazzles my tired eyes. I think of his illness and his sad look this morning. "Are you very unhappy?" I ask.

"I am not unhappy at all," he answers. I hear the ironic edge in his tone that tells me there is more than he is saying.

"What happened?" I ask. My heart rises. We will be friends again and talk of everything.

Mr. Serle throws away the grass and rubs his hand across his forehead, pushing his hat back. "She released me from the engagement last fall."

"Are you sure?" I feel doubt, remembering Anna Moses touching his arm, demanding his attention. "Will you tell me what happened?"

"I should not." Mr. Serle gazes away to the bubbling water of the falls. "You will think less of me."

"I want to be your friend," I reply. "I have not seen you for more than a year. I felt so close to you when I was a child. Now that I am grown, I wish to understand your life."

Mr. Serle's dark eyes regard me seriously.

"You really want to know?" he asks.

"I wish to know," I say.

Mr. Serle leans back. He is silent for a moment, and then he seems to make up his mind and speaks quickly. "The lady asked me to accompany her and her brother to Baltimore," he says. "She had an engagement there. After her performance, she invited me to have supper with her in the hotel. It was a private room. She had ordered champagne and oysters. She expected me to make love to her, I knew. We were engaged to marry, after all."

"Oysters?" I cannot help but ask, remembering our talk on the ship in the harbor of New York long ago.

Mr. Serle shrugs. "She does not care about such rules. Everyone eats oysters."

Life and religion remain mysterious, I think. There are rules, but then, sometimes, there are not rules. I wait, silently.

Mr. Serle sighs. "She had sung gloriously. The audience was carried away, and, of course, she knew she had triumphed. She was elated. I had sent crimson roses to her because I knew she loved them. They were in a vase on a side table. When we entered the room, she admired them, and then she turned to me. I took her in my arms—"

He stops.

"You are sure you wish to know this?" he asks.

"Yes," I say.

To believe that he is free of her, I must know how it ended.

"I kissed her with passion, I think," he says. "It seems unreal now, but I suppose I felt it at the time. As I kissed her, I pulled the combs from the black knot of her hair. I thought it romantic. I thought her black tresses would cascade about her pale shoulders. I thought some fairy-tale romance nonsense of the lover wrapped in his mistress's rich waving locks. I pulled the combs out as I kissed her, and then, when the whole great knot of hair came down, most of it came off in my hands. I was embracing the lady, and then I held her and her hair separately. I was startled, to say the least. It was like waking bewildered in the middle of a dream. She was furious. She seized the vase of roses in both hands and threw it at me. What can I say? Romance was over on both sides."

I cannot help myself. I begin to giggle, and then I laugh out loud. I try to control myself, and begin to hiccup.

"You are not flattering my manly image of myself, Miss Pigot," Mr. Serle says, but he is smiling.

"I am sorry," I say. "I am sorry."

I rise and walk to the pool, wade in a little, scoop a handful of cold water to bathe my face, and breathe slowly to regain myself.

"So you were set free?" I say more soberly, returning to sit on the blanket under the tree.

"Free indeed," Mr. Serle tells me.

"I feel sorry for the lady," I say.

"But why?" Mr. Serle asks me. "You should feel sorry for me, who was thrown over. She broke the engagement, and she kept an expensive ring too."

"She chose her own dignity over your love," I say. "She made a foolish choice."

"You would not choose so?" Mr. Serle is looking at me attentively. He has pulled another blade of grass and laid the end between his lips, tasting the green of it.

"Of course I would not choose so," I say. To my chagrin, just as I would wish to appear romantic myself, I yawn prodigiously.

Mr. Serle laughs, a sudden, joyful sound. I cannot remember hearing him laugh since we talked of mistresses in the Columbia House Hotel. "You are sleepy, *cara*," he says. "You had better rest."

"I am sorry," I say. I so want to talk to him. "But you were unhappy? You loved her?"

"It was a kind of love, I suppose." Mr. Serle brushes an adventuring ant from the blanket. "I was lonely when Guido left, and I was flattered by the interest Anna and her brother took in me. There is a richness and beauty to their lives that is not just from their money but from art such as I never knew before. Only in the end, I understood that they wanted a return for their investment."

"A return?" I am puzzled into wakefulness.

"Anna wanted a man to manage her business affairs, to tend to her needs, to make her feel loved even when she was not singing." Mr. Serle pauses, gazing at me, and then his eyelids hood his dark eyes as if he feels pain to see me as he speaks. "I could desire her—a hungry man does not turn easily from a tempting meal. I could admire her art. She wanted a husband to stand guard between her and the world. I wanted a family and a home. Living as I did in hotel garrets or mean, rented rooms—how I yearned for family. I made romance where none existed."

"How sad for you," I say.

"More than sad," Mr. Serle says abruptly, as if something wakes anger in him. "Dangerous. Such delusions hurt others and destroy our selves."

"But you need a family," I tell him. "You deserve love."

"We will see," Mr. Serle says. His mouth curves in his ironic smile. "You are drooping like a wilting rose, my dear. When you have had your rest, we will discuss what I might deserve."

"We will talk more later," I agree, my eyelids dropping against my will. Then I am asleep.

I have a dream of being lost in a great field grown over with rosebushes. It smells like paradise. In my dream, Mr. Serle is on the other side of the field. I wish to speak to him, to tell him that I am going to pick roses to make an essence of the flowers. All the rosebushes bar the way. I look for a path, but branches thick with thorns grow everywhere. When I search for a place to walk, my dress catches on the brambles, and I must stoop to release it. The heavy fragrance of the flowers dizzies and confuses me. I reach to put a branch aside, and now my hand is caught in the thorns. I awaken with a start and slap at a mosquito on my arm.

"Ow," I exclaim.

Mr. Serle is watching me, his book open in his hand.

"Are you all right?" he asks.

"Have I been asleep long?" I ask him.

"Not long," he says.

He closes his book with a snap and puts it in his pocket. Light catches something in his hand that flashes golden, then is gone. What did he hold besides his book? I wonder.

"Have you heard Tobias call?" I say.

My mouth tastes as if I have been eating wool.

"No. Is he likely to wander?" Mr. Serle asks me.

"If the dog is here, Tobias cannot be far away," I say. "Rafe is his guardian angel."

I go to the pool and tuck my skirts up to wade in the cold water. I splash my face and neck for the coolness of it and to wake myself. I cup both hands and scoop cold water to rinse my mouth. Where is the child gone to? I wonder.

"Tobias! Tobias!" I call.

"I am coming!"

I hear his voice from the meadow above us. Almost immediately, Tobias comes running down the path, carrying his hat in front of him. Rafe leaps from his rock and follows him.

"Mother, Mother, I have a surprise for you," Tobias shouts. "Lie down on your blanket, close your eyes, and I will bring it."

When I obey him, he comes to sit close to me. I hear him breathing from his run. He nestles in at my waist.

"See what I found? Taste one." He must be speaking to Mr. Serle.

"Excellent. Very sweet," comes Mr. Serle's voice.

"Open your mouth, Mother," Tobias whispers to me.

"Wait a moment." Mr. Serle is whispering too. He sounds closer than he was. "Take the stems from the berries. She will not like to eat the leaves and stems."

"You help," Tobias whispers. "You clean them, and I will feed her."

"Yes," Mr. Serle murmurs. "Here we are."

He must have handed Tobias a strawberry, because Tobias says to me in a severe little voice, "Now, keep your eyes closed and open your mouth."

His little fingers insert a berry between my lips.

"Mmmm," I say. "It is very sweet and good, Tobias."

"Keep your eyes closed," he orders. "Here comes another one."

"Not too fast," Mr. Serle says softly.

Tobias feeds me two more strawberries.

"Mmmm," I say again.

"She doesn't always like to eat," Tobias says in a confiding tone. "I have to trick her."

"How do you do that?" Mr. Serle speaks very quietly as if I am really asleep.

"I tell her stories," Tobias whispers. "Sometimes I say she is a fairy living in a tulip house, and I feed her bread and honey that the bees made for her."

"That is a good story."

I wonder if it is right to let Mr. Serle encourage Tobias in his fantasies.

"Yes," Tobias says. "And I know a good trick. I ask her about the stories she tells me, like how the cook in the great house in England made her special pancakes, *crêpes*. She makes them for me just the way he made them for her. Then she forgets she isn't hungry, and we eat together."

Tobias tucks another strawberry into my mouth.

"And what is the story now?" Mr. Serle asks.

"She is a sleeping princess," Tobias whispers. "The magic strawberries made her sleep. We have to kiss her to wake her up. I will go first, and then it will be your turn."

I feel his sticky lips against the corner of my mouth. He has been eating strawberries too, I think.

Honor's and Guido's voices, calling over the sound of the bubbling water of the falls, interrupt. They climbed to the top of the hill and now have much to tell us about the beauty of the lake seen from above. Tobias wants them to taste his strawberries. Everyone is talking at once except Mr. Serle, who strolls away off up the path that Honor and Guido have just come down. Honor and Guido eat the rest of the strawberries. Tobias follows Mr. Serle, and they stand by the rock where Rafe lay earlier. Tobias points at something in the field or the woods beyond. After Honor and I shake out the blankets and collect the damp towels and our swimming clothes from the bushes where they have been drying, we call them to come back.

On the way down the hill, Tobias and Rafe lead the way. Honor puts her parasol up and takes her husband's arm. Mr. Serle and I, carrying the lemonade jug and the blankets, fall a little behind.

"Are you happy here, Mina?" Mr. Serle asks me.

I think of the beauty of this place and of the stored goodness of the pantries and cellars at the farm. Already this year I have rhubarb preserves laid by and extra to sell.

"I am content. We will never go hungry with such a good farm to support our needs," I tell Mr. Serle.

"The fear of famine never leaves you?" he asks me. I hear sadness in his voice.

I shake my head no. " 'Best safety lies in fear,' " I tell him. "Do you think we can ever be free of fear? Should we wish to be, if fear is the lesson the past has taught to make us safe?"

"Happiness is not the absence of fear," he says, "nor is it safety."

Walking beside him, I cannot see his expression clearly. Besides, the dappled light as we pass along the path through a grove of birch confuses my vision. Just as I am about to speak, Honor stops suddenly and makes a little shrieking sound. A bee is buzzing about the artificial flowers on her hat. We have to try to shoo it away, and when that only makes it buzz more angrily, Guido insists she exchange hats with him so that she wears his shady straw and he her daisies.

When we resume our way, "They have succeeded in love," Mr. Serle says. "I am glad to see my friends happy."

We are in sunshine now, and when I look to see his face, he is smiling down at me.

"Do you wish Tobias to call you Uncle Benjamin?" I ask him. "I meant to ask you this morning if you would like it or not."

"Tobias and I discussed it," Mr. Serle says. There is a bubble of something in his voice, laughter perhaps, but I am not sure. "Tobias tells me Rafe advises against it."

"Oh dear," I say. "What did he say?"

"I am not at liberty to explain," Mr. Serle says. "Tobias tells me it is a secret."

"Oh dear," I say again. "It is difficult knowing how to care for a child. Do you think his fantasies should be discouraged? He seems really to believe Rafe talks to him."

"I would like to know more about Tobias," Mr. Serle tells me. "How did you come to care for him?"

"I want to talk to you," I say. "Only I feel it should be more private. There is never enough time."

At the house, we put the picnic things away. Lily heats water to wash the dishes, glancing sideways at the visitors. I need to be in the kitchen to steady her. She has a tendency to break things when she feels awkward. Anyway, I have preparations to begin for supper. The Carltons are coming to join us. I wonder if Mr. King reminded Henry Carlton about the fish.

"Can I help you?" Mr. Serle asks me.

Remembering how I felt this morning, watching him work, I am tempted. Wait, I tell myself. I know how I feel about that. We must let our friendship grow or die.

"Not just now, but later we will cook together," I say. "Wait here. I am going to get my book. Keep Tobias out of the pickle jar, would you?"

I hurry to my room. I pray that Mr. Serle is truly my friend again. I want him to know me even if I am changed.

"Here," I say. "You gave me this. For a year now, I have thought little of being in a church. My book is my confessor. I thank you for that. Begin here where it says *January 1852* and read as much as you want after that. It goes to last week."

"Are you sure?" Mr. Serle asks.

"Oh yes," I say. "Your visit is so short. There may be no time to talk tonight or tomorrow with so many people to care for. It is the only way." I stop. I remember that I wrote of kissing Maurice Clemens. I must be brave. "I remember that you said there are not many people in the world we can trust with our selves. Even if you think ill of me, I must be honest with you. I will trust you with my life."

Tobias has crawled out from under the table.

"I have to learn the rest of my psalm before supper," he announces.

"I will try to deserve your trust and to return it," Mr. Serle says. "I need your friendship." He accepts the book from me and goes away to his room or to the outdoors.

When he returns, the day is almost gone. He meets me on the path from the garden, where I have been cutting asparagus and also herbs for a salad. The storm clouds are piled higher in the west and the air is even heavier than it was at noon. Although the wind has risen a little and a growl of thunder comes from far away, we have no rain yet.

"Honor said you would be here," he says. He holds my book

in his hand. "I will exchange. Take your book, and I will carry the basket for you."

"Do you understand about Tobias?" I ask him as we walk to the house.

"I understand that it is impossible to know much," he says. "I am glad you found him and his poor mother."

"It has been a gift for me," I say.

"I understand that, I think," Mr. Serle says. "I am grateful to know the truth of your life this past year. There was a part of your story I hesitated over."

"Which part?" I ask. I wonder if he is going to ask me about Maurice Clemens.

"You really wanted me to read about the doctor?" he asks.

"Oh!" My hand flies to my mouth, and I feel my cheeks flush. "I forgot I wrote all that down too. I am sorry."

"It is all right," Mr. Serle says. "I am glad to know you found help in your trouble. Only it seemed very private."

"I make you share my secrets whether you wish to or not," I say ruefully. "Oh!" I say in horror. "I wrote something about Aunt Jane. I betrayed someone else's secret. Promise me not to tell."

"I promise," Mr. Serle says. "Although it did not surprise me. The man has been courting her again."

I would like to ask him if he thinks Honor recognizes her father.

He continues quickly before I can speak. "I suppose you wrote to Mr. Clemens once you settled here?"

"No," I say. "I have not needed to see or hear from him since I last saw him in Albany."

Mr. Serle looks into my face. There is a hesitation in him. "I am not proud of my role in your story. I caused you pain," he says. "I am grateful that you still cared for me last summer, but after a year—" He hesitates again. "You speak of him as sunlight on water."

"Oh!" I say and smile at the thought. "He is like that."

"He summons you to the joy in life."

The thought Mr. Serle speaks should be glad, but he sounds troubled instead.

"Sunlight on moving water sparkles beautifully," I say. "But some people see the beauty in a quiet pool. There is a pleasure in gazing into a depth and seeing mysterious plants, gleaming stones, and darting fishes. Still water reflects the trees, the clouds, and the changing sky too. Light on a surface is only itself."

"Fishes?" Mr. Serle asks.

He looks directly at me with a different interest in his eyes. His mouth curves.

"It seems yesterday, not a year ago, that I spoke to you in Tompkins Market," he says. "Are you still angry with me?"

"No," I tell him. "Only I wonder if we are changed. If I break a plate and do not mend it immediately, the edges may become more chipped and cannot ever be glued together evenly to make a whole. It might be like that. Over time friendships may grow, but they can die too."

"*Ahi me.*" Mr. Serle makes the sound a sigh. "Friendship."

We have come to the porch of the summer kitchen. Mr. Serle sets the basket on the step. The sun today heightened his color, and his dark hair curls beautifully at his temples. I am holding my book with both hands at my breast. The wind pulls at my hair and blows a strand across my cheek. Mr. Serle lifts his hand as if to stroke it away. I remember standing at the door of the kitchen at Fourth Street. I feel a terrible fear. He will say good-bye now.

Without thinking, I step back. Mr. Serle drops his hand.

"You look frightened," he says. "What is wrong?"

"Nothing," I lie.

I feel confusion. I wish that he would touch me. He kissed me once. What am I afraid of? Even if he must return to New York very soon, he is my friend and—I am sure now—more.

"It is nothing," I lie again, but I know inside me it is not nothing—it is everything. I cannot kiss and part. My heart would break in shards of ice completely. I must know his choice in life before I give myself up to my desire—or his. Mine is not a kaleidoscope world. "I must go in and put my book away and cook the supper for us," I say. "It is getting late."

Mr. Serle nods. He looks withdrawn into his thoughts.

"May I help you?" he asks.

"Of course," I tell him. My heart is no longer jumping in my breast. "Nothing would give me greater pleasure than to work with you. But I must warn you. This is not an easy kitchen."

Before Mr. Serle can speak again, Eben comes from the barn.

"We will have rain before the night is over," he says. "Henry Carlton remembered and sent the fish up. Did you see it in the pail with ice? And a letter came for you from California. It is on the kitchen table."

"Give me your orders, my lady," Mr. Serle says, "and lend me an apron. I will begin dinner. You must read your letter."

I opened the letter from Daniel gingerly and then read with growing joy. In his letters now, his truth emerges more and more. *I have seen the elephant from trunk to tail,* he says. That is a California expression. He means that he has experienced his life and is beginning to understand it. He lives with a woman and has for almost two years now. When Guido left, he thought he would perish of loneliness. He thought of returning to New York City, and yet, he liked his work, he liked the striving life. Just as he despaired, he found Belle. *Guido knows her,* he says. *Guido knew her well before I did. We consoled each other when Guido left.* Belle asked my brother for work in his store because she hated the ladies' house where she was. I think my brother means to tell me Belle was a prostitute and cannot bring himself to say it outright—nor should he. Her dignity deserves his protection. They have a son, born in March just after he wrote to me last. Joy expands my heart in my breast. I have a nephew. My family grew without my knowledge.

Daniel is buying out his partners. He will own his business all himself. He wants to settle money on me at the same time. I will have to go to New York, he thinks, to set up my accounts as I wish. He sends a bank draft—three hundred dollars—to cover my expenses for the trip. Seeing the draft reminds me I have money in the bank in New York that I have not thought of in a year.

And then—the taste of my thought is bitter in my mouth. My brother did not trust me with his life until I demanded truth. He informs me of his marriage—if it is a marriage—two years late. He sends me money. He says his love at the end of the letter. It is a politeness. Money comes so much cheaper than trust and love.

"It is not bad news, I hope." Mr. Serle speaks quietly. He stands by the sink with a knife in his hand. He is about to scale the fish.

"No, not really," I answer. I am still in Daniel's world and trying to understand if I am happy there. It is a pleasure to think of Daniel's son. But I cannot show this letter to Honor, I think. Guido's private actions are in it. And I do not know if Guido knows that Daniel has taken this Belle, who must have been his lover too. I see that asking for another's truth is not such a simple thing. Our lives are braids, not single threads.

"You look sad," Mr. Serle persists.

"Life is so strange," I sigh. "Daniel says the partnership with you and Guido and the others will be dissolved. Did you know?"

Mr. Serle pauses. "No," he says. "I imagine the letters are in New York waiting for us." He sweeps the knife up the length of the fish and silvery scales fly.

"He is settling money on me. I will have to go to the city myself, he thinks."

"Ah," Mr. Serle breathes, a sigh of satisfaction. "You will come to New York. I am glad. I have been puzzling how I will see you again soon. One day is not enough for us."

While I was reading, he was thinking of me. Our eyes meet, and I feel the blood mount in my face. He has a fish scale on his cheek, silver and iridescent against his darker skin. Laughter sounds on the porch. Guido and Honor are coming back from feeding the geese with Tobias.

I put the letter in my pocket. "Well, we will talk of it. First, there will be twelve of us at dinner tonight."

Mr. Serle pumps water at the sink to rinse the fish. Lily brings a cheese from the cold pantry and sets it on a plate. I made extra bread, cakes, and stock for soup in anticipation of the visitors. Everyone wants a task. I set Aunt Jane to helping Tobias learn his psalm, so they are out of the way in the corner. Honor must pick flowers and arrange them for the table. Guido helps wash the salads and vegetables and then assists Honor to set the table while Mr. Serle and I cook. Lily cleans the pans and dishes as we finish with them. We stuff the fish with herbs and braise it with field mushrooms, allspice, and brandy.

While the fish is cooking, I give Mr. Serle the task of preparing the George Washington omelets.

"I have learned about another founding father," I tell him. "We have to honor his memory by eating a dish he approved. It will make us more American, don't you think?"

His mouth curves in the way I love as he smiles at me.

"Tell me what to do," he says.

He will make four omelets soufflé of four eggs each: one with sautéed apples, one with asparagus, one with herbs, one plain except for a sprinkle of cheese. They must be made and served together, overlapped on a hot platter. I help to set the ingredients ready, and then while I am thickening the fish sauce, he will cook the omelets.

"Be careful at the fire," I tell him. "The andirons are really too small. When a log splits, the pieces sometimes roll forward."

He knits his brow and frowns at me.

"I hope you are careful yourself," he says.

"Georgina Carlton told me how to fireproof my petticoats and cooking aprons with a zinc wash," I say. "I do not like the feel of it, but it is safer." Then I think perhaps I should not have mentioned petticoats and how they feel. It might upset Aunt Jane.

Mr. Serle does not care, for he nods and says, "Good."

I would like to stop my work and watch him, but with the spinach needing a sauce and both the soup and the fish to finish, there is too much to do. Mr. Serle makes a beautiful dish of the George Washington omelets, with chopped herbs for a final garnish around the edge of the platter.

"This is fine enough for a state dinner," I tell him.

He smiles and says he enjoys a new recipe. He expects it will indeed make us feel more American to eat it. Just as everything is ready, the Carltons arrive, and there is much bustle and laughter as everyone settles themselves. As I am about to put a bowl of pickled butternuts on the table and sit down myself, Honor looks at me with a meaningful frown. I take off my cooking apron and hang it by the sink.

Because Silas King is not here to look reproving, we all talk more freely. Eben brings out his stone jug of cider and one of my bottles of Madeira. He pours the glasses, according to what each wants. The children are allowed a teaspoonful of wine in a glass of water. Tobias studies how Mr. Serle drinks a little at a time, slowly, and imitates him.

"A meal without wine is a day without sunshine," Guido says, raising his glass.

"Did you make the bread, Mina?" Aunt Jane asks me as she takes a piece.

"I had to," I say. "There is no bakery in Uncas Falls or even Sawyerville. It is not at all like the city here."

"It is very good," Mr. Serle says. "I remember you have a deft hand for baking."

When everyone had satisfied their first hunger, there were toasts about the table.

"Courage!" Mr. Serle said, lifting his glass to me.

"Understanding!" I replied.

Guido toasted Honor with love, and Henry Carlton said, "To infinite patience!" to Georgina. Eben toasted, "The faith of friends!" to Tobias and Rafe. Tobias looked at him, his bright eyes wide, and said very seriously, "To popcorn, Uncle Eben," making Eben chuckle.

The conversation ranged widely. We live in a time of such interest—the new railroads will affect all our lives. A new president will be elected in the fall. Benjamin Serle and Henry Carlton began to talk of trees and whether there is a trade to be made in collecting wild nuts. And then Henry wanted to tell us about the microscope he has ordered from England for his studies.

"The wonders of the unseen world are as great as what is obvious around us," he said. "Paradise is under our noses."

"Science is his religion," Georgina said affectionately.

"Guido and I may have another marriage ceremony in a

church," Honor announced. I suppose the mention of religion woke the thought in her.

From the expression on Aunt Jane's face I think she wants to tell Honor to stop.

"But why?" I ask. "Is it allowed?"

"My mother is coming to America," Guido responds in his cheerful way. "I have sent passage for her and for two of my cousins to bring her. *Cara Mamma.*"

"Guido's mother tells us she looks forward to attending the church in our parish and to meeting our priest who married us. Her own priest in Trastevere wrote the letter for her," Honor says.

"What will you do?" I want to know.

Honor shrugs. "Whatever is needed to make her happy," she says.

"But—" I begin.

"Let us change the subject," Aunt Jane manages to interject.

I suppose it is not proper to talk of marriage at the dinner table. I wonder why not. I cannot vote or run a railroad, but I know married people. I feel troubled suddenly. Aunt Jane expects me to keep her secrets—even from Honor, who I believe has a right to know. And Honor knows the truth that Aunt Jane is her mother and will not say it to her. Guido has a secret too. He had a mistress in California, and now my brother has the woman. I have my own secret. I love Mr. Serle—I see his dark head kindly bent to hear what Georgina Carlton, pecking at her plate, is confiding to him; I see the beauty of his strong hand serving Tobias food; I remember the liberation of his honest words to me by the waterfall. There are too many secrets at this table.

Henry Carlton does not seem to have heard Aunt Jane. "Perhaps extreme measures are necessary to placate a mother-in-law," he says. His sharp-cut profile turns hawklike toward Honor. "But will your own conscience rebel?"

"No," Honor replies. "In marriage one must consider the needs of all one's connections. One marries one's spouse's relatives too. I accept that."

"Some would disagree," Mr. Serle says. "Some think marriage a very private matter between two people."

Sometimes there are no relatives with needs, I think.

"I have read of marriage," I say suddenly. The devil in me wants out. "On the Erie Canal, my friend Celeste showed me a pamphlet about a new community in the western part of New York State. It is the Oneida Community, where every man is married to every woman and every woman to every man. They claim marriage is a form of slavery if there is not complete freedom."

Aunt Jane looks truly horrified. Honor regards me as if she wants to laugh but does not dare.

"And what do you think of such an idea, Mina?" Mr. Serle asks.

He regards me with a curious expression of amusement and surprise. I have been very improper.

"I think it shocking," I say. "Such behavior would not be marriage at all but sin."

"Well!" Henry Carlton exclaims. "It is the very opposite of the Shakers' communities, which do not permit marriage of any kind. I visited the Shakers. They are wonderful farmers."

"They sell the best seeds," Lily says shyly, her first contribution to the talk, and the conversation turns again. Guido and Honor and Aunt Jane tell stories of the fashion for spirit rappings in the city. Everyone has an opinion about whether the manifestations are real or frauds. Lily looks quite frightened.

The night is warm and oppressive. I rise to swing a window wider to catch the air. Pausing with my hand on the casement, I look about the table. My mood eases. What good people! We are very American, I suppose. Guido is rich now by his own work; Lily is poor. Aunt Jane has known both states. Georgina Carlton's ancestors were born in this land for generations back. Mr. Serle and I touched the cobbles of a New York street less than four years ago. Now, brought together by the turns of fortune's wheel, we sit down together.

The others are laughing at some remark of Guido's, but Mr. Serle is watching me.

"The pleasures of the table combine our human need to eat with our need for sociability," he says. His face is golden in the lamplight, and I can hear in his voice that he is quoting one of his books. "We are like travelers who wish to arrive together at the same destination. At the end of a well-savored meal, both soul and body enjoy well-being."

"A toast to that, *Beniamino*," Guido declares.

"Come sit, Mina," Mr. Serle says. "You haven't tasted the omelet yet. Pass your plate, and I will serve you."

After dinner, we let the fire die and stayed in the summer kitchen. The parlor is a dreary place, and with the windows wide the kitchen freshened quickly. Honor said that it was now the duty of the guests from the city to entertain their hostess and her friends.

Guido became master of the ceremony and introduced each person. Tobias recited the One Hundred Twenty-first Psalm, the one that begins *I will lift up mine eyes unto the hills, from whence cometh my help*. After private conferring, Mr. Serle and Honor borrowed my copy of Shakespeare and read a scene from *Twelfth Night*. Honor took the part of the lady Olivia and Mr. Serle was Viola, who has disguised herself as a boy. My heart turned over in my breast when Mr. Serle read, *Build me a willow cabin at your gate and call upon my soul within the house,* and then looked up at me.

Guido sang "Open Thy Lattice, Love"—while Honor blushed—and "Stay, Summer Breath," which made Georgina take out her handkerchief. After that Eben played on his pennywhistle, and Henry Carlton on his fiddle. They gave us "Turkey in the Straw," and then we all sang "Yankee Doodle" and many other rousing tunes. There was much laughter and applause.

I was tired beyond words when at last I fell into my bed and into deep and dreamless sleep. I do not think even the thunderstorm breaking would have awakened me if it had not frightened Tobias.

"Mama! Mama!" I heard him shriek.

The windows shivered blue-white with lightning striking on the lake. I hurried across the room to him as the light streaked down again and again. Tobias was screaming in fear as I took him in my arms.

"Here, darling," I said, "your mother is here."

"Mama!" he whimpered into my breast.

Thunder crashed about us as if warring giants had made our roof their anvil and were hammering out their sword blades on it. It was so noisy that I do not think Tobias could hear at all the murmur of my voice at his ear. As the thunder growled itself away into a waiting silence, there was a tap at the door. I tied my wrapper about me and went to see who was there.

"The storm awakened me, and then I heard the child scream," Mr. Serle said. "Is everything all right?"

"I think he had a bad dream as the storm began," I said.

The thunder clanged again over my words, and Tobias cried out. Rafe pushed against my leg to go from the room.

"Let us go to the kitchen and stir the fire," I said to Mr. Serle. "Warm milk will help him sleep again. The storm will pass, and then it will be quieter. Come with us?"

In the kitchen I give Tobias, who is weeping still, to Mr. Serle and fetch the milk jug, a pan, the tin box with maple sugar, and a spoon. I take Tobias again, and Mr. Serle stirs the embers and puts a log on the fire. He sets the pan of milk to warm on the spider. All the while the violence of the storm assaults us. Even Rafe stays close instead of lying out of the way by the door.

"Remember the storm when we were on the ship?" I ask Mr. Serle in one of the silences between the lightning and the thunder.

He nods yes, because it is useless then to speak. As the groaning of the heavens dies, we hear the rain begin, a sweep of sound down the hillside and then drumming on the roof. The smell of the air changes. A little water drips in the chimney, and the fire hisses at it. Mr. Serle looks toward the sound, and I remember his tale to me of the flood that killed his son and his wife.

"The lake is well below us," I say quietly. "This house has never been flooded, not even the basement in the spring when the snow melts. It all runs away down to the lake."

"Thank you," he says.

Tobias whimpers in my arms.

"Hush, my darling," I say. "The storm is passing. The dream is going too."

"Mama cried," he whispers. "We lost our way."

I rock him in my arms.

"We have found you," I tell him.

Just then the thunder crashes as if it will beat in the doors. I hold Tobias tight.

"Remember we prayed together on the ship?" I ask Mr. Serle.

"At least we do not face such danger tonight," he says. "I feel a safety in this stone house that I never did on the wild Atlantic Ocean."

"On the ship it comforted me to hear your Hebrew prayer," I say, remembering Mr. Serle's arm about me with longing. "Perhaps it will soothe Tobias."

Mr. Serle looks doubtful. "Perhaps," he says.

"Would you like to hear a prayer, Tobias?" I ask him.

He nods and whispers yes.

"I can say the psalm that Tobias recited for us earlier," Mr. Serle says. "Perhaps he would like that."

As another roll of thunder died away, Mr. Serle began to speak quietly. The sound made me remember the peace at the center of the storm on the ship, but Tobias stiffened in my arms. It was as if a thrill ran through him like the tingle of lightning in the air before the storm breaks. His hair even seemed to stand up higher on his head and to curl tighter. He pulled my head to him with both hands.

"Did my papa teach him?" he whispered at my ear.

"I do not think so," I say, startled and puzzled.

"What is it?" Mr. Serle sees that we are distracted and stops.

Tobias wriggles from my lap and pads across the room to Mr. Serle, who stoops and lifts him in his arms. As he does so, the dog, Rafe, rises and, instead of going with Tobias as I expect, comes and sits by me, leaning his great head against my knee. Together, we watch as Mr. Serle bows his head and Tobias whispers in his ear.

They whisper for what seems a long time. I stroke Rafe's shoulder. The feel of the warm, soft feathers of his fur soothes me. I can see from the tilt of Mr. Serle's head that he is asking Tobias a question. Tobias lifts the front of his little nightshirt and asks Mr. Serle a question in his turn. Mr. Serle nods yes.

At last, Mr. Serle looks up at me. His dark eyes glisten with feeling.

"Tobias is going to tell you something," he says. "Are you ready?"

"Yes," I say.

"Go to your mother, Tobias," he says gently, setting the child on the floor.

Tobias comes to me. I lift him to my lap. As I do so, Rafe lies down and rests his great head on my foot. I feel the warm weight of it, anchoring me.

"Tell me, Tobias," I whisper.

Tobias leans into my breast and speaks at my ear in the small voice he used all the time when I first found him.

"My name is Tobias de Fonseca. I am four years old. My mama is Clotel de Fonseca, born Clotel Zimmer. My papa is Sabato de Fonseca, a peddler. My grandmama is Elise Zimmer, a Jewess, betrayed and sold as a slave by Mr. Simon Clare of New Orleans, may God curse him. I must find my papa's cousin in Montreal, Canada. Please help me."

"Yes, I will help you, Tobias," I whisper. "Thank you for telling me."

"My grandmama taught me," Tobias says. His voice is louder now. "Mama made me practice every day on our journey so I would not forget."

"I am proud of you, Tobias," I tell him. "You did not forget."

"Can I have milk now?" he asks. "I am thirsty."

Mr. Serle stirs maple sugar from the tin into the pan of milk and pours a mug for each of us. I set Tobias on a chair close beside me and bid him hold the mug in two hands and drink slowly.

"What will we do?" I ask Mr. Serle.

We talk without a clear conclusion. I cannot leave everything here suddenly to go to Montreal. I speak neither French nor Hebrew. De Fonseca is a Spanish name, Mr. Serle thinks. But there are Spanish Jews who went to Constantinople and to the Caribbean islands too, he says, and to Italy as well.

The Fugitive Slave Law makes everything difficult—we cannot put a notice in the newspapers, as some do when they seek a relative. Mr. Serle says he will talk to friends in New York. There must be a way to search for the father. Mr. Serle will learn the names of the religious leaders in Montreal and write to them. He can write to the synagogue in New Orleans also since Tobias mentioned the place. He will use a lawyer's address for the reply, he says. Even to ask for an announcement in a synagogue is a risk. Not everyone hates slavery, Mr. Serle points out. And some who hate slavery still believe in the rights of the states to make their own laws even if they are bad ones.

I hesitated before I wrote down what Tobias's grandmother and mother made him memorize. It is dangerous to have such a record, for it could be used against my beloved Tobias to steal him from this home. But Tobias is so little still; he might forget the words. To erase the history of another, too young to know what the past will mean to him someday, seems wrong. I must not be selfish just because I love him. And yet, to keep a record that Tobias is the son of a slave—however wrongly the woman and her mother were enslaved—is very dangerous.

"Could you ask Mr. King about finding the grandmother?" Mr. Serle says. "You said he is an Abolitionist."

"I do not wish to," I say as Tobias sets his empty mug on the table and seeks my arms again.

I tell Mr. Serle that I fear the use Mr. King and Zipporah James would make of a beautiful child. Their cause is just, but they think of the greater glory of all, not each humble life. I remember Zipporah James trying to slap Tobias's hand when he reached for a biscuit before she was served herself.

"You will help Tobias more than they could," I say.

Tobias dozes in my lap. The lightning and the thunder passed as we talked, but the rain patters at the window softly. I drink a little milk. The strange sweetness of the maple still surprises my tongue. It is the murmuring forest itself offering its savor to us.

I should take poor Tobias to his bed, but I do not want this night to end yet. To sit with Mr. Serle in a kitchen and talk as friends—it is the goodness of the past returned to me.

"Do you believe in hell in your religion?" I ask Mr. Serle.

"What?" Mr. Serle sounds very surprised. His eyes are shadowed and distant with fatigue or trouble. His thoughts have been elsewhere entirely.

"Do you believe in hell?" I repeat.

He looks at me doubtfully. "Hell? Why do you ask?"

"I want to know," I say, and then I worry that I have been rude. "I am sorry," I say. "Perhaps it is not proper to discuss such things."

"It is perfectly proper, if you wish to know," Mr. Serle reassures me.

I look at Mr. Serle, waiting.

Mr. Serle takes his time. "The Bible—the Old Testament to you—does not include hell. The Talmud talks of *Gehenna,* where the evil are purified. Some of our folktales include ideas of heaven and a sort of hell, but in the religion itself? No. There is no hell with fire, devils, and sinners cast down into the flames. We believe—I believe—that we must live in the world we are given as best we can." He looks at me somberly. "I suppose that for me hell would be to choose evil and to live out my life on earth knowing that I had deliberately done wrong."

"You are a very good person to believe that," I tell him. "Thank you for answering my question."

Tobias nestles his head on my shoulder. His eyes flicker open and close again.

"I must take this child to his rest," I say to Mr. Serle.

My arm and leg are cramped from Tobias's sleeping weight. When I stand, I stagger, so I set him gently on the chair, where he wriggles, half awake, and lays his head on the table beside him. I stretch and then move to the fire to take the almost-empty milk pan from the spider.

"I will put water in it for you," Mr. Serle says, anticipating my need. He sets the mugs in the sink and pumps water into the pan that held the milk.

As he does so, the dog rises, yawns widely, and, going to the door, noses at the latch to lift it. I pick up the hearth shovel. I will just rake the coals up and bank the fire, I think. The rain is gone. When the dog opens the door, the clean air will refresh the kitchen.

It happens with bewildering speed. Tobias dozes, Mr. Serle stands with the milk pan in his hand, the door swings in, the dog bounds out, a gust of night air blows my light summer wrapper just as the last of the logs cracks and breaks into red embers on the hearth.

Before I can cry out, Mr. Serle pulls me away from the fire, empties the pan he holds against me, dousing the first sudden flare of flame, drops the pan, seizes my cooking apron to wrap my legs, and smothers the last glow of danger. In the shock of it, my knees give way and we fall, me half fainting, Mr. Serle supporting me.

We lie on the floor for a very long time without speaking, our arms tight about each other. A strange lethargy overtakes me. Fear saps thought and action. If I wished it, I could not move. We will stay here, I think. I need never let him go. His breath on my cheek breathes life in me. We will be one. I will open a door in my breast and he will live beside my beating heart forever.

The room smells of singed cotton, and of our fear, and of the wet, lightning-rent night air. We hear water drip, slow drop by slow drop, in the sink. Slowly, time, which fell all in a heap like a skein of snarled wool, untangles itself again into a smoothly unwinding yarn. Slowly, slowly, our panting breaths quiet, our racing hearts begin to ease.

Mr. Serle strokes my hair gently, kisses my temple, begins to murmur in my ear. I cannot understand him and think for a moment that the fear of fire has addled my mind. Then I comprehend that he is speaking several languages all mixed together.

"*Carissima, carissima,*" he whispers. "*Je t'aime. At mefakhet? Non hai paura.* You are safe, Mina. You are safe, *mia amata. Lev sheli. Liebchen. Amóre mio.*"

I lay the palm of my hand against his beloved face. "We are safe," I tell him. "We are safe. I love you so."

We might have lain there, whispering to each other, until love and relief and the wonder of our living bodies pressed to each other kindled into passion, but Tobias awakes and whimpers. He slides from his chair and comes for comfort. We pull him down and hold him between us. He too is safe. And the dog returns, shaking himself and scattering rain everywhere. With two such chaperones, what can we do but pull ourselves, stunned by dread and yet alive to joy, back into the world?

We rise and examine each other's hurts. It is still almost impossible to talk coherently. Mr. Serle's right hand has an angry red burn, but it is not blistering. I find the sweet oil and soothe some on the place. My legs are dirty with soot. Mr. Serle helps me to wash at the sink. Miraculously, I am not hurt at all, only, I suddenly realize, quite indecent in my torn, wet, and singed night shift. In his passion to save me, Mr. Serle tore my wrapper completely away, and it is lying tattered and burned on the hearth.

Without my speaking, Mr. Serle takes off his dressing gown and puts it on me. In his haste earlier, he just thrust on his trousers, which are buttoned crooked, and put on his dressing gown. I see the beauty of his bare chest and the strength of his shoulders; under the little curve of his navel, a black line of hair on his flat belly disappears into his clothes. I feel more unsettled looking at him undressed than I did when it was I who was exposed.

"Come, *tesòro,*" he says, knotting the sash of the dressing gown at my waist, "it is very late. We are both exhausted. We must rest."

With Rafe and me trailing behind, Mr. Serle carries Tobias to his bed and pulls the covers over him tenderly. Rafe settles himself on the floor. Tobias—who is already asleep again—will not be able to get up without stepping on him. We stand there for a moment, silent and dazed still by the fear we have shared. Tears slide on my cheeks.

"Come," Mr. Serle says, taking my hand. "The dog will guard the child."

He draws me with him to his room. The window stands open a little, and the murmur of the rain-swollen creek sounds loud in the silence of the night.

"Come," he says again. "Lie down with me. You need warmth and comfort. You are trembling still."

"You have saved me," I say. "I will do whatever you wish. My life is in your keeping."

In the darkness, Mr. Serle gives a little chuckle of laughter. "You sound resigned to your fate," he says. "I am not going to ravish you, *cara*. Tempting though you are, that is not what you need in this moment."

I hear the scratch of a match and then see the spurt of blue flame. Mr. Serle lights the oil lamp on the table. The flame wavers in the night air, and he swings the window closed.

"Come," he says, "lie beside me, and I will pull the blanket over us." He stoops to grasp my foot. "Your feet are freezing," he declares.

When we walked down the path from the falls, there was an ease in our pace together. When we worked in the kitchen to make dinner, we each moved according to the other's need. Now the comfort I felt, holding him, returns. Our bodies fit one to the other. Mr. Serle wraps the blanket about us, adjusts the pillow, pulls me close with one arm, caresses my face with his left hand, which I see dimly lit in the lamp's glow.

"Tell me your thoughts. You wish to live in Uncas Falls?" he asks.

"I feel at home here in the country by the lake." My heart opens to his warmth as I tell him my truth. "You told me you dreamed of such a place once, and my brother and I talked of a farm and horses long ago. Perhaps I treasured those dreams because they speak to my nature—to my soul. Village life suits me, and for so long as I am given to protect Tobias, it is healthier for him."

"If you need this life, you must have it," Mr. Serle says.

There is a silence. Wrapped in love, I feel safe now. Like the ice that breaks and melts and floats away down the lake under the warming sun of spring, the terror and shock are flowing from me. I watch the shadows thrown by the lamplight dance on the wall.

"Why didn't you write to me?" I ask. "Your engagement was broken off; you could have written to me."

He sighs, a light movement of breath against my temple. "Honor read me your letters—or parts of them. I did not hear that you thought of me—and I did not feel I deserved your thoughts. I knew I hurt you, even when I pretended to myself that I had not. Then, in the autumn, Sadick Meyer showed me drawings he bought from this artist Maurice Clemens in Albany. He thought to tease me. One drawing showed a woman with a knife in her hand peeling an orange. There was everything of you in the gesture. *M. dreaming of her lover,* was written under it. 'See,' Sadick told me, 'the artist loves to talk. He told me the tale of his boy-girl Mina. You were a fool not to take her when you could.' I knew I had been a fool, but not for the reason Sadick suggested."

"You have read my book," I say. "You know my story. Do I have to say who it was I dreamed of?"

"No," Mr. Serle says. "But I did not know you might forgive me until you wrote to me. And then I was ill and low in spirits and afraid to hope too much."

I remember when I was angry at Mr. Serle. I told him he threw away an innocent love. That was a truth—only it comes to me that such a child's love had to die. I can remember that childish adoration now; it is like a candle flame, wavering before a sacred picture. I want a love that fills the room. I want to be grown from the inside out and to taste everything. And death waits in the hot ashes of the fire, in the icy depths of the flood—under the beauty of the brief day is the dark of endless night. We are given so little time. Grown-up love cannot be innocent. I will extend my hand to my desire and accept what comes.

"I have to ask a favor of you," I say.

"Yes?" Mr. Serle sounds sleepy now. "What would you like, Mina?"

"I should like to kiss you," I tell him.

He tastes of wine and almonds. I smell bay leaves and the musky soap he uses when he shaves. I want to breathe him into me. When I stop at last, his arms tighten about me as if he would tell me that I please him. It makes my heart beat loud inside to feel his strength.

"What would you like, Mina?" he asks again. He sounds very awake now.

"I want," I say, "only to love you. You hold my heart. You protect me. I will be your mistress."

Mr. Serle sits up, throwing the blanket into a tangle. His face is very still. Only the sound of his breath through his parted lips and the flush of red high on his cheeks tell me he is stirred. His dark eyes glitter in the lamplight.

"My mistress?" He sounds shocked.

"I have thought about it very carefully," I tell him. "The priests say to know love just for love is a sin and means hell. They say Jews go to hell. I accept God's will. I have decided. I will go to hell. I will be with you forever."

"Tesòro mio." Mr. Serle seizes me so tight in both his arms that I cannot breathe. When he releases me, he holds me from him so he can look at me. There is a silence.

"I have no words," he says at last. "Only my blood speaks to you."

I put out my hand to touch his face.

"Was that why you asked me about hell?"

I nod yes. "If there were a hell in your religion, God might send you to a different place. But if the only hell is the one I have heard of, then it is all right."

"All right?" He kisses me gently on the cheek. "You are my heart," he says, "but perhaps not a competent theologian." He kisses me again, more vigorously. "You smell of roses," he says, "and clove." He kisses my neck under my left ear. "Your hair is cinnamon and honey," he murmurs, pushing the dressing gown—and my night shift too—down from my shoulder, "and your skin, almond milk."

A summer storm is breaking over me. I am swept into this moment. I will give myself up to be one drop of water in a deluge.

"Am I frightening you?" he asks, his lips at my ear.

"A little," I admit. "I thought for a moment you might make a meal of me."

"I might do that," he says. "I have starved for a very long time."

There is another silence. Mr. Serle traces his finger along my jaw and around the shell of my ear and then down my neck and my shoulder as if he is outlining me, drawing me in the air. His head bends to me. The lamplight glazes his hair like a halo, but his expression is hidden from me.

"Well, Miss Mina Pigot," he says at last. "Here you are in my bed. You are fully compromised. My duty is to marry you."

His voice sounds very satisfied.

"Marriage?" I wonder at his words. "I did not think you could marry me."

"Why not?"

"I will not ask you to choose between me and your faith," I say.

Mr. Serle is silent again. Then he straightens the dressing gown about me so that I am decently covered. He takes my hand in his.

"There is no choice," he tells me. "Love that sleeps cradled in the heart's darkness for four years and awakens again in the light of one afternoon cannot be denied. Love that lifts the soul cannot be wrong. Our beliefs are sincere—the forms of our individual worship are immaterial."

"Is it really all right?" I ask. "Sometimes I am so afraid."

"Tell me what you feel, Mina," he says.

"I was so happy when I was a child at home in Ireland before the famine, and now a whole world is gone. I must be very careful not to ask too much. When we hold happiness too close, it disappears, as warmth and smoke drift upward from the fire, leaving ashes."

Mr. Serle does not let go of my hand. "You have never asked too much," he says. "Never. Now I am troubled that I must ask something of you. I cannot be married by a priest. I cannot be married in a church."

"That is easy for me," I confess. "I know my own heart. I will not be ashamed to offer it direct to God when I die. In this world, I will trust love to guide me. God does not speak to us, and men make such foolish rules for Him."

"God will care for Himself," Mr. Serle assures me. "You and I will marry according to American law."

"When?" I ask.

"Do you have any objection to tomorrow?" he inquires. "Shall we ask Henry Carlton to marry us tomorrow morning?"

"Yes," I say. "Yes, we will."

Listen," he says. "The founding father Thomas Jefferson wrote about religion thus: *Divided we stand, united we fall.* Do you believe that?"

I think about it. Then—"Yes," I reply, "I believe it. My faith does not take from yours nor yours from mine."

"All paths end at your door," Mr. Serle says quietly. "I thought I could make my journey alone. And then, just as I miss your companionship most—there you are, walking in a market or sleeping by a waterfall. My heart tells me I will never be complete without you. I want to keep you safe."

"My safety is knowing that when you truly love, it is a strength forever," I say, kissing him. His beard is beginning to shadow his jaw. I am free now.

Mr. Serle strokes the hair back from my temple and twists a strand about his finger. "I have to tell you something more. Do you remember the gold coins you earned in England?"

"Of course," I reply.

"Last spring when I learned you had left New York, I took the gold to a jeweler. He made me a ring, a signet for my little finger. I told myself so long as I kept it safe you would be safe. I thought I would wear it, but I was too afraid it would slip off and be lost. I work so with my hands, you know."

"I know," I say.

Mr. Serle stands up. He reaches to his vest, where he hung it. The gold winks in the lamplight as he takes the ring out.

"You wore it today by the waterfall," I say, remembering the flash of brightness as he closed his book.

"Yes, I did," Mr. Serle says, sitting on the edge of the bed now. "It has your name written on the inside, Mina." He goes on before I can speak. "Perhaps it was not a proper thing to do. Forgive me, but telling the jeweler to do that brought me to understand myself."

"What did you understand?" I ask.

The room is dark all around us. In the wavering light, I see

Mr. Serle's face half golden, half shadow, and his hand holding the ring. His voice drops, hesitates, and then gains strength as he speaks.

"I must be honest with you. I understood I would never marry Anna Moses. The engagement would fail because in it I wronged both you and her. And even if you were gone, it was an evil because I could desire her body and admire her art but I did not love her soul. The morning the ring was delivered, I put it on my finger. The next post brought a letter from Honor saying you were safe. You make my heart alive in me. This ring is my need for you made visible."

"How beautiful," I tell him. "The hero of one of your novels might think of such a thing."

"Will you wear the ring?" Mr. Serle asks. "Please, Mina, forgive me for the past."

"Forgive you?" I wonder at the idea. "I love you. At first I loved you as a child loves, without thought. Then I loved you as a friend, because you are so kind to me. I have loved you just for yourself for a year now. I love you, all of you—just as you are."

He puts the ring on my finger and kisses me and touches me with his beautiful, clean hands until I feel—well, I cannot write down what I feel without blushing. Anyway, writing the feeling is useless because it does not exist in words. It is the body's knowledge that is part of me now.

When I can breathe again, I ask, "When we go to the jeweler to make the ring smaller, can we add your name to mine inside it?"

"You would like that?"

"Oh yes," I assure him. "Can it be written in your language?"

"Italian?" he asks.

"No, Hebrew," I say. "I would like it to be your name as your God would speak it."

Mr. Serle does not say anything, but he takes my right hand in both of his and kisses the palm.

"Come," he says. "I must take you back to your room across the hall."

"But—" I begin to object.

"I will not compromise your name here," he tells me. "Guido

and Honor would understand, but not the others. This is a small place. We are going to make our life among these people."

"But no one will know," I tell him.

"We will know," he answers me. "No—no passionate nights and regret in the morning. I see my way. No paramours or mistresses for me. If you want me, you must marry me."

"Oh," I say.

I look down at the rings, one on my right hand and one on my left hand. I sigh and let my heart ease itself in my breast.

"My mother would have wanted it so," I whisper.

"She would," Mr. Serle tells me, touching her ring on my hand. "And mine too. Now you must go before I lose control of my conscience, or rather, before my conscience loses control of the rest of me."

At my door, he puts his arms about me and holds me against him secure and silent.

Then—"Go," he says. "Sleep, *amóre*. Tomorrow."

"Yes," I answer. "Tomorrow."

"A Christian virgin and a Jewish child," he says softly, his lips curved in his ironic way and his eyes dark and unreadable. "It is a terrible responsibility."

"Yes," I say.

"We will find our way," he says.

He kisses me then and leaves me. I think I will lie awake or dream of fire, but peace comes quickly. Comforted by the scent of him, I sleep in his dressing gown for all that is left of the night.

I waken abruptly to the sound of screaming from the summer kitchen. By the time I have dressed myself and hurried out, the place is a babble of people. Lily arrived and found my burnt wrapper on the hearth, where I forgot it. She stands like a rooted tree in the middle of the room, clutching the tattered garment to her breast and sobbing in great gasps. Eben shouts at her, but she seems deaf to reason and the world. Aunt Jane is wringing her hands. Guido questions Tobias, who hangs his head. He is probably whispering and cannot be heard in the uproar Lily is making. Rafe goes about the room, bumping his head into people as he does when he wants them to notice something.

"Here she is!" Honor seizes me and kisses me. "Are you hurt?"

"I am all right," I say. "Where is Mr. Serle?"

"Here I am," he says, coming sleepy-eyed into the room. "What is all the noise?"

Honor eyes us sharply and takes charge. "Tobias, go to your mother," she says. "Aunt Jane, get a mug of cold water for Lily so she can collect herself. Eben, why don't you help Lily to sit down? She had a shock, but now she can see that no one was hurt. Guido, you and I will begin work on breakfast." She pauses. "Rafe," she says, "go lie out on the porch until Tobias needs you."

"Thank you, Honor," I say. Tobias is clinging to my skirt. "Darling," I say, stooping to him, "you buttoned your shirt crooked this morning. Let me fix it for you."

"You didn't wake up," he whispers in my ear. "I kissed you, and you didn't wake up."

"Benjamin," Honor says briskly, "I suggest you and Mina take Tobias outside or into the parlor for a few moments. There will be breakfast ready when you come back, and you can explain what happened. I imagine you may even have news for us—"

I was interrupted in my writing just then.

"Do you have us married yet, my darling?" Benjamin asks me from across the table, where he sits, writing letters. We have been sharing the ink bottle. "You have been very intent, and you blushed as you wrote a moment ago. Tell me what you were thinking, so I can watch the flame rise in your cheek again."

"Hush, *caro,*" I say, looking to Tobias, who sits at Benjamin's elbow, copying his alphabet and pretending that he too is writing letters. "I had come to when Honor took two hours and organized our wedding and a lunch and made arrangements for everyone— even the cow and the poultry—so we could have private time together."

"If that woman commanded an army, her cause would surely

win," Mr. Serle declares. "When I look back to the year we spent apart, there are two great goods—you found Tobias, and Honor Corbett became my friend as well as yours."

Tobias yawns.

"I will write the ending another night," I say.

SUNDAY, JUNE 20, 1852

I have found a moment for my book again. Now I return in thought to Friday, May 28, and the beauty of it.

The rain of the night scrubbed the air clean. The morning is fresh and bright and busy. My life changed forever, and yet the world perks on. No one seems greatly surprised that Benjamin Serle and I intend to marry.

"I knew you would need a new dress," Honor says, kissing me again.

Lily, calm now, pours boiling water into the French coffeepot slowly, as I have taught her. "Congratulations, Miss Mina," she whispers to me, "he is a fine-looking man."

I planned to make the fish left from the night before into a breakfast dish with cream, but there is no need for it. Guido and Honor set out cheese and smoked ham, and Lily scrambled eggs as well as toasting bread.

Over breakfast Honor organized us. Honor says that we cannot be married until noon, because I must bathe and have my hair dressed properly. After the wedding and a simple meal, which Georgina, her help, and Lily will make, Eben will drive the DiRomas and Aunt Jane to Albany. Aunt Jane agrees that she can manage to return to New York without Mr. Serle. In two weeks, when the DiRomas are home from Niagara, Mr. Serle and I will go to New York City. Really, Honor thinks of everything.

Eben went out early to see if the storm did damage to the fields and reports that a great oak by the upper pasture was struck by lightning. Everyone—except Honor, who goes down to talk to Georgina Carlton—troops up to see the fallen giant struck through its heart, and then Guido DiRoma and Mr. Serle take off their coats and spend an hour helping Eben to begin sawing the split trunk into lengths the horses can drag down by the barn. Oak wood burns long and hot.

After cool drinks for everyone, Honor returns, and Guido DiRoma and Mr. Serle go off to the Carltons' with Lily and Tobias and baskets of food. Of course, Rafe accompanies them.

Lily heated water for me and filled the bath before she went down to work with Georgina. Honor helped me to wash my hair at the sink and rinse it with rose water. I wound a towel about my head and lay in the bath. Being immersed in warm water is such a luxury—and on a weekday morning! As I soaped my arms, I could see that the scar from the night Jasper Westervelt gave me the hasheesh is a thin white line, almost invisible. The scar on my arm and the deformed little toe of my right foot where the pony stepped are marks life left on me as it pushed me forward.

I am slim, but muscle rounds my arms and legs. There is a strength to me now. The white mounds of my breasts with their outward-turning nipples are not abundant but womanly enough. At my groin, the springing darker red hair makes a contrast to the white smoothness of my belly. When I look down myself, I am satisfied that I am grown to be a woman. Soap bubbles wink their iridescence all about me as I wash in the soothing water.

Later, after I had rubbed lotion all over me, I sat by my bedroom window to comb and dry my hair. I wore Mr. Serle's dressing gown as a wrapper. Honor came in to be with me, raised an eyebrow when she saw it, and then smiled. "I made that for him last winter," she said. "I am interested that he has given it away."

I confessed more of what happened last night. Honor embraced me for relief that I am alive and that Mr. Serle saved me. Then she said that love that conquers death will conquer all doubt. Aunt Jane heard our voices and tapped on the door. Guido and Benjamin returned, she said, and were walking up to bathe at the falls again, but Georgina Carlton had kept Tobias with her.

We talked of everything: how Aunt Jane cared for me when I was drugged and how sorry I was that I had gone away so foolishly. Only it was good, really, Honor pointed out. I found Tobias. I told them about Doctor Walker, and her helping me to know I was not raped. Aunt Jane was very glad, she said, although she cannot bring herself to think of Bloomers as ladies.

"It was my mind, not my body, that had to heal last summer," I tell them. "When I had bad dreams and wakened fearful in the night, I would try to think of something good to soothe myself. I thought of you both, often, and also once that Mr. Westervelt acted honorably."

Aunt Jane turns bright pink and purses her mouth at the mention of Mr. Westervelt. Honor looks from her to me, her eyes narrowed with thought.

"I like him too," she says. "He asked me last week if he might bring his daughter to call soon. Did he mention it to you, Aunt Jane?"

Aunt Jane nods yes, picking up and toying with my comb.

"He said his daughter, Sarah, needs a woman friend," Honor says. "He said perhaps I might encourage her in society as an older sister would."

I hold my breath. Honor is all intent on Aunt Jane now.

"Did Mr. Westervelt mean me to understand something behind his words?"

Aunt Jane does not reply, but she grips the comb tight.

"What do you think, Mina?" Honor asks.

She still stares at Aunt Jane, her face a mix of pain and hope.

I hesitate, and then I say, "When I worked for him, he wanted to know if the Miss Corbetts were well. He asked me the age of Miss Honor Corbett. I always liked the kind expression of his gray eyes."

Honor looks at me sharply; her own gray eyes opening wide suddenly.

"I have wondered," she says.

I promised not to speak, and so I only look at her. Honor puts her arms around Aunt Jane, whose head is still bent. She holds her for a long moment, her cheek against her smooth brown hair, her eyes closed. For Honor, she is very still. Then energy flows in her again. She takes the comb from Aunt Jane and hands it to me. She takes her handkerchief from her pocket and presses it into Aunt Jane's hand.

"Later we will talk more," she says softly. "Now, my darling, we must help Mina dress for her wedding."

Aunt Jane arranged my hair for me. Her hands shook at first, but then she bent and kissed my cheek and steadied herself. When I put on my chemise, I hesitated. I made a place to tie my ring in it just as I have in all my underthings.

"What is that, Mina?" Honor asked me as I stood with the ring in my hand.

"It is my ring my mother gave me as she lay dying," I said. "I wear it always over my heart."

"You never told me," Honor said.

"How pretty," Aunt Jane said. "Do you never wear it?"

"Only at night to keep my mother near me," I said. "I used to be afraid to wear it in case it was stolen. Now I fear it will be lost when I am working."

"Well," Honor said, "you will not work today."

"I will wear it for my wedding," I answer, putting it on my finger.

Honor was very satisfied with how I looked in my green and white silk dress. I wore my brooch, of course. At the last moment, I took out my fan that Guido DiRoma gave me. I thought the picture of the waterfall on it might give me courage. Honor and Aunt Jane both said I looked a beautiful bride and very ladylike. I felt like a cake in a pastry case.

I suppose that Mr. Serle's novels end when the hero marries the heroine, because that is the point of their stories; marriage is all the characters yearn for. Perhaps the authors are embarrassed to talk about the marriage nights, or they think it is dull to be married. Perhaps they believe that waiting and loneliness is a better story than a man and woman united in a bed or working together in a kitchen.

This is my private book and not a novel, so I am free to write as I please. The DiRomas, Aunt Jane, and Eben walked down the hill with us to the Carltons. The children had gathered wildflowers to decorate the parlor. Henry Carlton married Mr. Serle and me and entered our names in his book of official records.

We ate our wedding meal together on the back porch of the Carltons' house, facing the lake. A breeze blew in to keep insects away. The lilacs in the yard were just coming into bloom and their light perfume mixed with the savory odors of the meal, the tang of the wet green weeds along the lakeshore, and the myriad spice, dried apple, and salt fish smells from the store. I cannot remember what I ate—nothing perhaps, for I had little appetite. And yet it was a very jovial and happy time, being with friends and floating upward on a wave of love and the joy of life.

We talked of plans over our meal. Of course, everyone has an opinion of what Mr. Serle and I should do. Guido DiRoma suggests we might become his agents to harvest ice on the lake.

Mr. Serle tells Eben frankly that he is no farmer. "I will see about this hotel that is building," he says. "They may want a chef." He looks at me and smiles. "You might have graham bread in your future after all, Mina," he says.

"If it is made with love, I am sure it will be palatable," I say.

"I think the village could use a bakery," Henry Carlton says.

"Mina makes excellent preserves," Georgina declares. "I would invest in a jam business myself."

Afterward, there was all the bustle of departing guests and being sure that Tobias—with Rafe, of course—had everything he needed to spend the night with Jem Carlton. And then—in the quiet house at the end of the afternoon, Mr. Serle and I were alone.

I wore my silk dress to be married, with its lace chemisette and my brooch. The brooch caught in the lace as I opened the clasp. Mr. Serle saw my trouble and unpinned the brooch carefully for me.

He weighed it in his hand. He has been so glad, and now, suddenly, he looks sad.

"I remember the day you gave it to me," I say. I wonder what he is thinking. "When we go to New York City, perhaps the jeweler where you bought it will write your name in my ring."

Mr. Serle looks surprised, and then he flushes.

"The brooch was my mother's," he says. "I did not buy it here."

I put my hands about his.

"Your mother's?" I am amazed. "Whose hair was in it once?" I ask.

"Mine and my brother's," he says. And then he takes a deep breath. "And my son's was added when Rachel wore it."

Tears well in my eyes.

"You gave it to me?" I say in wonder.

He is looking down at the perfect rose on its blue stone sky.

"I wanted to see you happy," he says, "but you cried when I gave it to you. I made you sad."

"I am crying now," I say, "for joy that you cared for me, that you trusted a child with such a treasure." I think of what the brooch must mean to him. "What did you do with the hair that was in it?"

"It is with my things," he says.

"We will put it back at once," I tell him. "I will keep your loves and mine together."

"Later," he says.

"No, now," I insist. "We will honor the past before we reach to the future."

The locks of hair were in a twist of paper in the back of his prayer book. We opened the brooch to put them in, and when all was safe, I set the lovely thing on the bureau.

"Now we can begin," I say. "Perhaps you can kiss the tears away." And then I feel uncertain. "Should I put a night shift on?" I ask.

"If you wish, *tesòro*," Mr. Serle tells me. "Will it distress you if I do not? My tradition teaches that clothing is an impediment to love. It is a duty even to set it aside."

"Is that my duty too?" I ask.

"You have no duty in our bedroom, *bella spòsa*," he says. "You have rights, which I must honor."

Mr. Serle drew me to him. He kissed my cheeks and my closed eyes. His lips drank the wet from my face. The mix of sorrow and joy in me separated itself and the sadness ebbed until all was sparkling light.

Doctor Lydia Mary Walker was right that I would find more pleasure than pain in my first experience. Mr. Serle seemed to be anxious that I was hurt or would cry, but I felt very happy. When mind and heart and body move as one, the world becomes centered in a kind of joy and mystery. I felt as if I lived at the heart of a rose. It was a revelation to me.

Later, we had to get up and pick all my hairpins out of the bed, so they would not poke us. And later still, with Mr. Serle holding me, I fell asleep. When I awoke, the last blush of daylight was fading in the sky, but he was not there.

I found him in the summer kitchen, setting out plates and food.

"Are you hungry, Mina?" he asked.

"Yes," I said, "I am very hungry."

"Are there candles?" he asked me.

"There are candles or the oil lamp, which gives more light," I told him.

"It is Friday night," he said. "I would like to light Sabbath candles."

I set the tapers in the sticks, and he taught me the simple prayer. Then we sat at the table and ate cold fish, salad, and bread and butter. I never had such a good meal in all my life. We talked of everything. Mr. Serle teased me that now I know all life's appetites and that he has found another way to help me to eat enough. When we had cleared the dishes away, we returned to the bedroom and lay together quietly. Mr. Serle said he must give me a wedding gift.

"But I have my ring," I tell him, "and I have you."

"Another present, then, to remember the day," he says. "I insist."

"A cookstove would be good," I suggest.

"That does not sound at all romantic," he objects. "And we must have one anyway. No more open fires, Mina. No, something for you."

I think for a long time.

"I would like a horse," I say.

"A horse? Not a garnet necklace or a portrait of me?" He winds a curl of my disheveled hair about his finger and gives a little tug. "You show signs of becoming a very difficult wife," he tells me.

"A gray mare," I say, "and a pretty cart for delivering the bread we will make."

So then—well—after a time I was hungry again, and we looked in the pantry and shared sponge cakes flavored with rose water.

I think I begin to understand why writers of novels stop at the marriage. The story could go on forever, and what interests me most in this moment is either the dailiness of life—the modern cookstove, the new bakery ovens, Mr. Serle's method of frying cauliflower in the Roman style, Tobias's need for a haircut, and the ripening Indian corn—or what is indecent to write down. It is our private love. Even my book cannot share in it now.

THURSDAY, JUNE 24, 1852

Today I received a letter that surprised and gladdened me.

> SAN FRANCISCO
> SUNDAY, MAY 16, 1852
>
> My dearest sister Mina,
>
> I have not received your reply to my last letter, but I think you will be eager to hear my news, and so I will not delay to share it. I have a strange tale to tell you.
>
> Two weeks ago a strange, uncouth, shambling sort of fellow came into our store. Not that strange, uncouth men

are such an unusual sight here, but this one seemed more incoherent and bewildered by the city than most. He is a large man but was very starved looking when I first saw him. I think the shop people were a little afraid of him, for Belle called me from my office immediately.

As soon as he saw me, the man began to exclaim. "It must be the brother!" he said over and over. He fished about in his pockets—I thought at first he was fumbling for a gun and put my hand to my own—and produced a dirty screw of paper. From that he took a lock of red hair, which he held up by my head. When he came close, I found he smelled dreadfully. "Yes!" he cried. "Yes, it is!" Then tears coursed down his cheeks. "Miss Mina says she loves you," he said. Tears came to my eyes too when I heard that.

Well, you will know by this description that Flint has found his way to California. I think he came on a ship last autumn. What he did after he arrived is not at all clear. He must have spent time in the gold fields, for he carried a bag heavy with gold and had nuggets in various pockets about his person. I think maybe he found a sick and dying miner in the backcountry and tried to nurse and help him. Or else he was working with a partner and they were attacked. I cannot get a straight story from the man, for he weeps when pressed to tell where he has been. He asked me in his innocent way what to do with the gold, and I helped him at the bank.

My pen hesitates—I do not wish to shock you, but you have asked for frankness. Near us in the city is a house of the kind they term a ladies' parlor house. Flint has been taken in there. The women seem very pleased to have him. He acts as a doorman and, often, as an escort when a woman goes out so she will not be bothered in the street. They have washed him, fed him, cut his hair, and refurbished his wardrobe. He seems very cheerful. He stops in to speak with me—it is the same conversation always—about you and your skillful cooking and kind ways. The women have comforted his body, but they have not yet succeeded in clearing his mind. Even so, you may be glad to know that he is alive. I think he was a friend to you or you were friend to him. That is my tale.

Do you wish to travel to us in California? The trip is long, and the truth is that I am not willing to leave my interests here to fetch you. If you decide to come, as your brother I will be glad to welcome you. There is always work in my store. Perhaps in your next letter you will send a lock of your hair. Flint refused to give me the curl you gave him. He says he needs it.

You will have my settlement on you soon, I expect. Meanwhile, I enclose the return on your investment, the gold eagle you gave me three years ago—a bank draft for two thousand dollars.

Your loving brother, Daniel

I thanked Daniel very much for the news of Flint and for his own honest words to me. I had written him already of my marriage, but now I wrote more of my love, and how Benjamin Serle and I will make our life together. *These past years since you left, I have lived in other people's houses in New York City and on a boat on the Erie Canal,* I wrote to Daniel. *Now I have my own dream.* I thanked Daniel for his gift of money and accepted it with gratitude.

I enclosed a lock of my hair.

Since I had no address for Flint, I also enclosed a letter to him in my letter for Daniel. I told Flint that I am pleased to be in the house where he grew up. The beauty of the lake, the bounty of the land, and the kindness of our neighbors sustain us. It is a healthy place for Tobias and for Mr. Serle. I asked Flint if he would sell the house and land to us.

Thursday, July 15, 1852

We made our journey to New York City—Benjamin Serle and I. It was a pleasure to see the DiRomas and to be their guests. We settled our business, and I went to my bank at last. Benjamin and Guido teased me that I could forget five hundred dollars and leave bank drafts lying in bureau drawers, but I would as soon have a good flock of poultry and a garden as money in a bank.

Honor insisted that I ought to have more clothes. It seems that married women need more dresses, shawls, and hats than single ones. I said I would have a new winter dress and a travel duster. Then I added that I had better have a new night shift too. Mr. Serle tore my best one when—well, I did not explain to Honor, and I will not write it either.

In the end, I spent more money at the shop for kitchen goods than I did for clothes. The newest ice cream makers are very nicely designed. Later in the summer, peach ice cream will be a treat for us all.

It was a happy visit, but it was a great pleasure to me when we stood at last on the deck of the steamboat. A sunset flamed up saffron and gold and violet in the western sky. As the day fades, we watch the twinkling lights of the city gleam bright and then dwindle in the distance. Darkness settles like a dream over the water. We are leaving the edge of America. We are beginning a new life in the heart of our country.

"What was the reason that Tobias would not call you Uncle Benjamin?" I ask.

"Ah, you remembered," Mr. Serle says.

"Tell me," I coax.

The wake from a passing steamboat makes our ship roll a little on the water. Mr. Serle steadies himself, one hand beside mine on the railing.

"We were standing above the waterfall," he says. "I asked Tobias if he would like to call me Uncle Benjamin. He said in a deliberate way, 'No, I will not call you Uncle. It confuses you.' I replied, 'What?' or something equally foolish. 'Rafe says you will make a good father,' he told me. 'It is a secret.' Then you called to us, and as we turned to go down the path, he told me, 'Rafe says, "Seek whom your soul loves." ' "

"Tobias said that? How could a child say such a thing?"

"I do not know," Mr. Serle says. His mouth curves. "How could a dog say such a thing?"

"It is a mystery," I reply.

"It is a wonderful mystery," Mr. Serle agrees and rests his hand over mine on the railing.

THURSDAY, DECEMBER 2, 1852

Yesterday's post brought a letter from Flint. Flint wants me to have the farm in Uncas Falls. *Zip hates the place and me,* he writes, *and your letter says that you feel love.* He encloses a lawyer's letter stating his intent. I am to present it to the family lawyer in Sawyerville and receive the deed. Flint's letter goes on:

Miss Felicitas helped me decide to give you the farm. She thinks in exchange you should write to me now and then of Uncas Falls, because your letter made me happy. I am going to live in a little house with just Miss Felicitas and Miss Caroline. We shared our gold to buy it. They do not want to live in the boardinghouse anymore. They say the life is for the young and the desperate. They are very good managers here. I like the food almost as well as what you cooked for me. I am going to die in California.

Flint has found kindness and comfort. He must be better in his mind if he no longer says he is already dead, a ghost. It will be a pleasure to write to him of our life in Uncas Falls. I sat with his letter in my hand and thought for a long time about goodness—there must be as many kinds of goodness as there are kinds of slavery.

TUESDAY, OCTOBER 14, 1856

This evening, I took my book from the back of the locked cupboard in the pantry where I hid it away four years ago. I must find a safer place. There were bounty men seen in Uncas Falls last Thursday. They are searching for a poor Negro man who is reported to have fled north from Delaware. He can be recognized by the brand mark on his cheek, they told Henry Carlton before he ordered them out of his store.

Mr. Serle and Tobias had gone to New York to stay with Herr Sadick Meyer and his wife and attend the synagogue for their New Year's observances. The first year we were married, I suggested Albany, but Mr. Serle says it is important for Tobias to know something of the greatest city in the world as well as our country life. I did not go with them this year, because with Leah Eliza fretful with teething and a little catarrh of the head, I did not wish to take her or to leave her with Georgina Carlton either. I was frantic with worry when my darlings were late returning home on Sunday night. Rafe and I were waiting on the porch when Eben drove them in safe at last.

The bakery is a success. The gardens and the orchards are flourishing. We hired another man to work under Eben and made a great profit on a shipment of apples to Liverpool last year.

"Well! We are in clover now!" Eben said when I gave him his share of the money.

The one apple tree that grew from the three seeds I brought from England bloomed beautifully dark pink this spring. I picked apples from the tree last month. The fruit is crisp and sweet as I remember, and yet—and yet—it tastes different here. It is the savor of this new world.

We talked about being American with Honor and Guido when they made their usual summer visit in August. We were sitting on the porch after supper, watching Daniel, their son, chase after the lightning bugs that flickered along the lilac hedge. Tobias sat on the bottom step with his arm around Rafe, who is an old dog now. We were drinking a little of the licorice-fragrant elderberry wine that Mr. Serle makes and calls *sambuco*. The baby was asleep in her cradle inside. I do not think we reached any conclusions in our talk. Honor says to be American is to dream, to strive, and to succeed. But Phoebe and Flint and poor John Deegan were born Americans.

I remember the moonlight made the lake all silver and that in the dark of the porch Mr. Serle held my hand. He gave me a book by Mr. Henry David Thoreau for an anniversary gift in May, and I was thinking of that too. *A lake is the landscape's most beautiful and expressive feature. It is the earth's eye; looking into which the beholder measures the depth of his own nature.* I wonder if we will ever finish knowing the depth of who we are and what we may become.

AUTHOR'S NOTE

The varied works—fiction, poetry, history, letters, diaries, memoirs, lyrics—of Louisa May Alcott, Tyler Anbinder, Irving Bacheller, Jean Anthelme Brillat-Savarin (in M.F.K. Fisher's translation), Charlotte Brontë, William Wells Brown, Byron, William Carleton, James Fenimore Cooper, Charles Dickens, Frederick Douglass, Stephen Collins Foster, John Fowler, Hyman B. Grinstein, Nathaniel Hawthorne, William Dean Howells, Henry James, Fanny Kemble, Vera Brodsky Lawrence, Edward Laxton, Herman Melville, Samuel Eliot Morrison, Russell Blaine Nye, Maureen Ogle, Edgar Allan Poe, Solon Robinson, Morris U. Schappes, Catherine Maria Sedgwick, William Shakespeare, Harriet Beecher Stowe, George Templeton Strong, Joseph Sturge, William Makepeace Thackeray, Fanny Trollope, Mark Twain, and Harriet E. Wilson inform the narrative and shape the language of *Bread and Dreams*. In addition, I am particularly indebted to:

Abbot, Jacob. *Marco Paul's Travels on the Erie Canal.* New York, NY: Harper & Brothers, 1852. As reproduced at http://www.history.rochester.edu/.

Abell, L. G. *A Mother's Book of Traditional Household Skills.* Reprint of 1852 Edition. New York, NY: The Lyons Press, 2001.

The librarians at the Brookline Public Library, the Blue Hill Public Library, the Boston Public Library, and the New York Public

Library have my enduring gratitude and admiration for their patience, resourcefulness, and willingness to share their skills and knowledge. With their help, I found the *New York Daily Tribune* for the years 1848 to 1852, the *Times* of 1851 and 1852, *Godey's Lady's Book*, Victorian menus and cookbooks, and the historical calendars that make the texture of Mina's world at least partially authentic. I owe thanks also to Mary Knapp of the Merchant's House Museum, the guides at Bellevue House National Historic Site, Merv Gard, Tania Langerman, Ginnie Gavrin, Elizabeth O'Neill, Sheree Conrad, Gaylen Morgan (who kindly permitted me to read the Canfield Family Papers), Jackie Cantor, and Lane Zachary for their interest, inspiration, information, critical reading skills, guidance, and support. Mary Manson and Judith Robbins are proof secure always of "the endearing elegance of female friendship." And at the last, but always first in my life, Robert Ceely, to whom this book is dedicated.

ABOUT THE AUTHOR

JONATHA CEELY grew up in Kingston, Ontario, and has lived in Turkey and Italy. She is a former teacher and administrator who lives in Brookline, Massachusetts, with her husband, a composer. Her debut novel, *Mina,* is available in trade paperback from Dell.